THE HEAT
ISLANDS

Also by Randy Wayne White

Sanibel Flats
Batfishing in the Rainforest

THE HEAT
ISLANDS

RANDY WAYNE WHITE

ST. MARTIN'S PRESS
NEW YORK

Sanibel Island, Florida, exists, though it—and all other places in this book—has been used fictitiously. In all other respects, this novel is a work of fiction. Names, characters, places, incidents, and politicians are either the product of the author's imagination or are used fictitiously, and any resemblance to actual persons, living or dead, events, or locales is entirely coincidental.

Design by Dawn Niles

Library of Congress Cataloging-in-Publication Data

White, Randy Wayne.
    The Heat Islands / Randy Wayne White.
        p.   cm.
    "A Thomas Dunne book."
    ISBN 0-312-06993-6
    I. Title.
PS3573.H47473H4   1992
813'.54—dc20   91-40458
                                                                  CIP

First Edition: February 1992

10 9 8 7 6 5 4 3 2 1

For dear, dear Deb

Turning and turning in the widening gyre
The falcon cannot hear the falconer;
Things fall apart; the center cannot hold;
Mere anarchy is loosed upon the world,
The blood-dimmed tide is loosed, and everywhere
The ceremony of innocence is drowned;
The best lack all conviction, while the worst
Are full of passionate intensity.

—*William Butler Yeats*

The savage in man is never quite eradicated.

—*Henry David Thoreau*

THE HEAT
ISLANDS

1

ON the morning that the most disliked man on the barrier islands was found floating, dead, Ford was aboard his skiff, balanced on the poling platform and looking for sea anemones.

He had switched on the portable VHF radio beneath the console, channel 18, so he could listen to the fishing guides talk. Ford liked the guides and enjoyed listening to the interchange of fishing data, sexual hyperbole and life lore; a daily soap opera in which the actors returned each evening, fish-slimed, sun-battered, and big as life, to the island marinas.

Tarpon season was a good time to listen because the guides got caught up in the action, and emotion overruled their sense of professional decorum—which is to say, they acted like themselves.

Unless the weather was bad.

If the weather was bad, or the fish weren't hitting, a few of the guides were prone to monologue, and that was boring. They talked too much and bragged shamelessly, as if past successes could somehow absolve them of current failures.

Which is how Ford knew that, on this morning, the tarpon weren't hitting. Too much conversation on the radio. There had been a bad storm, and he wasn't surprised, but he was getting tired of listening to the constant talk talk talk. He was about to swing down from the platform to switch the radio off when something the guides said caught his attention.

Not so much what they said, really, but the tone of their voices.

Captain Dalbert: "Hey, boys, I see something weird over here—you see that? *Really* weird."

Captain Javier: *"Sí* . . . ees right, ees right—Nels, what ees that *theeng* there floating?"

Captain Nels: "Uh-oh . . . hold the phone. . . ."

Captain Dalbert: " 'Bout the size of a Immokalee orange crate. Floatin' there, chubby as a pig—"

Captain Javier: "I see it now! Something that looks . . . bad. . . ."

Captain Nels: "Well, shit the bed, boys. I think we got ourselves a floater. . . ."

The radio went silent and Ford knew all of the guides were listening. Then, a little out of breath, Captain Nels said, "Somebody call the Coast Guard! Man, my anglers don't need to be seeing this. I thought it was like a oil drum or something. Yeew, this guy's got crabs on him—crawling outta his damn *ears.*"

Over the radio, from farther away, another guide, Captain Felix, cut in. "Beers? If you're taking orders, better count me in. A beer is what I could use right now. Crabs and beer. . . ."

Captain Nels said, "This dead guy, you coconut head. That's what I'm talking about. Ears, not beers. *Jeezus.*"

As he listened, Ford poled his flats skiff along the sandbar bordering the mangrove bank that created Dinkin's Bay. The bar broadened to the northwest, forming the bay side of Sanibel Island, a curving barrier island of palms and expensive homes that separated the Gulf of Mexico from mainland Southwest Florida.

Ford lived at the end of Tarpon Bay Road, next to Dinkin's Marina, in a house built over the water. He ran a small company there, Sanibel Biological Supply. From that house he caught and sold marine specimens to schools and labs around the country. He had recently received an order from Bowling Green State

2

University for twenty-five live sea anemones, which is why he happened to be on his flats skiff.

Normally, he would have spent the morning on his trawl boat, seining for tarpon larvae. In three weeks of continuous dragging, he had found no tarpon larvae—hadn't really expected to find larvae. But it was part of his work and he wanted to continue seining for at least another week, for he was doing tarpon research now.

Then he got the order from Bowling Green University, which is why he wanted to get out and collect anemones early on the dawn low tide.

But there had been a morning rain squall.

Then his friend Tomlinson stopped to see if he wanted to drive to the mainland to hear a lecture on the three pillars of Zen and maybe hit at the Line Drive batting cages in Cape Coral.

Then Dewey Nye stopped, saying she wanted to talk about her tennis game, but ended up talking about romantic problems instead.

All this before 10 A.M., with rain still dripping from the tin roof of his stilt house. Which is why Ford got a late start and was now trying to collect anemones on a June flood tide just one day before the full moon.

Elevated on the poling platform—a fiberglass stand above the motor—Ford pushed the boat along, using the long pole he held in both hands. He was thinking: *The guides aren't getting much time to fish today, what with squalls and dead bodies.*

And they weren't. Finding a corpse would probably put them off their pace, but no more so than the storm that morning.

Some storm. It had come from the Gulf, a black canyon of clouds churning like smoke and pushing a thirty-knot wind. He had sat on his porch and followed its progress across Dinkin's Bay: watched the clear sky yellow, then turn a throbbing, tumid green, amplifying sound, freshening odors until the first gust of cool wind. Then there was no sun, just sizzling lightning blasts through a hazy, ecliptic light, like sitting in a cave, looking through a waterfall.

But the storm had passed now. It rumbled over the mainland, casting great columns of sunlight through the moving clouds, illuminating the docks at St. James City and the dripping mangroves on Woodring Point, leaving Pine Island Sound washed and slick as raw glass.

On the radio, one of the guides said, "Perfect day for spotting bodies. Never seen one better, the water's so flat. Sight-cast corpses, take 'em on light tackle—how's that for an adver-tisement?"

The water *was* flat. Clear, too, in the shallows. Ford could see his own shadow on the sandbar as he pushed the boat along. In a patch of turtle grass, a cowfish nosed a scallop shell. Then a stingray spooked, making a brief explosion in the sand. There was a big whelk shell, its operculum thrown back, feeding on a dead mullet—one of several dead fish that had washed up on the bar. Attached to the whelk were the buds of a tulip snail egg case. Beyond that were the spiraling egg cases of whelks, like prehis-toric snakes, and the sand collars of moon snails.

Ahead, Ford could see the tracks of horseshoe crabs furrow-ing the sand . . . then the animals themselves, tan shells as if stamped from plastic: three smaller males attached to a big fe-male, locked in a slow fight to copulate.

A foot beneath the surface, the bottom was alive, one continuous interconnecting cycle, everything going on simulta-neously and without pause: egg, sperm, death and decay; all obliquely keyed by tides and heat and a million years of having survived. Yet each random event, anchored in the moment of its viewing, implied small dramas that, to Ford, were as interesting as the source of his own breath.

Why were there so many dead fish today?

Ford wondered if there might be an outbreak of red tide—something he could check later by taking water samples.

A pair of tube-dwelling anemones lay ahead, their tentacles thrown open, leaning in the current like wildflowers. But Ford pressed on until he was sure the anemones were part of a larger colony before he drove his pole into the sand, tied his boat, and got out.

From the radio, he heard Captain Dalbert say: "The Coast

Guard's standing by twenty-two alpha. They want one of us to stay with the body. I told them it was a man. That's right, isn't it? A man?"

Captain Nels: "He's floating facedown, but, yeah, a guy. Short hair. Looks like a guy. . . ."

Captain Billy: "That was a heck of a storm. Maybe he got washed over."

Captain Dalbert: "Naw, he's been in the water *awhile.* . . ."

Captain Javier: "Maybe was last night. Rain last night, too; *una puta.* Lightning it was so bad, I could not sleep. Big storm, going boom boom."

Wading barefoot by the boat, Ford took a small trowel and carefully dug beneath one of the anemones. At his touch, the animal's tentacles retracted, imploding into a leathery tube the size of a shotgun shell. As he transferred the anemone into a bucket of seawater, he heard Captain Felix ask, "Hey, Nels, you say they're a bunch of crabs around? Pass crabs, huh?"

Captain Nels said, "Yeah, crabs . . . uh-huh."

Captain Ramsey broke in, saying, "First that jerk Rios screws up his own tarpon tournament by not showing up for the start. Then the rain; now this. And we've all got anglers after the big money. Who has time to stand by?"

Ford was counting the anemones in the colony. There were more than two dozen, and he decided he could harvest five from here without doing harm. As he reached to take another, he heard Captain Felix say, "We're going to need bait if we have to fish tarpon in the pass. Any of you guys have crabs? Anybody think we'd be this desperate, we'd have to fish the pass?"

Captain Ramsey said, "We could all damn sure use some crabs, that's true. What with the rain. They dollar-size crabs, Nels?"

There was the garble of two people trying to talk at once on the same channel, then Captain Nels's voice broke through, saying, "You think I'm picking bait crabs off a corpse, you can kiss my butt on the county square," not at all amused. He said, "What we got to figure out is who's going to miss the tarpon

5

tournament and a day's pay standing by this body? If my anglers have to stay, I think everybody's ought to stay—"

Listening to the guides on the radio, Ford put four more anemones into the bucket, then transferred them from the bucket into the bait well. He waded back and, in a plastic collecting bag, placed a dead mullet and a dead trout—each about a foot long and already starting to stink.

From the wide pocket of his khaki shorts, he took a disposable Pyrex culture tube, filled it with a water sample, and stoppered it.

Back aboard his boat, he found a towel, wiped the sweat off his face, cleaned his glasses, then took a liter bottle of water from the ice and drank.

Clouds had scattered; tendrils of mist drifted off the water like steam in the harsh sunlight. It was hot now, and the odor of heating mangroves touched the air, mildly acidic.

Looking northwest, toward the power lines that crossed to Bowman's Beach, Ford could see the guide boats, a half dozen gray husks shimmering in the heat.

The boats were in an area of deep water known as the Mud Hole, just off Hardworking Bayou, where tarpon sometimes congregated. Several of the guides had anchored there, preferring to sit out the storm with baits in the water rather than retreat to a marina.

Ford knew that each of their clients had paid a two-thousand-dollar entry fee for the first annual Two Parrot Bight Tarpon Tournament, grand prize eighty thousand dollars, and they wanted to fish, not sit.

Over the radio, he heard Captain Nels calling his boat—"Sanibel Biological, Sanibel Bio. You out, Doc?"—and Ford was not surprised.

Taking his portable VHF from its place beneath the console, he pressed the transmitter button and said, "I've been listening, Nels. You sure the guy's dead?"

"You heard what we found? Man, I thought it was like an oil drum or something. Or like a chunka dock after that storm."

"He's dead for sure?"

6

"No mouth-to-mouth for this guy, no sir. Not from me, anyway."

Ford said, "I'm only a couple of miles away. I'll come out and wait for the Coast Guard so you guys can get back to work. That what you were calling about?"

Captain Nels said, "Aw, man, Doc, yeah—great. You wait for the Coast Guard, and . . . and we'll make sure you get any tarpon brought in for mounts. That sound fair? We'd sure appreciate that."

Captain Dalbert said, "You can by God count on it, Doc."

The guides or the taxidermist would have given Ford the dead tarpon anyway, but Ford said, "I'll be right there."

He nudged his boat off the bar and climbed in, the hydraulic trim whining as the oversize Mercury pivoted into the water. He started the motor, then launched the skiff onto plane, feeling the power of the motor through the trembling fiberglass and the abrupt speed surge that made his eyes tear and magnified each ripplet into a rhythmic water grid. Sitting at the wheel, only a foot above the water, he had the sensation of sailing across an ice field striated by wind; the horizon rushed toward him.

Fifty yards from the guide boats, Ford backed his skiff down, letting his own wake catch him, rolling past. Everybody was looking at him: six guides and maybe twenty fishermen, drifting in the heat and nobody fishing; nobody looking at the thing floating down tide, either. It was a dark shape, bloated like a garbage bag, facedown but with arms thrown wide, like someone falling, unable to stop. Ford idled toward the shape, then shut down his engine.

In the silence, Captain Nels said, "Felix is up by the river. With Hervey and Marshall. But we told them on the radio. Who knows where Karl is. He and his girly friend are fishing the tournament on their own. But we sat out the rain here all morning. Didn't see a fish; didn't get a hit." Avoiding the corpse in speech now, too.

Ford said, "Oh? Well . . . he certainly looks dead."

In Spanish, Captain Javier said, "We would stay, but this

7

tournament is very important. Much money is involved, and we get a share of the money if we win."

In English, Ford said, "I know."

He had drifted closer to the body and could see that it was the body of a man. The man wore tan slacks and a dark-blue knit shirt stretched tight over a back that looked to be more flab than muscle. Short dark hair, probably gray when it was dry; short legs and short fingers that were a pallid white in the green water. The corpse wore boating shoes.

Ford called over, "Any idea who it is?"

Captain Dalbert said, "Hadn't even thought of that. Probably some *turista* from a rental boat. We didn't want to get too close. Hayvee-air here says it's bad luck to touch a dead corpse." Smiling like he was talking about a child.

Javier shrugged and said in Spanish, "I did not say that. I said we should not touch the thing because of the police. There will be an investigation."

In Spanish, Ford said, "Of course, and you are exactly right," before saying to the other guides, "Well, the tide's starting to take him toward the mangroves. Better get a line around him."

He took a mooring line and looped it, then tossed it toward the man's left ankle, but missed. On the third try, with everyone watching, the rope missed the man's ankle but skipped toward his right arm.

Ford waited until the loop sank, then carefully pulled it tight. The unexpected weight of the corpse swung his skiff around, and the body rocked then bobbed like a lopsided cork, and suddenly the face and belly rolled toward the sky, eyes wide, crabs scurrying, mouth open, escaping gases making noise.

Ford heard someone say, "Jesus Christ, that's awful," and Javier say, *"¡Madre santo!"* and someone else say, "Hell, it's *him,"* for they all recognized the dead man now: Marvin Rios, owner of Two Parrot Bight Marina and the man who had organized the tarpon tournament.

Ford cleated off the line and turned toward the fishing guides, who were looking at the body, looking at each other uneasily, their faces showing the strain of a big-money tournament, and the rain, and too many days fishing during the busiest time of the year.

In the long silence, Captain Dalbert asked, "Anybody seen Jeth Nicholes today? Anybody seen him since he had that fight with Rios yesterday?"

Captain Nels snapped, "Don't even mention that; why you even bring it up?"

Captain Javier yelled, "Jeth did not do this *theeng!*"

"I wasn't accusing him—"

"Just shut up, damn you!"

Captain Billy said, "Rios drowned; anybody can see that. Missed the chapter where it says don't inhale salt water. Jesus, look at that face, like he's still screaming."

Captain Javier said, "We have peoples aboard! It is not a matter to discuss."

"As if you don't feel like celebrating—"

Captain Dalbert said, "Does Raggedy Ann have cotton tits?"

Captain Robert yelled, "You boys behave now! The asshole's dead. Show some respect."

Ford cut in, saying, "Hey—hey!" giving it a genial touch, waiting for the guides to exchange glares and settle themselves before he said, "I can take care of things here. Maybe you ought to get back to fishing."

"Yeah—Doc's right. Let's get the hell back to work."

Ford said, "But I wouldn't mention Rios's name on the radio. He has a wife, and the authorities ought to be the ones to tell her. Mention on the radio he's dead, the whole island will know in an hour."

Nodding, Captain Dalbert said, "Good news does travel fast," and started his engine.

Ford watched the six boats wheel away slowly, then faster, fanning into formation toward Lighthouse Point, his own boat and the late Marvin Rios bobbing in their wakes. On the radio, from miles away, Captain Felix was saying, "It's not like you'd

9

have to use your hands, Nels. I don't want you touching no dead people."

Silence.

Captain Felix again: "We going to sit around fat, dumb, and baitless, with no tarpon in sight?"

Static and silence.

"You want me to beg, Nels, I'll beg! I need *ammo,* man. I need surefire tarpon-catching crabs. So how about you dip those little darlings out with a net. . . ."

2

THE sheriff's deputy said, "I've seen a lot of drownings, but I don't think this guy drowned."

Ford, anchored now, sat and listened to the deputy while watching the five-man Coast Guard team in their blue ball caps, blue fatigues, and bright orange life jackets try to wrestle the body of Marvin Rios onto the flush deck of their thirty-foot cruiser. The sheriff's deputy, who had rafted up in the department's gray twenty-five-foot Mako, talked right along, leaning over the stern to help when he could.

The deputy said, "A person who's drowned usually has a lot of white stuff around his nose and mouth. Like a kinda foam. And when they've been in the water awhile, they get something like that all over them. But I forget the name of it."

Ford thought *adipocere,* but said nothing.

The deputy said, "Like a kind of jelly."

Grunting with effort, one of the Coasties said to the deputy, "Hey, knock it off. You trying to make us sick? Grab his legs and lift if you want to help. We got a softball game this afternoon."

The deputy said, "It's just that I've seen a lot of them, that's all. This guy didn't drown . . . but, jeez, he's *stiff,* huh?"

Ford had sat at anchor in the Mud Hole, just off Ding

11

Darling Sanctuary, for nearly an hour waiting for the Coast Guard to arrive. He had switched his radio to channel 22 so that he could talk to the cruiser's helmsman and direct him in. While he waited, he checked the anemones in the bait well, and he neatened up his skiff, and he watched the surface for rolling tarpon.

He saw several rays break the water, their wings cutting the surface like sharks. And he saw a cobia cruise by, its dorsal fin wagging back and forth in synch with each slow tail thrust.

Mostly he avoided looking at the body that tumbled slowly in the now-strong outgoing tide, fifteen feet off the back of his boat.

He saw no tarpon.

Ford had met Marvin Rios only once: a small man with bitter blue eyes, elevator shoes, and a driving insolence that projected the daily war he waged on life and the people around him. The previous January, Ford had attended Rios's annual New Year's Eve party, open to the whole island. But, with Rios watching from the shadows, the party was less like a celebration than a way of exacting tribute, and Ford hadn't stayed long.

For Rios, Ford guessed, wealth was a sophisticated score-card, a casualty list of enemies. He had made a fortune on island real estate and kept his hands in various developments and invest-ment ventures; then, two years ago, he built an extravagant marina and restaurant at Two Parrot Bight.

Two Parrot Bight was a paw of land that created a small harbor midway between Dinkin's Bay and Sanibel Marina near the toll bridge to the mainland. According to local folklore, the bight had been named years before by fishermen who noticed a pair of parrots, presumably feral, nesting in a gumbo limbo, and which squawked madly at any osprey or fish crow or fisherman who came near.

Rios had taken the name for his marina, a marina that was instantly successful—not because Rios was liked, or respected, or gave fair dollar service, but because dockage was hard to find on the islands. People had to moor their boats somewhere and, since

12

the other marinas were always backlogged, Two Parrot Bight was the only alternative.

It was getting that way all over Florida. A marina didn't have to be good. No matter how surly the management, no matter how inept the mechanics—if the place offered docks and sold gas, it flourished.

What Ford knew about Rios, he had learned from the fishing guides. There were three fishing guides at Dinkin's Bay Marina, several at Sanibel Marina, and three guides at Parrot Bight. All of them detested Rios because they were his prime targets for abuse: a small man who took real joy in bullying bigger men. Ford had heard about Rios humiliating his guides in front of their fishing clients, screaming that if they didn't like the rules at *his* marina, they should take their boats and get the hell out. But the Parrot Bight guides—Dalbert Weeks and Javier Castillo—could not get out, because the guide slots at the other marinas were filled. They had no options. But they did have families, mortgages, and boat payments. So they endured, allowing this tiny man to abuse them.

The deputy said to Ford, "You say you knew this guy?"

Ford looked up from the anemones in the bait well. "I knew of him."

The deputy was writing on a pad now while the Coasties took photographs and went through Rios's pockets. "He have any family? Someone we should call?"

"He had a wife."

"And you say he manages Parrot Bight, the marina over there. I mean managed. Past tense, right?"

Ford said, "Owned and managed, I think. Oh yeah, he's got a brother-in-law. A guy named Sutter who's kind of a fishing guide. More family. Karl Sutter."

Holding Rios's billfold, one of the Coasties gave a low whistle. "There's more than two grand here. Fifties and hundreds. If money floated, this guy'd be alive right now."

Water was draining out of Rios's pants, small rivulets losing momentum and draining across the deck into the scuppers. A wedge of distended belly showed beneath the dark shirt. In the water, his skin had appeared white. But now, lying on the white deck, his face and hands were the color of wet clay; his eyes black holes in bloated flesh: a soggy thing, swelling in the heat like road kill.

The deputy said, "Whata you mean, kinda a fishing guide? Like he just does it part time?"

Ford said, "Karl Sutter? I don't know much about him, either; Sutter or Rios. Anything I tell you would be third- or fourth-party hearsay."

But Ford had heard a lot about Rios's in-law, Karl Sutter, too.

A little more than a year ago, Rios had brought in Sutter as head guide, which meant that, each day, he was the first captain to be booked. Traditionally, the position was given to the most senior guide and, to add to the outrage, Sutter was a bumbling failure as a fisherman. Yet only the guides and a few experienced fishermen recognized the man for the incompetent he was. New tourists to the island, intere̶s̶t̶ ̶i̶n̶ a day's fishing, naturally gravitated to the biggest marin̶a̶ ̶t̶w̶o̶ Parrot Bight. And, as neophytes, they naturally wanted to fish in the biggest, newest boat—Sutter's. And when they met Sutter, who was an innate con man and, by all accounts, an outrageous liar, they willingly plunked down the sizable chunk of money it took to go out.

This hurt all of the guides, because novice anglers who fished once with Sutter would never want to fish the area again. Probably never fish with a guide again. Nor would their friends. And Sutter, who rarely caught anything, shifted the blame by complaining bitterly about his clients' lack of skill.

As Jeth Nicholes, the stuttering guide from Dinkin's Bay Marina, told Ford, "You know how some people get a creepy feeling when they see a sna-na-na-ake? That's the way I feel when I'm round Rios and Sutter. There's something ain't right 'ba-ba-bout them. Like a sickness. And I'm the kinda guy who gen'rally likes snakes."

As an interested outsider, Ford had listened to these stories over the past year, gauging the growing disgust with Rios and Sutter. He suspected that at least some of the horror stories had

14

profited from too much beer and too many days on the water, stories exaggerated by the guides to better illustrate the hatred they felt. But the hatred was real. Ford was sure of that. Just as he was sure that it would somehow, some way, come to a head.

Now perhaps it had. Rios was dead.

The deputy asked, "Was his brother-in-law one of the guides who found him?"

Ford said, "No," and named the guides who had discovered the body, then gave the marinas where they could be reached. "Sutter doesn't fish with the other guides," Ford said. "He's new."

"You know if the deceased has any history of heart problems, or high blood pressure? Any health problems? What is the guy, 'bout fifty-five? Not that old." The deputy was writing away, filling out a form, and Ford considered the deputy's hands for the first time: nails bitten on both hands, the habit of a nervous childhood. Slight pale band on the ringless ring finger of his left hand: separated from his wife within the last three months, the divorce probably already under way. Smoked cigarettes; had a few acne scars on his face, enough to suggest some tough teenage years; and, with those forceps marks on his temples, his mother had suffered while birthing him. The deputy, Ford judged, was twenty-six years into a difficult life, a guy who found refuge in his work.

"What?"

The deputy said, "I asked how old the guy was."

"His wife would know that."

The deputy said, "Male Caucasian." He stood on his toes to get another look at Rios. "Looks like that's a kinda cut on his head. Big slice. Under obvious injury." Then he said, "You know anyone who had a reason to dislike the deceased; hear anything recently about any problems?"

Ford thought about Captain Dalbert asking where Jeth Nicholes was, mentioning an argument. He said, "You need to ask someone else. I do know that Rios was supposed to be at the start of a tarpon tournament this morning. He sponsored it at Parrot Bight. I was told he didn't show up."

15

The deputy said, "Oh, yeah—hey, right. The one with the big prize money. I heard about that. The one with the big entry fee. And this guy ran the show, huh?" He said to the Coast Guard, "We'll be on the news tonight, boys. We've got a solid citizen here."

One of the Coasties said, "Did you get Mr. Ford's number? We'll need it for our report." They had just tied a tarp over Rios's body, and Ford could see that they were anxious to get to their softball game. He didn't blame them. Wrestling a corpse on a clear Florida day leached a little sunlight from the air; added a mortal pale that forced a grim Sunday tint upon the morning.

Nodding and writing, the deputy said, "Way I see it, Mr. Rios here probably had a heart attack or a stroke and gave his head a whack when he fell in. You watch, I'll bet the medical examiner says the same. Dead before he hit the water." The deputy closed the stainless-steel folder that held his notepad. "That wraps it up for me."

Ford said, "I'm surprised to hear you say that."

The deputy said, "What?"

Ford said, "If Rios had a heart attack or a stroke, there's something missing."

The deputy waited.

One of the Coasties said, "You don't get it, do you? This guy didn't swim out here. And he sure didn't walk."

The deputy said, "Aw, man . . ."

Ford said to the deputy, "You would have thought of it. Wondered how he got out here. . . ."

The deputy snapped his fingers, saying, "Unless he could'a floated. Like from an island. Drifted," and looking at them to see how this was accepted.

Ford was rubbing his chin with his fist, wondering if the drift and set of a corpse could be calculated.

But then the deputy said, "Never mind, never mind, I better do it. Go look for Mr. Rios's boat."

Ford banked his skiff through the cut at Woodring Point and into Dinkin's Bay, past the old Woodring house squatting in the shade where chickens scratched at the water's edge, feeding, it appeared, on dead fish that had washed ashore.

He reminded himself again to test the water sample he had taken for traces of red tide.

Ford followed the markers to Green Point, then cut behind the fish-house ruins. Pelicans and egrets flushed off the spoil islands, their wings laboring in the heat and heavy air, gaining slow altitude as their shadows panicked baitfish in the shallows.

Ford ran straight across the flats, but at reduced speed, concentrating on the water before him. It was an area often inhabited by manatee—huge, slow-moving mammals that cruised the shallow bottom, feeding on grasses and tunicates. Ahead was a tiny clearing; wooden buildings, a few cars, and docks: Dinkin's Marina. It was the only break in the great ring of mangroves that formed Dinkin's Bay.

Ford's house and lab were just a few hundred yards east of the marina, two weather-bleached cottages under a single tin roof, all built on stilts, and connected to shore by ninety feet of old boardwalk. At Ford's approach, his flat-bottomed trawl boat—the one he used for drag netting—swung idly on its mooring. The stern of the trawl boat read SANIBEL BIOLOGICAL SUPPLY. As he tied off, he searched for Jeth Nicholes's boat among the cruisers and sailboats and skiffs docked in a line at the marina.

Jeth's slip was empty.

Using a bucket, Ford transferred the anemones to his fish tank. He planted them carefully on the sand bottom, stepping back to admire his own work.

He had built the fish tank on a reinforced section of the platform, using half of an old wooden cistern built like a whiskey barrel. Raw water was constantly drawn in by the Briggs pump housed onshore, aerated and clarified by a hundred-gallon upper reservoir and subsand filter, then sprayed as a mist into the main tank. The water in the tank was clear, two feet deep, and alive with snappers, shrimp, whelks and conchs, reef squid, sea squirts, and, a recent addition, four immature tarpon, all about a foot long.

17

Ford found the tarpon and watched them for a time as the fish held nose-first into the current created by the aerator; thin bars of silver that seemed to create their own light.

He stood watching the tarpon, mentally trying to retrace his steps from the morning; trying to picture Jeth's dark-blue fishing boat, an old Suncoast.

Had Jeth's boat been at the dock when he left in his flats skiff?

Ford hadn't noticed.

Not that it was important. Jeth Nicholes was no murderer.

About 2 P.M., Ford heard someone yell to him from the boardwalk; someone coming up the ramp, calling, "Hey, Doc . . . yo, Ford! . . . ready to have your butt run into the ground?"

Ford was sitting beneath the roofed walkway that separated the stilt house's two rooms. He lived in one of the rooms. The other was his lab.

He was reading the new issue of *Copeia,* the Journal of the American Society of Ichthyology; taking notes and listening to Crosby, Stills, Nash and Young do "Guinnevere." Because he had lived in the stilt house without electricity for the first five months, the place was furnished half like a boat, half like a house, so his stereo was a Maxima marine with Micro 100 waterproof speakers. Not big wattage, but they handled CSN&Y just fine, diffusing the intricate chord patterns through the screen windows and screened door, spreading a soft mood.

From the boardwalk, the voice said, "No excuses, you coward. Get out here or I'll come in and drag your ass out."

Ford put down his magazine, went inside to get his shoes, and looked up when the screen door creaked open. Dewey Nye, all five feet ten inches of her, probably 140 pounds, stood with a humorous expression of mock challenge on her face, blond hair pulled back in a loosely braided rope and wreathed with a blue sun visor above gray-blue eyes, saying, "Shit, you're not even ready yet. I told you two P.M." Looking at the stereo, she let the screen door slam behind her. "What kind of music is that? Rich widow bait? Whew, like Lawrence Welk." She lifted the phonograph arm as if touching a soiled diaper, and mimicked Ford's wince. "Your fish are out there trying to fight off sleep; I'm getting dozy myself. This is a personal favor I'm doing here." She found a contemporary rock station, all synthesizers and tribal howls, and turned it up a half dozen notches, yelling, "Buy a calendar, Ford. They've got a thing now called rock 'n' roll. Which they play on CDs, not phonographs. This is your personal invitation into the current decade."

Ford reached over and turned down the noise. "Nice to see you, too, Dewey."

She said, "You big sweetie," mussing his hair, then straightening his glasses for him before stepping back. "About ready?"

"Tomlinson says Crosby, Stills, Nash and Young produced some of the most articulate rock and roll of our time."

She tapped her watch, hurrying him. "I've heard, I've heard; Tomlinson the old hippie. Like 'American Bandstand'; Dick Clark. The Fab Four. Back when 'Saturday Night Live' was funny. The good old days. Get your ass in gear."

Dewey Nye had one of those California beach faces, but without the vacuous leer; all cheekbones and chin with deep-set eyes that missed nothing; a face formed by generations of European farm stock sailing among the New World's gene pool. But Ford liked her face not for what it said about her forebears but for what it said about her: the crooked nose, broken in a field hockey game; the stubborn, jutting jaw; the tiny scar at the corner of her right eye—maybe she'd been hit by a swing when she was a kid. Or, more likely, someone's fist. She had a good smile and a catalog of gawky expressions and a vocabulary more commonly associated with sailors than with one of the country's best tennis players—which she happened to be.

Ford said, "What I don't understand is why we have to run when it's so hot. Why at two P.M.?"

"You're not going to whine your way out of this, Doc."

"I've never whined in my life."

"So now I've got two things on my shopping list: a calendar

19

and something to record your whining with. Because I like the heat. Why else? I like to sweat. Hurry up."

Ford was tying his Etonic running shoes, looking up at her: all legs and muscle cordage beneath Day-Glo orange running shorts. The shorts were pulled over a silver latex body stocking stretched taut from lean waist to shoulders. It emphasized the anatomy, streamlining all the soft curves and heavy swell of breasts; a high-tech look, as if she had been created in a wind tunnel. Ford said, "If you run in that, cars will be going off the road. Guys will be hooting and honking."

"No one's going to bother me with you along."

"It's nice you have confidence—"

"I mean with that belly, you look like a pro wrestler." She was braced against the wall, stretching her calves. "Who's going to mess with a guy who has Hulk-a-mania?"

Ford said, "Belly? Where?" He was looking down at his own chest, seeing a navy-blue T-shirt that had gone gray from years of washing. Small gold letters above the breast read B.U.D.S./S.E.A.L.S.

Dewey said, "The belly of the future. I'm looking at what happens when a guy your age doesn't work out."

Ford said, *"That* belly," walking past her out the door, snapping the elastic of her shorts. "Four miles?"

"Four-point-eight. But you need to stretch first. I'm not slowing down if you pull a hamstring."

Ford said, "Then maybe I should I track down my cane."

They ran among the mangroves along the marina's shell road to the intersection of Tarpon Bay and SanCap Road, then turned west onto the bike path, picking up the pace in the sunlight and the heat.

Dewey said, "Let your arms relax. Relax your shoulders a little. My God, you run like a weight lifter."

Ford said, "You're telling me how to run now, too?"

She said, "I'm starting to sound bossy, aren't I? Jeez, I hate bossy people. Don't let me boss you, Doc."

Ford said wryly, "I'll try my darnedest."

20

She said, "Let your hands relax. You look like you're going to punch somebody."

Ford said, "There's an idea."

From long habit, Ford ran four or five times a week, usually a total of about twenty miles, but seldom fast. He liked running at dusk, when it was cool and the island's animals were foraging, or late at night, especially in August during the Perseid meteor showers. But now, after only half mile of trying to keep up with Dewey, his lungs burned, his thigh muscles itched from oxygen debt, and his whole body poured sweat in a frantic effort to cool itself. Without looking at her, he said, "Let's slow down. I'll never make it at this pace."

"Sure you will. Push yourself. Whatever happened to male pride?"

"Male pride was invented by women. Slow down, god-damn it." His wire-rimmed glasses were a blur of sweat; the bike path, a dark vacuum before him.

"Another half mile at this pace, then we'll slow down."

"No."

"Don't pout. Talk to me. It'll take your mind off it. What did you do after I saw you this morning?"

Talking in spurts as he exhaled, Ford said, "Some of the guides found a body. The guy who owned Two Parrot Bight Marina. I stayed with the body until the Coast Guard picked it up. That's what I did. Out in the bay."

"A dead body."

"Yeah."

"Yuck."

"Exactly. Yuck."

"Did you know—hey, wait a minute!" The woman stopped running for a moment, looking at Ford, then jogged to catch up, both of them going slower. "The guy who ran Two Parrot Bight—you don't mean Rios? Marvin Rios?"

"Yeah. Dead."

"Marvin Rios?"

"Yes."

"But how? You're serious."

21

"Heart attack, maybe. They couldn't tell. Maybe a stroke."

"God, I can't believe it."

"I didn't even know you knew him."

"Holy shit, he's really dead?"

"Yes!"

"I knew him."

"You never mentioned it."

Dewey said, "That's because you don't talk about people you hate. At least I don't."

"Wait a minute—"

"No, no, no, I do. I mean I did. I did hate him. Probably the only man I've ever hated. Well, him and my second tennis coach. Now he's dead? It's like being a balloon and having the air let out." Her voice had a contemplative quality, both horrified and wondrous.

"But why?"

She quickened the pace a little, saying, "It's something I don't talk about."

The island's municipal pool, lime green in its cement basin, was nearly empty. The pool was almost always empty, but there were kids on the playground making a nice noise among the cabbage palms and live oaks. In the training room, Dewey went to work on the weight machine, throwing herself into the stations, losing herself in the dull labor, blowing and heaving, sweat dripping off her crooked nose, whispering, ". . . thirteen . . . fourteen . . . *fifteen*."

Her attention, focused on the weights, drifted once when a hawk screamed from a gumbo tree outside, then again when the lifeguard banged up the volume on some song Ford had heard before but did not recognize. Dewey danced alone for a moment, tall blond girl in the deserted weight room, mouthing the words until she seemed to remember something, then stared at Ford: "Christ, you've just sitting there playing with—what is that, a lizard? *Gawd!*"

"Key West anole. See the markings?"

She was pulling at his arm but staying far from the anole.

22

"Off your butt, Thoreau. Just let it go—*not in here!* Then it's sit-ups. And pull-ups."

He went to the pull-up bar, and when he finished, she was looking at him, smiling. "Not bad, Doc, not too bad. Almost impressive. Eighteen pull-ups."

"Nineteen. You lost count."

"That's *good*. I've never been able to do more than twelve. Shit, you're *strong*."

There was a time in Ford's life when he'd had to do twenty-six pull-ups before each meal. He said, "And at my age, too."

She threw an arm over his shoulder, hugging him briefly, sweat like hot oil on her arms and face. "I'm too rough on you."

"Naw. . . ."

"I'm sorry. It just the way I am."

"The way you are what?"

She was fiddling with her watch, one of those plastic computers on a black plastic band. "We ran up here at a seven-fifteen pace. Let's try to get back in under sevens."

Ford said, "I thought we were going to swim."

"We are. But not in the pool. In the bay, when we get back."

"But look at the pool. All to ourselves. Nice and cool; nice lane markers—" But she was already out the door.

Halfway back to Dinkin's Marina, with Ford fighting for what seemed to be his very life, the woman said, "About two years ago, my fifth year on the circuit, I went to a party. One of those grand-opening kind of deals, I forget what, but they wanted celebrities, and that was back when I still liked the idea of being recognized."

Ford said, "Uh-huh," not realizing, for a moment, that she had decided to tell him about Marvin Rios.

She said, "I was—what?—twenty-two and getting my picture in magazines. Getting interviewed. For a girl who'd spent her life like a hermit, always on the tennis court or studying, it was hot stuff. So I went to this party, and Rios was one of the main guys. Like a host. It was on island, and the local big shots were there. Everybody getting drunk and trying not to show it.

23

All the usual bullshit, but I was too naive to realize what a crock it was. No, not naive. I don't think I've ever been naive. Probably just full of myself, and a little too polite, too."

Ford said, "Uh-huh," thinking, *how can she run so fast and still talk?*

Dewey said, "He must have followed me out into the garden or something, because somehow we ended up alone. I knew he'd been eyeing me all night, and I had to get away from all that smoke, and there we were. He starts off asking me about my tennis sponsors, and were they treating me okay. Very authoritative, as if he could underwrite the whole bill himself. Talking like he could do me favors.

"He's standing there talking about money and tax breaks, speaking to me like a child, and the whole time I'm thinking, How in the hell can I get away from this chubby little nerd? I make a move to get past him, and he takes me by the arm—not hard, but holding me. He's looking up at me with those piggy little blue eyes of his. I go to pull my arm away, but he just moves with me, looking in my eyes. Then he puts his other hand on my breast. It still gives me the shivers, thinking about that. Not hard, but moving it around and staring at me.

"If that sort of thing happened in the movies, the girl'd smack the guy in the face. Or scream maybe. But it's different when it happens for real. I froze. You know how a mouse freezes when a cat has it? Like that. Like an animal feeling. Like shock. My ears were ringing and I couldn't look at anything but his eyes. Then he takes his hand away, but I feel it fiddling with my skirt. I'm backing away real slow, and he says, 'I can help you a lot. You know that.' He says, 'What you need is a man.' That's exactly what he said. 'A man.' "

Listening, Ford wasn't thinking about the pain in his chest now, or his legs.

Dewey said, "And I stood there. Makes me sick, now, I let him do that. He *touched* me. You know for how long I couldn't sleep at night, thinking what I should have done, what I should have said?"

Ford croaked, "Not your fault."

24

"I was an idiot for letting him get me alone like that. A jerk."

Ford wanted to say that victims always blame themselves, but he couldn't. He said, "Unh-uh."

Dewey said, "Then I hear like a zipping sound. Maybe he's unzipping my dress, but I don't have a zipper on my dress. I can't look at anything but his eyes, and I feel him take my arm and try to move my hand down, and then I know what zipper. But I wouldn't let him do that. I yanked my arm away and, at the same moment, the glass doors slide open and some other people come out, talking loud. Well, that did it. That snapped me out of it. When he tried to pull my hand back, I let him pull me, then gave him a hell of a shove. I must have screamed at the same time, too; yelled something, because the people heard me. We were behind some trees, but they came running. Rios was lying there trying to get his zipper up, and I wanted to kill him, and I was crying, and people were asking, 'What's wrong?' and all I could think to say was, 'take a look at this twerp's dong. Wouldn't make a meal for a bird!' and I left the party."

His mouth open, scooping oxygen, Ford grinned.

Dewey said, "I should have hit him. Hit him right in his goddamn fat face, then called the cops. But I didn't. I figured just let it go. I mean, it was *humiliating*. Then . . . Christ, this is the worst part . . . *then*, a few months later, my friends begin to hear rumors. It's getting spread around that I'm gay."

Ford said, "Oh?"

"None of the people I know would've started anything like that. My personal life is strictly nobody's business. *Nobody's.*"

Ford wondered just what that meant.

She ran in silence for a time, then said, "Then one of the investigators from the tennis association calls me and says she has information that suggests I've been using steroids. Damn! So I submit to more tests than they already make us do. Then a reporter from a sports magazine calls, very polite, and hints around at it, but finally comes right out and asks if it's true I've tested positive for AIDS. He's gotten an anonymous tip. Then my mother calls from Chicago, practically hysterical. She's *crying*

25

because she's gotten a call, too. Someone's asked her about this crap."

"Rios," Ford said.

"I think so; can't think of anybody else who'd do that . . . that sort of garbage. But my lawyer said there was nothing we could do unless we found someone who would testify he was starting all this stuff. We hired an investigative firm. Cost me like five grand. All they came up with was it was maybe Marvin Rios or a male accomplice, but nothing solid enough for a suit." She said, "I'd hurt the little shmuck's ego in front of some Sanibel hotshots. He was out to plow me under. I mean, a purely evil little son of a bitch."

Finally, they were at the shell road into Dinkin's Marina, and Ford came clomping to a stop at the entrance to his stilt house, bending at the waist, hands interlaced over his head, sucking air.

Dewey said, "Seven-ten miles. Not bad, old man." Sweating, but not breathing that hard, studying her watch.

Ford said, "Why haven't I heard any of this stuff . . . this stuff about you and Rios?"

Dewey said, "I told you: I don't talk about it. Besides, you're the kind of guy people tell their problems to, but not the real creepy stuff, the real dirty stuff. Be like trying to tell their chemistry professor; someone who's above that sort of crap."

Ford said, "Oh," looking at her to see if she really believed that.

She said, "Plus, between you and me, I didn't want anyone but my attorney to know."

"I guess that makes sense."

"Yeah. I'd have never done it, but I couldn't help thinking of ways to have that bastard killed."

Going up the walkway to Ford's house, stripping off her running shorts and throwing them over the railing, she said, "But now, it doesn't matter. Like freedom." Dewey said, "Ding dong, the witch is dead."

3

AT 6 P.M., stretched out on a lawn chair on his porch, writing in his notebook, Ford watched across the water as the guide boats filed back into the marina. Jeth Nicholes's boat was not among them.

He wrote: "T = tide; W = wind; R = resistance; L = lag; U = unknowns. $TW_1 - TW_2 +/- 2[L] +/- U \times R = X$."

He puzzled over the formula for several minutes, then carefully erased it, as unsure that resistance factors could be computed as he was certain there were too many unknowns.

He knew that drowning victims sink for a period of time, which varied with water temperature and salinity, but certainly the victim's own body composition must play a role. But did people sink who entered the water already dead? Probably. If so, though, the tidal current near the bottom would be different from the surface current, and the body mass would change as body gases contracted at depth, and then expanded with decomposition. And in South Florida, in June heat, decomposition would begin the moment a man's last breath was taken.

It was a complicated problem; gruesome, too, though that did not bother Ford. But the fact that the problem was composed of factors that could not be calculated did.

Aw, screw it. . . .

Closing his notebook, he settled back to watch the guides, Felix Haynes and Nels Langford, begin the evening wash-down, stowing their gear, popping their first beers beneath the giant sea-grape tree beside the office, talking matter-of-factly but not laughing much, and Ford knew they had not won the tarpon tournament.

It was Friday night, official end of the workweek at marinas all up and down the Florida coast. Saturday and Sunday were the busiest days of the week, but Friday night was still the traditional gathering time for the live-aboards and marina employees. It was the brief quiet time before the weekend rush, when they came together as a community. When they drank and laughed and complained and lied, with no one around to hear, just them, and the marina became a private thing, like a secret.

Music already echoed inside Noel Yarbrough's forty-foot Grand Banks. Rhonda Lister and JoAnn Smallwood had hung Japanese lanterns on the stern of their wood-rotted Chris-Craft cruiser, and had changed into sarongs—an unspoken party invitation underlined by the bright pink hibiscus blossoms each woman wore behind her ear. Men in sandals and shorts roamed the docks with women in coral-bright blouses, their hair freshly washed, laughing, with drinks in hand, their elongated reflections like oil on the water, blending with the darker reflections of coco palms, which feathered over the seawall behind them. All the boats floated motionless in their slips—the Makos, Aquasports, the larger cruisers and trawlers and candy-colored fiberglass sailboats—stirring only when someone stepped aboard to fetch bottles of beer from the ice.

Graeme MacKinley, the New Zealander who managed the marina, came out of the office wearing a long-billed fishing cap and flip-flops, carrying his ring of keys, and began to padlock the bait tanks and the rod-rental closet, closing shop. He looked over toward Ford's stilt house and waved briefly, then held up an invisible glass, meaning cocktail time. Ford had had no alcohol for three months, yet he held up his hand in acquiescence. A cold beer would be good right now. And after his workout with Dewey, he had earned it.

Stiff, leg-sore, Ford forced himself out of the lounge chair to change clothes, but then saw Tomlinson heading across the bay in his little wooden dinghy. So he sat down to wait, and soon there was Tomlinson wearing a hot pink Hawaiian shirt, blond scraggly hair down to his shoulders, black beard cut short, hopping up onto his dock and grinning: "Dr. Ford, I presume."

Ford said, "And you're no Stanley. What time's your date?"

Tomlinson straightened himself, gazing around with that dreamy look, saying, "How you know that, man? Only the second date I've had in . . . a year? Yeah, like ten months."

"Second time I've seen that shirt. Nice, too."

Tomlinson pulled the shirt away from his jeans, as if seeing it for the first time. "Hey, this is pretty, isn't it?" he said. "Imported." He was fingering the material, studying it, his psychedelic eyes softened by experience and years and the objective inspection he now made. "Yep, imported . . . I'm pretty sure. I don't think they make shirts like this in America." He looked up. "Colorful, huh? I'm having dinner with a woman."

"Someone you met today at the Zen lecture?"

Tomlinson said, "Not a lecture. An oral sharing," holding up a long, bony finger, the kindly teacher correcting the reluctant student.

Ford said, "Ah."

"She was there, but I've known her since college. She still lives in Cambridge; teaches at the university—the one I went up to visit last month. Clear to Boston on a plane."

Tomlinson had returned after a week, his behavior even more esoteric and preoccupied than usual—which was saying something for Tomlinson.

"The one who wanted to marry you, you mean?"

"Not marry me, just use me," Tomlinson said miserably. "That's right—she's the one. I'd forgotten. Now she shows up on my doorstep—what the hell's got into women?"

"That's quite a thing to forget."

29

"I was busy with the Zen retreat. You should have come. Very . . . cleansing. About fourteen of us in a little room. Did a short sesshin—about two hours of meditation."

"Two hours of sitting on the floor," Ford said. "And I missed it."

"A good group. No breakthroughs, but a nice stillness; a nice clarity. Dr. Rocky Kaplan-*sensei* was the guest. Very damn spiritual. Then I went to Line Drive and used the pitching machine." Tomlinson was swinging an imaginary bat, head down, throwing his hands. "Finally got my stroke back. Really beat piss out of the ball."

Dr. Rocky Kaplan-*sensei*? Ford was tempted to ask, but didn't want to risk a lengthy explanation. Instead, he said, "I'm going to the marina for a beer. You have time?"

"You? A beer? Sure. I never understood why you quit in the first place."

Ford said, "Let me get some clothes and we'll go."

Tomlinson followed him up into the house, talking right along, saying Ford was starting to look a little gaunt; a little flushed; concerned until he heard about the workout with Dewey Nye: four-mile run, mile swim in the bay, plus the other stuff.

Tomlinson said, "I thought she had a boyfriend. What's-his-name, the rich kid."

Ford said, "As of yesterday, she doesn't. As of today, she still doesn't. I just want to get back into shape, and she's helping. Besides, I'm at least ten, twelve years older than her. And she's pushy."

"You were always running, swimming—everything before you met her."

Ford said, "So?"

Nodding, smiling, twisting his hair with his fingers, Tomlinson said, "Three months ago, maybe less, you meet this pretty woman—on a golf course or something, right? Dewey."

"She was golfing, I was fishing one of the lakes, trying to get a baby tarpon. Right. 'Bout three months."

"Within a week of meeting her, you quit drinking beer.

You never drank more than three a day, but you gave it up. Every night, I sit there on my boat, I look over here, and you're doing pull-ups. You're doing sit-ups. Now you take a breath, I can see your ribs. You've lost weight. There's a reason. And you're letting your hair grow longer. High time, I might add."

Ford owned five shirts, three pairs of long pants, and a half dozen sets of T-shirts and shorts. He said, "All this logic, Tomlinson—doesn't it make you thirsty?" as he searched through the neat stack of clothes.

He selected faded gray shorts and a blue denim shirt washed until it felt like silk, then slid on a pair of worn leather sandals from Guatemala as he said, "I quit beer because it was getting to feel like a habit. And I work out because I feel like crap if I don't. There are all kinds of ways the human body adapts to its role in an industrialized society—none good. So I choose not to adapt. A conscious decision."

"Industrialized society—*right*. Human adaptation." Tomlinson was shaking his head, accepting none of it, making Ford grin when he said, "Plumage, man. That's what you're doing. Brightening up the colors. Toning up the package for a mating display. And I've seen the way that girl looks at you."

"Oh, Lordy."

Tomlinson said, "If you ever need to borrow this pretty shirt of mine—"

Ford said, "I know, I know."

On the docks, Captain Nels was saying, "That jerk, that's who won the tarpon tournament. Captain Goof. The psycho liar. You know the guy. Everybody's buddy."

Captain Nels was hosing out his boat, standing on the bow, not looking at Ford, who was leaning against a piling, swatting at mosquitoes, having just asked who won. Nels stopped long enough to pack a pinch of snuff in his lower front lip, and said, "Karl Sutter won the eighty grand. Eighty frigging thousand dollars. Most fish, biggest fish. Out there all alone with his fat girlfriend," sliding the snuff tin into his shorts. Copenhagen.

Captain Felix was on his boat in the adjoining slip, dipping

31

out pinfish, putting them in a floating cage, talking to Nels and Ford both, saying, "Don't ask how he did it, man. Landed five fish. All that rain. All that wind. Like God was telling us that idiots shall inherit our chosen field of occupation." Felix, a big man, six five and wide, but reserved, was shaking his head as if amused with his own disgust.

"In-frigging-credible."

"There—that sums it up."

Nels said, "We work our butts off, using all the tricks. Dalbert and Javier, the guys from Parrot Bight, land five tarpon between 'em. My anglers got two. Felix's got two. Most everybody got two—released them all. Even the amateur boats. Sutter hasn't landed two tarpon in his career, but he comes in with five dead ones strung up. Hanging off the bow. Strung from the fly bridge; a damn funeral parlor for tarpon. Man, I couldn't stay down there at Parrot Bight and watch it. Someone says, 'Hey, Sutter, you're breaking the game laws. Only allowed to keep two.' Sutter says, 'I got the tags.' We tell 'im, 'Hell, doesn't matter. Still only allowed to keep two.' He says, 'So you guys are going to be bad sports about this? That's childish.' "

Felix said, "That's just what he said. 'Childish.' "

Nels said, "Felix and me just said adios to our clients and left. They were pissed at us anyway, wasting so much time with Rios's corpse. Shoulda just let the crabs eat him. No tip, either, and those people all had plenty of money."

Ford asked, "Sutter killed all the fish?" He was surprised. Tarpon were a game fish, not a food fish. These days, even novice fishermen knew it was bad form to kill a tarpon.

"Sure he did. But had tags for all of them, like he said. Fifty-buck tags from the state. Came in saying he was going to have 'em all mounted with the prize money. 'Nice profit,' he says. 'Cover my whole den.' The mounts will cost him maybe two grand, but that's not the reason he brought them in."

Felix said, " 'Cause no one woulda believed he caught that many fish, that's why he killed them. He was out fishing so deep, he says, he couldn't reach any of the committee boats on the radio. . . ."

32

Nels said, *"Right."*

"... but won't say where, like he's got a secret fishing hole. The tournament party they were supposed to have was canceled. Rios spoiled it, dying and all. And I just couldn't stand another minute of watching Sutter trying to act sad about his brother-in-law dying, but happy about winning all that money. Like watching a guy trying to rub his belly and load his pants at the same time." Felix was still smiling at himself. "Understand—it's not like we're *bitter* or anything, Doc."

Ford said, "Of course not," smiling with him.

Tomlinson was standing at the head of the dock near the marina office talking to MacKinley: MacKinley, thick, with short legs, looking up at the tall man with long hair.

As Ford walked up, MacKinley was saying, "... so I reckon Jeth threatened to kick Marvin's butt right there. On the docks in front of all these people down there at Parrot Bight. Said I'll put your midget ass in the hospital. Clever, like that. Pretty quick, for Jeth. Of course, he was stuttering, and that just made it worse."

Ford said, "Jeth, huh?"

"You heard about the argument he had with Rios? I was just telling Tomlinson."

Ford said, "A little."

MacKinley said, "Yesterday afternoon, Jeth pulled into Parrot Bight with clients. They wanted lunch. I guess Rios yelled at him for tripping over a gas hose; spilled some gas. Something of that sort. You know how clumsy Jeth's been lately. If all he does around here in a full day is spill some gas, I feel lucky.

"Jeth tries to explain it was an accident, but Rios chides him about stuttering so badly he can't understand anything; write it down—like a joke—and Jeth snaps. Embarrassed and all in front of his clients, plus the guides have a thing for Rios, anyway. Really loses it, like he's going to deck Rios right there, but Rios grabs a ball bat. Very ugly scene. I guess Jeth decided he'd had enough."

33

"Bad karma," said Tomlinson. "That whole place, Two Parrot Bight, has such a bad feel to it, I won't even go there. Sanibel Marina's okay; Jensen's great. But not Parrot Bight. Went once, but never again. Rios was a nasty little predator."

MacKinley was giving Tomlinson a familiar look, like standing in a zoo, looking through bars.

Ford was looking at him, too; strong words for Tomlinson. Ford said, "Where's Jeth now?"

MacKinley shrugged. "Stormed off last night in his boat. Haven't seen him since. I guess he called his clients last night and said he wouldn't fish the tournament. They showed up here bright and early, seriously pissed off. Reckon I made ten, twelve calls finding them another guide. I like Jeth, but he'd better not ever put me in a spot like that again. He's been acting very strange lately."

"Did his clients say what time he called?"

"Yeah. They said late. They were asleep. They had to get up for the tournament." MacKinley was looking at Ford, both of them thinking the same thing. "I don't think Jeth could've killed Rios," MacKinley said. "I really don't see him as a killer, no matter how mad he got."

"I don't think he could, either. I was just wondering where he is. A little worried, too."

Tomlinson said, "What? Kill somebody? Kill Rios? No way, not Jeth. I don't even know the man that well, and I can tell you."

"Karma?" said MacKinley.

"Exactly. For sure."

MacKinley said, "Jeth's probably with one of his girlfriends. I've never seen a man the women loved so much. Decent women, too."

Ford said, "It's just that he picked a bad time to disappear." He looked toward the mouth of the bay, watching a lone boat jolt abruptly, kicking mud in the shallow water—a pilot who didn't know the channel and couldn't read the water.

From the docks, Ford heard Captain Nels hoot. "Looky

34

there, boys! Over by Green Point. It's Karl Sutter coming to pay us a call. Out there plowing bean rows."

Karl Sutter was talking to himself, saying, "Aw damn, aw damn, aw crapola," thinking: *If the idiots around here would just mark the channels a little better.* . . .

He had run his boat through the mouth of Dinkin's Bay, planning to give those assholes Felix and Nels a quick flyby kick in the ego. No plans to stop, just sweep past the marina docks not even looking at them, letting these five big tarpon swinging on their ropes do the talking for him. Then out through the narrow opening in the wall of mangroves it showed on the charts, the one that led out into Pine Island Sound, where he could dump these damn fish, then get home and get to bed.

Christ, he'd only gotten—what?—three hours' sleep last night? Not much.

But before he could head for home, he'd have to wait out on the water for another half hour so the sun was completely down and no one would see him. Make sure to take the metal tags off the fish, too. But shit, the water wasn't deep enough to run a boat, not his boat, anyway; not outside the channel in this shitty little bay with its worm-eaten old posts for markers. Plus he couldn't even see the opening that was supposed to be there, so the bastards who made the charts were really to blame; a good lawsuit would serve them just about right, and he had the money to do it now.

Fuckers!

Sutter had his big gold Suzuki outboard tilted nearly out of the water, blasting a soup of gray marl twenty feet in the air, his engine screaming like some juiced-up Japanese dirt bike. He cut the wheel this way and that, gunning it, rocking it, spooking about a hundred birds off the little islands at the edge of the channel, pelicans and those birds with the long necks—cranes, he guessed, but maybe that wasn't right.

Then his boat begin to move, breaking the suction of the mud bottom, nosediving for a moment like a wild sled before jumping free, back into the deeper water of the channel, and

35

Sutter could feel the guides and everyone else at the marina watching.

Great! Now what?

There was no way he could make it to the little opening the chart showed—he still didn't see it—and if he just turned around and headed back out the channel, Felix and Nels and the rest of those assholes standing there would think he'd changed his mind about coming in, too embarrassed 'cause of running aground.

Sutter had a brief mental picture of his mother standing over him, big fat woman, wagging that one finger, saying, "They're just jealous, Colin, 'cause they know you're so much better. They ain't got the brains to know how to treat people like us."

Crazy old fat woman, but she knew people; knew them for what they were, the shitheels, the snobs, everyone acting high and mighty, stealing all the attention. Which is maybe why his mother was always on the move, one town for a year, the next town for two, then she'd get wise to the people, the way they'd stab you in the back if they had a chance, and they'd just pack up and leave. "Screw the rent," she'd say, "after the way they treated us here."

And the things she used to tell people. His dad had been a bomber pilot but got killed in the war. His dad had been a Hollywood actor—she'd name some actor—but they'd gotten divorced because she just couldn't stand Hollywood, too many fakes and all those wild parties. Of course, she'd kept the divorce out of the papers. She wanted her privacy and knew how to get it. And the one where they'd left New York because he was a boy genius and the college professors were after him, but they just wanted a simple life, so they'd skipped, left the bank account and everything, even though they had a lot of money and, of course, would someday go back and claim it.

Big woman in a cheap baggy dress with sweat stains, sucking on a cigarette with the ash growing; inhaling like nobody he'd ever seen with those big lungs, touching him while she talked, always touching him.

Shit, people would believe anything—for a while, anyway.

36

Then they'd get that look in their eyes, like she was some kind of weird bug, looking at him the same way, too, that high-and-mighty look, but a little uneasy, like the bug might bite. Marvin Rios was born with that look, his brother-in-law. Karl'd known it the moment they met, saw that look in Rios's eye, like no matter who Marvin shook hands with, he was doing them a favor, pulling away even as he was reaching out, like he didn't want to get his hand dirty.

But he'd married Marvin's sister, Judy, anyway, a woman with a shrill laugh he despised and a soft white body that just lay there, letting him do anything he wanted like she'd probably let a hundred other guys do. But she didn't have that look, which was important, and she knew how to get money out of Marvin, which was even more important.

So after four years of her, and after that little accident Judy'd had, Marvin says to him, "You think just because my sister's dead it cancels the money you owe me?"

As if he hadn't earned it, putting up with that crazy slut, the way she botched the two businesses he'd tried to start, never once getting off her fat ass to help, so he'd had to file Chapter 11, bankrupt because of her.

But Marvin wouldn't hear it, saying, "I know how your mind works, bub—and I also know how to put people like you in jail," giving him that look, shitting all over him, the little shyster, which was how he'd become Marvin's employee, not just an ex–brother-in-law.

But Marvin Rios had gotten exactly what he deserved—and, the best thing was, he hadn't had to lift a finger to do it. Not a finger. It was like God actually did him a favor for once; actually did him some good instead of ignoring him or crapping on him while He gave breaks to every other scum bucket on earth. Sending all that debt with Rios to the grave, and making him a free man with tournament money left over, all good luck, though he'd thought of doing it himself more than once.

Like that slut Judy with her laugh like a bird screaming. He hadn't needed God's help at all with Judy.

As his mother used to say, sucking that cigarette and waving it around, "Sometimes I just feel like killing them. . . ."

Karl Sutter slid his boat into gear and pointed it toward the marina, idling in now, feeling the familiar shallow-water tightening of stomach, trying to keep his boat in that shitty little channel, no wider than a ditch.

Sutter could feel Felix and Nels looking until he got between the marker ropes that funneled boats into the marina basin, then no one was watching, intentionally averting their eyes, refusing to look at the tarpon hanging on his boat, knowing these fish had made a lot of money for him, but probably too jealous to acknowledge it.

Like a bunch of damn kids. Childish, that's what they are.
. . .

Sutter's stomach tightened even more as he approached the dock, spun the wheel furiously and lurched into reverse too late, banging the dock—*whunk*—then hustling over to get a rope around a cleat before his boat drifted away.

He climbed out of the boat, nonchalant now, taking his time, removing his long-billed Hemingway cap to wipe his forehead, hand resting on the fishing pliers belted to his khaki shorts, trying to catch Nels's eye, already knowing what he'd say to the guides, the excuse for him coming here.

There were people on the docks, a few pretty women, and men with money acting like hotshots on their shiny cruisers, and Sutter made a show of tightening lines, checking the way the tarpon were tied to his boat, letting them see more big fish than most of these bastards had caught in their lives.

Near the office, the foreign guy who ran the marina—Mack-something they called him—was standing with two men. One was a big guy in a baggy T-shirt and wire glasses. And this other dude with long hair and a bright tourist shirt, some fucking zapped-out old hippie.

They were staring, and Sutter called, "Mind if I tie up for a while?"

The foreign one, Mack, said, "Long as you want. But if you

38

need something from the store, tell me now. I'm about to lock up," talking with a kind of accent, maybe British, adding, "You're Karl Sutter, right? They figure out what happened to Rios?"

Sutter, thinking, *As if you really give a shit,* said, "We're still in what you call shock; everybody at the marina's real upset. Marvin was a great guy, but he woulda been the first to admit he didn't what you call know a lot about boats and stuff. Being on the water."

The guy, Mack, said, "Is that right."

Sutter said, "Yeah, we figure he went out on the dock fishing or something. Maybe took one of the rental boats, 'cause his big boat's still at the marina, then somehow got knocked in, 'cause Marvin, he didn't swim so good."

The guy with the wire glasses, the one the hippie called Doc, said, "He didn't tell his wife where he was going?" Staring, not blinking. Not friendly or unfriendly, just looking at him.

Sutter didn't like this guy's eyes at all. Pale-blue eyes magnified by the glasses, not showing a thing, but a lot going on inside. Like a librarian on vacation with those glasses.

Sutter shrugged. "His wife, Candy, isn't in what you'd call a real talkative mood. I guess most guys who were me woulda spent their evening dumping down the champagne—I won the tarpon tournament today, ya know. Eighty thousand bucks. All mine. But I called the doctor to get her some pills. Had to kind of take care of things at the marina." He looked at Mack, and couldn't resist giving him the knife, adding, "Parrot Bight isn't like this place. Lot to be done with all the business it gets."

MacKinley, kind of smiling, said, "I can imagine."

Sutter said, "Tell you the truth, I had to kind of run things even when Marvin *was* there. He was a great guy and all but, like he was the first to admit, he wasn't what you call an expert about boats and things. But a truly great individual. Reminded me of my dad. My dad was a big bomber pilot, got killed in the war."

The hippie said, "Really? Hey, man, I'm sorry, I really am," and Sutter could see that he meant it, his expression sharing the hurt.

39

What a shmuck.

Sutter said, "Yeah, World War Two."

The guy with glasses seemed interested. "What unit?"

Sutter's mind scrambled, and he said, "Air force," then turned away quickly, looking for the other guides. "I gotta get going, gentlemen. Just stopped in to give your boys a few tips. But—hey—Mack? Just 'cause Marvin's gone doesn't mean our two marinas can't still work together. I'll make sure my people still send our overflow, smaller boats and stuff, straight here."

MacKinley said, "So you're running Parrot Bight now?"

"Well, you know women don't have the brain for that sorta thing, and I guess me being family, Candy's not gonna have nobody else to turn to." Sutter shook his head as if a little tired. "Christ, I sold my business up north 'cause I wanted outta the rat race. Made all the money I needed. But, hell, she's family, so what choice do I have?"

"Sounds like life has you in a corner, Sutter," giving it a tone, like he didn't have time to listen anymore. MacKinley stood there with a smile on his face, but not really smiling, just crapping all over him, and Karl Sutter couldn't think of a thing to say in return.

Asshole!

The two Dinkin's Bay guides, Felix and Nels, continued talking even though they could hear him walking toward them on the dock, hear his footsteps over the noise of the music and the women laughing, and Sutter heard Nels saying, "Know what they say about Key West? You drop a reel on the docks in Key West, you best kick it clear to Marathon before bending over to pick it up."

Sutter laughed louder than Felix, striding right up, letting his weight be felt through the wood of the old dock, saying, "You didn't know that, Felix? You really didn't know that? Fucking queers, man, they *own* Key West." Standing there looking eye to eye with Felix, who maybe weighed a little more but wasn't any taller. "I used to have plenty friends down there;

Duval Street scotch-drinking buddies. Hell, taught some of those guides how to fish the flats."

Nels said, "We were just watching you fish the flats. Out there."

"Huh?" Sutter said, giving him his shitkicker look. "What's that supposed to mean?"

"Lesson number one, is what it means: Don't drive your boat where the birds are standing."

"What? You guys thought I was aground? You shitting me. Just blasting some grass off my prop, that's all I was doing."

Nels and Felix were looking at each other, nodding, like they were trying not to smile. "So *that's* what happened."

Sutter said, "Didn't want to come in here at all, what with me still carrying those fish, but the goddamn taxidermist didn't show up at Parrot Bight, so I figure maybe he came up here by mistake. I mean, you guys didn't get any mounts today, right?"

Felix said, "Even if we did, we don't kill the fish. All you have to do is measure the damn thing and let it go. You get the same mount either way. Made out of fiberglass from a mold, and we still get our twenty-five percent from the taxidermist. You saying you don't know that?"

Sutter said, "You do it your way, I'll do it mine, 'cause my way seems to be working," looking across the dock at Jeth Nicholes's empty slip, with the sign that had his name in black and BACK COUNTRY FISHING / GUARANTEED FUN in orange. "Why didn't Jeth fish the tournament today? Figure too much competition?" Grinning, really giving these two hicks the knife.

"Skipped out alone in his boat last night. Didn't show up this morning. You'd have to ask him why."

Sutter said, "You don't say?" still looking at Jeth's empty slip. "Last night all by himself. You sure?"

"That's what I said."

"What time about?"

"How the hell should we know, Sutter? Late, for Christ's sake."

Sutter said, "And in that storm," noticing that the guy with the glasses, the one who'd been talking to Mack, was standing

41

looking at the tarpon hanging on his boat, but not touching them. Sutter asked, "Hey, who is that guy, anyway?."

Nels said, "Him? That's the guy that lives in the old fish house, Doc Ford."

"Like a real doctor, you mean?"

"Naw, a marine biologist. That kinda doctor, doing research. He's a good guy."

Sutter said, "Oh yeah. I heard Dalbert and the nigger talking about him. The scientist. At least that's what they think he is."

Felix said, "You better never let Jeth hear you talking about Javier like that."

"I know, I know. Jeth and Javier, big buddies. The hick and the spic."

"Knock it off!"

Sutter was still watching Ford. "Well, he is, isn't he? Javier. Cuban nigger. That's all Javier is. The way he talks about you guys, I wouldn't figure you'd be so fussy what I call him."

"And what does Javier say about us?" Sick of this guy, Felix was showing it.

Sutter shrugged. "The nigger and Dalbert both, telling people you're no longer the hot guides you used to be. Taking your old clients. But if you don't want to hear it . . ."

Felix said, "Karl, you're so full of crap, how do you still breathe through your nose?"

Putting his beer bottle on a piling, Nels said, "Thing is, Felix . . . wait a minute, I'm trying to remember. . . . Karl may be getting at something."

"Aw, come on."

"No. You know that dentist from Cleveland you fish? The old guy with the pretty wife. Yeah, the thing is, I saw Dalbert fishing that guy two weeks ago. I meant to tell you, but, hey!" He snapped his fingers. "Come to think of it, Dalbert had some of my old clients out last week, too. That son of a bitch, I never put two and two together."

Sutter held his palms up, a presto gesture. "Dalbert and the nigger, both of 'em. I tried to talk to 'em, but with Marvin in charge, all he cared about was getting the people booked, making the dough. But that shit's going to change now. You got to have ethics in a business like this."

"Ya know, you think you can trust a fellow guide. . . ."

Felix said, "Whoa, can't you see what this guy's trying to do, Nels?"

Nels said, "I know, I know, but it's just that things are starting to add up," draining the rest of his beer.

Sutter was watching the guy with glasses, who was now touching one of the tarpon hanging on his boat. Inspecting it. Studying the fish's eyes. Getting up on his tiptoes, trying to look into the fish's mouth.

Sutter said, "What the hell's that guy doing?" Then he yelled across the docks, "Hey, what the hell you think you're doing? Get away from my fish."

Felix said, "It's not like he's going to steal a dead tarpon, for Christ's sake," but Sutter was already walking down the dock, then walking faster, calling, "You got a hearing problem, man?"

But the guy with glasses, the one called Doc, was still messing with the fish. Not exactly ignoring him, but not paying attention, either.

Sutter went up to him fast, bumping him a little as he stopped, saying, "That's my private property you've got your hands on there, man."

The guy looked at him through those librarian glasses but made no move to step away from the tarpon—the biggest fish, probably 150 pounds, all gray, not silver now, except where blood had bloated it, and that part was black.

The guy they called Doc said, "Since the taxidermist is just going to dump them anyway, I didn't think you would mind—"

"I do mind. What the taxidermist does is between me and the taxidermist, okay?"

The guy had his hand on the fish again, turning it around and looking, but saying, "You're right. I should have asked first," and Sutter knew everyone was watching, judging him, every single one of these bastards just waiting for an excuse to

43

dump on him. And this asshole wouldn't take his hands off the fish.

"Okay, then, so get away from my boat."

No notice, no sign that he was moving; this guy was showing complete disrespect.

Sutter said more loudly, "I'm not going to tell you again."

The guy turned to him. "Where did you gaff this fish? I can't find a gaff mark on any of them," turning back to the tarpon, like he was reading those big scales . . . talking loud enough for Felix and Nels to hear, and Sutter knew he had to stop it.

Sutter grabbed the guy's arm, trying to pull him away. And the guy said, "Wait—don't do that."

Then, when the guy resisted, Sutter swung him hard toward the edge of the dock, thinking he could knock this guy right in, no problem.

Real cold, the guy said, "That was a mistake."

Then something happened; a blurry movement . . . then a hazy white light flashed in his eyes, like a flashbulb had exploded in his brain. And Sutter tried to refocus, realizing it must be because the guy had hit him, realizing that he was now on his back on the dock.

The guy with glasses was bending over him, had his arm locked around his elbow. Had his fingers jammed up under his jaw, creating so much torque and pain that all Sutter could make was a squeaking sound when he tried to talk, thinking in a panic, *This man is going to crush my throat.* . . .

Knowing this guy could do it, too. No doubt. Could break his arm or ruin his windpipe; looking up into the guy's face, seeing no rage, no hatred, nothing at all but a kind of blank indifference in those blue eyes through thick glass lenses. Like he was looking into a scope with cross hairs.

Sutter made his body go slack, submissive, closing his eyes, no longer struggling, and felt the guy's grip immediately relax a little. He heard Felix's voice say, "I think he's had enough, Doc."

44

Heard the guy say, "Does he always act like this?" Kind of perplexed, but interested.

Heard Nels say, "It's not worth getting into trouble over a weird one like him, man."

Then he felt the guy release him, and he stood up.

Sutter opened his eyes and got quickly to his feet, backing away, trying to speak, wanting to say something that would show this asshole he didn't know who he was messing with. But when his mouth opened, all that came out was a raspy sound, no words.

The guy, Doc, said, "You'll be all right in a little bit. Why the hell did you try to hit me like that? I was just looking at your fish." Like he was genuinely surprised.

Sutter was still rubbing his throat, backing away, and stepped into his boat, feeling everyone on the dock looking at him, giving him that buggy look, the men, the women; hearing his mother lecture, "You see they way they are?"

Karl Sutter freed the lines and started his boat, pulling away fast with a big wake that rocked the other boats, looking at the guy Doc, giving him his shitkicker look, trying to let him know.

You're a dead man, motherfucker. You are dead.

4

DEWEY Nye had asked, "You want to go fish nine?" talking to Ford over the phone from her Captiva Island beach house, where the VCR was playing, and Bud Collins was on the television screen, saying, "Even at her age, Martina is capable of playing the running serve and volley, cutting off the court, entirely dominating this younger player."

Dewey said, "I'm going nuts sitting here in the house watching tapes, getting my butt kicked over and over. I've got to be doing something."

Ford told her, "I thought we were going to work out this afternoon," which was his way of trying to say no. With him, it was always work, work, work. Dewey knew that to have a good time, she practically had to force him.

She told him, "We are going to work out, we are. But why not fish nine right after the storm? What, usually rains about five? So we go after the storm when all the other golfers have been run off. You fish and I'll bring the clubs and hit. Then we run later, when it's cool, and you won't bitch so much."

"A very kind invitation." Being a smart ass, like he had a tendency to be sometimes.

"See? Just thinking of you." Showing him she could be just as smart-assish.

So now they were at the thirteenth fairway of the Osprey Country Club, having parked along the road in this exclusive development with its piling homes shut tight among the trees, big air conditioners whirring; no one outside. Like a well-kept ghost town because of the heat and the mosquitoes.

Ford took the fly rod from the bed of his Chevy pickup, fitted it together and threaded line through the guides while she got her clubs out. "Hey," she said, "I just saw one roll. There's another, right there."

She had a good eye for fish—he'd told her that more than once, and she took real pleasure in proving him correct.

Ford followed her gaze to the water hazard, a small pond linked to a series of other small ponds and then a cement weir that, when flooded, led to the bay. An expanding circle in the water marked the spot where a small tarpon had just surfaced— one of many that had been trapped in these ponds over the years. Ford said, "No golfers, either. Lightning spooked them."

"Or these goddamn bugs. JEE-zus, why are the no-see-ums so bad right after a rain? You want some Skin So Soft?" She was rubbing the oil on her face and wrists, looking good in worn jeans and a white blouse, her blond hair long. The gnats drifted around her head, luminous as dust particles in the harsh sunset light.

"I'd rather have the bugs. Mineral oil works just as good, you know. Like flypaper on your skin; same concept."

"You already told me, but this smells better. Christ, they can bite."

"You don't actually feel the bite. No-see-ums—sand flies, really—they deposit a microscopic speck of acid. It dissolves the flesh. That's what you feel. Are you going to hit from the tee?"

"Nope. Working on the irons today." As she walked past him, clubs making a marching sound in her pro-size bag, she reached up and gave Ford's neck an affectionate squeeze, brushing him with her hip, thinking, *Doc's so damn dull sometimes, I believe you'd have to book an appointment. Tell him exactly what you wanted, and when. . . .*

He walked along the edge of the pond until he saw another

47

tarpon carousel at the surface. He tied on a tiny silver and white streamer fly, then began to strip line off his reel, letting it fall in a pile at his feet in the fairway grass. He shook the rod, goading the first thirty feet of line through the guides, and then began to false cast. Because the front section of line was slightly thicker and heavier, the rod fulcrumed the line easily, fore cast and back cast; a nine-weight Loomis graphite rod with a cork grip that moved as rhythmically in his big hand as a conductor's baton.

Checking over his shoulder on his back cast—he didn't want to hook Dewey—he could see that she had thrown golf balls at random around the fairway and had selected three irons, two of which lay on the ground behind her. She was studying her first shot, lining it up, as she pulled on the Easton batting glove she wore for golf, and Ford noticed again that her right wrist and forearm were huge from so much tennis. Much bigger than her left. And he could see the tiny white welt where she had had recent elbow surgery.

Another fish surfaced, twisting as it dove, and Ford shot line toward it, trying to get the fly in front of the fish and a little beyond. Behind him, he heard Dewey's club cutting the still air and then the green-twig crack of metal against golf ball, then silence, then the distant skip and splash of the ball landing in water.

"*Shit!*"

Looking at the spot where the ball had hit, Dewey thought, *Why is it my first few golf shots suck and it's just the opposite in tennis?*

It made no sense to her—because she enjoyed golf so much more. Not that she had played that much of it, hell no. With her parents, it had always been tennis, tennis, tennis. There was a color photograph her mother had kept on the mantelpiece for years: of her in pigtails, swinging a pro-size tennis racket, age four.

That's they way her life had gone.

Her father was a tennis fanatic—no other way to describe him. He'd wanted desperately to play pro tennis during the days of Poncho Gonzales, Rod Laver, Ken Rosewall, and Stan Smith, but he'd never had the talent—not that he would admit that, no.

48

In his mind, coaching was all he'd lacked, so he made damn sure that she had all the coaching she could bear, and then some.

Because her father had made a bundle of money at insurance and could afford it, she had been one of the youngest players ever accepted into the Nick Bolliteri Tennis Academy. Which meant that, all through adolescence, she lived in a dormitory, not at home. Which was hell at first, but then she grew to know the other girls so well that they were more of a family than her real family. After that, it wasn't so bad. In fact, it was pretty good.

She'd spent some time at the Harry Hopman Auzzie Camp, too, and played all the USTA tournaments, and won her sectional at fourteen, which was considered a hell of a thing to do in those days, and then she won her age group in nationals, two years running, so going pro was the next logical step.

Only it had never crossed her father's mind that she would someday grow tired of tennis. Tired of *him* first, really, and tennis second. But she had, sure enough. So weary of both of them that she could hardly bear to think of it. So she only talked to her father about once a month by phone. And, since the elbow operation, she only worked at tennis when her best friend from NBTA, Bets, who was Romanian, chided her into it.

Otherwise, she played golf. Which she loved—except for the first few shots, in which she really sucked.

Goddamn it!

Smiling, Ford let the fly sink through the murk and began to strip it back slowly, his concentration vectoring on that unseen point where his lure and the fish should intersect . . . but they did not. This time, anyway. He made several more casts, listening to Dewey's running commentary behind him, talking to herself as if no one was there to hear.

"Oh Christ, look at this divot—I want the mineral rights on this one. . . . That's right, Nye, hit *another* one in the water. Russian judge gives that about a six. Good height, bad entry. . . . Military golf, that's what Miss Nye is playing today, folks: left, right, left, right."

Ford reeled his line in, watching her. "Having fun?" he asked.

She looked up, jaw set, eyes intense. "Hold it." She stood over her last ball, brought the club up slowly, then swung down through it. Ford watched the ball start low, rising on a line, then hit once on the distant green before kicking back toward the flag.

"Finally," she said, gathering her clubs. "Two to the left, five just off to the right, and one on the dance floor."

"How far is that?"

"Hundred sixty yards, maybe one seventy."

"My gosh."

"You want to try?"

"Naw."

"Why not?"

"I already told you, I played golf once. It was like tennis. I spent the whole time apologizing."

Dewey said, "Hit just one, and maybe a little later I'll try to catch a fish. I can give you some tips."

Ford said, "Okay, just one," and laid his rod carefully in the grass, taking the club the woman offered, and stood over the ball as he had seen golfers on television do.

Dewey was saying, "Don't try to hit it hard, just hit it solid. Keep the club face square; don't let your body get out in front."

Ford said, "Right, uh-huh, okay," then hit the ball like a rocket toward the green, but it sliced way right, where it disappeared toward the line of trees and houses.

Dewey had been squatting down, watching, and now she stood, taking the club from Ford. "You're right," she said.

"Huh?"

"About golf. You suck."

Ford was still looking where his ball had gone, and Dewey said, "Hope some kid's dog wasn't over there playing or something. Well . . . if it was, it's dead, and there's nothing you can do about it now. Or maybe an old lady out watering her flowers."

"Fine golf coach you'd make."

"Wait till I try to teach you tennis."

50

"After my next golf lesson. You're so encouraging."

She cupped her hand around the back of his neck. "Aw, I *am* too tough on you, aren't I, Doc? I guess that's why you never ask me out. Is that the reason? It's always me that asks you." Joking with her voice, but not joking with her eyes, looking at him.

"You mean, like a date?"

"You do catch on quick, buster." Smiling a question with her expression, then answering it herself. "I'm too abrasive, huh? Maybe too young for you—you said that once."

"I don't remember ever saying—"

"Well, maybe you didn't. Just an idea, that's all."

"And you just called it quits with your guy Doug. On the rebound—isn't that what they call it?"

"Mr. Have Porsche Will Babble? More like on the short hop from him. No romance; strictly buddies, and then that wasn't enough for him. Dougie reminds me too much of that guy on the reruns . . . Alan Alda? Talk, talk, talk, like he was imitating Groucho Marx all the time, but not funny." Dewey was shouldering her bag, ready to move to the next hole. "Besides, you're the only guy I've ever hung around with where I actually learned something. And the only one who didn't try to give me advice on my ground stroke. Talking about bugs and fish and stuff. I like that. I always was sort of a nature buff."

"Your what stroke?"

"See?" Grinning, she gave him another one of those squeezes, communicating on a whole different level as she brushed past him, saying, "Don't forget your rod, dearie."

On the next hole, Ford made a steady series of casts without a strike, while Dewey hit irons, talking about tennis more, it seemed to Ford, to put distance between the talk of dating than to actually discuss the sport. She said, "The thing with tennis, you absolutely work your butt off to qualify for the Grand Prix Circuit and, once you qualify, you still have to work like a maniac to maintain your ranking. Mucho pressure. There's a major tournament someplace every week of the year, except Christmas, so that means you better by God be there on the

51

court, ready, or you begin to slide in the ratings. You live in hotels and planes. Really sucks after a while. More than once I woke up and had to find the telephone book just to remember where I was."

She was hitting balls, nearly every shot straight now, relaxed and enjoying herself, but introspective, too. Ford hadn't seen this side of her.

"The way it works is, the whole thing's computerized. Computer figures the weight of the tournament—that's how many seeded players—then figures in the purse, gives a bonus if you beat a seeded player, and that all works out to a single number. You're better off making the semis in two big tournaments than winning two small ones. Complicated."

He said, "I see that."

"Miss a few tournaments, your number slips. Last year, playing full time, I was ranked nineteenth in the world. This year, with the injury and all the time off, sixty-fourth. Three years ago, my best year, I was thirteenth. Lucky thirteen. You can make a lot of money just beating seeded players, not even winning, but I made a lot more on exhibitions, endorsements. But that's changed now. Even the big manufacturers aren't giving long-term contracts anymore. Strictly year by year, and all incentive-type stuff, unless you're Graf or Martina."

Ford said, "Yeah?" wondering where she was going with this.

Dewey said, "You know what bothers me the most?"

"What's that?"

She hit another long iron, the ball's trajectory creating a brief laser streak, catching the remnant pink flare of sunset. "I've been playing tennis nearly every day of my life since age five. . . ." She began to put her clubs away, done now, her face sweaty and standing close enough so that he could smell the woman mixture of sweat and body lotion. "I've been on the circuit nearly eight years now . . . and the thing that bothers me is that I wasn't born for it. Not born just for that. Tennis, I mean."

"Oh?"

"No."

Ford waited, thinking she would explain, but when she didn't, he said, "What, then?"

She started to say something, stopped. Something serious, but then she made a joke of it, explaining, "Here's what I was really born for—golf. Born for the LPGA."

Ford said, "For a second, I thought you were going to tell me you were retiring."

Dewey thought, *Jesus God, he's scary sometimes.* . . .

But she said, "Well . . . maybe transfer, but never quit. Skip the French Open and maybe surface in the spring at Augusta. Take the summer off tennis, then make my bid as a links star. That would shock the shit outta the sportswriters, wouldn't it?"

She was moving closer, making too much of the joke, and Ford knew that she really had almost told him—told him that she was thinking of quitting. He lifted his arm, and she slid under it, and he could feel her ribs beneath his fingers, warm inside the damp blouse.

For Dewey, it was like being alone together for the first time.

Ford said, "You want to get something to eat?"

"Bullshit, we run first. Then eat."

"Okay, okay."

She turned her face and kissed him flatly on the cheek, a real smacker, before pulling away. "See?" she said. "Asking me out isn't so hard."

Ford was in his lab beneath the gooseneck lamp that threw a wafer of yellow light over the wooden floor and onto the walls, showing the stainless-steel dissecting table, a wooden chair, shelves with books and chemical jars, and rows of larger jars containing preserved specimens: nudibranchia, brittle stars, anemones, eels, unborn sharks, and tiny tarpon, all floating motionless, adding to the night silence as he sat alone over his microscope.

But then there was a sound: the combustion ratchet of a hand-crank outboard starting, the boat getting closer and closer.

Ford waited until he felt his stilt house jolt slightly—the impact of a skiff landing at his dock—before he got up and took a bottle of beer from the little refrigerator. He placed the bottle on the empty chair, then returned to his Wolfe stereomicroscope, looking and making notes.

There was the thumping vibration of someone coming up the steps, then, over his shoulder, Tomlinson's voice said, "You have company? Thought you might have some company."

Ford said, "Nope."

The screen door opened and closed. "There's a car parked out there. By the mangroves down from your walkway, like they didn't want to be seen."

"Oh?"

"Yeah, I just saw it."

"Probably a couple of kids parking, looking at the moon."

Tomlinson said, "Yeah, it's bright tonight. Bay's pure silver." Then he said, "Ho boy, my favorite refreshment," opening the bottle of beer and sitting down. "God blessed this earth with forests and oceans and plenty of brewers, huh?"

Ford looked at him, rocking back in the chair and drinking. Tomlinson wore no shirt, no shoes; his abdominal oblique muscles showing on the skinny torso, his long arms with veins, probably wearing the same ragged cutoffs he'd worn at Woodstock or Altamont.

"How'd your date go last night?"

"Nice; very nice. This woman is a truly enlightened human being, Doc. Harry, that's her name. Really brilliant, which is no big deal, but spiritually awakened. Not a bad set of dials, either."

"Dials?"

"You know, running lights. Knobs. Berks. Diddies. Love snorbs."

"Ah."

"Yep."

"Harry's the one wanted you to marry her?"

"Well, yeah—father her children, at least. It's one of those genetic deals. She considered all the guys she's ever known, and

54

decided I was the one who had the most to offer. She's only human."

"From Boston, you say?"

"Yep. Her name used to be Musashi Rinmon, but she changed it." Tomlinson took a long drink, reflecting. "After that, it was Moontree, which I liked a lot. That was her name when I first met her, but she switched to Harry as a kind of a protest thing. Glad she didn't show up in time to see you smack Sutter. That was very ugly. *Very* ugly. I personally didn't approve."

"So I just stand there and let him knock me off the dock?"

"Why not? The guy's disturbed, man. You don't feel that in him? I do. Damn dad gets killed in the war dropping bombs on people—enough to disturb anybody. So he knocks you off the dock. So what? We have to learn to absorb indignities, Doc. You're too big a person to let the small stuff bother you."

Still looking into the microscope, Ford said, "You're wrong."

"Well, *I* think you're too big a person."

"Wrong about that, too, but Sutter's father wasn't killed in the war—at least not dropping bombs. He said his dad was in the air force. The air force didn't exist during the Second World War. It wasn't founded until a couple of years later, after the atomic bomb was dropped. It was the army air corps. The sons of war heroes don't make that kind of mistake."

Tomlinson said, "I'll be damned. But he was so convincing, like *he* believed it. Well, I'd rather be naive than cynical."

"I'm aware of that."

Tomlinson was watching Ford concentrate. "Find any tarpon larvae yet? Solve the mystery of where tarpon spawn?"

The tarpon was one of the most popular game fish on earth, but almost nothing was known about its life history—not even where the animals spawned, though there were indications that spawning took place far offshore.

Still looking through the microscope, his glasses balanced on his forehead like goggles, Ford told Tomlinson it was going to take more than one researcher working in one area to solve

55

the mystery. He straightened and rubbed his eyes. "But that's not what I'm looking for. Yesterday, when I was up by the Mud Hole—just below Captiva?—I took a water sample. I saw some dead fish floating around up there, so I'm checking for red tide."

"Aw, man, I hope not. Couple years ago, I was anchored up off Sarasota. Siesta Key, and we got a real bad red tide. Man, these bloated fish floating everywhere. Every kind of fish; some real weird-looking eels, too. Like the whole ocean had died, and you take a breath, your lungs burned. This guy I talked to, this guy who'd lived there forever, told me every time oil companies started dropping sample wells, they got a red tide. Pollution, man, it's going to kill us all one day."

Ford rotated the calibrated dial on the microscope, increasing magnification, and said, "Most researchers wouldn't agree. Not about pollution, but about what causes red tide. Most say it's a natural phenomena. It's worldwide, you know. Some are studying if maybe increased agricultural runoff—phosphates, nitrates from fertilizer—maybe catalyze increased blooms, but most think it's just something that happens."

Tomlinson said, "I don't know, man."

Ford was looking through the microscope again. "Well, red tide only describes discoloration caused by plankton bloom. It might or might not be toxic. The nontoxic blooms can still kill fish, because if it's concentrated in an area where the water doesn't flush, it depletes oxygen. Fish suffocate. Usually at night, when plant plankton can't manufacture oxygen, so has to take it from the water. See?"

Tomlinson was listening, so Ford continued. "Take the bridge they built from the mainland to Sanibel back in the sixties. The spoil islands interrupt the natural flushing of the bays. The water's shallow, so plankton blooms become even more concentrated. Result: same amount of red tides, but they're more deadly to fish. Peripheral impact—that could be an ecological science."

"Yeah," said Tomlinson, "or like an epitaph. Florida's. Died from peripheral impact. But it's the same thing, man. You see that." He was becoming animated, using his arms to talk.

"It's greed. A destructive force. The progeny of light casting a dark shadow."

Ford shrugged. "I don't see it that way; I don't think you believe that, either. It's just the way we are; the way we make it as a species. Sometimes we're too successful."

"Right."

"You know—*successful*."

"No, what?"

Ford said, "Like . . . well, say a tribe of orangutans lives in the same small valley for a hundred years. In, say, Sumatra, feeding on a few big mango trees. Then one day, one of the orangs discovers that he can knock all the mangoes off the tree using a stick. Doesn't have to climb. But the mangoes they can't eat rot on the ground. Soon they're starving."

"Uh-huhmmh," said Tomlinson. "A destructive catalyst."

"No, it's a process. We exist as a species because we adapt our environment to fit us. Ants and bees have the same ability. Nothing ugly about bees, is there? Very few species travel through history in a straight line. There are a few exceptions: horseshoe crabs, certain sharks, maybe tarpon. A few others. But most go banging back and forth, traveling blind alleys, making special mistakes, then finding new ways to survive. The orangutans leave the valley and become solitary nomads. See? We're the same way. It's not a matter of it being ugly or greedy or sinful. It's a process, a way of evolving."

Tomlinson pondered that, then looked at his empty bottle. "You want one?"

Ford said, "I meant to have a beer yesterday. So sure. Tonight I had dinner with Dewey and she's got a thing about alcohol. I think her father had a drinking problem."

Ford switched slides as Tomlinson went across the walkway to the refrigerator, letting both screen doors bang behind him, thinking his way back as he handed Ford the beer. "So explain this," he said. "Thirteenth century, Genghis Kahn conquers China, and his grandson Kublai Khan, same thing in Russia. Scorched earth. At the very same time, the Seventh Crusade is preparing in France. Same phenomenon occurs off and on throughout history. The Second World War; Hitler. That's fucking inimical, man, not a process."

Looking up briefly, amused, Ford said, "What the hell does that have to do with what we're talking about?"

It had become a game with them: present a single concept, then follow that concept through its various branchings, induce the narrowing arteries of thought until they exited out onto larger platforms of truth or nonsense.

Tomlinson, who spent his days reading esoteric books on world history and doing God knows what else, was prone to make intuitive leaps, forgoing linear thought; leaps that produced some interesting conclusions. Which is why Ford kept beer in the refrigerator for Tomlinson.

Tomlinson said, "Those blind alleys you were talking about. Special mistakes. Spee-shell, as in species?"

"Yeah."

"You agree that worldwide killing is a special mistake?"

"Well . . . sure."

"Happens when one or more leaders takes a group down one of your evolutionary blind alleys. Right? Like Hitler led the Germans."

Ford said, "Okay."

"So replace the guns with earthmovers and replace the bullets with nuclear-waste dumps, pollution, oil spills—"

"I see what you're getting at."

"—and instead of just the population of a society following along, make it the entire world population because of advances in communication. Replace Kublai Khan with technology. Technology is the world's new dictator. And everyone following it right down a blind alley, picking up the mango stick. Trouble is, we're not just taking the fruit, we're killing the entire valley. That's not a process; it's a kind of hysteria. Like world war."

Ford said, "You're taking the analogy too far."

Tomlinson said, "Nope, nope; damned if I am. A destructive force sparked by a catalyst, that's what I'm talking about. The catalyst can be a man, or an idea, or a method—like the

58

orangutan with a stick. You don't see the parallels in nature? Introduce an unstable cell into a body of living tissue, and the result may be cancer. Introduce an unstable atom into a chain of atoms, and you have a nuclear holocaust. The microcosm and the macrocosm, man. What's true of the tiniest unit is true of the whole. A basic principle."

"All I was trying to do was explain red tide, Tomlinson—"

But Tomlinson was standing now, walking around the room, flapping his arms, thinking aloud. "The reaction to the catalyst, though, can be positive or negative. Yin and yang, that's another basic principle. But it's different for man than the rest of nature. See why? Because we can consciously decide whether to be constructive or destructive. That's important."

Resigned to listening, Ford took the cold bottle in his hand as Tomlinson said, "That option implies a higher force. Absolutely; a higher consciousness. That single option is the hot line to the force of good and the force of evil." He stared at Ford for a moment. "You can't doubt that they exist."

Looking at the bottle, Ford said, "Well, actually—"

"And I'll tell you why you can't doubt that good and evil exist."

In a louder voice, Ford said, "I'm trying to concentrate on this slide."

Tomlinson said, "It doesn't seem to apply at first, but it does: The reason you can't doubt is because a body in motion has a greater mass than a body at rest. That's a fact of physics that applies to all matter. But where does the additional mass come from? No logic can explain it. Yet it's there. The sum of the whole is greater than the sum of its parts. Like saying two plus two equals four, but two hundred plus two hundred equals five hundred. It's mathematical nonsense, yet it's a fundamental truth. The effects of this mysterious force can be measured, but the force itself can't be isolated. You know why?"

Ford was pushing his chair back, standing, saying, "No, I don't—here, have a look at this."

Tomlinson said, "Because it's the universal positive and the universal negative. It's an adhesive phenomenon; doesn't exist until a catalyst is introduced. We can access it positively or access it negatively . . . but we need to be damn careful, because the destructive path is almost always the path of least resistance. Yeah, that's true—but why? Why the hell is that? . . ."

He let the thought trail off, his mind pondering, but he was already straddling the chair, confronting the microscope. After a moment, he shook his head and said, "What're we looking for here?" as if he just woke up.

Ford said, "Dinoflagellate. I finally found the kind I wanted."

"Hum. . . . How'd you adjust this damn thing? My eyes must be different from yours." Tomlinson was squinting into the binocular tubes. "Oh . . . okay, now I see. Tiny little animals, man. Bunch of 'em."

"There's one near the middle, a real slow mover. Kind of a yellowish green, moving with its pointed side first, and like it has ribbon wrapped all around it."

"Sure, yeah—I got it. Weird, man. The water's alive."

"That dinoflagellate is *Gymnodinium breve,* which causes toxic red tide. It doesn't suffocate fish. *Breve* dies after it blooms, sinks to the bottom, and becomes neurotoxic as it decomposes. That's the one that causes your lungs to burn. It accumulates in bivalves, like oysters, and makes them toxic to humans. Can cause massive fish kills, too."

"So it's here, huh? We got red tide in the bay . . . well, crap."

"No, there's not enough of them. By my count, anyway. They're always in the water, but sometimes, for some unknown reason, they'll begin to multiply like crazy. Split asexually, billions of them, and that's when the trouble starts. That's what they call a bloom."

Tomlinson considered that for a moment. "But something causes the bloom."

"Yeah. Of course."

"It's just that no one knows what."

"Right."

Tomlinson said, "The *X* factor, man. The catalyst that keys the destructive force. I rest my case."

Ford said, "Oh, boy," moving to the window, listening. Then he said, "There's a boat coming in. Running across the flats without lights. Somebody who knows the water."

"Probably a mullet fisherman."

Beyond the window, the bay was swollen white, smooth, and Ford could see the scarecrow shapes of the channel markers and the charcoal sketch of mangrove islands. The boat was a small black void, moving fast, casting a wake like silver sparks in the moonlight.

Ford said, "No. Not a mullet boat."

"What is it, after midnight? Somebody out fishing late, or just coming in from dinner at Cabbage Key. Got caught in the Heineken trap at the bar."

Ford turned and said, "Let's walk over to the docks."

"Sure. You want a beer for the road?"

"Grab three. I think that's Jeth's boat."

Stepping out into the summer night was like stepping into warm water, but with sounds and odors. Fragrance of night flowers. *Thunk-whap* of jumping mullet. Sulfuric gas oozing from the mangrove muck like a long, hot breath; the moon sinking in the west and so bright the two men threw shadows as they stepped off the boardwalk onto the path that led to the marina parking lot.

"Somebody's been here smoking cigarettes, man. Smell it? Still strong."

"Where was that car parked?"

"Just over there. Probably those kids. They must have just left, but I didn't hear the engine start."

"I did. You were talking."

"Kids out here parking and smoking. Probably doing heavy petting while we're in there talking about the end of the world. I like that."

Ford said, "Me, too."

"I don't think I even know anybody who smokes anymore, do you?"

"A couple of the guides, no one else."

"High school, I didn't do anything. Young Democrats and baseball, that's all. College, though, man. Like someone plucked my brain out and said, 'Hoo, this thing could use a little *color*.' "

Looking, Ford said, "Yeah, that's Jeth's boat. I can see the lines." They ducked under mangrove limbs, then zigzagged between boats on trailers that showed in the marina's high, bright mercury lights. When they got to the docks, Ford stopped at the bait tanks, suddenly feeling as if he might be intruding.

"Let's just stand here and see if Jeth wants to talk."

"Gotcha; know exactly what you mean. Guy's been gone two days, maybe the reason's personal. And it's not like we're the only ones up."

From the rows of darkened boats came the low whisper of night voices . . . muted laughter . . . live-aboards awake in the moonlight. Ford watched Jeth Nicholes idle his old blue Suncoast skiff through the entrance of the marina basin, then dock it smartly with a brief sternward burst of throttle, reaching out to take the dock lines. He looked toward the bait tanks, looked again, then called softly, "That you, Doc?"

"Hey, Jeth."

Tomlinson said, "We got a little welcome-home present for you. Got a dear little beer for you." Waving the bottle at him. "Where the hell you *been,* man?"

Ford cringed.

"What?" Jeth was pulling the scupper plugs, tilting his engine, not paying a lot of attention.

"Something cold. Drink it right down."

Not even listening, he said, "I know you're different and all, Tomlinson, but don't be calling me dear." Nicholes took the key from the ignition and looked up. "I don't go for that stuff."

"We've got a *beer* for you."

Jeth said, "O-o-o-h, that's better. Ran out of ice on the way back this morning, then ran out of warm ones 'bout noon." He was talking as he climbed stiffly out of his boat, clomping toward them, waving shyly, big thigh muscles knotting with each step beneath his shorts: man in his late twenties with straight black hair, all shoulders and narrow hips, and the kind of loyal face found on linebackers in high school yearbooks.

He took the bottle and tossed the cap into the water, saying, "We meet again," as he drank off half the beer, wobbling as he tilted his head back, and Ford wondered if he was already drunk.

"Must have been kind of a long trip, huh?"

Jeth said, "What makes you think that, Doc?"

"You said you ran out of ice this morning, so you had to be someplace you couldn't buy it. Way offshore, or way south. Ten Thousand Islands, maybe? You grew up in Everglades City, so I thought maybe you made a trip home."

"Yeah, down to the islands, but I didn't stop in Everglades. Kept going south. Get down around Cape Sable, not many marinas where you can stop and buy ice. That's smart, Doc."

Cape Sable was the southwesternmost point of mainland Florida, all raw mangrove islands and wilderness between Flamingo and Marco Island, a stretch of more than a hundred miles of undeveloped shoreline—undeveloped only because it was part of the National Park System.

Ford said, "I'd call Cape Sable a long trip. And in an open boat."

Jeth said, "Yeah, well . . ."

Ford stood waiting for him to continue, not wanting to press the issue, but Jeth remained silent, oddly vacant and a little dreamy, too, leaning his weight on the bait tank as he finished his beer. The way he was behaving made Ford uneasy.

Finally, Ford said, "You see any tarpon down that way?"

Jeth said, "A few."

Ford waited again before he said, "Any big schools moving north? That's what a lot of people say, you know: tarpon come up from the Keys to Sanibel and Homosassa."

"One big school down off Lost Man's River, but I don't believe that, anyway. People like to talk. They gotta have a reason for everything."

"And the fish didn't seem to be moving north?"

63

"Naw, not so's I could tell." Jeth dropped his bottle into the trash bin and said, "Well, nice talking to you fellas," moving off, looking up at the dark windows of his apartment built over the marina. "I better get up there and get some food out for Crunch & Des."

Crunch & Des was Nicholes's large black cat, named for two famous fishing guides.

He said, "I don't feed him for a couple days, he gets mad and pisses on my pillow."

Ford said quickly, "You hear Tomlinson had a date last night?" trying to keep the conversation going.

Jeth stopped, mildly interested for the first time. "No kiddin'," he said. "She pretty?"

Tomlinson said, "Gorgeous, man. Black hair down to her waist, plus she is truly a spiritual human being. Good dancer, too."

Jeth was turning away again as he said, "That's good, Tomlinson. Never date an ugly woman, 'cause you never know when you're going to fall in love," but then he stopped suddenly. "Hey, you guys know what I saw down there? Down there off Shark River?"

"What's that?"

"I saw the green flash, man. Right at sunset, out there all alone in my boat. I did; I really did see it."

Tomlinson said, "Wow," impressed.

Jeth said, "People'd told me about the green flash, but I'd never seen it. And with all the days I've spent on the water, I just figured, hell, it's just a bunch of bullshit. But I really saw it. Watched the sun go right down behind the Gulf, and the moment it disappears, all red and orange—*poof*—a bright green flash. Like a green flashbulb had gone off. I mean it was bright! Always thought the islands'd be the perfect place to see it. Sky's so clear, and there it was." Jeth was smiling, not looking at them.

Ford said, "That's why you ran clear to Cape Sable? Mac-Kinley said you canceled your all-day tournament trip."

Jeth shrugged. "Naw, I went because I wanted to. Just had to get away, that's all. Had to get someplace where I couldn't see

64

buildings. Threw some extra fuel cans in the boat and just took off. Ran most the night Friday. Ran out of a big thunder squall off Fort Myers Beach. Other than that, it was nice out there with all those stars. But Christ, has this coast been built up. One condo after another; didn't even realize how much it'd changed."

Tomlinson said, "Put your life in four-wheel drive, man. That's the way to do it. Climb out of the rut."

Speaking directly to Tomlinson now, Jeth said, "You know, when I saw that green flash, it was like a sign. It really was. You'd understand that. That's just the way I felt, not seeing it my entire life, then finally seeing it. Like it meant something. A great big flash outta nowhere."

Tomlinson was nodding his head. "Absolutely, man. No doubt. Signs try to speak to us every day, it's just that almost no one listens. The Indians knew it."

Ford said, "I was out yesterday morning, and Nels and some of the other guides found a body. It was Marvin Rios, dead. They found him up at the Mud Hole by Hardworking Bayou."

Jeth was nodding. "Heard it on my AM radio on the way back. Rios was a prick, only the radio didn't say that. Radio just said he had a broken neck, maybe murdered."

Ford said, "Murdered?" He hadn't listened to the news all day, and it was the first he'd heard it.

"Yeah, the radio said maybe he was beaten to death."

Tomlinson said, "Like about two weeks ago, this owl lands on top my mast, going 'hoo, hoo, hoo.' Next morning, I'm stepping over these owl pellets all over my deck and I stub the shit out of my toe. Just as I'm bending down to hop around, the boom swings over my head, coulda knocked me right over."

Jeth said, "Trying to warn you."

"Exactly, the owl."

Ford said, "That was on the radio?"

"About Rios? Yeah, about an hour ago; I was just off Naples beach. A Naples country station."

Holding his foot out for inspection, Tomlinson said, "Here, look at my foot. The damn nail's about to come off."

Jeth said, "That owl saved your life."

Tomlinson held his palms upright, a can't-argue-with-the-evidence gesture.

Jeth said, "Those are the kinda signs I never thought about."

Tomlinson said, "It's because we don't pay attention, man. But they're definitely there."

Ford said, "Who do you think would've killed Rios?"

Jeth said, "Probably the first sane person to get a good chance," walking away, showing them with his expression that he didn't want to talk anymore. He called to them, "Well, 'night," and unlocked the door to his apartment, where the cat was already meowing at his feet.

On the way back to the stilt house, Ford said to Tomlinson, "He didn't stutter. Not once. Before this weekend, Jeth couldn't put five words together. Now he doesn't stutter."

Tomlinson was nodding, gliding along beside him. "The man definitely seemed different."

"He even moves differently. I can't put my finger on it."

Tomlinson said, "To me, he seems very aware. Very in tune. Plus, he could have been real drunk. Hard to tell with Jeth."

"In tune like a zombie, that's the way he seemed to me. Acting strange. Something happened to him."

"Saw the green flash, man. An awakening. Hey—" Tomlinson stopped walking for a moment. "What the hell's the green flash, anyway?"

"You've never heard of it?"

"If I did, it's lost now. Maybe I did. I can't be sure. It just sounds so neat. *Green flash.* And the way Jeth described it, like a giant flashbulb. I want to see it, man; I'm gonna start looking."

Ford said, "Don't get your hopes up. It has something to do with the distance sunlight travels at the earth's horizon. The light travels farther, something like that. The distance bends and separates the light, makes the sun seem visible after it has already sunk below the horizon. If conditions are just right, the yellow of the sun mixes with the blue of the sea, and it's like a chemical reaction. Volatile. Like an explosion; a great flash of green. But the atmosphere has to be perfectly clear. I've seen it other places in the world, but only twice in Florida. Once at sunrise, once at sunset, and that was years ago, before all the cars. With the monoxide fumes, you don't see it."

"You're telling me it needs a pure canvas?"

"Well, in a way, yeah."

"O-o-o-oh, this is great. I *have* heard of it. Only I thought I dreamed it. The perfect metaphor. Nature's litmus test—tells you when she's healthy by flashing you the green light. All systems go. Man, my mind; my mind . . ."

Ford said, "Could use a good scrubbing."

"No, it's like getting to live everything twice. Sometimes three, four times."

"Uh-huh."

"That's what happened to Jeth. He saw the great sign, the green flash, and it's changed his life."

Ford said, "Well, I don't think he stopped stuttering because he saw a pretty sunset, or because he heard an owl call, or any of that kind of stuff. Something's happened to him, and I just hope to hell it has nothing to do with Rios."

Tomlinson started to say something, but then he touched Ford's shoulder. "Hey, is your skiff caught under the dock or something?"

Ford could see the boat in the moonlight, the bow straining upward, the stern sitting way too low; he took off running. The whole back deck was nearly underwater, the engine riding barely above it. He grabbed an empty bucket and began to bail, leaning over from the dock because he knew his weight on the boat would probably be enough to roll it.

Tomlinson said, "You got some kind of pump running in there. Hear it?"

"Probably the bilge pump, but it's not pumping water."

Tomlinson was leaning over the boat, fishing his hands into compartments. He said, "You left the bait pump running, Doc.

67

That's what happened. You got the kind of bait pump that brings in raw water from outside?"

"I didn't leave the bait pump running. I've never done that." Ford was still bailing, starting to make a little progress.

"Yep, that's what happened. The overflow scupper got plugged." Tomlinson was holding up a plastic bag—a used ice bag, which he placed on the deck. "Sucked this thing right up it, that's what happened. Here—" He leaned over with his long arm and hit a toggle switch on the boat's console, and the humming of the pump stopped. "Now your boat's not sinking anymore. You've got to be more careful, Doc."

Still bailing and beginning to sweat in the night heat, Ford said again, "I didn't leave the bait pump running," meaning that someone had tried to sink his boat.

5

FORD was usually out of bed by 6:30 A.M., but the next morning, Sunday morning, the mosquito bombers attacked Sanibel at dawn.

Lying in bed, his eyes opened at the first distant rumble, and he thought the noise was thunder; that they were in for another morning storm.

But then the noise translated itself, that deep engine roar, and he threw the sheet back and walked naked to the window, looking out into the pearly light to see a formation of old DC-3s, World War II prop planes, flying in low over the mangroves, off Pine Island Sound. There were three planes, flying in tight formation, and, one by one, their spotlights burst on as they neared the island, coming in low over Dinkin's Bay, pointing right at his stilt house and the marina, as if on a strafing run.

Damn.

Ford ran to his bed, stripped the sheet off in a single motion, then was out the screen door. The roar of the planes was deafening now—Christ, they couldn't be more than a hundred feet off the water—and the entire framework of the stilt house vibrated beneath his bare feet. He threw the sheet over his fish tank and worked frantically to get it anchored in place, imagining a vague kinship with long-gone sailors on, say, the *Arizona,* December 7, 1941.

He worked and watched at the same time as, within the DC-3s, unseen pilots hit switches, and all three planes began to exhaust massive plumes of gray fog—mosquito spray; malathion.

Ford ducked instinctively as the beams of the spotlights and the planes swept over him, feeling the wind wake trying to draw him along as the DC-3s banked northwest and made their way up the island.

Still pouring fog, all three planes looked as if they had been hit by flak and were about to crash.

He stood fully for the first time and laid a plank across the tank to hold the sheet firmly, feeling oily drops of poison fog landing on his shoulders.

If the insecticide had gotten into the tank, it would have killed the few delicate squid he kept there, and maybe some of the fish—just as the poison would kill fish larvae in tidal creeks and shallow ponds all up and down the islands, everywhere the bombers sprayed.

There was a thin clapping noise, four or five people applauding, and Ford looked across the water to the marina's docks, to see Captains Felix and Nels, and several of the live-aboards—men and women—laughing at him, giving him a mock standing ovation.

"What time's the next show, Doc? I'll bring my video camera!"

Ford waved regally, not even bothering to cover himself now, and started back inside, but then stopped suddenly, looking at the empty dock below him; stood dumbly for long seconds.

His skiff, the one that had almost sunk last night, was now gone. That's what he finally realized.

He hurried inside, pulled on nylon running shorts, then walked along the railed platform on which his house was built, casting his eyes back and forth, searching west to east.

Marina docks . . . marina basin . . . oyster bars . . . Dinkin's Bay, all flat water, no empty boats floating . . . distant spoil islands with mangrove trees, wind beaten, solitary; no boat there . . .

more bay, more water, pelicans skimming . . . brightening eastern sky, swath of white light . . . high bars of pink clouds glowing like the inside of a conch shell . . . no boat . . . rim of red sun, the slow amphitheater of sunrise as the spinning earth spilled light over Miami, over the Everglades . . . more water, old pilings, long sandbar that could catch a boat—and there it was. Ford could see the blue fiberglass glisten of a boat wedged among the mangrove roots beyond the bar—his boat showing itself in the harsh pink light that was already beginning to radiate heat across the Florida peninsula.

Ford went down the steps to his dock and found the lines that had once held the skiff still cleated there. He took one of the lines, inspected it, and saw that it had been cut.

What in the hell was going on here?

He went back inside and pulled on his white rubber boots. He lighted the propane stove and put coffee on to boil before wading down the sandbar to his boat.

Karl Sutter was in the late Marvin Rios's house, sitting at the late Marvin Rios's desk, going through the late Marvin Rios's papers. Behind him, the door of the floor safe was open—he had watched through the window, once, and saw where Marvin kept the combination—and now he had papers stacked everywhere, going through them one by one, putting them in order.

A place for everything, sweetie, and everything in its place.

Karl would look at a sheaf of papers and say, "Bullshit," reach over and put it in the bullshit stack. He'd look at another sheaf and say, "Money on the hoof," and put it in the pile with other deeds and mortgage papers, then make a notation in the notebook he was keeping for himself. He'd open another envelope and say, "Little golden egg," and put the bond or the certificate of stock issue in the pile with the stock portfolio, and make another notation.

Not that he'd try to liquidate any of this stuff himself. No, that would be dumb. Couldn't even think about touching any of it until it went through probate and until Marvin's wife, Candy, received her cut from the lawyers and the government

71

and the rest of the fucking bloodsuckers who always took a little piece of the corpse.

Candy'd be left with, what? Maybe half the gross value of the estate. Naw, more than that. But not much more, because that greedy damn Marvin had kept everything in his name, like maybe he'd someday divorce her. Which he probably would have if Candy'd ever put up a fuss about all the women he was screwing; those barter whores who took their payment in trips or clothes or apartments, because that's the only way that little dwarf Marvin could get a girl.

On the bright side, Candy was Marvin's only heir. Parents dead—probably out of embarrassment from spawning a midget like Marvin. No kids, either, and his only sister, that slut Judy, drowned while on vacation in Mexico—so full of the vodka Sutter'd forced into her that the greaseball mortician down there in Cancún probably didn't even bother to use embalming fluid. What the hell did the mortician care? He'd gotten a free look at a white woman's tits, and him and that beaner coroner probably both diddled her before sending the body back with a certificate that said "death by misadventure."

So Candy would get it all. What was left, anyway. What was left minus the $13,660 in cash Sutter had found in the safe—all sweet fifties and a few twenties—plus nine gold coins, old American double eagles probably worth four grand, maybe more. Plus the note he and Judy had signed, borrowing $37,500 from Marvin; man, was he happy to find *that*. All of it stuffed into the big pockets of the safari jacket he brought for just such an occasion, the cash folded over with the weight and shape of thick paperback books.

If Candy asked him on the way out, he'd just tell her he was going to do some heavy reading.

Sutter was looking at another folder of papers. He gave the papers a quick glance, and when he saw they didn't include a deed or a bond certificate, almost put them in the bullshit pile. But then words midway down the first page jumped out at him—*Mayakkatee River Development, Inc.*—and he stopped his hand above the pile and gave the papers a closer look.

72

The folder included just three pages stapled together, all original documents, and he skimmed over the first page through a lot of party-of-the-first-parts (some company named Griff Inc.) and party-of-the-second-parts (that was Marvin) and saw that the papers comprised a contract concerning Marvin's big development, Mayakkatee Estates.

Sutter knew about Mayakkatee Estates, a twelve-hundred-acre parcel of oaks and mangroves on the Mayakkatee River where Marvin's people were already clearing out trees, planning on putting in high-income housing. Hell, just last week Marvin had sent him up to the construction site to get the plastic explosives he said he knew so damn much about. Sent him up there at night with a note to the watchman saying it was okay to go into the warehouse trailer to get what he needed—which was two five-pound boxes of stuff labeled PRIMACORD. Two small boxes, heavier than they looked 'cause the stuff was packed real tight, wrapped in cellophane, this coiled plastic cord like yellow clothesline, only it felt like the clay he'd used in grade school. You could mold it.

Marvin had said what pissed him off was he was putting on this big tarpon tournament, eighty-grand-cash first prize, and all he was getting out of it was a little percentage and some free advertising. Letting it dribble right through his fingers, that's what pissed him off. "The trick to making money," Marvin had told him, "is find people smart enough to have money to give you, and dumb enough to think you'll give it back."

So, wondered Marvin, what if his brother-in-law won the tournament instead of one of those shmuck sportsmen? That way, his brother-in-law could pay off the goddamn money he owed him, plus maybe prove to the other fishing guides that he wasn't a complete moron and knew how to catch tarpon.

"Trouble is, Karl," Marvin had said to him, giving him that buggy look, "you couldn't catch the clap in a Harlem whorehouse. But I know how we can fix that, if you'll go along with the deal."

Sutter had said, "Hell, I *like* the idea, Marv," thinking, *You*

73

fucking little midget, I bet you got to goose yourself in the ass each morning just to find your dick.

So he got the explosives Marvin said he knew so much about. Then, the night before the tournament, they each got into one of those shitty little rental boats—they had to have two boats, Marvin had insisted, so they could drop charges at the same time but at different places—and they went fishing. Lightning and raining like hell, the two of them out there on Pine Island Sound bouncing around in separate boats, which Marvin said was perfect. With all the thunder, nobody would ever suspect what they were doing.

Only thing was, the water was so rough, there was no fucking way he was going to try to detonate the Primacord; leave that crazy business to Marvin. Tell him he couldn't get the fucking fuse ignitors to light; make up some excuse like that. It was so damn dark and raining so hard, Marvin probably couldn't even see him from his boat, let alone see what he was doing—sitting in the bottom of that shitty little rental skiff, hating all those black waves.

Well, Marvin was right about one thing: It was perfect. Because that was the end of Marvin. Only now, the police were saying that Marvin had been murdered. At least, the television news last night had said foul play was suspected; that Marvin had been beaten to death. Not blown up. He'd had his neck broken.

Into Sutter's mind came the glittering image of Marvin standing up in that little boat during a lightning blast, holding something in his hand. A weird-looking thing to see across two hundred yards of waves and rain, and then the ocean gave a great belch—an explosion—and he never saw Marvin again. Just found the rental boat about an hour later, the seats broken and everything a mess but empty, so Sutter had taken care of that.

So why in the hell did the police think Marvin had been beaten to death? Shit, the police doctors would know the difference between a guy who got blown to pieces and a guy who'd had his neck broken, right?

So what the hell had happened?

Maybe a boat had followed them out there—Sutter didn't

like that thought. Gave him the creeps, the idea of someone following them through all that darkness. But it was possible. With all those clouds over the moon, they never would have known it.

Or maybe the cops *were* wrong, and Marvin had just been blown up and it looked like he'd been beaten. Fucking cops were so stupid, but he knew they'd want to paw through Marvin's things looking for clues—*dumb asses*—so he'd better hurry.

Sutter was reading the last part of the contract, the one concerning Mayakkatee Estates.

It read:

> Whereas both parties are in agreement as to the terms of the sale of the described properties known as Mayakkatee Estates, and whereas the terms of this sale have been duly recorded, it is also agreed and entered into willingly by both parties the following, hereby known as addendum clause A: It is agreed that, if the aforementioned properties are sold *in toto,* then a full sixty percent (60%) of realized gross profits revert back to the original seller, or party of the first part (Griff, Inc., or Robert M. Griffin), to be paid upon demand by the original buyer, or party of the second part (Mayakkatee River Development, Inc., or Marvin A. Rios). It is also agreed, willingly and faithfully, that copies of this clause, Adden-

dum Clause A, shall not be publicly filed nor duplicated, though
it also be agreed that all matters
pertaining to this contract and the
aforementioned described property shall not violate any custom
of the industry. . . .

Sutter pondered over that, wondering: *If Marvin decided to
sell the land and not develop it, why the hell would he agree to pay the
original owner 60 percent of the profit?*

That was weird; didn't sound like Marvin at all, fucking
little shyster. But maybe it was the only way he could talk this
Robert Griffin guy into selling.

Robert Griffin? Shit, he'd heard that name before . . .
Robert Griffin . . . *Robert Griffin* the goddamn state senator, that's
who this guy was!

Sutter banged his big fist on the desk, pleased with himself
for remembering.

Hell, he'd met Griffin at one of Marv's famous assholes and
high-fliers parties. Tall guy in a suit, with dark hair, like he'd
used a whole can of hair spray. Smile like it was painted on by
a PR firm, but a lot of nastiness in that weak Florida-southern
accent when he didn't think anybody was listening.

"Senator, this is Karl, was married to my late sister. Anything you want, just tell Karl. He's the marina flunky."

Well, fuck you, Marvin. Look who's sitting at your desk
now. . . .

Sutter reread the clause, not understanding it all but certain
there was something stinky about it. Marvin and the senator had
entered into some kind of secret agreement—that copies "not to
be publicly filed or duplicated" said as much. And that business
about "shall not violate custom of the industry" was just some
kind of legal out. Yeah, that was it. Something to say they had
no plans to break the law, but they sure as shit did have plans,
because why else would they want to keep it secret? And why

else would a tightwad like Marvin ever agree to give away 60 percent of his company's own profits?

Sutter folded the contract and placed it on the desk in front of him. He shook a cigarette out and lit it, holding the cigarette between his teeth as he stared at the paper.

"You got to remember, darling, people in this world will stab you in the back first chance they get. That's why you got to stab them first. . . ."

Sutter could hear noise down the hallway, someone in the kitchen. There was the sound of a cupboard opening, then water running in the sink. Christ, Candy was up already. He wondered if he should jam all the papers back into the safe. Then figured, naw, what the hell, he had to handle Candy sooner or later.

But he wanted to keep this contract, keep it until he figured out just exactly what it meant. Then maybe he'd give Senator Griffin a call, say something like, "Hey, Robert, you remember that flunky you met at the party 'bout a year ago? Turns out I'm your new partner." Really shit all over the guy, a fucking state senator.

Sutter took the contract and folded it into one of the big pockets of his safari jacket, right there with all the cash, thinking, *Little golden egg . . .*

Candy Rios stood in the doorway, pale eyes darting back and forth, taking in the open safe, all the scattered papers, and said, "You're not robbing me, Karl, are you?" Standing there with both hands holding the pink housecoat tightly at the neck, looking at him, then looking away when he tried to meet her eyes.

"You awake already, Candy? I was hoping you could get some rest. Maybe those pills I got from the doctor aren't any good."

Candy said, "You shouldn't be in here. Marv's attorney said I shouldn't let anyone touch anything till he gets here tomorrow for the funeral. He said the police are going to want to interview me, and everything in the house should be just the way it was." She stood there, not looking at him, a tiny little

77

woman with bleached hair and a voice like a bird, so beaten down and nervous after living with Marvin that she was like one of those frightened animals in the cartoons, a chipmunk, maybe. She said, "I have to ask you to leave, Karl."

Speaking softly, Sutter said, "Anything you say, Candy, but I'm just trying to do what's best for you. That's why I've been kinda taking care of the marina for you, that's why I went to the doctor so you wouldn't have to. That's what I'm doing *here,* going through all these papers. Here, look for yourself," and he held up the notebook on which he had logged the various bonds and deeds. She took a few steps closer, squinting to read, as he said, "I was kind of Marvin's right-hand man, you know. That's how I know Marvin might have some stuff locked away he wouldn't even want his attorney to see; stuff the IRS can get their hands on and make all kinds of trouble."

Candy said, "Oh? Oh dear."

He held the notebook out farther so she could take it. "Check it yourself," he said. "Everything listed you'll find right here on this desk. I swear to God. All yours. But I know Marv woulda wanted me to kind of help him out here; make sure what the government was going to get a look at. Marv and me was what you'd call pretty close, you know. That's why Judy and me came down here. Hell, he's the one gave me the combination to the safe, just in case."

Candy placed the notebook back on the desk, sighing, still holding the housecoat at the neck. "All he told me was that it was because you owed him some money. And then I saw you in here, and . . . well, I hope you don't think I'm accusing you of anything, Karl. I'm just upset."

Sutter allowed himself a gentle chuckle. "I paid Marv that money a year ago. Got the receipt back at my place if you want to see it—"

"No, I trust you—"

"I know you do, it's just you're upset because you're all worn out. Damn it, those pills shoulda helped!"

The woman jumped slightly when he raised his voice—plain-faced little woman, but with nice high cheeks, so she might

78

have been pretty before age caused the skin to go loose. Or maybe Marvin screaming at her had loosened it up, made her whole face sag. A guy like Marvin, his mouth was worse than his fists. But Candy had nice skin, very smooth when you looked close, as Sutter was doing now. He'd never noticed before that Candy might have been pretty once.

Candy used one hand to pat the pockets of her robe, and Karl said quickly, "Have one of mine," offering his pack of cigarettes to her. She took the cigarette in her fingers and leaned over the lighter he held out, sucking the smoke in deep, and Sutter felt a brief adrenaline stir in his abdomen, watching her.

"God," she said, "these are strong."

"Lucky Strike means fine tobacco. It'll relax you."

She took a seat opposite him, brushing hair back off her face, inhaling deeply again and exhaling smoke through her nose. "Those darn mosquito planes went over about six, and I never really got back to sleep. You wouldn't think they'd spray on Sunday."

"Bunch of what you'd call smart asses in those planes, probably old combat pilots the way they fly."

"But they're so *loud.*"

"Doesn't bother me, Candy. My father was a pilot. He got killed bombing the Japanese. D Day."

Candy looked at him for the first time. "Oh, you poor thing. You must have been just a baby."

"I don't even like talk about it. I just said it to let you know I know a little bit about what you're going through, Marv dying and all." Sutter had his head down, talking softly. "And, of course, there was Judy. . . ."

"That's right, dear Judy. Oh, Karl, it never even dawned on me how much you've been through." Candy was silent for a moment, smoking, but with something on her mind. He could tell. Finally, she said, "Karl . . . can I ask you something?"

"Anything. Name it."

"Last night, real late, I woke up and was going to the kitchen to get a drink and Marvin's bedroom door was open. I

79

saw you in there at his dresser doing something with one of his hairbrushes. Holding it. Why were you doing that?"

Sutter still had his head down, and as she talked, he brought his hands up to his face. Pressing his eyelids back with his index fingers, he touched his eyeballs, rubbing them round and round, and when he felt the tear ducts open, he looked up, tears streaming down his face. His voice choked, he said, "It's . . . it's just that I missed him, Candy. . . . I just wanted to be near him, that's all. . . ." Letting her see his face, see him weeping, until her own face went and she began to cry, holding her arms to her chest, making a sort of mewing noise.

"You two *were* close, weren't you?"

"Yes. Like a brother."

"I just didn't know."

He stood and moved around the desk to her. "He was a great man; people didn't understand him." And he slowly put his hands on her shoulders, feeling her tighten immediately. "He was what you call way ahead of his time, and I'd love to get five minutes alone with the guy who killed him." He began to massage her neck gently, rubbing the warm skin of her neck and her shoulders with his big fingers.

"I just didn't know, Karl. Marv never told me anything. Never told me anything ever. Like we were two strangers; we never even talked. Even Thursday night, the night he was killed, he was just here for a while and left, didn't tell me where he was going, anything."

She was beginning to relax a little beneath his hands, but still uneasy with him touching her—he could tell—and she reached out to put the cigarette in an ashtray. Why did she have to do that? Sutter had a good flow of tears going now, really crying, but he wanted her to hold the cigarette while he touched her. He tried to think of something to say, but then she took the cigarette in her fingers again, inhaling once more deeply, and Sutter thought about his mother, the way it had been, her sitting there naked in the bathtub, smoking, while he watched. Seventeen years old and furious because she had grounded him, moving closer and closer to the electric heater beside the tub,

80

wondering if he could really do it while she lounged beneath the suds, not at all worried because he knew she liked it when he watched, sucking that cigarette.

Sutter said, "I've always thought the world of you, Candy."

"I . . . I've always liked you, too, Karl."

"I've never really had a family of my own."

Which made her cry again, her body shaking softly beneath his hands. She looked up with her red eyes and said pitifully, "You just need to be held, don't you?" and let him move around the chair to lay his head on her housecoat, holding him and stroking his head. "I've lost my dear husband, and you lost your father and your wife—"

He wailed, "And my mother died when I was seventeen!"

"My God, you poor man." Stroking him, and Sutter took one of her hands and kissed it, then kissed her arm, then turned his head upward and kissed her on the lips, tasting her tobacco breath.

She pulled away, very tense again. "Karl, you can't do that; don't do that—"

He pulled her face to his again, forcing her until she let him, and then he could tell that she would let him do anything he wanted, anytime he wanted—anything at all. He said, "Candy, we need each other. You need someone in control now. I'm in control."

He slid his hand between the lapels of the housecoat and found her left breast, way lower on her belly than he suspected, like a partially deflated balloon, and she began to struggle again, but not much. She whispered, "This isn't right, it just isn't right—"

Sutter said, "There ain't nothing that's wrong in this world," and forced his lips to hers again.

An hour before sunset, Ford steered his flat-bottom trawl boat across Dinkin's Bay toward his house on stilts. The nets were winched up tight so that the boat, with its gray hull, looked like a huge bird with folded wings, and the little diesel engine *pop-pop-popped* along, loud, but not so loud he couldn't hear the

81

drifting hint of church bells, the electronic chimes coming across Pine Island Sound from the chapel at Shell Point Village.

Oh come, all ye faithful, joyful and triumphant . . .

Why were they playing that now, the Sunday before the summer solstice, the first day of summer?

It gave the day a holiday softness, a quality Ford recognized but ignored.

Ahead, he could see his house caught in the tilted sunlight, the white paint peeling, rust streaks of the tin roof glowing orange in the rich light; the west side of the house catching the sun, the east side in shadow, as if the house were a small planet, standing in the water on its crooked stilts, caught in an eclipse.

Ford thought: *I'd hire somebody to paint it, but the paint fumes might have an effect on my fish.* Then dismissed the idea, as he had dismissed it a dozen times before.

There was someone standing on his back porch by the roofed but open walkway that separated his lab from his living quarters, and Ford recognized Tomlinson. Tomlinson wore only shorts and thongs, as usual, leaning toward him over the rail, one hand tugging at his straggly hair. Like something was on his mind and he wanted to talk.

Ford brought the trawl boat in and swept past the anchor buoy a little too fast, missed it when he reached out, and had to bring the engine into full reverse to get back to the dock. Then he reached over the side, clipped the anchor buoy to the stern cleat, and nosed the front of the boat up to the dock, where Tomlinson was waiting with a line.

Ford said, "I think I might like boating—once I get the hang of it."

Tomlinson was cleating the boat off, one foot on the boat, the other on the dock. "This thing must steer like a truck anyway, with that little engine and all that flat bottom."

"Yeah, but you'd think I'd know how to handle it by now." Ford was already bending over the big Igloo cooler filled with water in the back of the boat, brushing away salt foam created by the aerator, and he lifted out two cheesecloth sacks. "I bet I have ten pounds of plankton here. Bound to have some fish larvae in it. I've got to strain this stuff, then filter it, then rehydrate it and pump it through another filter." Ford held the dripping bags for Tomlinson to take. "Pretty long process. If you've got time, you could help."

"Time, yeah, I've got time, but there's something going on here."

Ford pulled himself up onto the dock. "Huh?"

"I said something's going on; some shit's been going down since you went out."

Ford took the sacks, carrying them up the steps to the fish tank on the main deck. "Someone else had their boat stolen?"

"No, but have a look." Tomlinson was pointing to the marina parking lot. Ford lowered the sacks of plankton into the water and used string to tie them to the sides of the bank. Fish spooked as his hands breached the surface, the explosive movements of the fish creating dull thuds that carried through the water.

Ford said, "Look at what?" but then he saw, parked right there by the marina and the door to Jeth's apartment, two white and blue squad cars with SANIBEL / FORT MYERS POLICE in big reflective letters on the side. There was a third car, a beige Ford, with an emergency flasher on the dashboard, but no markings.

"Oh no," Ford said.

"First one got here about half hour ago; two cops in uniform. Jeth was on the docks helping MacKinley reprime the bait pump, and they talked to him for a little bit, and they all three went up to his apartment. I was out on my boat, and Mack told me they wanted to know which boat was Jeth's, and then they said they wanted to talk to him."

"They didn't advise him of his rights or anything?"

"Mack didn't say anything about that."

"That could be a good sign."

Tomlinson said, "Then the other cop car shows up, and two more uniforms go up, then that unmarked car pulls in. Guy in a sport coat, fucking gun clipped to his belt, and he goes up without even knocking." Tomlinson was glaring at the windows of Jeth's apartment. "Fucking pigs are probably slapping the shit out of him right now, working him over up there."

Ford said, "Come off it," walking down the dock, headed for the marina. Tomlinson had an irrational dislike of policemen that Ford didn't share.

"I don't know, man. I don't trust those fuckers. I never did."

"The guy without the uniform, it wasn't Lester Durell, was it?"

"Who?"

"You know, that police major I went to high school with."

"They all look alike to me, man. All I see is their guns and their beady little eyes."

"And you're normally so fair-minded."

"Well . . ."

As they got to the marina, two of the uniforms and the plainclothes cop came out of Jeth's apartment, talking among themselves. Plainclothes was carrying a large black briefcase, and Ford knew he was part of an evidence team. It wasn't Les Durell.

They were walking toward the docks, and Ford increased his pace to catch them, calling when he got close enough, "They're making all you guys work on a Sunday?" Trying to fix his smile just right; curious but relaxed.

All three men stopped, their eyes latching on to him—taking in Tomlinson, too—and Ford said quickly, "I'm a friend of Jeth's. What's going on?"

One of the uniforms said, "Police business—that's what's going on," like slamming a door in his face, but plainclothes said, "How well do you know Mr. Nicholes?" fixing his own smile and opening the door a little.

"Pretty well. I see him just about every day."

"Oh?" Still wearing that easy expression, but there was nothing easy about plainclothes's eyes; a short man, but huge in the shoulders, with a plain face that seemed bigger because he was nearly bald, and with big hands showing from the brown blazer he wore. Ford knew that plainclothes was sorting him out, probably just as he had sorted out that blazer, having to buy off the rack because he couldn't afford anything else, and now he was trying to figure out which rack Ford belonged on.

Ford said, "I live over there on that stilt house." He pointed beyond the fish-cleaning table, through the mangroves. "I spend a lot of time around the marina."

"So you work here?"

"No."

"I thought you might be one of the fishing guides."

"No, I'm a biologist. My name's Ford." He held his hand out to plainclothes, not surprised by the cop's slow acquiescence, his reluctance to shake hands. "And you are . . . ?"

"Detective Fuller. Maybe you wouldn't mind showing us which one is Mr. Nicholes's boat."

Behind him, Tomlinson cleared his throat, meaning the cops already knew where Jeth's boat was, but Ford said, "Sure, be happy to," playing right along. Plainclothes would want to pump information out of him, but maybe he could get some information in return.

As Ford started to lead them down the dock, Tomlinson called, "I assume you people have a search warrant?" Giving it a chilly edge, standing his ground, not following them. "You need one to get on a private citizen's boat."

Detective Fuller turned and looked at him for a moment, then just smiled and walked on. To Ford, he said, "Your friend with the long hair seems upset about something."

"I think he had a bad experience at the 'Sixty-eight Democratic Convention."

"What? Oh, I get it!"

Ford said, "It's not a joke."

"No kiddin'? Well, you know what, Mr. Ford? I don't blame your friend. Don't blame him a bit. I remember those days, but I still believe the cops did what they had to do." Very congenial, playing the good guy to put Ford in a talkative mood.

Ford said, "That's Jeth's boat, the blue one. See the sign?"

Fuller stopped at the dock above the Suncoast, a plain open fiberglass boat, no wood, no chrome, a pure work boat with a center console and good live wells. He was opening the big briefcase, handing out a miniature vacuum and a smaller aluminum case to the two uniforms, saying, "Lance, you sweep first, then—Harold? You dust for prints right behind him. Keep your eyes open."

Ford said, "My gosh, Jeth isn't in some kind of trouble, is he?"

Replying innocently to Ford's innocent question, Fuller said, "Naw, this is just routine," playing right along with Ford now. "You heard about Mr. Rios dying? Well, a guy with that much money, we have to do a full investigation. We're just trying to talk to anybody who might have been out on the water the night he was killed."

"Murdered," Ford said.

The detective shrugged, watching the two uniforms work. "Medical examiner's report says Rios died from some kind of blunt trauma, but that doesn't really tell us much. Could have just slipped and hit his head. Just a lot of confusing medical talk; a C-two fracture—"

"Which is a broken neck. That's what Rios died from?"

Fuller looked at him coolly. "That's right."

"So you're talking to everyone who was on the water Thursday night, and taking evidence from their boats? You fellows have a lot of work ahead of you. Just on the chance Rios was murdered."

Fuller said, "I didn't get your first name, Mr. Ford," wanting to reverse the momentum.

"Marion. But people around here call me Doc."

"A Ph.D.?"

"That's right."

"In biology. And you've known Mr. Nicholes for . . . ?"

"Nearly two years. Jeth's a good man; he was born and raised in this area, a lot of people know him. And he's very . . . kind, in his way."

"Uh-huh. Childlike, that's the way Mr. MacKinley described him."

So they'd already talked with Mack.

Ford said, "Well, maybe boyish, but he's not dumb."

"And kind."

"Right."

"People at Two Parrot Bight Marina told me that Nicholes and Rios had quite a fight Thursday afternoon. Some threats were exchanged. From some of the things Nicholes supposedly said, he's not always so kind. I don't guess you were there?"

Ford said, "So that's what this is about." Like he didn't know.

"We're just talking to a lot of people, trying to get things sorted out."

"I heard Jeth and Rios had an argument, not a fight."

"Right, right; semantics. Bad choice of words. An argument, not a fight." Fuller was smiling, letting Ford know that the concession didn't bother him a bit. "So you weren't there."

"If you guys have to get search warrants for everyone who had an argument with Marvin Rios, you're going to need reinforcements. And more judges."

"Well, don't quote me on it, but I heard the guy was a real asshole. Rios, I mean. I know the type. Too much money and too much ego."

"Whoever told you they saw Rios on Jeth's boat made a mistake, that's my guess."

Fuller said, "Yeah, but we have to check it out—"and stopped suddenly, realizing what he had just told Ford. Then he said, "What makes you think somebody told us that?"

"You got a judge to sign a warrant on a Sunday, I just figured it had to be more than an argument—"

"Did you see Rios on Mr. Nicholes's boat?"

"No, I doubt if he ever was—"

"Then that's a very odd thing to say, Dr. Ford."

"Not really. It's a reasonable assumption."

"You're sure you're not trying to protect him?"

From the boat, one of the uniforms, the one with the little vacuum, said, "Hey, Roy, check this out." He had his face close to the transom, the plank of fiberglass that separated the back of the boat from the engine. "I got some hair here, and maybe some blood, too."

Ford thought, *Oh, shit* . . .

Detective Fuller, whose first name must have been Roy, looked at Ford; a frank expression, still amused, but not about to take any more crap. "Been nice talking to you, Dr. Ford," dismissing him, just like that.

"I don't mind waiting, if you have any more questions—"

"This may come as a surprise to you, Dr. Ford, but I get along just fine working on my own. In fact, we usually put up yellow tape to keep civilians out of the way, but if you just move back there by the marina, we won't have to."

Fuller waited until Ford turned to go. He stepped down into the boat.

MacKinley was saying, "The detective, the one without the uniform, asked me a few questions. His name was . . . Fuller. What sort of person was Jeth, how long was he out in his boat this weekend, had he been acting odd lately? Made quite a point of how strong Jeth looked. I told him yes; hope I didn't do anything to get him in trouble, Doc."

"Yes that Jeth was strong?"

"That, too, but that he really hasn't been himself lately. He hasn't been—you know that. I've been wondering if the bugger had started using drugs. He's just so . . . spacey. All month he's been like that. Maybe longer."

Ford said, "Never lie to a policeman; they always find out."

MacKinley was sitting on the bar chair behind the cash register, feeling miserable, while Ford stood at the glass counter, going over Jeth's charter schedule, a black appointment book that had seen a lot of rough use. From the apartment above them, they could hear water running. Jeth hadn't been down since the police left half an hour ago, and now he was taking a shower.

Ford said, "What's it mean where you've taped over dates here, then written over the tape?" Ford held up Jeth's appointment book so MacKinley could see.

"That's where charters canceled, but I later rebooked the time slot."

The marina booked all the guides and took 15 percent of the gross as an agent's fee.

MacKinley said, "There's a lot of that in Jeth's book because people call in here wanting a guide, so I book them—tell them to mail in a deposit—but Jeth comes in and looks and says the tides are bad that day, so he calls them and has them rebook later. Then, when it's busy, I end up having to book him for the bad tides, anyway. It's a pain in the butt."

"Felix and Nels don't do that?"

MacKinley thought for a moment, then said, "I guess they do. They all do that." He smiled. "I guess they're all a pain in the butt. But they bring people into the marina, especially during the summer for tarpon, and that's the island's slow time. And the people buy suntan lotion and hats and beer, so I profit two ways."

Ford said, "And Jeth has written 'do not book' on days he doesn't want to fish?"

"Right. That costs me money, but I just let them do what they want. Trying to organize fishing guides is like trying to organize a bunch of snakes. I think that's why they hated Rios. Rios treated them as hired help."

Ford was counting. "Jeth cancelled the whole first week of June. Then he fished on the eighth, took off the ninth and tenth, fished the weekend, took Monday off, then fished through Thursday. He's hardly worked at all."

"Uh-huh. First week of June, he said his grandmother was sick and he wanted to visit her. You knew that."

"I knew he was gone, but I didn't know why. Is that a normal amount of days for him to take off?"

"During tarpon season last year, he was fishing two or three four-hour trips a day, seven days a week. You know Jeth. He's always short of money because he can't turn down anybody who asks for a loan, and he has all those girlfriends, plus he's always breaking stuff on his boat. Tries to fix things, and it just snaps in those hands of his. And he's gotten worse. Last week, he came in here, tripped over something, knocked that whole rack of T-shirts over, fishhooks and sinkers flying everywhere, then just sat there on the floor like he was going to cry. A twenty-eight-year-old man."

"Did he say why he was taking so many days off?"

"I asked. He just said there were more important things in life than being a fishing guide. Like maybe he was spending a lot of time with a woman. Or out looking for another job, but I didn't pursue it."

"Did Detective Fuller look at this book?"

"Never asked, so I didn't offer. People think guides work a regular schedule; they don't think about them keeping calendars."

Talking more to himself than to MacKinley, Ford said, "And he doesn't stutter anymore."

"What?"

Ford said, "When Jeth came in last night, he didn't stutter. We talked for maybe ten minutes, and he didn't do it once. Have you noticed that?"

"No-o-o-o. Well, I'm not sure, really. I saw him briefly Thursday late, and he was stuttering so bad, he could hardly get it out about the argument he had with Rios. Then he took off, so I didn't see him Friday or Saturday. Then today, I didn't see him much—he chartered this afternoon—then he helped me with the bait pump and . . . come to think of it, I can't remember him stuttering. He was telling me some long story, about something he saw down in the Everglades."

"The green flash."

"About a sunset or something, exactly. But you know how it is with Jeth—sometimes you just tune him out when he gets to talking."

Above them, a door closed, and there was the sound of steps on the stairs and, through the big window, they watched Jeth Nicholes exit onto the cement walk beside the parking lot. His hair was still wet and he was wearing dark-blue sweatpants and a white T-shirt that showed his biceps. He waved at them, an embarrassed grin on his face, then opened the marina door and poked his head in. "They just wanted to ask me a lot of questions, that's all."

Ford said, "Did the police tell you it was about Rios?"

"Not at first, but I'm not dumb. All straightened out now, though. I told them what I did; my boat trip."

"You gave them the names of the people who saw you down there, right?"

Jeth was shaking his head. "I didn't see anybody down there. I mean, I saw a few other boats off Marco and the Ten Thousand Islands, but I didn't stop and talk. And I didn't see anybody around Cape Sable, except a few canoeists."

"You talked to the canoeists? You did, didn't you?"

Jeth appeared taken aback at Ford's tone. "Hell no. Why would I talk to anybody crazy enough to canoe in an area like that?"

"And you didn't stop at any marinas, not even Flamingo."

"No, why should I? I had extra fuel. What're you worried about, Doc? The cops knew I was telling the truth. I liked that one guy, Fuller. He fishes."

Ford said, "Yeah, Fuller is a gem."

"Well," said Jeth, "I'm going out to see Tomlinson now. He's going to teach me how to meditate."

MacKinley and Ford were looking at each other, their expressions pained. Jeth said, "Tomlinson is a very spiritual person. I wisht I'da realized it sooner."

During the second decade of his life, Tomlinson had wanted so badly to be wise that he sometimes embraced beliefs in which he had no confidence and many times spoke words in which he had no faith. He alternately embraced and rejected politics and religion, religion and politics, spewing out dogma while ingesting pills, powders, and psychedelic mushrooms.

His brain seldom got a rest.

In the tumult of that time, he projected the many roles he played as the manifestations of a single truth. But even his belief in that single truth added to a growing confusion in him. Gradually, the horror dawned that he was just one more player in a generation of bad actors, and that The Truth was just another

91

buzz phrase, not unlike "Where's your head at?" and "Get your act together."

This revelation came to him on a Wednesday outside Spokane when he should have been tending the commune's herb garden but instead had joined in a peyote feast with a sweating, naked teenager named Andrea and a Paiute Indian called Billy Three Fires. After eating six peyote buttons, the careful scaffolding of his own life collapsed in a haze of swirls and starburst colors, and he saw his theatrics for what they were. The realization was so frightening, so ripe with black panic that, by Monday, he was in a Chicago facility known as Elms, making billfolds and signing his letters "Sincerely as a Fucking Loon."

It was a painful time.

Yet the quest for wisdom did not die there. Indeed, Tomlinson's fledgling legs first found purchase on what he now thought of as The True Course during that period—the True Course being a personal compass assembled from his own knowledge, his own pain and the pain of others.

Like it or not, he felt what others felt; hurt right along with people in trouble, strangers or friends. It was the way he was; the way he had always been, like one of those strange plants with leaves that wilt at a human's touch. It was not a triumph of the intellect, though he had always been gifted in that way, too. Facts did not fall on Tomlinson's brain as snowflakes, they embedded themselves like diamond shards, and he could clearly remember the astounded looks of adults who listened as he, then in grade school, recited long passages of prose from memory, or solved complicated math problems in his head. This ability was what adults called genius, yet he sensed even then how wrong they were.

These days, his cognitive powers were not so reliable. Years of synthetic exploration and all that peyote had exacted their toll; had torn bits and pieces from the mental fabric, maybe even burned a few sizable holes.

It did not trouble him.

The ability to calculate the square root of seventeen was a feat, a trick, like someone who was born double-jointed. It was nothing like his intrinsic empathy for people. Tomlinson felt that was his true gift; his gift or his curse, for there were nights, even now, when the collective pain of the world settled upon him, and the old black panic threatened; nights when the very stars seemed to echo the screams of the anguished.

Suffering through such nights made all quests for wisdom contentious. Like the petty aspiration of someone who wanted to spy on a party but not participate, it was a way of remaining aloof. In fact, the quest for wisdom, he came to believe, was a form of escape.

Tomlinson no longer wanted to escape. Nor did he want to mislead, as he must have done in the days of his second decade. He knew he had the ability to influence, so he took pains not to influence. Which was probably why he felt so comfortable with Ford. Ford was one of the few men to whom he could say any damn thing that popped into his mind. With Ford, he could argue any cause, could assemble any chain of reason without fear of offending him or, worse, swaying him. Debating Ford was like arguing with the multiplication tables, for that was the way Ford saw himself—a man of cold reason—and while Tomlinson suspected there were warmer levels to the man, he had also learned to respect as reality another person's own self-image.

With anyone other than Ford, though, he took pains. He was careful. He tried to speak only the few true things he knew, really knew, and tried to say them so simply and clearly that there was no room for confusion.

Like with Jeth Nicholes now.

The two of them sat in the main salon of Tomlinson's old forty-two-foot Morgan sailboat; Tomlinson sitting on the settee berth, with the table collapsed, so that it was like a wide bed. Jeth sat eagerly across from him, his fingers interlaced, tapping his thumbs together as he said, "That's neat the way you do that, but I don't think I can." Meaning the way Tomlinson was sitting, his legs meshed in the full lotus position.

Jeth pulled his right foot up so that it touched his left thigh . . . *Ouch, ouch, ooh* . . . then tried to fold his left leg over his right calf . . . *Aw-w-w-w, that hurts!* Untangling himself, he said, "Man, if I have to do that, I don't think I'll ever learn how to meditate. My legs haven't been working too well lately."

Tomlinson smiled. "Just takes a little practice, man; get the ol' joints loosened up. But it's not necessary right off. Just fold your hands like this, get your back straight; try to center yourself and let your eyes go soft. Yeah, that's it. Now just count your breaths, one to ten. Get to ten, start back at one."

"That's it?"

"For starters, yeah."

"Just count."

"Uh-huh."

"Like damn grade school, you ask me. But I'll try." Jeth did try, taking deep breaths.

Watching, looking at Jeth's face, Tomlinson was reminded of one of those American film characters, the simple country kid destined for glory. He knew Jeth was not simple—no one was. But Tomlinson, who believed in the glory of the individual, thought the last part might be right. One never knew.

Jeth sat motionless for no more than a minute before saying, "Ah . . . Tomlinson?"

"Yes?"

"What if you have an itch?" A little embarrassed, like he didn't want to break any rules.

"Itch all you want. Then concentrate on your breathing."

"I can do it now, if I want? Scratch, I mean."

"Sure."

Jeth scratched his nose, his crotch, then another two minutes passed before he said, "There's a lot of stuff I've been wondering about lately. That's why I want to learn this."

Tomlinson did not reply.

A few more seconds passed. "It's just that, sometimes, nothing in the world seems to make sense."

Tomlinson stirred. He said, "I hear that," agreeing.

"You told me this meditation stuff helps you see things more clearly."

"For some, it does. Even if it doesn't, it's a good way to relax."

"That's what I want—to understand things."

Tomlinson said patiently, "Relax and count your breaths," as his own breathing took control, sitting there with his legs folded, back straight, feeling the earth absorb him. But then he jumped as Jeth unexpectedly bolted from his seat and smacked his hand against one of the galley lockers.

Bang!

"Cockroach," Jeth said in explanation, wiping his hand on his sweatpants. "Big fucker."

Tomlinson winced.

"I hate those things."

Tomlinson said gently, "I don't want to put you off, man, but killing something during meditation is a bad deal, karmically speaking."

"Oh." Nervous, like he might start stuttering again. "Like respect for all living things, you mean."

"Pretty much."

"Like that business about how, after we die, we come back as cows and bugs and stuff?"

"Some people believe that."

Jeth was staring at the cockroach, worried. "Christ, I hope this guy wasn't an American. It's stone-dead, not even wiggling."

"It's done, man. Live in the present, not the past."

Jeth was nodding. "I'm not going to kill no more again. I see exactly what you're saying. Hell, I wouldn't want to get smashed like that. Poor little roach. No more, ever. Not even fish."

Jeth became quiet, and Tomlinson disappeared once again into cerebral nothingness, feeling himself, at once, shrink and grow.

More minutes passed. Then an hour. Then maybe two hours. Tomlinson wasn't sure; he never was. He kept no clocks.

After a long time, Tomlinson stirred, then unfolded his legs, stretching himself. He felt clear. The bulkheads of his boat, the books on the shelf, the incense burner smoldering on the hanging locker, and the brass barometer seemed to sparkle with the vibrating structure of their own molecules. He stood and took a bottle of water from the icebox, tasting the water. Good. Clear. Real. Outside, something thumped against the hull. An owl spoke, *Hoo-hoo-hoo,* maybe the one that had been dropping pellets on his boat. Ford would know what kind of owl it was. The voice of night.

Tomlinson turned and looked at the settee berth, where Jeth sat, head back, snoring softly.

Jeth had fallen asleep almost immediately.

Tomlinson took a towel from the water closet and spread it across the big man's chest, feeling, as his hand brushed Jeth's shoulder, an abrupt jolt of darkness, of confusion, like an electrical shock.

He stepped back quickly, wondering for a microsecond if he had *been* shocked—that's how strong the sensation was.

He stared at the man's peaceful, sleeping face, but felt no peace there.

Tomlinson went up the companionway steps and urinated into the bay, making slow circles in the water beneath the drifting moon. Then he lay down on the cockpit locker. The stars above moved and moaned, and he could not sleep.

In the morning, before the guides left, MacKinley came out in one of the little yellow rental boats and told Tomlinson to wake Jeth; the police wanted to talk to him again.

Later that same morning, MacKinley told Tomlinson the police had handcuffed Jeth while arresting him for the murder of Marvin Rios.

MacKinley said the cops didn't have to tell him, but they did: There had been an eyewitness.

6

THE woman on the phone told Ford that visiting days at Glades Detention were Tuesday, Wednesday, Saturday, noon to four, so there was no way he could see Jeth Nicholes today.

A man at the clerk of courts office told him Nicholes was scheduled for his first court appearance tomorrow, Tuesday, a bail hearing.

"If he doesn't have an attorney," the man said to Ford's question, "the arresting officer's probably already contacted the public defender's office to get one appointed. If they didn't, the judge will see to that tomorrow, too."

Sitting in his stilt house, looking at the black plastic telephone on the hatch-cover table, Ford considered making one more call. He had grown up in South Florida, had played high school baseball and football before leaving at age eighteen for the navy, then government service, and had not returned to the region for nearly fifteen years. As a result, he had former friends in the area whom time and absence had reduced to distant acquaintances. One of those was Lester Durell, who had graduated from high school before him, and was now a major with the Sanibel/Fort Myers Police.

Finally, Ford picked up the phone, dialed, then waited to

be transferred. He recognized the voice that answered, and he said, "Hey, Les, Marion Ford. How's it going?"

There was a short pause at the other end, then Lester Durell said, "Oh shit, what now?"

"Maybe I caught you at a bad time."

"Before you even get started, Marion, just tell me one thing. Does this have anything to do with official police business?"

"In a way. Maybe."

"Uh-huh. You recognize that noise?"

"Yeah, you're taping the call. You just turned it on. That's fine."

"Thought you might recognize it. Or maybe you have one of those resistance meters hooked up so you can tell when a line is bugged? Working for the CIA and all."

Durell was having fun with this.

Ford said, "I don't work for the CIA. I never did."

"Sure. Now maybe you can tell me what it is you want."

"A small favor, that's all. A friend of mine, a man named Nicholes, was arrested this morning by your people and I—"

"For what? What was he arrested for?"

"Ah, murder."

"It figures."

"You know the Nicholes family, out of Coconut below Hendry Creek? A few in Everglades City, too. They've lived around here forever. Jeth Nicholes."

"I know the family, so what? I've heard of Jeth; supposed to be a hot fishing guide. It doesn't make any difference."

"I know that, Les. But one of your guys, a Detective Fuller, is working the case, and I was wondering—"

"Wondering what? If I could tell Fuller you're a good guy and to open his files to you? Tell Fuller you don't think the guy is guilty, so to lay off 'cause we used to play on the same football team? That's what this is about, isn't it? Your buddy's not guilty, same old shit we hear about every murderer that comes in here—"

Raising his own voice, Ford said, "I don't know if he did

98

it or not. I just want to know can you get me in to see him today."

Durell waited for a moment before saying, "That's it?"

"That's it."

"But today's not a visitation day—unless they've changed the schedule."

"I'm aware of that."

Durell said, "Sorry. If the prisoner puts you on his visitors' list, the days are Tuesday, Wednesday, Saturdays. If you're not on the list, you've got to file a written request."

"Come on, Les, this is such a small thing—"

"And being familiar with our line of work, I know you wouldn't want me to break any rules."

Ford started to stay something else, but Durell cut in with official formality: "Anything else I can help you with, don't hesitate to call," and hung up.

From outside came the miscellaneous noises of a marina workday: the rhythmic grating of someone scraping barnacles off the bottom of a boat, the whine of a drill, an occasional voice lifted above the noise of a running outboard motor. Ford went out the screen door and made a contemplative tour around his porch. Beneath his house, he could see mangrove snapper wheeling around the pilings and pods of mullet darting past. He checked the fish in his tank. The sea anemones were all packaged, ready for UPS and the trip to Bowling Green State University, but he had left three anemones in the tank, and they looked very delicate and pretty there beneath the water.

The sun was up now, a vast white glare that leached all color from the sky, and already hot, hot, hot.

Finally, he went back inside, turned the fan on his face, and found his address book on top of the little refrigerator. He dialed the Two Parrot Bight Marina number and was glad that a young man answered, no one he knew. Speaking in what he hoped sounded like a prim, official tone, Ford said, "My name's Johnson, from the county census office. I hate to trouble you, but I'm afraid we need a couple of Social Security numbers right away to get our records straight."

The young man said, "What? Oh, you'll have to call back; the manager isn't here right now."

Ford wondered who the young man considered the manager to be. Sutter, maybe? He hoped so; hoped Sutter wasn't there. Sutter might recognize his voice. He said, "I'm afraid we're in a hurry. You must have some kind of pay schedule in one of your files with the numbers. We need them for a Mr. Rios and a Mr. Sutter, Karl Sutter."

The young man said, "But Mr. Rios's . . . no longer; I mean, he died a couple days ago. The funeral's right now, today. That's why the manager's not here, his wife, neither. Mrs. Rios, I mean."

"That's exactly why I need the information now." Giving it some urgency, as if they couldn't bury Rios until the county census office had the Social Security numbers.

The young man said, "Oh!" and put the phone down. Ford could hear customer noises in the background, someone asking why they couldn't pick out their own bait shrimp, someone asking was this all salt water? Then the young man was back and gave him both numbers, which Ford noted on a yellow pad.

"But why do you need Captain Sutter's number?" the young man asked.

Borrowing Les Durell's tone and style, Ford said, "For our records, of course," and thanked him.

Ford took up his address book again, and dialed a number with a Washington, D.C., area code, and left a message on the recording machine he knew would answer.

To the recorder, he said, "Sally, this is Ford," now looking through the thin Sanibel phone book as he spoke. "I need information on two men. One, a guy named Marvin Rios, ah . . . I don't have a middle initial, sorry, but he lives here, on the island. You know which island, the one where you said you had so much fun last September. The other is Karl . . . Karl B. Sutter, same place. Antecedents unknown, probably the Midwest. Probably no military background, but I'm not sure. I have both Social Security numbers. . . ."

For the recorder, he matched the numbers with the names, then went outside and stepped into his flats boat.

Ford could see Dewey grimace slightly each time she brought the racket around, giving the ball wicked top spins, blasting it across the net into impossible corners of the opposite court where the electric server *whoofed* fluorescent green tennis balls at her.

At shaded tables, spectators sitting over drinks beneath umbrellas at the exclusive Punta Rassa Tennis Club didn't notice; about twenty people and at least two reporters watching Dewey Nye, once ranked thirteen in the world, in her first full tennis workout since having elbow surgery. But Ford saw the slight involuntary grimace and knew that she was in pain.

At the refreshment bar, he bought a bottle of Coors Light, and, as he turned to find a seat, a man wearing a shirt bearing the club logo touched him on the arm. "Excuse me, sir. Is that your boat parked at the dock?"

"Tied at the dock, yes."

"Are you a member here? Your boat doesn't have a sticker."

"No, I'm waiting for Ms. Nye."

The man's cool tone dissipated. "Oh, you're a friend of hers?"

"That's right."

His smile became magnanimous. "In that case, excuse the inquiry. We have to be careful, you know."

"Absolutely," said Ford, who had never belonged to a tennis club—or any club—in his life. "Can't be too careful."

There were no empty tables near the court, so he sat on the grass in the shade, drinking his beer, a whole complex of courts to his right, most of them in use. Tennis courts, he decided, had an odor different from any of the sports facilities with which he was familiar. An odor of damp chalk—clay, he guessed—and neatly trimmed grass with just a hint of rubber; nothing cloying like the perfume worn by some of those women at the tables, but

101

with a subtle tang to it, maybe like the interior of one of the Porsches baking in the heat out there in the parking lot.

Dewey caught his eye, grinned, and held up one finger—almost done. Her white knit shirt was soaked with sweat, hanging limp on her wide shoulders; her hair a dark gold now, as if she had just climbed out of a swimming pool. He watched her making shots near the net, forehands and backhands, grunting with the effort of each stroke, a low guttural noise with an animal intensity. Something about that noise did not fit here; the quality of brute determination created an off-chord sound quickly deflected by these neat surroundings, all these neat people watching.

We have to be careful, you know. . . .

In that instant, Ford sensed what it was that attracted him to the woman, though it was difficult to pinpoint. Were it not for her skills, she would not be at this place—that was part of it. Not only would she not be on the court, she would not be at one of those shaded tables, watching. But it was more than that. Along with the innocence, there was a displaced quality about her, too—the strange quality of one who would have fit more comfortably into a different time, into a different place; a person who achieved, who prevailed, yet never quite meshed with the circumstances of her own life. Screens shielded her—her humor, her gruffness. Shielded others as well as herself.

It was a quality familiar to Ford. Why, he wasn't sure.

There was a woman tagging along with Dewey; a tall woman, brown hair cropped short and brushed back, with wide brown eyes in a lean European face. The woman wore standard tennis dress—trim green shorts and a dark-blue designer shirt that had a sweeping burnt orange stripe across the back and chest. Long arms and longer legs, yet she moved fluidly, everything easy and relaxed, as if conserving energy; an athlete, physically sure of herself, and oddly attractive because of it, with her plain outdoor face.

Ford studied her a moment, considering the woman's wrists, her calves, the sunburn flush, the patched shoes, the

102

charm bracelet, the style, the smile, and he thought: *East German or Eastern European. Is politically aware. A tennis player. Right-handed, likes gold jewelry. Isn't married; probably hasn't been in Florida more than a day or two.*

The woman had been the first to Dewey's side when Dewey finished her workout, helping her zip rackets into their cases. Then she had produced an ice pack and was now securing it to Dewey's elbow, wrapping a flesh-colored athletic bandage round and round while Dewey sat on a folding chair inside the screened court, talking with the few spectators who had come in to meet her, and the two reporters, one with a notebook, the other with a tape recorder.

Like some kind of trainer, but she wasn't dressed that way. Didn't have the earnest professional look. Plus, she and Dewey were exchanging too many grins; laughing a lot together, and the reporters were talking to the taller woman, as well. A pro tennis player, probably, and Dewey's friend—though Dewey hadn't mentioned a friend visiting, or any female friends in the area. Which was just like Dewey.

Ford waited in the shade until they came through the gate, the two women together, and Dewey called to him, "Hey, Ford, I got someone I want you to meet. Just flew in yesterday, my old buddy Bets," meaning the tall woman, who held out a firm hand, her expression friendlier than Ford had expected, but nothing shy about it, looking him right in the eye.

Dewey was chuckling, nudging Bets like a kid in school. "I told you he wouldn't know who the hell you were."

Bets said, "Yes, it is kind of nice; I see what you mean," with an Eastern European accent that had lost the thudding *dahs* and *vhats*, probably abraded smooth by many years of speaking English.

Her amusement at not being recognized was real, but Ford still felt obliged to apologize, saying, "I don't follow sports like I should, I'm sorry—"

But she was already laughing it off, listening to Dewey say, "The guy doesn't even have a television. Still listens to records. Doesn't have a microwave!" The two of them looking at him like he was a zoo oddity, someone who had just crawled out of a cave, but putting him at ease, too, by cutting through the awkwardness usually present when a new friend meets an old friend.

Bets said, "You had better have a shower before you become chilled."

Dewey was flapping her shirt like a bellows, still wearing the ice pack. "My God, it must be ninety in the shade. But, yeah, I'm going to start stinking pretty quick." Checking for Ford's grin, and getting it. "Did you drive over?"

"I came by boat."

"Hum, that's a problem. Bets and I drove, so—I know!" Her face brightened. "You take us for a spin in the boat, then drop us back here. Then we meet tonight for dinner . . . at the Lazy Flamingo. Raw conch salad and beer."

Making them a threesome, just like that.

Ford was still grinning, but now at the way she took complete control. "Sure, but on Monday nights—"

"Damn, that's right." To Bets, she said, "On Mondays, Doc boats up to Cabbage Key—that's a little island; a neat little hotel there—and watches Monday-night baseball on the tube. A real guy thing to do. You know, male bonding at the bar."

Bets said, "That sounds like fun."

Dewey said, "Bets loves boats. She grew up on the—what sea was it?"

"The Black Sea."

Ford thought, *Romania,* and knew immediately who the woman must be as she said, "When I was a little girl, only the fishermen and the party people had boats, everyone was so poor. So, yes, I enjoy boating now."

"She's got like a fifty-foot sailboat she keeps on Long Island. Runs it herself."

"Fifteen meters, which is a little smaller? Yes. A pretty ketch. I may have it transported home now that my people have taken our country back."

Dewey said, "Bets has got like five sisters—six? Yeah, six.

A whole crew back there in Romania to take care of it. So if you know any eligible guys, Doc . . ."

Bets said, "No, no men until I get their teeth straightened," smiling and showing her own teeth, which were capped and hadn't yet lost the brace scars.

Ford was thinking: Walda something-tovski, one of the better known names in world tennis. Walda *Bzantovski*, only the press had a different nickname for her; he couldn't remember what—not Bets. The only reason he knew was because when the Romanians overthrew dictator Nicolae Ceausescu, he had heard a report about this woman on National Public Radio. About her withdrawing from some major tennis tournament to rush home to join the liberation militia; the interviewer hammering delightedly at the irony of this tennis star who had defected to the United States years before, trading a skirt for the battle fatigues and the side arm she apparently wore during the interview.

He remembered one short portion of the interview, Bzantovski defending the Revolution's street executions of the Securitate, members of Ceausescu's secret police; remembered it because of the weary cast to the woman's voice, as if she had seen some things, maybe done some things. Nothing at all like American celebrities who cloaked themselves in stylish causes with all the theatrical severity of children playing in the attic. Something in that voice had touched him; something in that voice knew how tiny a tennis court really was.

Ford said, "Then we'll all go to Cabbage Key. My friend Tomlinson usually goes, but I think he has a friend visiting."

Walda said, "At night, I would love that. There will be a moon?"

"A nearly full moon in June."

"Hot damn." Dewey turned. "I bet I could squeeze a gallon of sweat out of this T-shirt. You two have something to drink. I'll make it quick." Then she set off toward the training complex without giving him the brief pat or hug that had become her standard greeting and farewell.

Walda called after her, "And make sure you drink some Gatorade while you are showering! You need to rehydrate."

Counting Candy, the minister, that pig Greta, and himself, only eleven people attended Marvin Rios's funeral, including four civic officials who were so used to brownnosing and ass kissing that the vacuum caused by the death of such a gigantic asshole probably sucked them right to the grave—or maybe so they could make sure the corpse was really Rios. Get it down on the books, make it official, so at the next council meeting they could say, "All those who think the little maggot is actually dead, say aye!"

The best news, though, was the head asshole was there, Senator Robert M. Griffin himself; two flunkies along looking just as bored as the big boss, all of them wearing vests beneath their suit coats, real hotshots in their shiny shoes, glancing at their watches like they resented wasting time on something so unimportant.

Which they probably did.

On the phone, Sutter had said, "Thing is, Senator, unless you make it down to Sanibel so we can have a little chat, I may have to what you call leak the contents of this contract I'm holding to the press. Maybe you can tell them why you and Rios agreed not to file it."

To which the senator had said, "Consult an attorney, Mr. Sutter, and he will explain that the law does not require contracts to be filed. That's a public misconception." Like he had ice in his mouth.

"You and Rios were just such good friends, huh?"

"We were distant business associates. Frankly, my firm handles most of my business dealings. I'm a little busy with my duties in Tallahassee—and I don't like your tone one bit."

"So forget it, Senator. You got nothing to hide from the press, more power to you. Hell, my dad was in politics; I know how things work. But I like a nice business deal, and I'm no Boy Scout, so if you want to discuss things, be at the funeral."

And goddamn if he wasn't there; obviously pissed, but standing right there in the morning heat of the Colonial Palm Cemetery, which was a hell of a shock to Sutter. Making that call to Griffin was like buying a lottery ticket—something that probably wouldn't pay off, but a chance to shit on a big shot just a little bit before the senator said fuck you, bozo, and slammed the phone down. But Christ, the guy was there; probably had to fly down in a private plane from the capitol at Tallahassee or wherever he lived.

A senator obeying my orders!

Sutter knew he was on to something; something really big. But he had to play it just right. Had to let on he knew more than he did. Had to get the senator talking; just sit back like he was in control, maybe let Griffin buy him off. Naw, the big money would be in the deal—whatever the hell the deal was. He had to play it cool, hope the senator would fill him in. And, if he didn't, then go for the buy-off.

Watching the minister drop dirt into the grave, Sutter thought, *Elevator shoes aren't going to help you now, you midget.*

Then he drifted toward the senator when the damn thing ended. Hugged Candy, who had been in a daze since their little party yesterday; was still in a daze, leaning on him for support. Which was good; show Griffin he was part of the family. Ignored Greta 'cause he didn't want to introduce a pig like that as his girlfriend, which she was—but not for long. Left Greta standing over there by herself wearing the dark chemise like a tent over the rolls of fat, that stewed-prune little mouth of hers all set to start yammering about half the tarpon prize money being hers because she'd gone along with the gag. Went right up to Griffin and said, "Maybe we can get together later, discuss some business."

The senator put on his politician's face, smiling, like he was talking to a voter. "We're staying on Captiva, South Seas Plantation. How about you come up for some supper." Giving it a southern twang; the good ol' boy not adverse to wheeling and dealing, but keeping it low so not even his two stooges could hear.

"I was thinking more like Cabbage Key. That's a little island just north on the Intracoastal—"

"Buddy rough," the senator cut in, "I've shaken hands and

fought and fucked in parts of this state tourists like you never even heard about yet. I'm fourth-generation Cracker; you don't need to give me directions any place, especially Cabbage Key." Twitching a little bit, angry, with a crazy look in his eyes, like he might lean over and take a bite out of him.

Sutter stepped back a little. "That's what we'll do then, tonight. Only don't bring your two friends. This has got to be what you call private."

Griffin said, "You're the one with all the mouth, Sutter. *You* keep that in mind." And walked off.

Sitting in the bar at Cabbage Key, Dewey had said, "Radical. I love this place. Like an old English movie, or a Bogart flick with all the ceiling fans."

Walda had stared at the wallpaper—thousands of one-dollar bills. She had said, "Except we're in America," as if nowhere else could you find wallpaper like this.

Ford was hoping the two of them wouldn't sit there talking, requiring his attention all through the game. He got the chance to watch baseball only once a week, and tonight was the night. Royals at Boston; an evening of classic left-handed hitters.

Dewey was saying, "Our own little island, and not a damn tennis court to be seen."

Meaning Cabbage Key, named for cabbage palms: a hundred acres of sand and mangrove upon which prehistoric Indians, the Calusa, built high shell mounds—the Florida equivalent of Central America's Mayan temples. Back in the 1930s, when the island was known as Palmetto Key, wealthy New Yorkers commissioned a large house to be constructed on the highest mound, among the poinciana trees and gumbo limbos. A winter estate, it was called in those days, built of hardwood and white clapboard, with guest rooms, a library, a dining room, and its own generator, because there was no electricity. Now the estate was a laid-back inn and restaurant where boaters and fishermen could sit on the shaded porch, or climb the wooden water tower and look out across the island to the other islands in Pine Island Sound. The place had an oasis feel to it, sitting out there all by itself, like it could have been Abaco or Tangiers or Caicos, soaking up the sun through the decades while travelers tromped up the shell path to the old house on the mound.

Now Dewey was up mingling, and Ford was sitting with Walda at a table in the little bar. He didn't think of her as "Bets." The nickname just didn't fit, looking at those dark eyes, set deep, like peering out from a cave, and the long jaw; a plain-looking woman of about thirty who fit nicely into the worn Levi's and the expensive Egyptian cotton safari shirt, as if she were still in uniform but for the rings and the heavy gold charm bracelet.

She said, "Then call me Walda," pronouncing it VAUL-dah, with a very soft *V*.

Ford said, "Okay, Walda," trying it out.

"But not Wally or Waldo. Not Wallaby, either—some reporter used that in Sydney. The Australian Open."

"Right. Walda."

Beyond, through the porch screen, there was moonlight on the trees and Pine Island Sound showed through the leaves in smooth portions of glazed silver—wedges of water that seemed to rock randomly, gently, as the tree limbs stirred, so that being in the bar was a little bit like being on a ship.

It was darker in the bar. Ceiling fans and muted light. Noisier, though only a few people still sat over stone-crab claws and steaks out on the back porch; two more couples at tables, eating the house dessert, key lime pie with whipped cream. A couple more men on stools at the bar. Old paintings and fiber-glass fish on the walls, the walls all papered with curling dollar bills—something visitors did here, signed dollars and taped them up. That had impressed Walda. Thousands of dollars on the walls, on the ceiling, peeling off like elm bark, giving the bar a tree-house feel.

"The wallpaper of capitalism," Walda said.

Ford smiled and nodded, trying to watch the game.

"And that fish. It must have weighed a hundred pounds!" Meaning the tarpon mounted on the wall. The tarpon was nearly seven feet long, and the taxidermist had reproduced the mirror silver scales nicely, had done a good job with the huge end-

109

loader jaw and the horse-size eyes. But he had painted the fish's back an iridescent blue-black that didn't do justice to the parallel striations of blue seen on a living fish.

Ford said, "That one weighed nearly two hundred pounds, a tarpon. It's a big one, but they get bigger. Supposedly more than three hundred pounds."

"Is that one of the fish you study? Dewey said that's what you do."

"It's my main interest now. Tarpon, I mean."

"And you're not sure how big the fish gets? It seems you should know that." Smiling slightly, Walda was watching for his reaction.

For the first time, Ford's attention wandered from the baseball game. "I know almost nothing about the fish. No one does. The tarpon is one of the most important game fish in the world, but its life history is a mystery." He looked at Walda to see if she was interested, and she seemed to be. He continued, "Every spring, tarpon migrate from somewhere offshore into the estuaries—shallow water. They come here by the thousands; you can see them rolling on the surface. Everyone assumed it was a spawning migration, but no fertilized tarpon eggs have ever been found in shallow water. They've been found forty miles offshore and farther, but never in shallow water. So that's what I'm doing now. Seining shallow water for fertilized eggs and larvae. It's been done before, but never on an extended basis. The shallow-water-spawning theory hasn't been conclusively eliminated, and that's what I'm doing. Looking for larvae."

"Netting tarpon eggs, hoping not to find any that have been fertilized." She smiled, amused, but following right along.

"Why would I have any hopes one way or the other? It's research."

"But it's something you like."

"Sure. That one unknown presents a number of interesting problems. Why do tarpon make a yearly migration? Why do they gather in groups of mature fish and swim in slow circles if it's not a mating ritual? Fishermen call it 'daisy chaining.' If they do spawn offshore, why are immature fish sometimes found fifty

110

miles up tidal creeks in fresh water? Where offshore do they come from? Do they cross oceans, do they travel coastlines, or do they just go out to deep water and stay there until the next spring? Opens all kinds of doors. Things no one knows."

"I meant you like the fish." She was looking at the tarpon on the wall again.

"Yeah. Tarpon're interesting. They're prehistoric. Their air bladder acts more like a lung so they can breathe surface air. They're pure muscle; one of the strongest animals on earth. And to humans, they're a mystery."

Walda Bzantovski was leaning on the table, her tan, plain face not looking so plain anymore, gathering character and a certain sexuality from the way her brown eyes held him.

"Then I like the tarpon, too. I want you to take me to see one. This week, before I have to leave. If Dewey can't go, that's okay."

Ford was looking back at her, thinking: *Yeah. I'd like that.* Ford turned his eyes back to Boston and Kansas City playing baseball on television. He said, "We'll see."

Walda was saying look how Dewey found friends no matter where she went, causing Ford's eyes to leave the television once more and find Dewey. She was over by the fireplace playing darts with three men Ford didn't know, probably with the group of D.C. bankers who, according to Terry, the dockmaster, had come down to fish Boca Grande Pass.

Ford had heard one of the dart players on the bar telephone earlier, his voice harried, apparently still trying to arrange for charter boats and transportation to the island for late arrivals, finally yelling into the phone before slamming it down: "Look, Ms. Bittinger, I've got a lot of important men to please. We need boats, we need guides, we need entertainment—we're short everything down here! So if it floats, flies, or fucks—lease it!"

Men with money taking a long weekend; not bad guys from the way they behaved, just out to have some fun. Drinking, fishing, now playing darts. Also getting their collective butts kicked by Dewey, judging from the expression on their faces.

Ford said, "Those guys aren't used to getting beat by a woman."

Walda was nodding. "If they are going to play with Dewey, they had better get used to it," looking at Ford, not smiling, but congenial, still wanting to make conversation, maybe beginning to feel the two Johnnie Walker Blacks she'd had, nearly finished with her third. She touched Ford's hand briefly, getting his attention. "Dewey speaks very well of you."

"That's nice."

"Forgive me for saying it . . . well, perhaps I shouldn't."

"Feel free. Say what you want."

"Okay. I was going to say you don't look like the men we normally meet. Your face, not handsome, but like you've been some bad places and it's made you kinder. No, not kinder. There's a phrase in Romanian: *Mai intelept decit batrinii*. That's the look you have."

Ford asked, "Which means?"

"If I could say it in English, I would." Like she wanted to do some verbal jousting, feeling him out. When he didn't react, she said, "It didn't bother you that I said you're not handsome? Some women would think you are. But the men we meet on the tour are often very handsome. And very rich. Does that make you uneasy?"

"Nope."

"No big ego. Dewey said that's one of the things she likes about you. She beats you, but you don't mind. She says you are an exceptionally strong swimmer, you could pull boats. But she runs faster than you, and you don't make excuses. That's a rare thing in men."

"And in women."

"Oh?"

"Yes."

"But I can give you an example. See that man's face?"

She meant the tall one, the one with the simmering look, holding his mouth like it was a steam valve while Dewey waved her arms around, yelling into his face, "Bullshit! That wasn't on the line! You don't know the rules, you shouldn't play!" Like

112

she apparently sometimes talked to tennis referees. Or umpires. Whatever they called them, Ford didn't know.

Walda said, "Men act like that. She says you don't. That's what I mean."

The television was on the upright piano near the dart board, and Ford could see the screen just past Walda's right ear. He was trying not to be obvious about watching. Usually, he sat at the bar with Terry, and Rob, the owner, but now they were over there and he was here.

On the screen, Boggs had doubled and now Mike Greenwell was up.

Ford said, "So it's hard to find guys who lose gracefully?"

"That's not exactly the point."

"She's a professional athlete, I'm not. Competing seems a little silly."

"Precisely!"

"We're in two different fields. Me trying to beat her at sports would be like . . . like her coming into my lab and trying to beat me . . . at . . . at—"

Greenwell hit a bullet with that great swing of his, but the shortstop flagged it, and they doubled Boggs at second. End of inning.

Walda said, "Beat you at what?"

Ford said, "At anything. Who cares?" He wasn't a fan of a particular team, but there were certain hitters he enjoyed watching—unless they got robbed with men in scoring position.

Walda was leaning toward him, nodding her head. "You are so right. In my own country, all over Eastern Europe, wives are kept pregnant until they produce a son. Did you know that?"

Ford knew it but said nothing.

"My own father and mother kept trying until they had seven daughters. It's absurd, the importance of a person's sex, when there are so many things going on. Important things."

"Yep," Ford said. Now he was watching Clemens take his warm-up pitches, bringing that fastball from right behind his head, it seemed.

"Exactly. Only in a society that has so much free time—and

113

so much freedom!—could the masses care about such matters. One group fighting against the other."

"Right."

"They don't communicate, they compete. Prosperity doesn't unify, it magnifies differences. That is why my country-men united so quickly. No prosperity, none. I'll know Romania is doing well when Romanians begin to fight among them-selves."

Three up, three down; Clemens, the rocket man, throwing gas right up to the commercial break: "I love what you do for me, Toyota." George Brett wouldn't get up until next inning. Ford stood. "I'm going to get another beer; you want any-thing?"

Walda swirled the ice in her glass. "Yes, but make this one something different. A margarita; a lot of salt. Hey, Dewey"—she was calling across the room, over the empty tables; these two women dominating the room—"why don't you try a margarita? They're not strong. Doc's going to the bar."

Dewey was pulling darts out of the board, distracted, proba-bly calculating her score. "I'll have another iced tea, but I'm buying. Give me about two more minutes, and each one of these D.C. cowboys is going to owe me ten bucks." Laughing, saying it into the faces of the three bankers, she was standing there in the black T-shirt and shorts that were loose enough on her to suggest all the taut curves beneath, which is probably why the men had asked her to play in the first place.

At the bar, Terry, with his Buddha eyes and shaggy gray hair said, "That's a lively little woman there. What, she doesn't drink?"

Ford said, "Guess not."

"Back when I used to womanize, that always added about an extra week to the schedule. A woman who didn't drink. Got so I avoided 'em."

"Don't say that to her face. You might get your windows tinted."

"What?"

"Smacked."

114

"Ah. She's pretty tough on those guys."

"Get on the wrong side of her, and Dewey's no day at the beach. They been here before?"

"Nope. They came in this afternoon. Bossy; they wanted everything their way, but that's normal when people try to push too much fun into too few days. I don't think your friend is fitting into their game plan."

Ford was waiting on the drinks, leaning against the bar. "With Dewey, you either fit into her game plan or you don't fit at all."

"I think one of those bankers is looking to make the creature with two backs."

"Instead, they got a night of Dewey. Must be a shock. I kind of feel for them."

"Are you with her or the one at the table?"

"Both, I guess."

"She's pretty, too—but in a different way." Meaning Walda. "The more you look, the prettier she gets. But not really pretty—interesting. That kind. But not romantic, huh? With either one of them?"

From so much sun, the skin at Ford's eyes crinkled when he smiled. "Having trouble concentrating on the game? I'm not even sure what inning it is."

"Who knows. I just sit here for the companionship. It's just that she doesn't seem like your type, the one playing darts."

"I guess that's why I like her. She's not a type."

Ford was taking the can of beer, the iced tea, and the wide margarita glass in his hands, turning, and as he did, he saw back into the corner of the dining room for the first time.

There sat Karl Sutter.

Ford recognized the wide back and the blond hair poking out from beneath the fishing cap, and the puckered outline of Sutter's tiny pink mouth.

Ford stood there for a moment, looking. Thought about detouring past the man, stopping just long enough to say something about Sutter cutting his boat loose; let Sutter know he knew; not even let on it was only a suspicion. Pretend he had

115

been seen parked in that white car back in among the mangroves. Pretend he knew Sutter had futzed up the bilge pump of his skiff, then snuck back later and cut the boat free. Put it on the line and see how Sutter reacted. But then Ford thought, *No, wait and see how far he'll take it. Give him plenty of rope.*

Sutter sat across the table from another man: executive-looking type with carefully sprayed hair, a tasteful knit sports shirt; wearing those clothes like a pennant, permission to socialize. They were both leaning across the table. Low voices; an intense expression on the face of the executive. A serious conversation, and private, too, way back there in the corner.

Ford said, "What about that guy, over there at the far table. You know him?"

"The one's Karl Sutter, kind of a half-assed fishing guide—"

"No, the one facing us."

Terry said, "No-o-o-o, but the face is sort of familiar. You want me to check?"

Ford said, "I'd appreciate that," as he watched Dewey returning to their table; watched her give Walda a locker-room squeeze, both of them laughing, sharing something between them. Watched the tall banker peeling off bills from a wad and throwing them onto the table, pissed but trying to act like it didn't bother him. Watched the banker lean and say something into Dewey's ear, then saw Dewey's face change; saw it pale from tan to mottled white, and Ford thought, *Uh-oh,* taking his eyeglasses off and placing them on the bar.

Then he watched a blurry Dewey twist to the right as if in slow motion . . . check herself, as if giving it careful thought . . . then twist back to the left before doubling her fist and hitting the yachtsman hard on the left cheek of his surprised face—could see the surprise in those wide, wild eyes of his—and watched him backpedal into the next table, falling over it backward, knocking off all the drinks, landing hard in the mess on the wooden floor as Dewey yelled, "Turd!" standing over the guy like a boxer, challenging him to get up.

By the time Terry said, "Oh, shit," Ford was already moving toward Dewey, watching the scene develop, people moving in all directions: people getting up from their dinner to see what in the hell all the noise was; Walda jumping up so quick her chair tumbled over behind her; the banker's two buddies charging in, one of them reaching out to shove Dewey away, but then Walda was there. Walda caught the man's arm as he was moving forward, then leveraged it downward and pulled, using his own momentum to swing him headfirst into the piano; hit so hard, the piano jolted sideways, knocking the dart board off the wall, signed dollar bills flying everywhere, swirling in the wake of the ceiling fan.

Ford caught the second guy in a loose bear hug just before he got to Dewey, holding him back and yelling at the guy, "She's done; she's not going to hit him again. Let's just stop it." But then the first banker got to his feet and Dewey did hit him again; smacked him right in the face, making a sound like plywood slapping together, and Ford knew his credibility was shot.

So he let the second guy break free, thinking maybe there was still hope of reasoning this thing out. But there wasn't. Not after the guy lunged at Dewey, trying to hold her, but instead fell over her as she ducked, both of them falling against the fireplace, swinging wildly, with Dewey still yelling things. Then the first banker was back into it, bleeding from the nose, and Ford jumped in front of him, getting his arms up, catching punches on his elbows and shoulders until a stunning impact buckled his knees, like being immersed in ammonia. Then he was on the floor, kneeling groggily, noise all around him, thinking he'd been punched—but then realized the slick substance on his face was pie filling, not blood, and saw the broken chunks of ceramic on the floor beside him.

Christ, he'd been hit in the head with a plate.

Someone was throwing plates . . . Walda, that's who. Taking desserts and coffee cups off the tables, then hurling them, driving both bankers out of the bar—now the third one, too, as he got shakily to his feet over there by the piano. The three men backing fast onto the porch, hollering threats, but mostly ducking as Walda bore down on them, her dark eyes intense, as if she was sighting down a Baretta instead of throwing plates of half-eaten pie. Caught up in a rage that had silenced the whole bar—even Dewey was just standing, watching now—then Walda seemed to catch herself, as if on the edge of something, visibly pulling herself back.

In the sudden quiet, she spoke to Dewey. "What did that bastard say to you?"

Dewey was looking at the porch, as if the bankers might return. "He said I'd screwed him, so now I should let him screw me. Only he didn't say *screw*." Toning down her language with people listening. "No one talks to me like that. Never again. That's why I hit him."

Ford was sitting on a bar stool, leaning his weight against the bar. He was aware that the dining room had emptied, all the guests stacked up at the bar entrance, watching the show. Sutter was there, taller than everyone, his eyes fixed on the two women, his expression strange, slightly flushed.

Ford didn't like the way his face looked, like someone who enjoyed car wrecks.

Walda turned from Ford to Dewey, then back to Ford, and said in the silence, "Do you normally bring ladies to dumps like this?" Using her hands to indicate the mess on the floor and the overturned tables. Which caused the people watching to laugh.

Ford said, "No, so I thought you two might feel right at home." Which made Dewey smile, then chuckle as she put her arm around Walda, then they were both laughing, roaring, letting the tension go.

Walda was pointing at Ford. "I hit you in the head with a plate! I'm sorry; I didn't mean to. But you looked so funny! The way you . . . the way you went down . . .!" Laughing so hard she couldn't talk.

Wide-eyed, Dewey said, "You hit Doc? You missed and hit Doc? Hah! On the melon?" Which doubled her over.

Ford said, "I have key lime pie in my eustachian tube," holding up his index finger for inspection. He said, "You think that's funny? You thought the bill for damages Terry gave you was funny. You thought that banker threatening a lawsuit was funny. You girls think everything is funny. I could go deaf."

"Women! Not girls. Women!"

Dewey and Walda were in the kitchen of Dewey's Captiva beach house, making drinks. Maybe more margaritas; he could hear the blender. Terry had refused them service after the fight, and now Walda said she wanted to get a little drunk. Dewey said, yeah, they had earned it, and she might have a drink, too—which was a shocker. So Ford had made the midnight crossing from Cabbage Key to Captiva Island, running the Intracoastal to Captiva Pass, then cutting across the flats, all that dark water, to the docks at Blind Pass, where Dewey kept a slip.

Now Ford was sitting in a deck chair by the screened-in pool, looking at the night sky. It was late, after two, and still. Summer-still, with insect noises, and the moon was gone. The darkness was compressed by the hour; the stillness of 2 A.M. and the fixed stars seemed to resonate, like being deep, deep underwater. Ford sat there looking at the sky, and found himself wondering if Jeth Nicholes was awake. Wondered if Jeth was studying these same stars through a window with bars. Jeth Nicholes the accused murderer, which sounded absurd, but that's the way things stood.

From the open sliding glass doors into the kitchen, Walda called to him. "Why don't you go for a swim? That would clean out your ear. Or get into the hot tub."

"I don't have a suit."

"Such a prude! I don't have a suit, and I'm going for a swim. Dewey and I are both going swimming!"

"Damn right, Doc. Get your puny ass in there!" Dewey's voice.

He could hear them both laughing, probably two or three margaritas gone, and then the pool's underwater lights went on, like a challenge. Ford poked his head into the kitchen. Dewey and Walda were beyond, in the living room, just opening some kind of a scrapbook. Wide living room with hurricane shutters closed tight, as if to shut out the world. Low modern furniture and floor cushions by the fireplace. Professionally decorated with

119

prints of sea oats, herons, and starfish. Cool colors and vacation home sterile. No trophies on the mantelpiece; no reminders of her profession in this big room, which had been the thing that first told Ford she was weary of tennis. An impersonal room in an impersonal house, which had never really been lived in until Dewey's elbow surgery, so it had the feel of an elaborate hotel suite; a place to relax between airports. Ford said to them, "I either have to boat home now or borrow your car and drive home later. It's late, and I've still got a twenty-minute run."

Dewey looked up from the scrapbook, and he could see that she was a little drunk, the way her eyes didn't quite focus. "So stay here, Einstein. Sleep in the guest room, then we can all go for a run early. On the beach."

Walda said, "As long as you don't snore."

Ford wondered if that meant Walda was also staying in the guest room. Or in Dewey's room. Or maybe the house had a third bedroom; he wasn't sure.

"Then I'm going to go down and check the boat."

"Then you'll swim?"

"Sure. Get my ear washed out."

He went out the pool door. Behind him was the gray beach and the open Gulf of Mexico. The Gulf made a breathing noise, the way the water lapped, calm. He crossed SanCap Road, then walked along it in the darkness, beneath the palms and casuarina pines. Even this late, there were a few fishermen on the Blind Pass Bridge, the bridge that connected Sanibel to Captiva. No matter what the weather, pouring rain or wind; no matter what time of day or night, there were always fishermen on that bridge. Same with the Matlacha Bridge on Pine Island. Same with the old Bahia Honda Bridge on the Keys. The really good fishing bridges always had fishermen, and Blind Pass was one of the best.

Dewey's dock was on the bay side, and Ford cut through a yard to his skiff. He checked the lines and dropped an anchor off to hold the boat away from the dock when the tide started out again, then found a diet Coke in the cooler and sat watching the silhouettes of the fishermen up on the bridge. Fifty yards or so down the pass, shielded by mangroves, someone banged around in a boat, and an outboard engine started. More late fishermen out to get a snook, or maybe a tarpon. Ford yawned, enjoying the night.

When he got back to Dewey's house, the pool lights were off, and he could hear the two women splashing around and talking softly. The screen door creaked when he opened it, and they both hooted and moved to the far end of the pool. Yep, they were naked, all right. Not that he could see them. Just two dim shapes glistening, the bodies indistinguishable, so that only Dewey's blonde hair gave her away.

"The water's nice, Doc. We won't look."

Dewey called, "The hell we won't! He watched us."

Ford said, "What?"

"You heard me."

"I was down at the boat. I didn't watch anything."

"Hah! I heard you out there walking around. Rooting around in the bushes trying to get a peek. When I turned down the music, I could hear you breathing, for Christ sake."

Ford said, "You're serious, aren't you?"

Dewey said, "Wait a minute—that wasn't you? Really? No shit now, Doc."

Ford went into the kitchen, walking fast. "You have a flashlight in here?"

"Hey, hold it. I know what it was. The neighbor's damn dog. That's what it was. Kind of a big mutt, like a shepherd. He scared me the other night like that, came sniffing around. I just figured it was you acting like a pervert. I'll have to shovel more dog crap in the morning."

Walda said to Dewey, "I never did hear anything. You said you could, but I didn't." Floating on her back momentarily, giving Ford a quick look: breasts flattening as her back arched; the dark symmetry of nipples; the grid of stomach muscles veiled in shadow, then gone beneath the water.

Ford felt a physical stirring, like an abdominal cramp— that's how long it had been.

He said, "Flashlight?"

"God, you're stubborn."

"Just a quick look around, that's all. Where is it?"

"There's one plugged into the wall, by the stove. It goes on when the power goes out. But there's no reason—"

Ford found the light and followed the wide beam out through the screen door into the backyard—a low-maintenance gravel yard, bordered by sand and casuarina needles, with isolated landscaped islands of date palms and bird-of-paradise plants. A privacy hedge, shoulder-high, had been planted around the pool, and Ford went slowly along the hedge, painting back and forth with the light, looking at the ground. Wood chips, really; some sand.

From inside, he heard Dewey say, "That's where I first heard it. Right where you are now."

Ford dropped down to one knee, looking carefully . . . and found a shallow crater of a footprint. Nothing detailed about it; a swale in the sand, but large. A man's footprint. Someone with some weight had stood near the hedge, toes pointing toward the pool. He moved out across the yard, but the gravel would not show prints. Found a pile of dog scat at the edge of the drive, not fresh. The dog had been eating grass and the bones of some kind of fowl. Ford worked his way around the house, twice, making wider and wider circles, then returned to the pool.

"See anything?" Dewey and Walda were back there in the deep end, holding on to the edge.

"Like you said, probably just a dog."

"You'll learn to listen to me."

Ford was stripping off his shirt, folding it, putting it with his glasses. "Your yardmen keep the yard nice. How often do they come?"

"You took so long, we're about ready to get out."

"Did they come today?"

"The guys who do the yard? Nope. Every Wednesday. So you're coming in anyway."

Ford said, "I've got to get that pie out of my ear," and stepped out of his shorts, and received a chorus of hoots before diving, gliding underwater, eyes wide, trying to pick out the outline of Dewey's legs. Found them—or were they Walda's?

122

Unsure, he surfaced, to find Dewey splashing away from him. He grabbed her ankle and pulled her to him . . . felt the brief softness of her breasts against his arm before she kicked away, saying, "No touching, buster!" Like she was kidding, but not really kidding. Suddenly tense.

Feeling like a rebuked schoolboy, Ford made no second attempt to get close to her. The three of them swam around. Talked about nonsense. Looked at the sky. Kept their distance. Then Dewey showed him to his room—a small room with hurricane shutters closed and a brass bed. As dark as a box with the door closed.

Ford slept.

It was like the dreams he had had in those early months . . . those nights after first losing her. . . .

He could put her out of his mind during the day, even in the first months. He was that disciplined. But at night, the dreams came. Never welcome, but he had no control and he despised himself for that weakness. Hated the depth of emotion that dominated him; hated the sappy juvenility of the love that he had never sought—indeed, had always thought was a song-writer's fiction. Or the invention of bad soap operas. Until he met her.

It was painful. It was privately embarrassing. Worse, it interfered with his work.

Yet the dreams came bubbling up from the unconscious like welts, with an acid clarity—her face, her eyes, her touch—so that, by morning, he was withered with the pain of missing her, but all the more determined that it would never happen to him again.

Pilar . . .

Not with Pilar. Not with any woman. Ever, ever.

Gradually, the dreams had dissipated. Then were gone as completely as Pilar herself was gone.

Until now . . .

Deep in sleep, Ford knew what was happening even before it happened; could feel her standing over his bed in the darkness, and he knew the dream had returned. Could sense her arms reaching out to fold the sheet back even before he felt the coolness on his stomach and legs. Could feel her long fingers on his chest as she slid into the bed beside him, covering his mouth with hers, her tongue flicking, touching, her hands moving, finding him and sliding smoothly up and down the length of him. The warm weight of her breasts on his body, her nipples hard enough to etch designs on his cheeks, his chest, then his abdomen as she moved downward, her lips and tongue tracing a path as her mouth found him.

Pilar . . .

Ford lay asleep, knowing he was asleep and dreaming, but aware of the good weight of her, aware of what she was doing . . . feeling, in this playful gift of hers, the unity of them together; the utter, utter peace of being with her, like coming home.

I just want to hold you. That's all, just hold you and never let go again. . . .

Speaking to her, finding her head with his hand and touching her soft hair, combing it with his fingers, not wanting to awaken, because to awaken was to lose her again; fighting to remain asleep, yet feeling himself drift upward into consciousness.

Don't leave . . . please don't leave. . . .

Then he was awake, startled by the realization that the woman in bed with him was real.

"Hey—hey . . . who are you? Dewey?"

There was a small whoop, a woman's cry of surprise, and Ford was sitting upright in the darkness. Seeing nothing but darkness in this closed room, aware of the chill breeze of air conditioning on his face, aware of a rushing movement. And calling out, straining to see. "Dewey? Is that you?"

The door to his room cracked open; a brief wedge of charcoal light into which moved a long female shape, head down, hurrying, then the door closed again.

Ford swung his arm around, trying to find the reading lamp beside the bed. Knocked into something, and there was a crash. Got out of bed, hands pressed out ahead of him, feeling for the wall. Touched the wall, following it to the door, then to the light switch. Bright overhead light that showed the reading lamp unbroken on the floor along with his glasses.

Ford found his fishing shorts folded on the chair, put them on, and stepped out into the hall.

The hall was illuminated by the light from his room; the entire house was dark. Down the hall were three doors, two closed tight and one open—the bathroom. He looked into the bathroom and switched on the light. Nothing. Went to the end of the hall and pressed his ear against one closed door, then the other. No sound. He went down the hall into the main house, switching on lights, hoping to find Dewey or Walda—whoever the hell had been in his bed—sitting there in the darkness, waiting for him. Even slid open the glass door and looked into the pool area.

But no one was up, just him, standing barefoot on the carpet, hearing the ticking of the kitchen clock. It was 4:15 A.M.

Ford retraced his steps, switching off lights. Stopped at the two closed doors once more. Tried one, then the other. Both locked.

Returned to his room; got into bed. But couldn't sleep, shaken by the illusion of being once again with Pilar, and then the surprise of the reality. He lay there trying to reconstruct what he had thought to be a dream, trying to latch upon some detail that would tell him who had come to his bed. There was no tactful way he could ask either Dewey or Walda, for to ask was to risk revealing the strange behavior of one to the other. And for all he knew, his visitor had been sleepwalking—answering the needs of her own private dream.

Ford sat in his room until the first pearl-gray lines of dawn filtered through the window's shutters, then dressed. He left a note on the kitchen counter by the coffee maker. The note ended, "Please keep your doors chained, just in case it wasn't a dog last night."

Then walked to Blind Pass and started his boat.

7

WHEN the telephone rang at 8:45 A.M., Ford thought it was Dewey calling to ask him why the hell he hadn't stayed to run. Hoped it would be Dewey, because then, by gauging the tone of her voice, he could tell if she was the one who had slipped into his dreams . . . and his bed.

Ford answered the phone, saying, "Sanibel Biological," but it was Terry from Cabbage Key who replied, asking, "So those two amazons got you home safe. I was wondering."

Ford said, "What a night, huh? I'm sorry; I truly am. You think the bankers are going to press charges?"

"Naw, I just talked to them. They're out there laughing about it over eggs and bacon. Talking like they're in love with those two ladies of yours, and I think they really are. That's some impressive pair. The bankers said they'd kick in half for damages, but no more."

Ford said, "That sounds fair. You give us the whole bill last night?"

"You're not going to pay it, are you?"

"I'll chip in with the ladies. I was the one who brought them."

"Then I'll send down the final one. And a request that they

126

not return. Not for a week or two, anyway. But if that's going to keep you away from Monday-night baseball, we'll let it slide. The bankers will be gone by Thursday. Fact, I don't think they'd mind the chance to make it up to the ladies. So forget the suspension; bad idea."

Ford said no, it was okay, they probably wouldn't be back for a while, before Terry said, "Oh, and I got the name of that guy you were wondering about. The one with Karl Sutter last night."

There was a pencil on a string beside the phone, and Ford wiped fish slime on his shorts before taking the pencil in his fingers. "Yeah?"

"One of the waitresses recognized him. A heavyweight. A guy named Bob Griffin, a state senator. An old Florida family. He's been in before, which is why he looked familiar, but I couldn't remember."

"Senator Robert Griffin, I've heard of him. But what in the hell was he doing with Sutter?"

"Having dinner. Skipped out right after the fight, probably worried about bad publicity. Best I can tell, they came in separate boats, but I don't watch the docks at night unless it's real busy."

"So he hadn't chartered Sutter."

"Not if they came in separate boats, I wouldn't think. But who knows. I'm just telling you who the guy was. Which doesn't make sense if Sutter is the screwup the other guides say he is."

Ford said, "I'm starting to wonder myself."

Terry said, "Christ, what a night. It belongs in the unofficial bar hall of fame."

"And I was a part of it."

"Your head okay?"

Ford touched his left ear, which was swollen. "My head's just fine."

Terry said, "Next time, don't bring women unless they're baseball fans."

When he finished on the phone, Ford selected another album—*Brother Moon,* Latin choral chants, which he loved. He

127

placed it on the turntable and turned the volume up loud enough to hear in the next room, then went across to his lab to finish the necropsies he was doing. The Latin chants moved through the rooms, ancient and stately, lending the mood of medieval stone churches to the wooden piling house, taking the edge off the fresh morning heat of a Florida summer.

On the dissecting table were the mullet and the trout he had taken from the sandbar on Friday, the day the guides found Rios's body. Two of several dead fish he had seen floating that day, which is why he had suspected red tide. But now he knew that red tide had not killed them. He wanted to find out what had.

Ford opened his notebook, wrote in the date, and picked up the mullet in his left hand. It was a common striped mullet, family *Mugilidae,* one of more than a hundred mullet species worldwide. A strange-looking fish, shaped like an old-time soap box derby car, but with bugged eyes and bright silver scales, which now, in death, were gray. Mullet were a staple fish of commercial netters (the roe was prized by Taiwanese buyers) but were valuable only as a bait to sportfishermen because they fed on microscopic animals and detritus, so getting one to take a hook was no easy thing. Ford turned the fish in his hand, studying it, and wrote, "No obvious external injuries. Slight extrusion of the eyes, possibly from bloating. Gills clean, slightly gray, with few parasites. Fins good. Scales intact."

Then he placed the mullet on the dissecting table and, using a micro scissors, opened the fish from anus to lateral fins, then clipped on hemostats to hold the belly open. Using a Mall probe and seeker, he began to survey the viscera. The inside of a mullet always seemed slightly muddy; black mud because of the decomposed mangrove leaves they often fed upon. The intestines, the gizzard, the grit-filled stomach, the liver all looked good—though he couldn't be sure unless he sent the organs off to a better lab where they had a histologist on staff. But no obvious bacterial infections; no obvious tumors . . . but something was wrong. What the hell was it?

Ford stood over the fish, looking. He pulled the gooseneck

lamp lower, wanting more light. He stood for several seconds looking dumbly at the fish before he finally realized—and it was so damn obvious! Where the hell was the swim bladder? The mullet had no air bladder layered in among the viscera. All fish had swim bladders; had to, to survive. But this one didn't—at least not that Ford could see.

He took the fine probe and began to move the stomach and intestines away, and there saw the pearly white lip of the missing bladder. It appeared to have been expelled outward, toward the mouth. Ford turned the fish and opened its mouth with the probe and his thumb—and there was the bladder, filling the whole throat cavity. As if the fish had stuck its nose into a vacuum sweeper and had this organ sucked out.

Ford took the sea trout in his hand and pried open its mouth. Same thing. Through the two sharp catch teeth, beyond the golden mouth, the air bladder clogged the entire throat.

This was a strange one. Very strange.

He washed his hands in the sink, then began to wash his dissecting instruments, drying them carefully before returning them to their case. Cleaning up mechanically, his mind scanning for an explanation.

If the fish had been in deep water and had been brought to the surface too quickly, it was possible that the air bladders might expand into their mouths because of the rapid expansion of air as atmospheric pressure decreased. That was a common phenomenon in deep-water fishing: reel up fish from the depths with their eyes bulging and their swim bladders bursting. But the water in the area where Ford had found the fish did not exceed thirty-three feet—and it would take at least that much water to cause a change in atmospheric pressure. Ford stood and checked the chart on the wall just to make sure. The Mud Hole, at its deepest, was twenty-three feet. So maybe someone caught the fish offshore and didn't dump them until they got in. Which seemed reasonable—except that mullet weren't caught on a hook; certainly not on the kind of hooks used by deep-water fishermen.

That left only one alternate explanation.

Ford finished cleaning the dissecting table, then placed each fish in double Ziploc bags, noting on the outside of the bags the date of dissection and the place where they had been collected. He put them in his fish freezer, then found his address book and thumbed through it while he flipped the *Brother Moon* album. With the music turned low, he called two marine biologists he knew, one with the Florida Department of Natural Resources, the other with Mote Marine Lab in Sarasota. Both confirmed his suspicion by voicing their own: Maybe the fish had been killed in an explosion.

Someone had been out in Pine Island Sound dynamiting fish.

Which suggested to Ford how Karl Sutter had won the tarpon tournament. And maybe how Marvin Rios had really died.

Ford told both biologists he wasn't sure he needed it, but he might, and would they would be willing to necropsy the fish and send him their findings?

They said sure, they'd be happy to.

Jeth Nicholes stood in his cell in Glades Detention, a new beige brick building with electronic doors and a big parking lot fenced with razor wire, built so far out in the palmetto scrub that decent people didn't have to pass it on the way to work. So far out nothing but rattlesnakes and feral hogs had roamed here before the bulldozers came in and scraped the acreage clean. But now a small industrial park was growing up just to the west, using the new blacktop road—Nicholes could see the roofs of the corrugated metal buildings poking up among the rank slash pine. Could see their beige shells through the heat if he pressed his face against the bars that protected the tiny Plexiglas window, maybe half a mile down the blacktop where the ditch was littered with pop cans and Big Mac containers.

Man, I could go for about three Big Macs right now. Extra sauce, hold those pickles.

Nicholes, wearing a bright-orange prison jumpsuit, sat heavily on his bunk, thinking unchristian thoughts about his fellow inmates. Across the corridor, a couple of skinny redneck guys sat in their cells, smoking filtered cigarettes, talking through the bars. Evil smiles with those bad teeth, sitting there with tattoos on their arms. Guys who'd probably never known a horny moment until the day their sisters bought running shoes. Nasty-looking fuckers here, but crazed flesh stompers on the outside once they got a bellyful of whiskey. Tooling around in their rusty pickups, sniffing out trouble—Jeth could just picture them.

One of the rednecks noticed Nicholes looking and called over, "You gat you ah probum, boy?"

Jeth stiffened, not about to take any shit from these prison sheep humpers. He stood. "How'd you like to go home and tell your mama some *boy* just kicked your butt so hard you could eat firewood through your asshole?"

"Okay, okay. Lighten up, man."

Jeth returned to his bunk.

Down the corridor, all the colored guys were hooting about something, talking all at once so it was kind of like one high moan, going, *Muhfuckah* this and *muhfuckah* that, like they only knew about ten words and had to space out the noise with something just to prove they were alive. Jumping around, reaching for spears but finding only their dicks to grab. Not like the black guys he'd played ball with. Those were decent guys. Hell, some of them had even gone on to college on scholarship. Doing good out there in the world. Or like Captain Javier. No better guy in the world than Javier. Took care of those pretty little kids of his, two girls and an older boy, always standing on their tiptoes and grinning when they saw their daddy coming. And the way Javier worked his ass off and didn't bitch even when Marvin Rios started demanding half his charter money or he'd turn him in to the feds as an illegal alien. Deport the whole family. Which is probably what had driven Javier to finally killing the dwarf bastard—if Javier had killed him—and good riddance.

But these guys, Christ.

Brain-dead spades and wormy rednecks. Be another two, maybe three thousand years before this spawn could rightly be

131

called human. Probably never eaten a fish in their lives that didn't have whiskers—but right at home here where food was served on plastic trays and eaten with spoons.

Correctional institution.

That was a laugh. Like it was a place to cure these egg suckers. A place for them to get a rest, more like it. Got more attention here than at a Holiday Inn, plus there was a basketball court and everything was free. A little pause in the rapes, murders, and dope snorting for this bunch. The Sin Pen, that's what the place ought to be called.

Sitting on his bunk, Jeth Nicholes imagined a neon sign outside Glades Detention: SIN PEN in soft green and flamingo pink. That was a good one. He'd tell that to Mack or Doc, maybe write it to them in a letter.

Sheep humpers!

And what pissed him off the most was, these guys were all probably healthy as horses and didn't have to lift a finger to be that way. Dancing all around death while getting more and more life forced down their throats.

Like he'd told that woman attorney just an hour ago, after the judge looked down from the bench and told him he'd appoint a public defender: "Miz Harper, my folks are both dead. I got three sisters, all busy with their husbands and kids, so they don't count on me for nothing. I got no wife, no children, so I might just as well go to the electric chair without a fight. Instead of trying to save me, why'n't you do us all a favor and get some of these other yahoos zapped while we're at it?"

That had seemed the best thing to say, and the best thing to do. Hell, Javier had kids depending on him. Javier had something to lose. He didn't.

Like Tomlinson had told him, "All the way to heaven was heaven." Whatever the hell that meant.

But it meant something, and that was exactly the sort of thing he needed to start figuring out. He needed to start understanding a few things. Needed to start coming to terms. After twenty-eight years of being dumb, it was time to get smart. Being cheerful and dumb had left him in a hell of a spot, 'cause

132

now he had to hurry; figure out the whys and the wherefores and be damn quick about it.

Maybe get back to Jesus. Maybe that was the answer.

Nicholes imagined himself at one of the outdoor revivals, like the ones his daddy and mama used to take him to. Sitting on folding chairs out there in the hot night beneath the tent; the whole thing set up at some supermarket parking lot or in a palmetto field so there was plenty of convenient parking for all the sinners and their kids.

No fun being a kid at those things. The way the preacher pranced around yelling and swinging his arms, sweating through his black suit, talking about the Devil waiting for them right outside. Then breaking down in tears—a grown man—crying about how bad they all were, and how they were going to burn in hell, letting his eyes go wild, singing out in the divine tongues.

"OHH-H-H-aalee-OHH-H-H-delah . . . rebah-rebah . . . JESUS!"

Man, he'd hated that divine-tongue business; all the adults going loony like that. Scary as hell for a little kid. But even worse when he got in his teens. Like those times his mama asked the preacher to heal his stutter.

"Want you to meet our only son, Preacher. He ain't smart, but he's got the goodest heart of any boy you ever seen. . . ."

Standing him up in front of all those sweating white faces and black faces, girls his own age looking on and embarrassed for him, while the preacher cupped his meaty fingers around his throat and prayed and prayed and prayed.

"Heal this sinner of his affliction, Jesus . . . cast out the evil demon that lives in the throat of this good boy. . . ."

Well, he had been a good boy. Sitting in his cell, face pressed into his hands, Jeth Nicholes could give himself credit for at least that. Only thing he'd ever intentionally hurt in his life was a gopher turtle. Found it out there on the shell road on the way to Chokoloskee and tossed it into a big puddle of oil at the asphalt dump just to see what would happen. Could still see that turtle blinking at him through the black smear, already dying and no way to help the poor thing. Thinking about it still made his throat catch, the idea of him doing something so cruel. Made him want to cry, really.

But before that and certainly after that, he'd tried his best to be kind to everybody and every thing. Had hardly even told a lie.

Well, that wasn't exactly true. He'd told some lies, but not many—and Christ, that wasn't the truth, either.

Fact was, he'd told plenty of lies, because what he did was tell people what they wanted to hear. His whole life he'd done that. A guy wanted to hear his boat looked nice, he'd tell him it was beautiful. A guy wanted to think he was a good fisherman, he'd say, Man, you're a regular fish hawk. Didn't matter if it was true or not, because the only thing Jeth wanted in his life was for people to like him. Wanted to get along. Felt people had reason enough not to like him, him being so slow and with that demon in his throat, so he just naturally bent over backward to please them.

Oh, he'd told plenty of lies, all right.

'Specially to women.

Thinking of that made Nicholes moan into his own hands.

God, had he told some lies to women. They'd come down from New York or Ohio or Chicago on vacation, lonely and frazzled from too much work, washed out from living in places that had no sun, nervous as hell and still acting like lawyers or doctors or important society women, even though they were sick of it and just wanted to let go for a while. So he'd talk to them. Talk to them real soft and shy, telling them the little lies they wanted to hear.

"Those sick people are damn lucky to have a woman smart as you taking care of them. . . ."

"You're just too pretty to be worrying about things like that. . . ."

Stuttering, of course, when he spoke, and he could see in their eyes that the stutter touched them; softened them right up, so the next thing he knew, they'd be out on some empty beach with the woman stripping off her bathing suit and running buck naked in the sun. Some looked like fashion models and some

134

looked like librarians, but they all looked good because they were laughing and they liked him.

Didn't seem like he'd been doing any harm. Lord knows, they all seemed happy enough about it. But, if there was nothing wrong with it, how did he happen to end up being engaged to two women at once that time? That was a damn sin in anybody's book.

Hell, who was he trying to kid? Once he'd been engaged to *five* women, two of them married. And four of them were still sending him Christmas cards. And he'd never had any intention of marrying any of them; just told them what they wanted to hear.

Jeth Nicholes shook his head miserably.

A liar and an adulterer were just about exactly what he was. A sure-enough sinner, just like the preacher had said, with a ball of evil in him the size of an Ocala grapefruit. Well, God had finally nailed him, and with good reason. He'd been out there adultering like a mad dog on borrowed time, and now the invoice was overdue.

From down the corridor came the echo of leather shoes on the hard floor. Nicholes listened as the footsteps came closer, expecting to see the guard pass by, but the guard stopped, standing there in his baggy blue uniform, looking down on him.

"Hey, Jeth, there's a guy downstairs wants to see you."

Nicholes said, "I don't want to see nobody right now. Just don't feel like it."

The guard said, "Sharon told him you didn't put no names on your visitors' list, but the guy says he's a friend of yours. Guy named"—the guard looked at the slip of yellow paper in his hands—"guy named Marion Ford."

"Oh. Hum. . . . Nope, tell him I'm busy. No, wait a minute—that'd be lying. Tell him I don't feel too good. That'd be the truth."

Beyond the bars, the guard shifted his weight, leather belt creaking. "Look, Jeth, I know you're new here, but you don't mind a little advice, stop being so hard on yourself. This place ain't so bad. It ain't no disgrace. Ev'body makes a mistake—"

135

"It's not that," Nicholes said quickly. "You guys do a hell of a job here. Keep it damn nice, you ask me. I've been treated real good. You people are real professional."

The guard blushed slightly at the praise. "Well, we try to make it smooth as we can. Keep a clean shop, though you wouldn't know it from the way these other guys bitch all the time. I tell them, 'You try to keep six hundred lawbreakers happy, see how long you last.'" The guard put his hands on the bars and leaned toward him. "But personally, I hate like hell to see a guy like you come in. Shit, man, you're a famous fishing guide, in here with all these . . . criminals. Just don't seem right."

Nicholes stopped him, saying, "Now don't go blaming yourself. I'm getting just what I deserve. I've been sitting here thinking about that."

"Aw, I think you're being too hard on yourself. Might do you good to talk to the people coming to see you."

Nicholes was thinking about Doc, the way he seemed to know things without even asking questions. Once Doc had said to him, "So the doctor said you weren't getting headaches because of your eyes, huh?" Figuring the whole thing out just by the way his pupils looked—those drops the doctor had put in his eyes. And he hadn't told Doc a thing about the headaches or going to see the doctor. Doc had just taken one look at him and said it. Figured the whole thing out by the way his eyes looked and because he wasn't carrying new glasses around. It was eerie. Nope, no way he could let Doc in here. Doc might take one look at him and see the truth.

Jeth said, "That lawyer woman said something about I could make two phone calls a week?"

The guard nodded. "Tonight and Thursday night for this block. I'll sign you up right now, you want."

"If you don't mind, tell the guy, Doc, I'll call him tonight. That okay?"

"You got it." The guard turned to go, then hesitated. He said, "You probably get sick of talking about fishin', huh?"

"No way, not me."

"You know, I'm kinda a snook fisherman myself. Not in

136

your league, a'course, but I get out there on the weekends and bang the bushes. Give 'er hell. I got a couple Shimano Speed-masters and an old President that's a beaut."

Jeth was nodding. "Some of the best snook men I know are weekenders. They do stuff us guides can't. Always trying new spots, picking their tides just right. You'd laugh your head off if I told you some of the tides we gotta fish."

"No kiddin'! You really think so?"

"I know so."

"Say, if you've got time later, you think me and a couple of the other guards could stop up and sort of pick your brain? A lot of us, that's all we do is fish."

If he had time—that was a good one.

Nicholes said, "Hell yes, I'd like that a lot."

The guard turned his head back and forth, looking down the corridor before asking, "Can we bring you something? Anything you need?" Talking low so those rednecks across the way couldn't hear.

"Well, I have been sort of sitting here thinking about a Big Mac. Lots of sauce, no pickles."

"You got 'em, Cap'n. All you want."

"As long as it won't get you in no trouble."

"Hell, a case of beer and a dancing girl would be trouble. Not that I couldn't work it out. But some burgers, hell. You just wait."

When the guard's footsteps had disappeared, Nicholes returned to the window, looking out, trying to see Doc's old blue pickup truck, but it wasn't in the side lot. Musta parked it out front at the entrance. Thinking about Doc being so close gave him a kind of homesick feeling for Dinkin's Bay. Made him feel sad, so he tried to think of something to make himself feel better.

In his mind, he assembled the faces and bodies of some of his favorite women, but that didn't work. Hell, he'd never see a woman again, except for his lawyer—who wasn't too bad with that shiny black hair and those big knockers beneath the business suit. But she was cold, cold, cold. Besides, the only way a lawyer would screw a confessed murderer was on the bill.

137

His mind cast around for something better to think about, and he thought about his trip south to Cape Sable.

There, that was something nice.

Great big sun ball. Yellow . . . red . . . orange . . . oily purple, then—poof!—*green*.

Seeing that green flash, sitting out there on the gray water all alone, was like the sign he had been yearning for: a sign that there was reason and a purpose to living in this world; a private wink from God, telling him everything was going to be okay. And just like that, his stutter was gone; the demon taken away. That sunset had done what the preachers couldn't. After all those years of being afraid; afraid to talk to strangers, avoiding those damn *D* words and *T* words, hating the way his whole body clamped up when that demon threw his head back and caused his tongue and jaw to spasm.

His own personal sign from God . . .

Thinking about it, Jeth felt the same warm swell of emotion, a rushing sensation of peace and safety that had left him sitting on his boat, bawling like a baby.

He'd had a lifetime of being bad. Now it was time to hurry up and do some good. . . .

Ford pulled away from Glades Detention, onto the open blacktop, thinking: *I have overlooked something, or I lack information. Which?*

Jeth had refused to see him. Why the hell would he act like that? Something was missing from the equation; maybe many things. But something that specifically concerned Jeth.

Ford shifted through the gears, his old truck gathering speed through the heat, the gearshift knob kiln-fired beneath his hand, the cab oven-hot but cooling slightly with the windows open.

What I ought to do is buy a new truck. No, I like this one. I buy a new truck, I won't own it, it'll own me. Maybe just have the garage add air conditioning. . . .

He drove through palmetto flats, then turned west into the commercial outskirts of municipal Southwest Florida, a burgeoning hedgework of asphalt and concrete that extended fifty miles in each direction, Tampa to Naples, pressed right up against the Gulf of Mexico. Real estate brokers, title-insurance offices, 7-Elevens, notaries, law firms, U-Haul rentals, and all the other service components of a society on the move. Here were the nuts and bolts of mobility; the infrastructure to which the rootless seekers and dreamers tethered their hopes of living happily in the sun. Many made it. They did good work, took pride in their lives, raised pretty kids. They earned and enjoyed their little chunk of success. But here, also, were the repo car lots, the boarded businesses, the pawnshops and bail bondsmen; the symptoms of dreams that had gone sour, and the agents who gathered up those broken hopes and resold them at a profit. It was the urban spore of a state on the make; a here-today, gone-tomorrow economic combat that left Ford anxious to get back to his house on the water.

But first he had to make a few more stops.

Jeth had had his first-appearance court hearing that morning. Ford had called the county clerk's office and found that out. Law-enforcement people, presumably Detective Roy Fuller, had submitted enough evidence on the booking sheet to have the court decree there was probable cause for charging Jeth with first-degree murder, no bail set. The judge had also appointed a public defender to work on Jeth's case, an Elizabeth Harper. Ford wanted to talk with Harper, and also try to get a copy of the medical examiner's autopsy report on Marvin Rios. Tell the pathologist about the fish kill, and see if it shed new light on Rios's death. Then maybe check at the newspaper library, find out a little more about Senator Robert Griffin. It didn't make sense, him having dinner with an oddball like Sutter. Rios had to be the connecting thread.

Ford drove along, mulling it over, troubled by something but unable to put his finger on what. Hugging the slow lane, thinking. Cars ahead of him, cars behind him, jockeying for position in the traffic and the heat, brake lights pounding out the thudding pulse of harried commuters.

A beer would be good right now, if I didn't have to pee so bad. Jesus, why am I even bothering with this? He's got an attorney now. The legal system is tilted to favor the guilty, so someone who is innocent—presuming Jeth is innocent—should skate right through. No need for me to go poking around.

So what was it that was troubling him?

As he drove, Ford began to organize the few facts he had assembled, putting them in neat columns, or as if on the trays of a lab scale. But then he stopped himself. He realized he was making a fundamental mistake. That's what was troubling him. The fundamental mistake was that he was theorizing in advance of the data. If one fell into that trap, then it was only natural to force all incoming data to fit the theory rather than assembling a theory from the facts. And he did not yet have sufficient information. Nor, he was sure, did Detective Roy Fuller, or the judge who had decreed probable cause, or Jeth's attorney, for that matter.

Which was why Jeth's position was so precarious.

Facts, Ford knew, could be stretched, torn, and reconstituted to support any proposition. That's why he followed his own strict lab procedures so veraciously. It was also why he had little faith in the legal system.

The legal system, Ford knew, was an abacus of shrewdness, not a scale of justice. Indeed, true justice was an anomaly. It was not that legislators, attorneys, and judges weren't good and decent human beings—though some certainly were not. The problem was that they and their legal forebears had gradually perverted the legal system for the protection of their own profession. Jurisprudence was no longer a moral process. It was a competition in which the competitors—attorneys—created their own rules.

It was the lone oversight in the carefully constructed system of checks and balances created by the nation's founding fathers. The oversight was this: Most legislators were also attorneys. The founding fathers had not foreseen it and probably had no reason to worry about it at the time. As a result, new laws favored the competition of law, not the society that the legislators were mandated to serve. Which was why social ethics and legal ethics—once nearly synonymous—were now strange antonyms,

140

orbiting in concentric circles. Professional behavior that would be considered outrageous by any society on earth was now perfectly acceptable behavior in the outlander orbit of legal ethics. Which was why attorneys could use videos to coach criminals how to lie more effectively to juries. Which was why accident liability had become a predatory device. Which was why judges, if the letter of the law allowed, could, in perfectly good conscience, release murderers, rapists, child molesters, and thugs back into the social maelstrom. The legal ethic was always served, but that ethic—like justice—was a façade, a careful illusion propped up by those who had helped to destroy justice at its roots.

Successfully negotiating the legal system, Ford knew, required that an individual be shrewd. Or wealthy. Or both. And Jeth Nicholes was poorly equipped on all counts.

Driving into the center of town, slowing for traffic lights, Ford considered the two options. He could give them the information, then stay the hell out of it. Or he could get involved.

He thought, *I'll see how it goes. . . .*

The county seat had once been a nice little town. Still was a nice little town, in fact: old offices built of brick and coquina rock on the bank of the Caloosahatchee River; small restaurants, bookstores, and barbershops. The explosive growth of the last two decades had wedged the town in tight against the wide tidal river and threatened to absorb it into the anonymous urban sprawl. But the old power structure had done a good job of protecting the town core. It still retained its old Florida feel, with its park and narrow streets; the fortress anachronism while modern Florida crackled along beyond its walls.

Ford parked near the shade of the big banyan tree outside the courthouse, then headed straight for the men's room. Then he took the elevator to the sixth floor and found the public defender's office. He told the secretary he wanted to speak with Elizabeth Harper, then sat leafing through a *Harvard Law Review* until a door opened and a woman's voice said, "You wanted to see me?"

Ford looked up to meet the eyes of a compact woman in a business suit and heels who was staring at him through black horn-rimmed glasses, a manila folder under her arm. Maybe thirty years old, judging from the backs of her hands, the skin starting to gather a bit. A pale, handsome face and weak chin that looked better for the light makeup she wore. Straight black hair cut conservatively to match the no-nonsense elegance of the dark tropic-weight jacket and pleated skirt; a full-bodied woman on a tiny frame, and with a severe expression, her owlish brown eyes like those of a strict high school teacher.

Ford stood. "I'm a friend of Jeth Nicholes, Marion Ford. Do you have a minute to talk?"

"It concerns his case?"

"Yes."

The woman checked her wristwatch mechanically. "I have to be downstairs in fifteen minutes, so if you can make it fast."

Ford followed the woman into her office, a neon cubicle with a cluttered desk and diplomas on the wall: Brown University, Stetson, Florida bar. Two photographs in a cabinet frame on the desk: an older man and woman, arm in arm beneath a maple tree; parents, probably, so she had grown up in the East or Midwest. Another photograph of a college-age Elizabeth Harper in khaki clothes beside a mountain stream, grinning into the lens. A woman-to-lover grin, but no wedding ring on her hand now. An electric bill among the papers on her desk, so she probably lived alone.

She sat across the desk from him, arms folded, leaning back in the swivel chair. "How long have you known Mr. Nicholes, Mr. Ford?"

"A couple of years. I live right beside the marina where he's a fishing guide. I see him nearly every day."

"And you have something you want to tell me that concerns the case."

"Something to tell you, Ms. Harper, and a few things to ask, too."

The woman sat up straight. "Don't bother asking anything about Mr. Nicholes, because I'm not going to answer. Attorney-client privilege. If that's why you're here, then I think you're wasting time I don't have."

"Then I'll tell you what I know, and you judge for yourself."

"I'm waiting."

Ford said, "Marvin Rios's body was found in Pine Island Sound. The night he died, on that same body of water, someone was out using explosives to kill fish. The tarpon tournament Rios's marina was sponsoring took place the next day. Grand prize, eighty thousand dollars."

The woman looked at him blankly. "So what are you telling me?"

"I'm telling you that someone used explosives to kill tarpon so they could win the tournament."

"And Mr. Nicholes was in the tournament?"

"No."

"Then how does that affect Mr. Nicholes, or me, or anything else?"

"Don't you see—"

"Mr. Ford, I have no interest in fishing, none. In the two years I've lived here, I've never been on a boat. So I'm afraid you're going to have to be a little more lucid"—checking her wristwatch again—and concise. *Please*." Impatient, or maybe trying to cover her unfamiliarity with the topic.

Ford said, "All right. Late Thursday night or early Friday morning—the approximate time Rios was killed—a person or persons took a boat or boats into Pine Island Sound and detonated explosives. There was a thunderstorm that night, so the noise was covered."

"So far, so good. Now, is Pine Island Sound a large body of water, or small?"

"Do you have a phone book? There's a map in the phone book."

"Well . . . yes—right here."

Ford leaned across her desk as she opened the book in front of him, sensing her uneasiness at his closeness; smelling the light perfume she wore and the stale coffee in the Styrofoam cup at her arm as he leafed through the pages. "Right here is the approximate area where Rios was found on Friday." He tapped his finger on the page. "Sanibel here, Captiva here, Pine Island Sound here. I waited with the body. Less than two miles away, that same morning, I collected specimens from a small fish kill. I'm convinced the fish were killed in an explosion."

"And how would you have known that?"

"I run a biological supply business, my own little lab. My findings were tentatively confirmed by two other biologists, and they're willing to review the necropsies if I want."

The woman closed the phone book and leaned back, putting some distance between them. "So I'll ask one more time: What are you telling me?"

"I'm telling you that Rios either caught the person or persons using the explosives and was killed by them, or he participated so he could profit from his own tournament and maybe was killed in an explosion. The man who won the tournament is a guy named Karl Sutter, who was Rios's former brother-in-law. Sutter works out of Rios's marina. I know from personal experience that Sutter is tricky and mean." Leaning on the desk hurt his back, bending like that, so he straightened himself. "I'm telling you that Sutter should be the prime suspect, not Jeth. Or that Rios died accidentally."

The woman said, "That's very interesting," now making notes on a yellow pad; a nice looping script.

"Did you talk to Jeth this morning, Ms. Harper?"

Still writing as she talked, she said, "I did, but I'm not going to tell you anything about it."

"I want to help."

"I realize that, Mr. Ford. And I appreciate you taking the time to come in." Putting the pen down, finished with the notes and him, and already rising to show him out.

"Ms. Harper, a moment ago you admitted that you knew nothing about fishing and very little about the area. I know a lot about both."

"I'm sure you do—"

"How many cases are you working on right now?"

"I don't see what that has to do with—"

"It comes down to how much time you have to invest. I know how overworked people in public law are—how many cases?"

That stopped her. She considered him for a moment, touching her fingers together. "Fourteen cases—no, fifteen, with Nicholes," dropping the shields just a little. "They put it on my desk this morning."

"Do you have an assistant?"

"No. But we have two investigators."

"Who handle all your cases, plus the cases of your fellow public defenders."

"I see what you're driving at, Mr. Ford. But I am not about to authorize a layman to—"

"And I'm not about to pass myself off as something I'm not, Ms. Harper. I have no secret fantasy of being a private eye. I have absolutely no desire to get involved with the legal system. I don't want to strut around and ask strangers for just the facts, please, just the facts. I'm very happy doing the work I've chosen to do. But you don't know the water, and you don't know the people who live around the water. I do. I can be your eyes and ears out there. Maybe I'll come up with something that will help."

The woman moved some papers on her desk, thinking, before she looked at the office door, as if to make sure it was closed, then looked at Ford. "What do you want to know? I'm not saying I'll tell you, but go ahead and ask."

Ford said, "I heard that someone claims to be an eyewitness. Who was it, and what do they say they saw?"

The woman nodded but made no move to reply.

"Well?"

She said, "Keep asking. I want to hear the questions."

"Okay. The police took traces of hair samples and what appeared to be blood from Nicholes's boat. And that was only a few hours *after* Nicholes washed down his boat. I was there—I saw him wash it. I'm assuming the police lab already did the DNA tests on the hair—I doubt if they had enough blood to do a precipitin test. But was the hair taken from Nicholes's boat consistent with the samples taken from Rios's body?"

Her eyes focused slightly in reappraisal. "Have you done police work before?"

"No, but I'm familiar with lab procedures."

"I see. Go on."

"And the last question is, what did Jeth tell you this morning? I was just out at Glades Detention and he refused to see me."

"I thought you said you were a friend."

"I am. That's why I want to know what he told you."

Harper was standing, checking her watch once more, and beginning to press Ford toward the door. "I'll tell you this, Mr. Ford. I asked him to sign a written invocation of rights this morning, and he refused to do it. Which means the DA or the police or anybody else can go to Mr. Nicholes's cell any time they want and ask him anything they want—which is very distressing for the person trying to defend the man. In other words, he seems to have very little interest in protecting himself. He told me he didn't want to make anybody mad by not talking to them."

"That sounds like Jeth."

"Yes. I don't let myself get emotionally involved with clients, but I must admit there is something . . . very childlike about Mr. Nicholes. A nice quality. Why he wouldn't talk with you, I don't know."

"I don't believe he's capable of murder, Ms. Harper."

"Which will be up to me to prove. Now, I would like to ask you a question. Can you think of any reason why Mr. Nicholes would be . . .abnormally concerned with the amount of time that passed between someone being sentenced to die in the electric chair and actually having the sentence carried out?" A serious question, carefully couched.

"Christ, he asked you that? Like he was guilty?"

"I'm asking you the question."

"And what about the questions I asked you?"

"Do you have a business card, Mr. Ford?"

"What? No. I mean, I don't use them."

Elizabeth Harper was holding the door open. "Then leave your number and address with the secretary. Think about my question. I'll get back with you."

Ford stopped at the medical examiner's office, and found a jolly pathologist and a jollier investigator laughing over coffee outside the double doors of the autopsy suite. Big new building with lab tile on the floors and a Cauzatron air filtering system that whispered refrigerated air into the place, removing most traces of human odor. Ford introduced himself, and told the men why he was there. As he expected, they told him they could say nothing about Rios unless it was cleared through the district attorney's office. Ford explained what he had discovered while dissecting the fish, hoping it would spark at least a minor reaction. It did not. The men were smart and articulate, and they weren't about to be steered anywhere.

Ford tried another approach. "Then let's consider a hypothetical situation. A man is in a boat, and he's killed in an explosion. What would you expect to find?"

The investigator looked at the pathologist, shrugged, and then they were both smiling again. "Oh, so you want to be hypothetical, huh? Sure, we can do that!" Which was good for another laugh.

Ford waited, smiling himself. These men were happy in their work; happier than most, perhaps because their daily dealings with death produced in them a more essential awareness of fragile, transient life.

The pathologist said, "Death by explosion is pretty obvious. A lot of major trauma to the side of the body facing the blast. In the case of a boat, probably a lot of wood or fiberglass fragments would pepper one side of the victim. Some thermal injuries, too, depending on the kind of explosion."

"It couldn't be confused with the damage done by a severe beating?"

The pathologist hooted. "See there, Keith, he's second-guessing us!"

The investigator said, "Sorry, Mr. Ford, but I don't think so."

"What kind of injuries would be consistent with a person who had been beaten to death?"

"Are we still being hypothetical?"

"Of course."

The investigator said, "Okay. In that case, it depends on what was used to beat the victim, and how he was beaten. If the victim was beaten and choked, you might find severe trauma to the strap muscles. The horns of the hyoid bones might be broken, too." He turned to the pathologist. "Right?"

"Right. If a blunt instrument was used, you might not see obvious evidence on the soft surface tissue, but you could find severe trauma beneath. Contused heart, bruised organs, an occluded airway. That sort of thing."

"Is that what you found in Marvin Rios?"

"Now, now, now, Mr. Ford, we can't talk about that. But I think even the newspaper reported that we had found evidence of a severe beating with a blunt instrument. Isn't that right, Keith?"

"Gee, I don't know. I only read the sports page."

Ford hadn't read the papers at all. He rarely did.

Through the rectangular windows, Ford could see a sheet-covered corpse atop a gurney. He thanked the two, saying he didn't want to keep them from their work.

"We have the most patient clientele in the world. Stop by anytime, Mr. Ford!"

Ford made one more stop, the local newspaper. Got a pass into what was once called the morgue, but what had now joined the casualty list of euphemism and New Age sensitivity—the clipping library.

Emily, the librarian, showed him how to use the microfilm machine and the rotating file system, and Ford spent the next hour piecing together information on Griffin, Senator Robert M.

Griffin was the middle child of a Central Florida land baron and dairy farmer, Denham Griffin, who had once been active in state politics. The Griffins were an old-money Florida family. Over the years, the newspaper had done several Sunday features on Griffin Pioneer Days, a family reunion that drew hundreds of family members back to the original Griffin homestead—a fat pine cabin preserved in the shadows of the family mansion. Robert M. Griffin had given his opening speech as a candidate at Pioneer Days when he first ran for the state legislature at age twenty-four. And it was to the Griffin Plantation that reporters came to question Griffin when his development company declared bankruptcy three years later. From what Ford read, that bankruptcy seemed to be the lone stumble in an otherwise solid career of real estate development and part-time state politics. In Griffin's fourth successful bid for the state Senate, his listed net worth was in excess of $2 million.

Now the man was forty-eight years old, divorced, with no children, and there was public speculation that Griffin would finally make the big switch and run for the U.S. Senate. Each story was accompanied with what, by now to Ford, was the familiar file photo: big beaming grin on a rugged down-home face that could garner a sizable percentage of votes on looks alone. The same man he had seen talking privately with Sutter at Cabbage Key.

Ford kept flipping through folders, making mental notes, and then he finally found the slim connection he was looking for. It wasn't much. A little more than a year ago, one of Griffin's companies (for he had several now) had sold off twelve hundred acres of pristine frontage on the Mayakkatee River and the eastern shore of Charlotte Harbor to a development group calling itself Mayakkatee River Development, Inc., in which Marvin Rios was listed as the major shareholder. According to the story, tax stamps reflected a sale price of nearly twice the going rate for raw acreage. A spokesman for Rios's group said they had expectations of building a planned community on the land, but refused to offer specifics.

Environmental groups protested the sale, and filed recommendations that the state purchase the land as a part of its Conservation and Recreation Lands Acquisition Program, acronym CARL. Griffin told the press that he agreed the land should be saved, but, as a businessman, he couldn't afford to pass up what was clearly a very profitable offer.

"I truly wish I could set aside that land as a sort of park for the people of this great state," Griffin was quoted as saying. "But I've got bills to meet, just like everybody else, and business is business. However, I'll do what I can on the legislative end to come to a compromise between the consortium that now owns the land and Florida's dire environmental needs."

Carefully enough worded to have been a press release, and it sounded reasonable. Griffin's company had made the sale, and it was now out of his hands. So why was he having dinner with Sutter? Even if Sutter was representing Rios's interests, why were those two together?

Ford considered cross-referencing to the Mayakkatee River file, but he'd already been in the library for an hour, and he had his own work to do.

He had found the connection; two connections, really. It was not easy for a private citizen to purchase explosives these days. They had to apply for state licensing, then file for permits. The entire process was carefully monitored. Ford knew about explosives. They had taught him all about explosives during his training at Coronado. Which is why he knew that mining companies and construction companies were the two best private-sector sources.

Mayakkatee River Development.

So what would he do with it? Sit on it for a while; let Detective Roy Fuller know, and let them finish making the connections.

Or he could turn it over to Tomlinson. Tomlinson liked doing research.

Yeah, that's what he would do. Ask Tomlinson to help.

Dewey and Walda were sitting in the main room of Ford's stilt house when Jeth called. Sitting on the floor laying out cards for some new board game Walda said she'd bought at Kennedy

150

Airport, a thing called Ravel. There was a thick stack of cards containing riddles and problems of logic in different categories. A player could ask five yes-or-no questions. For each yes, the player moved his piece one space. Move completely around the board or solve the riddle, and the player was given an icon that fit into a cube. Win four icons, win the game.

Ford was at the propane stove frying fish in a skillet, listening to the women. They had arrived about an hour ago, gone for a swim in the bay, and done some pull-ups on one of the beams that connected the main room with the lab.

Now they sat on the floor, relaxed and having fun, their hair still wet from the swim. It gave this room a nice homey feel, with music on the stereo, laughter, and the moon up outside. Produced in him the realization, like a minor shock, how alone he had been living here on the water and how . . . lonely?

Not lonely, just alone . . .

"Hey, Doc, are you gonna cook or are you gonna play?"

"Can't I do both? You roll the dice and move for me."

"But you must concentrate. This game is very hard." Walda's voice. "Have you heard some of these questions?"

He had heard some of the questions. He said, "Then I'll play after we eat."

"See, Bets? He's trying to chicken out."

"Hah!"

He had tried to decipher, from eye contact and body language, which of them had come to his bed. Dewey or Walda?

Nothing.

He had watched them climb out of the water after their swim, trying to match one of the bodies with the body that had pressed against his.

Too much alike. Both long and lean and fit.

It was a private riddle more complicated than the ones he heard being read from the cards.

Walda was reading one of the cards now. " 'An anthropologist went to the Arctic on an expedition. There he found a man and woman frozen and perfectly preserved in a block of ice.

151

Upon seeing them, he turned immediately to his assistant and said, "We have found Adam and Eve!" How did he know?' "

Ford flipped the fish—small snapper fillets—then took English muffins from the toaster, glopped on butter, and sprinkled them with garlic salt. Then he began to cut fresh limes into wedges, enjoying the fragrance. Through the window, he could see the dock lights of the marina and beyond, Tomlinson's sailboat on its mooring buoy on the other side of the channel. All the portholes were dark; Tomlinson's tender gone. Probably out with Harry, his old girlfriend.

Dewey was asking questions. "Was Eve holding an apple?"

"No."

"Was the guy missing a rib? Adam?"

"No."

"Am I warm? . . . That's not an official question. You can't count that one, damn it."

The phone rang, so Ford slid the skillet off the burner and answered.

"Hey, Doc. You mad at me?"

It was Jeth.

"Hold on a minute." He pulled the cord along behind him and shut the door, standing outside on the porch. He said, "How you doing, Jeth?"

"Well, are you?"

"Mad, you mean? No. But why wouldn't you see me?"

"It's just that I wasn't feeling too good, plus a lot of the guards were standing around, talking about fishing. I didn't want to interrupt. They brought me Big Macs for supper. Nice guys. They snuck them in."

"I talked with Elizabeth Harper today, Jeth. Did you tell her you killed Rios?"

"Is that what she said?"

"No. But that was the impression I got. Why'd you tell her that?"

"Doc, I just don't want to talk about it—"

"Jeth, you're in a hell of a lot of trouble, so you'd better talk to somebody. If not me, maybe another lawyer. I've got some

152

money. We can hire a good lawyer for you. MacKinley said he'd chip in, Felix and Tomlinson, too."

"It don't make no difference. I'm not telling you why, but it don't. Believe me, Doc, it just don't! It's not like I got three little kids and a wife to take care of. I'm doing what I think's best."

Ford thought immediately of Javier Castillo, the only guide he knew who was married and had three children.

Into the phone, he said, "You've got about three weeks to think this thing out, Jeth. By that time, a grand jury is going to be involved, and they're going to have to hand you over for arraignment. You'll have to enter a plea. I just don't want you to do the wrong thing, that's all."

"That's exactly what I'm not going to do, Doc—the wrong thing. All my life I've been doing the wrong things, and this is my chance to do right. Just trust me, okay?"

"If you just tell me one thing."

"What's that?"

"When you took off the first week of June, where'd you go?"

"Now see! That's exactly what I'm talking about! Why I didn't want to see you today—"

Ford said, "It wasn't to visit your sick grandmother, was it? Were you getting therapy for your stutter?"

"No!"

"Then what did you do?"

There was a silence, and Nicholes said, "I've got to go, Doc; they got a time limit here. I don't want to get into trouble."

"You're already accused of murder."

"Yeah, but I don't want to upset the guards here. They're nice guys."

"Will you call me again in a couple of days?"

"Well . . . sure, Doc. Just so long as you're not mad at me."

Ford carried the receiver inside and replaced it on its cradle. Beside the phone, on the table, was the information he had received from Sally Field, who worked for the Operations Data Board of National Security Affairs in Washington, D.C. The

153

information had been FedExed and arrived late that afternoon: three computer-fresh pages that capsulized the public lives of Marvin Rios and Karl Sutter.

Ford, who had worked for NSA for more than ten years, had seen thousands of such data sheets, and his eyes touched automatically upon the pertinent data. For Rios, it was tax audits: two, both of which had included stiff fines, and a third review pending. For Karl Sutter, it was the final line on the heavy printer paper, a non-sentence that said he had died five years earlier of natural causes at the age of seventy-one, in Denver, Colorado. End of file.

Ford returned to the stove and placed the skillet on the fire while, behind him, Dewey still worked on the Adam and Eve riddle.

"Was there a snake at their feet?"

"No! You get one more question, then you take a card and ask me a question."

Dewey called to him, "Hey, Doc, have you been following this? How'd the anthropologist know he'd found Adam and Eve? Give me a good question to ask."

Ford thought, *No umbilical cords, no belly buttons,* but he said, "Let's eat first. Then maybe go for a boat ride."

Dewey was standing, disgusted. "That's fine with me. I told you, Bets, I hate games like this."

8

KARL Sutter was standing in the living room of his girl-friend's shithole Sanibel apartment, thinking, *I got to play this one just right. Make just the right moves, play it smooth. Real smooth and clean, and I end up rich enough to shit on all the assholes in the world. But if I give this bitch time to tell someone about the tarpon gag, I'm screwed. . . .*

Standing there waiting for Greta to pack her bags, just like he'd told her on the phone, saying, "You know what I think we ought to do, baby? I think we ought to enjoy some of that prize money and surprise all your friends. Just sneak off for a few days to Key West, or Disney World, maybe, and come back married."

"Karl! Baby!" Christ, could she shriek. Made him want to put his fingers in his ears. "Do you mean it, darling? Do you really mean it?" Starting to blubber right there on the phone, the big old cow. "Wait till I tell Suzie, that little bitch'll take back all the bad stuff she said about me dating a guy your age. But she should be there, Karl. Suzie and me have been through so much, sweetie. We're practically like sisters."

Her best friend, Suzie, was a big old cow, too.

"Are you sure you didn't tell Suzie about the tarpon deal?" Asking Greta for about the hundredth time.

155

"I swear to Christ I didn't. Didn't I already tell you? She was gone all weekend, then we didn't get a minute to talk yesterday, and I would'nta said anything anyway, babe."

"Good. Don't tell Suzie this, neither. That'd ruin the surprise."

"But she'll know I went someplace. We work in the same office, and—"

"Then tell her you're driving to Miami to see about . . . something. A new job. Something you can work from here, but have to go to their office in Miami to apply. A lot more money, tell Suzie that. But don't mention me, or she'll put two and two together. Ruin the whole thing. We'll just run off and do it, come back and say, 'Look at us, Mr. and Mrs. Karl Sutter.' "

"Baby, you're so romantic. Just what you say, I'll do it. I promise. I'll be such a good wife to you—" Beginning to bawl again. He could picture the chubby fat-girl face of hers shiny with tears and snot. "And with all that money, and with Marvin dying and leaving you with a good business to run, we should do real fine. Let's make it Disney World, darling. Find a preacher or a notary republic, then honeymoon at the Magic Kingdom."

So now he was in her apartment, waiting for her to pack. Musta been ninety-five in the shade outside, just hotter than hell, and stuck waiting in this nasty little apartment of hers where the window air conditioner didn't work worth a shit, burping and banging so loud he could hardly hear her yammering away in the next room while she folded clothes into a suitcase—not that he minded not hearing her.

Looking around the apartment, he thought, *God, what a pigsty*.

Peanut cans for ashtrays, stuffed full. A Motley Crüe poster taped over the stereo. Jesus, a twenty-three-year-old heavy-metal fan. A little ceramic plaque on the wall—GOD BLESS THIS MESS—and another of a sea gull flying toward the sun. Her mom had probably given her those. Dirty clothes thrown everywhere, dishes in the sink and something yellow that had dripped down the tiny stove and hardened. Egg, probably. The place stank, too, like she had a hamster for a pet.

After this, it's only beautiful women for me. Clean women with nice hair.

Sutter thought about the two women that asshole Ford had been with at Cabbage Key. He knew the one; knew where she lived, at least, because old dead Marvin had had a thing for her. Dewey Nye, some kind of rich tennis star. Marvin wanted to shit all over her, probably because she'd told him what a dwarf he was, though Marvin hadn't said. Just said he wanted her place checked out, see if she was doing anything weird they could maybe report to the cops. Then Marvin had had him make a few phone calls, give some anonymous crap to some reporters about her being a lesbo and stuff like that. Really trying to hurt the bitch. Then Marvin had called him off, said to stay strictly away.

Well, Marvin was out of the picture now. . . .

Sutter was thinking about watching the tennis star and that other woman from the bushes while they wiggled out of their clothes and dove into the pool. Gave his penis a little zap, like electricity, thinking of that. Man oh man, what bodies. Those tits with big pointed nipples because they were cold, and so skinny he could see their stomach muscles.

He could hardly stay away from something like that. Plus, it would be just the right way to get back at that asshole Ford. Show him he couldn't mess with money. Not the kind of money he was going to have, anyway.

Greta came out lugging two Samsonite suitcases, a big green one and a small overnight case. The floor was carpet over a cement slab, and the suitcases had some weight when she dropped them on the floor. "A trip like this"—she beamed—"you have to pack the same way you would for a month. Like you would for Paris or someplace like that." Sliding into his arms, the observation really a request, so he knew what she was going to ask before she asked it. "Karl, you think we could go to Paris sometime? That's something I've always wanted to do. I took French in high school, you know. Two years. And it's not like we can't afford it."

Already spending his money.

"Sure, baby. Paris, England, you name it. I know them

157

both pretty good. Maybe in the fall when things here get straightened out."

"And we can buy a house, too. A nice house. With a pool! Sweetie, I just love laying out by a pool. Wouldn't that be fun, you coming home from work and finding me out by the pool?" Pressing her wide hips into his, letting him know what she meant. Now she'd already quit her job on his money.

Sutter held her away; could hardly bear to look at her, that dumpy white body beneath the jeans and pink Led Zeppelin T-shirt, her tits squashed down like mounds of lard. That big wide mouth of hers on a big white face with little blue eyes peering out beneath the blond bangs, looking up at him. "Wouldn't you like that? Great big Karl coming home every day to sweet little me?"

"Hell yes, I'd like that fine."

"And you know what I'd do for you every day you got home? Guess, baby." Grinning at him while her hand moved down to massage his crotch. "Any day you wanted it, anytime."

Sutter automatically slid his hand up under her T-shirt, but then pulled it away, thinking, *I can't waste any time here. What if someone stopped by and found us?*

"Hey, we've got plenty of time for that. Let's get going."

"You sure, darling? I just feel like I want to give you something nice, let you know I'm all yours." Trying to snuggle against him as he turned her roughly toward the door and gave her a little push. "Oh-h-h-h, you're so mean to me, I'm going to be after you the whole drive to Orlando." Pouting but wicked; a wicked little-girl look on her face.

In the parking lot, Sutter put Greta's luggage in the backseat of Marvin's white Lincoln, but stopped her when she tried to get in. "You've got to take your car, baby. Don't you see why?"

"Hey, where's your luggage?" She was looking in the Lincoln's back window.

"In the trunk. Did you hear me?"

"You mean I'm supposed to follow you all the way to Orlando? And what about your birth certificate? Did you remember for the wedding?"

Sutter had his arm around her, steering her toward her new Mazda, the one she'd just gotten with a bank loan. "You follow me to the airport. We park your car there, then get right on the interstate. You leave your car here, Suzie might stop by and catch on."

"But she's not going to stop. I already told her—"

"Do you want this to be a surprise or not?"

"Okay." Pouting again as she unlocked her car door. "But you just wait till I get in your car. Am I going to make you suffer! And you brought your birth certificate—"

"In my luggage in the back."

"And you got cigarettes?"

"Yes!" And he shut the door, looking down on her through the window.

Sutter slid into the Lincoln, taking a quick look around. No one outside the apartment complex this hot Wednesday morning. A UPS truck over there, but no one watching him. He reached his hand under the seat until his fingers touched the checkered handgrip of the nickel-plated 9 mm Taurus auto hidden there. Big silver pistol with the laser night sight clamped beneath the barrel. Turn on the laser, touch and shoot—so simple. Wicked-looking bastard, which is why he'd bought it from that backseat pawnbroker. Like a space gun.

Well, no one had stolen the damn thing while he was inside the apartment. These days, you couldn't leave a car alone for a minute without worrying.

Sutter put the Lincoln in gear and motioned to Greta in the mirror, telling her to follow.

Early Wednesday morning, Ford telephoned Detective Roy Fuller, but Fuller wasn't in, so Ford left his number and a message: "Check SS records; Karl Sutter died five years ago in Colorado." Then he got in his flats boat and idled across the bay to talk with Tomlinson.

Tomlinson's forty-two-foot Morgan had once been bright white with blue trim, but the hull had gone gray above the green bottom paint; a fiberglass voyager that had pounded a lot of sea and had bleached in the harbor sunlight of islands around the world. Now it sat on its mooring line, high and still, like a workhorse dozing in the pasture; a quiet gray pyramid on the flat blue bay.

Quiet until Ford shut down his engine and drifted to the boat's stern, catching the line that held the tender. Which is when he heard Tomlinson's voice saying, "OU-OU-OU, that's just about exactly where I want it!"

Ford thought: *This is bad timing.*

He heard Tomlinson again: "My head's starting to focus now! The cosmos is beginning to gel!"

Then a woman's voice: "Is it good, Sighurdhr? Is that the spot?"

Then Tomlinson: "OU-OU, baby, it's . . . it's two outs . . . blazing sliders . . . it's fucking infield in, baby!" Half yelling, half moaning.

Ford looked at the sky, twisted around and stared at the marina, didn't want to look at the boat at all.

SEA-gurd . . . so that's how Tomlinson's first name was pronounced.

But couldn't they hear his boat coming? Probably not. Not with the music turned up loud, The Doors singing "This Is the End," a Heart of Darkness kind of tune, as if the earth had caught fire and was drifting off its orbit.

"What about here, Sighurdhr? Is that good, too?"

"I'm rounding third!"

"And here?"

"Missed . . . the fucking . . . cutoff!"

"Now, now, *mi amor*, that's all for the moment."

"What!"

"Seventh-inning stretch, my pet. I think your friend has come to visit. I heard a boat outside."

Ford wished he could just disappear, or maybe somehow pull his skiff up and hide beside the hull. But too late. There came Tomlinson, scraggly-haired and shiny with sweat, digging a fist into his eye, hitching his baggy shorts as he stepped out into the sunlight. "Hey, Doc! Good to see you, man—"

160

"I just remembered something at the house. I'll stop back later—"

"No, man. You got to meet Harry first." Meaning the woman who had changed her name from Musashi Rinmon to Moontree to Harry. Tomlinson was smiling at him, not the least bit embarrassed. "She's great. You know what she was just doing? You got to try it."

Ford thought, *Sometimes he's just a little too weird.*

"Maybe not right now."

Then a woman ducked out of the main cabin behind him; stood there holding on to a halyard, smiling down. Nice-looking Asiatic woman, Japanese judging from her face, with long black Navaho hair, good skin without makeup, wearing a blue denim shirt. A medium-size woman who had been around, who looked as if she took joy in things; probably liked camping, used organic soap, and read *Mother Earth* magazine.

She said, "Tie up your boat, please. I've heard so much about you. I'll make tea." She went back down the companionway steps into the salon.

Ford stepped out of his boat, with Tomlinson grinning at him. "I mean it, you've got to get Harry to do it to you—"

"Tomlinson—"

"It's called shiatsu, man. An Oriental thing where she uses pressure points on your body to release all the poisons—"

"What? Oh-h-h-h."

Tomlinson was moving his head around experimentally, testing his neck muscles. "Only she combines it with a thing called Rolfing, so it hurts like crazy, the way she digs into the old muscle fiber. I mean, like you want to scream. But leaves you feeling like you've just been born."

Ford said, "Fascinating, Tomlinson. I've read something about it—" Talking stiffly because he felt so relieved.

The three of them sat around the dinette table over tea, the music turned low, making introductory conversation. The cabin smelled of diesel, kerosene lamps, sailcloth, and sandalwood incense—or maybe that was the perfume Harry was wearing, the

161

sandalwood smell. Finally, Ford said, "Look, the reason I stopped by is because I want to ask a favor."

"Sure, Doc—name it."

"But I'm reluctant because it's going to interrupt your vacation." Finding it strange to call a woman "Harry," he pointed the question right at her.

She said, "If I choose not to help, I'll say so. What's the favor?"

Ford described seeing Sutter with Senator Griffin; tried to illustrate the strangeness of that by talking about Sutter, explaining the whole thing for Harry, who did not know the man and who did not live in Florida.

"A tourist area attracts some pretty strange characters," he said. "Maybe it's the same with a college town. Both are ideal cruising grounds for transient types, people with the rogue mentality. Because no one knows them, they can create the illusion of being anything they choose to be. Their lies go unchallenged. Understand? In a land populated with strangers, the illusion of fact is more important than the facts themselves. So they're accepted without question." Ford looked at the two to see if they were following along. They were—probably even a little ahead of him.

Harry said, "I'm aware of that personality type. And this is in reference to this man Sutter, correct?"

Ford said, "I think so. Tomlinson, do you remember how Sutter lied about how his father was killed? In the air force, he said."

"I believed him." Tomlinson looked at Harry and said, "This guy comes off very sincere, but he has seriously bad karma. Like a negative force."

The woman patted Tomlinson's hand, still concentrating on Ford.

Ford said, "I think the reason he seems so sincere is that he actually believes the lies he tells people. Which is one of the characteristics of a pathological liar, correct?"

He was asking them both, but Harry answered. "One of the indicators, but it's also commonly noted in other forms of dys-

162

functional behavior. From psychoparesis to the psychopathic. It can run the broad spectrum. It doesn't necessarily mean that the man is dangerous, Doc." Giving Ford the clear impression that, back in her Moontree days, Tomlinson was the only one who specialized in substance abuse. All her little neuron passages were still fast tracks.

Ford said, "You're right, of course. I'd be willing to bet that if you checked the credentials of every person who lives in this area—successful people, too—you would find a small percentage of people who have found ways to profit from an invented past. Faked college diplomas, criminal records left unmentioned. That sort of thing. They probably live peacefully and do good work.

"But Sutter *does* strike me as being dangerous . . . Harry. For one thing, I have proof he's living here under an assumed name. He's violent by nature—Tomlinson can tell you that. And he's a cheat. We had a big tarpon tournament here recently, and there are indicators that he killed fish with explosives so he could win the prize money."

"Did he? Win, I mean?" Harry was asking.

"Yep. But here's the thing: I also believe he's manipulated evidence to suggest that Jeth murdered Marvin Rios. I'm not sure of that. No one will talk to me about the evidence. But it's the only explanation that makes sense."

Tomlinson said, "So you think Sutter killed Rios? He's setting up Jeth to protect himself. That conehead!"

"No, I don't think so. I don't think Sutter did kill him. Rios had more than two thousand dollars on him when he was found. Sutter likes money. He would have taken all of it. No, make that most of it. Sutter's shrewd. And he would have tried to weight down the body, or hide it. Even if he hadn't planned to kill Rios—which you have to assume, because Rios was beaten to death, not shot or stabbed. Even if he hadn't planned it, he would have tried to hide the body. Pathological liars—and psychopaths—are very methodical. They don't panic. Covering their tracks is a way of life. Isn't that right?"

The woman smiled wryly. "In many cases, yes."

"So if Sutter didn't kill Rios, who did?"

Ford said, "I have a couple of ideas, but I can't be certain until I find out if there is a serious connection between Sutter and Griffin. There probably isn't. Why would a senator deal with someone who is clearly bad news? But, if there is a connection, it suggests all kinds of possibilities. So what I'm asking is, would you two be willing to do some research? I'm going to tell the police what I know, but it'd be nice to give it to them in a whole package. If we can outline all the possibilities, they might just cut Jeth loose. The way it stands now, the police're trying to prove him guilty. They have their man, so that's the only case they're trying to build."

Harry said, "And Florida has the death penalty, doesn't it? They could electrocute your friend; an innocent man."

Tomlinson was nodding. "Which is the stupidest thing in the world. Killing people doesn't deter criminals. It just adds to the tragedy. Barbaric, is what it is. Like the old saying, 'Fighting for peace is like fucking for virginity.' Same thing."

Ford said nothing because he didn't agree.

Tomlinson looked at Harry. "I'm up for it. Put the ol' brain in research mode and maybe right some wrongs." To Ford, he said, "Same thing we were talking about earlier: the disruptive influence. That's what we're tracking down, isn't it?"

"That's it exactly. We need to find the disruptive hinge."

Tomlinson was using his hands to talk, a clear sign he was enthusiastic. "Harry and I used to work together a lot. Back in the sixties, we put out national research papers. You ever hear an SDS speech? They used our stuff all the time. We were *good*. But we'll need to borrow your pickup truck. We'll need to do some driving around."

"You've got it."

Harry looked at Ford, the look of joy on her face replaced by a studied concern. "But to get started," she said, "we'll need more information."

Ford had Xeroxed several of the newspaper stories about Robert Griffin. He took them from his pocket, unfolded them, and began: "Are you familiar with the Mayakkatee River?"

★ ★ ★

164

Ford had returned to the marina, and now he was talking to MacKinley. It was 11 A.M., so the guides were all out, but there was still plenty of activity: people renting boats, getting bait, buying hats and souvenirs, tapping on the glass counter so Mack had to get up from his chair and work the cash register or list what fish was fresh today.

"The snapper is very nice. The grouper is good. No, the oysters come from Apalachicola, but we got them in yesterday."

Every time he rang the cash register, Mack would smile—a private joke. "They're playing my song," he would tell Ford, meaning that he loved the American dollar.

Now MacKinley was sitting in his chair behind the counter, listening to Ford.

"So what I'm saying is, if I could just have a look around Jeth's apartment. Maybe check out his truck; just take a quick look."

"I have the key to his apartment, but not his truck. I've been feeding his cat."

In reply to the expression on MacKinley's face, Ford said, "I know—I don't like the idea of going in without his permission, either. But it might help him."

"The police were already up there. I don't see the point."

"The police were looking for something to prove he killed Rios. Not to prove he didn't. That's what I'll be looking for."

MacKinley shrugged. "It's fine with me, cobber. I trust you. But I have no authority"—he was standing, looking at keys hanging on a hook on the wall—"to give you permission, so you'll be doing it without my consent." He handed Ford a key ring. "The brass one goes to the downstairs door; the silver one to the porch. Use the porch steps."

"I'll do it."

As Ford was going out, MacKinley said, "While you're up there, I'll straighten a coat hanger so you can pick the lock on his truck."

"But you're not involved."

"I have my personal ethics to consider."

Ford stopped and turned. "One more thing, Mack. Does Jeth have insurance through the marina?"

"What? You mean like for his boat and stuff? Or health insurance—that sort of thing?"

"Both."

"Nope. All the guides are on their own. It's an independent kind of contractor deal. They keep their own books, pay their own insurance, handle their own taxes, everything."

"That's what I thought. I'll be back in about twenty minutes."

Jeth's apartment was over the marina office, a one-bedroom efficiency with a broad view of the docks below and of Dinkin's Bay. A few small boats out there drifting, fishing for trout. There was a desk with a reading lamp, and books piled in the corner: *McClane's New Standard Fishing Encyclopedia; Chapman's Piloting,* the *Ashley Book of Knots,* and other standards on the sport.

Ford began to go through drawers; found Jeth's personal calendar with the first week of June blocked out, but no explanation. Found Jeth's personal phone book, and jotted down the telephone numbers of Jeth's three sisters.

Maybe they would know something. If need be, he could try to call them later.

As he went through Nicholes's private papers, the big black cat, Crunch & Des, sauntered past, brushing Ford's leg once, then jumped up on the desk to watch.

Ford liked dogs, and he liked cats—if they weren't the neurotic variety that demanded constant attention. Crunch & Des was not. As Ford went through the papers, he sometimes paused to scratch him behind the ears—a gesture that Crunch & Des accepted with apparent indifference.

Electric bills, bills for tackle, a payment book for Jeth's outboard motor, a payment book for the shiny Ford Bronco sitting out there in the parking lot, an unpaid Visa bill from May—all symptoms of the New Age fatal flaw: the acceptance of a life on credit. Jeth wasn't keeping his head above financial waters, which was no surprise.

Ford put the stack of bills away carefully, then went

166

through the next drawer and the next. He found insurance policies for the boat, for the truck, and a commercial-liability policy for Jeth's passengers, but that was all.

He made one more stop, the bathroom medicine cabinet. Old Spice, Aqua Velva, shaving cream, Tylenol, wintergreen rubbing alcohol, two condom foils—well, at least Jeth was being careful that way—bandages, a container of fishhooks—yep, fishhooks—aspirin, Alka-Seltzer, a container of Everglades Seasoning, and a bottle of Antivert tablets, which was the only prescription medicine.

Unlike the Everglades Seasoning, the Antivert tablets made sense.

Ford checked the apartment once to make sure he had left everything just as he had found it, then gave Crunch & Des a scratch. "You can come and stay with me tonight—long as you don't bother my fish." He took the cat, locked the apartment's porch entrance and went downstairs, into the marina office.

MacKinley was at the register again, and he said over the heads of two gray-haired ladies who had just purchased straw hats, "You find anything?"

"There was something I didn't find."

"What's that?"

"I don't think Jeth has any health insurance."

MacKinley said, "Probably no life insurance, either. He's a fishing guide, for heaven's sake, what do you expect? So what does it mean?"

"I'm not sure." Ford waited until the ladies had left, and then he said, "Do you have the coat hanger?"

"I do. Here, I'll go out with you. I need a break from this place."

Jeth had a blue Bronco with bucket seats and a rod rack clamped to the roof. It took them a few minutes to fish the coat hanger in through the door seal and pop the lock. Once in, Ford checked under the seat, pawing through the litter of hook containers, popping-cork boxes, and crushed beer cans.

"Jeth left this vehicle of his a mess, huh? I keep waiting for him to grow up."

Ford said, "He hauls bait in here, too. Smells like dead fish."

In the glove compartment, he found a Florida map folded to the north-central section of the state, then he found another map, a Gainesville local with the University of Florida professional complex circled in ink.

Shit!

Ford studied the local map closely, thinking there should be a telephone number written on it, but there wasn't.

Ford closed the glove compartment and backed out of the Bronco. "We can lock it up now."

"I ought to get the keys from Jeth, anyway. Start it every day so the battery doesn't go bad." MacKinley pressed the door closed. "You find what you wanted to find?"

Ford said, "I found what I didn't want to find."

Ford parked his old ten-speed Trek bicycle at Two Parrot Bight Marina just after noon, a bright place with white aluminum siding covering the restaurant, the ship's store, and the big boat barn, all roofed with metal and designed by an architect to fit into the Old Florida clapboard and tin tradition. The place had been professionally landscaped, with propped-up coconut palms and hibiscus. Hawser rope and pilings marked the footpaths, so it looked as clean as public facilities at a national park, and just as sterile.

Ford checked the docks as he rounded the marina basin. All the guide boats were in for lunch, including Sutter's. He didn't want to see Sutter now; didn't trust himself to be around the man. But there was Captain Javier over there behind the marina office, sitting in the grass eating a sandwich. Captain Dalbert Weeks, too. Both of them off by themselves, probably trying to hide from the afternoon fishing clients; wanted to enjoy their hour break without interruption.

They both waved casually as Ford approached, and when Ford was close enough, Dalbert said, "Too bad about ol' Jeth, huh? You talked to him since he got arrested?"

Ford stopped, hands in pockets. Dalbert, though he advertised himself as a native guide, had spent most of his life working citrus near Orlando before coming to the islands. He was a talker; did more talking on the VHF radio than fishing, according to the other guides, and Ford didn't want to get him started now. He answered, "I talked with Jeth on the phone last night. He's doing okay."

"That's the first thing that popped into my mind when we found Rios, that argument he had with Jeth. I've never seen Jeth that mad." Dalbert hesitated for a moment. "You think Mac-Kinley will be getting in a new guide, with Jeth gone and all?" Obviously interested in the position himself, or trying to find out who the competition would be.

Ford said, "I think that would be premature. I don't think he killed Rios."

"This ol' country boy hopes you're right, but are you sayin' it because you're wishin' it or because you got some evidence?"

Dalbert was fond of calling himself an old country boy, a persona that excused stupidity while implying an innate shrewdness he did not possess. Ford was looking at Javier, hoping he'd take the hint so they could go off and talk alone. To Dalbert, he said, "I guess the police get paid for finding their own evidence."

"Mister man, that's just what I want them to do. But Jeth sure was mad that day. Boy oh boy."

Javier stood, wiping his hands on his jeans: a lean black man, average height, thin lips but a broad African nose and short black hair beneath the wide straw plantation hat he wore. "I must get baited up for the next trip. I see you out there, huh, Dalbert?" Then to Ford, he said, "Can I show you something? A *feesh* you want to know about?"

Ford walked with Javier along the docks beside the marina, and when they were far enough from Dalbert, Javier said in Spanish, "I have been wanting to talk with you. I am happy you have come."

Ford said, "It is because of Jeth, is that correct?" his mind shifting easily into formal Spanish, but listening carefully because Cuban Spanish was a rough and ragged language, filled with colloquialisms and strange accents.

169

Javier said, "He telephoned me early Monday morning, our friend Jeth."

"The morning he was arrested."

"Yes. The police had come for him, and he told me there was a thing he knew but would not say. To the police, he meant."

"Talk to the police about you? Is that what he meant, Javier?"

"I think that was his meaning. It was very early. I was getting ready to leave for my charter when Jeth made this telephone call. Our friend told me to listen, not talk. He told me that he knew who had killed Mr. Rios, but that I should say nothing. That I should act as if I knew nothing about it, and to have no fear, for he would not argue with the police. If they wanted to believe that he killed Mr. Rios, then it was the will of God."

"Jeth believes that you killed Mr. Rios."

"Our conversation, it was very strange. Yes, perhaps that is what he meant."

"Why would Jeth believe that?"

Javier was standing, looking into his open boat, an old twenty-four-foot Aquasport he had bought used and tried to fix up. He turned and sat on the gunwale, his feet still on the dock. "There is a reason," he said.

Ford waited.

Finally, Javier said, "I will tell you the reason because I trust you. But first I must explain something. And what I tell you must remain between the sea and us."

Ford nodded. The sea and us—it was an old Cuban expression, and it had been years since he had heard it.

Javier said, "I have been a fishing guide on this island since Mr. Rios opened this marina, and it has not always been an easy thing. But I did not ask for more because my life has never been an easy one. I was a young man in 1980 when Fidel told all Cubans that if we wanted to go to the United States, we need only sign a paper that gave all our possessions to the state. I happily signed this paper, as did nearly a million other Cubans,

170

for poverty and hard work were my only possessions in that terrible place."

Ford listened, standing in the heat.

"But it was not so easy for my young wife, Ellfreda, who was then pregnant with our son, Felipe. For three weeks, in Mariel Harbor, we lived in a wire cage with a thousand others, praying that we would be put on a boat to the United States. In the sun! With no food! Do you see this thing? My pregnant wife had nothing to eat but a few mangoes and a kind of soup of coconut milk made by the other women. The pain I felt for her, I cannot express."

Ford said, "Yes. Mariel Harbor was a very difficult thing." Ford knew about Mariel. He had spent twelve days there during the boat lift, doing surveillance.

"But we endured," Javier said fiercely, his nostrils widening, taking in air. "We found a boat. But, on the boat trip across the Florida Straits, the gringo captain called for our attention. There were more than a hundred refugees on that boat—a shrimp boat that should have carried no more than twenty! The captain called for our attention and said that he had learned from the radio that the American government was now arresting boat captains for carrying refugees and taking their boats. He said that he could not afford such a loss, and that he must take us back to Cuba. We spoke with this captain. We told him that we had been through too much to ever go back. Fidel would have killed us! The captain and his crew were very frightened because we were many and they were few."

"You took the boat," Ford said.

"Yes," said Javier. "To protect our families. The young must be allowed to survive—the captain would not understand this. On that terrible night, there were those among us who said we must kill the captain and his crew. We had taken them and tied them, and the crew were crying for their lives, but not the captain. He was a brave man. I liked that man! I argued that they must be spared. I argued that it was wrong to enter this new country and our new lives as murderers. Ellfreda says that she was very proud of me that night. I saved the lives of those men! I

171

became the leader that night—me, a young man among many older men."

Ford asked, "How did you get past the Coast Guard at Key West?"

Javier smiled. "We did a simple thing. We did not go to Key West. We spent two more days at sea. When planes flew near, we covered ourselves with tarps. We lowered the net booms as if we were really shrimpers. We sailed east to the Bahamas, Andros Island. The Bahamian government is a sloppy thing, and we went ashore unnoticed in a rural place. We were hungry, like animals. We foraged for turtles and conch. But we conducted ourselves as men. We released the crew unhurt, and they sailed away in their boat. Because my wife was pregnant, the villagers were kind to us. Ellfreda and I found passage to America on a fishing boat that I knew was carrying marijuana, but I did not care. That boat brought us to the Everglades coast, to Everglades City. There we met another woman, a woman who was very kind to us. She took us in, even though she had many children of her own. My son, Filipe, was born in that woman's house."

"Jeth's sister. That was the woman?" Ford knew from Jeth's address book that Jeth had a sister still living in Everglades.

"Your mind is very quick." Javier smiled slightly. "After Filipe was born, I worked as a migrant laborer for a few years. It was easy to blend in, picking fruit and vegetables around Immokalee, but I also loved to fish. I met Jeth. He was as kind as his sister. Jeth helped me get a boat, and he told me about a new marina opening on Sanibel. I could not get a captain's license, of course, because I had entered the country illegally, but Jeth said that Mr. Rios might not ask for it, and he was right—for a time, anyway. Then, about three weeks ago, Mr. Rios did ask for it, and I realized that he had suspected all along that I was an illegal immigrant. Mr. Rios said he would take half my chartering money, and if I would do small jobs for him, he would not notify the authorities."

Ford said, "I see."

"Yes, he did that to me."

172

"He—"

"Made me his property. Exactly. Or tried to." Javier Castillo checked his watch, swung his legs over into the boat, and began to straighten rods, move buckets, getting ready for his next charter. "Jeth was very angry when I told him this thing. But not so angry as I. I told Jeth that I would kill Mr. Rios before I let him hurt my family in such a way. We have come too far."

"And no one but Jeth and Rios knew. About you, I mean."

"And now you." Javier stood and looked at Ford. "I know what Sutter calls me behind my back. And Dalbert, too, sometimes. And perhaps others. They talk as if I am from the slums of New York and not a man who has worked so hard to live in this country."

"I have never heard it," Ford said.

"They would not say it to you. But most of the guides judge me for what I do, how hard I work, not by my color, and that is the way it should be. But I have little to gain from trust, and much to lose."

"You thought Jeth killed Rios to help you."

"Yes. And because Jeth was so mad. Mr. Rios was an evil man."

"Jeth thinks you killed him."

"I see that for the first time. You have made that clear."

"But you didn't?"

"Kill Mr. Rios? Perhaps I would have, but I did not have the chance. I was trying to think of a way. I even spoke with Jeth about it, but such plans do not come easily to me. Would I let my friend go to jail for something I did?"

Ford said, "I'm certain you would not." He had sat on the dock while Javier told his story, and now he stood. Across the marina basin, Captain Dalbert was getting his boat ready, but Karl Sutter's boat still sat empty, the vinyl console cover buttoned tight. Javier noticed Ford looking, and he said, "He canceled his charter this morning. His people were very angry." Javier allowed himself a smile. "They did not know how lucky they are. He is evil, that one . . . Sutter. More evil than Mr. Rios, and he catches no fish. He is the one who calls me 'nigger' and thinks I am dumb because of my English, yet he speaks no Spanish at all."

Ford said, "The dumbest fisherman catches the biggest fish." Another old Cuban expression.

Javier said, "I have caught something else, I think."

"Oh?"

"Are you certain that Jeth did not kill Mr. Rios?"

"Yes," Ford said. "I am."

"Then the thing I have caught is one of the marina rental boats. I had a shelling trip yesterday morning, and I found it hidden in the mangroves. Mr. Rios had to be in a boat that night, correct? The night he was killed. I would have reported it, but I did not want them to find further evidence against my friend Jeth."

"Can you take me to this boat?" Ford asked.

"Now? This afternoon? I have my work to do. I cannot. But I can tell you where to find this boat. When I take people on shelling trips, we walk the sandbars by the mangrove islands. When the people begin finding shells, I go into the mangroves and search for driftwood. Beautiful driftwood, and Ellfreda makes pretty things from the wood, which she sells. That is how I found the boat. If I tell you about this island, perhaps you can find it on your own."

Ford said, "I'm sure I can." He was looking across the marina basin again. Captain Dalbert was leaving on his afternoon charter, already talking away to his four clients, who sat blinking back at him. Probably giving his "I'm just an ol' country boy" introductory lecture as he backed out of his slip, beside which sat Karl Sutter's boat.

"There is one more thing, Javier."

"Then I must go. My people are waiting for me."

"You have told me things in confidence. There is something I would like to keep in confidence."

"Between us and the sea."

"Yes. I want to take a quick look at Sutter's boat. I need to board it."

Javier shrugged, untying his own lines. "Dalbert is gone. And I am already not here. Who is there to know?"

Ford was in his lab, bent over a tiny scale taken from one of the small tarpon in his fish tank. On the dissecting table before him were his microscope, two tabs of litmus paper, a prepared slide, and several larger tarpon scales. At the end of the table was a tiny piece of something that looked like yellowish brown plastic rope but was really a Class 1 explosive sold commercially as Primacord. Ford had snipped the piece from a slightly larger length he had located beneath the broken seat of the rental boat. The remainder he left where he had found it.

He had discovered the boat right where Javier had said it was: wedged into a narrow tidal cut and shielded by mangroves. Hidden right there in the mangrove bank near the Mud Hole, the back side of Ding Darling Sanctuary.

Ford tried to picture it. The night Rios was killed, Sutter had probably dragged the rental skiff across the sandbar. It meant that Rios died around midnight, since the tide had to be up. It also meant that they had been in separate boats. Probably took rental boats just in case someone saw them. Rios had died in one of the rental boats, and Sutter had found it, realized that Rios was probably dead, so he stuffed it into the first handy spot. He would have had a flashlight, and there would have been lightning to help.

Even if Sutter had wanted to, he couldn't call the police. What would he have told them—that Rios had disappeared while the two of them were out killing tarpon to cheat in a fishing tournament? That would have meant no prize money. So Sutter had pulled the boat into the mangroves and tried to sink it. Probably tried to beat holes into the hull, then attempted to swamp it, using the bailing bucket, but fiberglass boats are not easy to sink, so he had left it there, hidden in the mangroves— seats broken out, the fiberglass cracked, littered with mangrove leaves, limbs, scales, fish slime, and debris—where no one would ever find it because no one in his right mind would try to walk through those monkey-bar roots tangled into the sulfur muck.

Unless they were looking for old bottles, or driftwood.

Sutter had removed the stick-on registration numbers, and the little hand-crank outboard motor and the portable gas tanks, too—just in case someone did find the boat, they would have no reason to salvage such a wreck.

Why he had tried to nail Jeth for the murder was anybody's guess. Maybe to get the whole thing settled quickly; draw attention away from why someone like Rios would be out on Pine Island Sound in a storm the night before his own tarpon tournament. Or maybe Sutter had done it out of a natural meanness; saw a chance to hurt a better fishing guide and took it.

There were only two things Sutter had overlooked, and one of those was the length of Primacord, a piece of which Ford had snipped off and brought back to his lab, just to make sure.

From his days at the Naval Special Warfare Center in Coronado, Ford remembered: "Primacord—rate of detonation, 27,000 feet per second. Wire bound for molding and perfectly waterproof. Can be primed electrically, or by using a dual waterproof fire assembly. For underwater work, store the M60 fuse ignitor in a knotted condom until needed."

He also remembered: "It's so easy, any fool can figure it out. So never let your issue get out of your hands."

Well, two fools had used it. And for the first time, Ford knew exactly how Marvin Rios had died. And he hadn't died in an explosion. The trouble was, no grand jury would entertain the evidence, and, if it did, certainly no judge would accept it.

The other thing Sutter had overlooked was that a friend of Jeth Nicholes might get to the boat before the law did.

Ford removed the slide from the microscope, placed it with the litmus paper, then turned his attention to the tiny tarpon scale. In his big fingers, the scale was translucent, silver, as delicate as a snowflake and just as beautiful to consider.

By telephone, Ford had contacted Roy Fuller's office. Fuller wasn't in—as usual—so Ford had left a message for Fuller to meet him at the marina as soon as possible. When Fuller arrived, he would help him find the broken rental boat and present him with some of the information—but not all of it. Just enough to put Jeth in the clear and let Fuller figure the rest out from there. That attorney, too, Elizabeth Harper. She hadn't called and probably never would.

"Can you think of any reason why Mr. Nicholes would be abnormally concerned with the amount of time that passed between someone being sentenced to die in the electric chair and actually having the sentence carried out?"

Let her answer her own questions.

He remembered Fuller standing on the dock by Jeth's boat, saying, "This may come as a surprise to you, Dr. Ford, but I get along just fine working on my own."

Well, let Fuller work on his own. Then see how Karl Sutter dealt with the full weight of the law-enforcement bureaucracy when it came down on him.

And it would. Ford had made sure of that.

9

EARLY Wednesday afternoon, Karl Sutter was sitting in the big white Lincoln, the air conditioner on full blast because of the damn Florida heat, getting ready to snake his way up the logging trail to the shell road that led to the highway where there was a small sign that read:

MAYAKKATEE RIVER DEVELOPMENT

DANGER BLASTING AREA

ABSOLUTELY NO TRESPASSING

The gate was open because the dredging crew was working. Not that Sutter had seen them, no. They hadn't seen him either; he'd been careful about that. But he could hear the diesel grumble of the dragline through the trees, a couple miles down the shell construction road that forked like a wagon wheel when it got to the Mayakkatee River, then dead-ended at the bay.

A few dump trucks had gone by, but there was no way the drivers could have seen him or his car, parked way down the logging trail as he was.

Once a truck had gone by, and Greta had screamed like a madwoman, begging for the driver to come help her.

178

That was a laugh. Like the driver could hear her over the sound of that big Mack truck engine. Well, bitches were all so damn dumb.

Just like Mom. That's just the way she sounded. Just like Mom.

Sitting with his huge hands on the wheel of the Lincoln, Sutter had a brief mental flash: Greta, naked, bent over with both hands on the trunk of a tree and looking back as he stood over her, her blond hair matted with leaves and twigs and stuff because he'd made her strip, then smacked her around a little. That wasn't part of the plan, but, Christ, just looking at her made him want to.

God, the way she could whine. . . .

"This is just a joke, right, Karl baby? You don't need a gun, for God's sake. You want to play, let's play."

Finding it hard to talk with her jaw gone puffy from the beating; her whole body trembling and tears dripping down the piggy face that never tanned, acting like she didn't like it, didn't like being bent over against a tree with him behind her.

Well, they all liked it, no matter what they said. No matter how much they screamed and scratched, they liked it just fine. Christ, they begged for it, the way they dressed, the way they acted, then when you try to give it to them, they put on the big act. Especially the pretty ones, the ones with the money and the pretty hair. They'd give him that look, right down their noses, shitting all over him. Like the college girls he tried to talk to when he got out of Denver Psychiatric. Stuck there in the juvenile wing because he was only seventeen and the hotshot quacks didn't know quite what to make of him, the way he handled it after the cops came and found his mom electrocuted in the bathtub.

"Do you have some relatives we should contact, son?"

"About two or three hundred uncles. You won't have any trouble finding them."

"What?"

"Just check the VD wards. That bitch ruined more circumcisions than Hitler."

The cops hadn't dug that at all. And they didn't dig what

they found when they starting piecing his school record together, making phone calls to other towns, other states. Which was his first lesson in the value of a healthy change in identification. A thing that was very easy to do. You just watch the obituaries, pick out a name, then apply for a duplicate Social Security card. After that, getting a driver's license and the rest was easy, as long as you moved to a new state. Which is what he had done after that college bitch gave him that look, and he'd bashed her in the face and dragged her into the car and gave her just what she was asking for, though she pretended like she didn't want it.

Well, they all wanted it. Like his mom, and he'd given it to her, too.

". . . ruined more circumcisions than Hitler."

Christ, that was a good one. One of the cops had even laughed a little bit. And he was only seventeen.

"You scored very high on the intelligence tests, Colin. You can do whatever you want with your life. It's just a matter of applying yourself."

His counselor at Denver Psychiatric had told him that.

Colin . . .

Colin Kane, which was the name he was born with, but there was no telling if that was right, either, the way his mother had moved around and changed names, the bitch. Well, he'd been through a lot of names himself. He'd been Keith Raybourne in L.A., and Kenny Mikovich in Seattle and Gainesville, then he'd gone back to Colorado and become Karl Sutter, which is where he'd met Marvin's sister, Judy, in Aspen, sitting in the Hotel Jerome, drinking Rusty Nails and chain-smoking, looking to get picked up.

Karl Sutter was easy; he liked it. It was best to pick out a name that sounded a little bit like your own, which is something he discovered when he took his first new name, Abe something. Christ, it was hard to even remember now, it'd been so long. The name of some old Jew he'd taken from the *Times* when he was living on the streets of Sunset Strip. The others would have to say "Hey, Abe!" about a dozen times before he realized who they were talking to, laughing at him like he was deaf, the bastards. So he got rid of that name, first chance he had, and after that he waited until he found one that fit easy.

Karl Sutter was a good one, maybe the best one so far. But, if things didn't work out here, he could always move on and find a new one. It wasn't that he liked moving around and picking out new names. It wasn't that he wanted the pretty women with nice hair to fight him. If they wanted to shit on him, that was their problem. He just gave them back exactly what they deserved. And he'd done it too many times to remember now.

Sitting at the wheel of the Lincoln, with the air conditioner blasting, Sutter made himself go over his little mental checklist once more. Had he worn gloves the whole time? Yes, he'd worn gloves. And he'd pulled a big green Hefty trash bag over his head like a poncho before he shot her; shot her in the back of the head, right at the base of the skull. He'd worn the poncho just in case blood splattered, but it didn't, not much, anyway, so maybe she was already dead. Then he'd put Greta in another Hefty bag with the poncho and her clothes, wrapped it all tight, and rolled it into the hole he had dug. He'd covered the hole with dirt and palmetto fronds, then wrapped the shovel in another garbage bag and stowed it in the trunk. The cops could match soil samples—Sutter knew that—so he'd have to clean the shovel, and he didn't want any dirt samples in the car. He'd also have to dump her purse and her luggage someplace safe. And store the 9 mm Taurus on the boat, just in case he had to sink it quick.

You have to go through so much bullshit for something like this. Why can't people just mind their own goddamn business!

Sutter put the car in gear and pulled ahead until he reached the section of logging trail where there was no sand, just mulch and twigs. He got out of the car and used a pine branch to sweep away his tire tracks—the cops could match tread marks, too—then drove on toward where the logging trail intersected with the shell road. He waited for a moment to make sure no dump trucks were coming . . . began to edge forward . . . then stomped the brake hard and ducked down.

181

Shit!

An old blue pickup truck was coming, bouncing along, going fast. Sutter waited, then peeked one eye over the dash. The truck was already past, but he could see it plainly through the trees. An old Chevy that had been restored with nice new paint. And carrying a man and a woman.

Son of a bitch!

He recognized the truck. An old truck like that stood out. He'd seen the goddamn thing at Dinkin's Bay Marina on Sanibel. What in the hell was someone from Dinkin's Bay doing up here? Who in the hell could have made the connection so quickly?

Sutter's heart was pounding, that trapped feeling all over again, and he knew it might be time to go looking for a new state and a new name; just have to go off and leave that beautiful deal with the senator and all that money and security, screwed by life one more time.

He pulled out onto the shell road and sped toward the main highway. Sutter was thinking, *Ford* . . .

Detective Roy Fuller came strolling up the boardwalk to Ford's cottage, his huge shoulders cramped beneath the same brown blazer he had worn the day he'd come to interview Jeth. Standing at the screen door, Ford said, "So you really do go to the office and check your messages. I was beginning to wonder."

Fuller was smiling, but not friendly—an official smile, as if he didn't appreciate having to get out of his unmarked car into this heat. Ford held the door open, but Fuller stopped on the porch, hands in pockets so that Ford could see the little revolver clipped to the waistband of his pants. Fuller said, "I got the one about Karl Sutter's Social Security number, which I've checked out. Then the one about coming out here right away because it was important. Which better be good, me spending so damn much time in traffic. I'm telling you."

"Come in, get some tea."

"If it's so important, I doubt I'll have time." Still smiling, Fuller was letting Ford know just exactly who was in control.

182

"You checked out Sutter?"

"Like your message said, the Social Security number and name belong to a guy who died in Colorado. I'd ask how you happened to find that out, but Major Durell told me not to bother."

"Les Durell, I knew him before he was a cop. Back in high school. Nice guy."

"About you, he says you're an ex-fed weirdo. Or was it spook?" Fuller had moved a little, so that he was standing in the shade of the porch roof.

"Well, Les always had an opinion on things. But that cuts me to the quick."

"Actually, he said eccentric. Same difference. But the ex-fed part's right, huh?" Looking at him, not expecting Ford to answer.

Ford didn't. He said, "So do you still consider Sutter a reliable eyewitness?"

Fuller gave him about a four-count I-don't-believe-this-shit stare. "Who the hell you been talking to?"

"Like my buddy Les said, don't bother asking. Did Sutter give a deposition, or was it just a hot telephone tip?"

"We're going to have a chat with Mr. Sutter, don't you worry your head about that. But not until we get answers to the rest of our inquiries. And I hope to hell you didn't make me come clear out to the islands just to ask me that."

Ford said, "Do you have time to take a boat ride?"

"Hell no, I don't have time."

"I think I know where Rios's boat is. The boat he was in the night he was murdered."

"You think so, huh?"

"Yep."

"But you haven't seen it yourself?"

Ford said easily, "I was waiting on you. If it's a crime scene, you should see it first, right? The person who found it said it was a rental boat from Two Parrot Bight, hidden back in the mangroves. Spotted it when he was out looking for shells." None of it a lie.

183

"Who found it?"

"Someone who knows what the Parrot Bight rental boats look like."

"But there were no rental boats missing the day Rios was found. I checked with the—" Fuller hesitated for a moment, and Ford finished for him: "You checked with the acting manager, who was Karl Sutter."

Fuller said, "Shit. I talked to the guy on the phone, so, yeah, maybe it was Sutter."

"It was Sutter."

Fuller looked at his watch. "Can you go right now?"

"Don't you want a crime-scene team to join us?"

The detective's jowly face described irritation. "How about I see the boat first, then decide if I need a scene team. That okay with you?"

"Sorry. Didn't mean to be pushy. I have a date to go fishing late this afternoon. Just trying to save time."

"You know where the boat is?"

"Not exactly, but I think we can find it. We'll have to get out and wade around. Do you want to borrow some boots?"

Fuller looked at his shoes, worn maroon wingtips. "I can't go barefoot?"

"I wouldn't. Oysters will cut the hell out of your feet."

"I thought you said you hadn't seen the boat. How do you know they're oysters out there?"

Ford let the screen door close and said through the screen, "God, you're suspicious, Fuller. All mangroves have oysters on their roots. Everywhere. I probably should let you go just the way you are. Ruin your whole outfit. Then you'd have to go back to Sears and spend another forty, fifty bucks."

"Major Durell said that about you, too. Don't expect any respect."

"And you better put on a pair of my shorts. Save those pants. Polyester probably doesn't last any longer than your average Hostess Twinkie. Couple decades, and you've got to go right out and buy them again."

Fuller opened the screen door and stepped into the house,

squinting to see Ford. "Like you're some kind of damn fashion expert."

Ford considered his own dress absently, as if he hadn't even noticed what he'd put on that morning—which he hadn't. Khaki fishing shorts, a gray long-sleeved cotton shirt to keep the sun off, and white rubber boots but no socks.

"Jeez," he said. "You're right." He held out shorts and his spare pair of boots to Fuller. "We both look like hell."

Fuller said, "That's more like it."

Dewey Nye was groaning, saying, "You're killing me, for God's sake. My hamstrings are about to tear!"

"Complain, complain, complain. That's all you do!"

"Just don't push any more. I feel like a wishbone."

"A wishbone? What is a wishbone?"

"God, don't they teach you people anything in Romania? *Not so hard.*"

Dewey sat on the wooden deck of the Punta Rassa Tennis Club's steam room, legs spread wide, nose almost touching the towels beneath her, while Walda Bzantovski leaned her weight onto Dewey's shoulders, helping her stretch. They both wore nylon Speedo swimsuits, soaked by sweat and the steam cloud gathered at the tile ceiling of the little room. They had been in the room for less than five minutes—the final station in Bets's elaborate prepractice stretching routine.

"Have you ever known me to have a muscle injury?" Bets liked to preach. "No. Never one. Never one muscle pull or torn tendon. It is because I stretch for an hour before each practice. I go into a sauna or steam room, no matter where I am, and stretch. Every day of my life. But you, you always have the injuries. So now I put you on my program."

"It's ninety in the shade outside, and you've got me in a steam room." Dewey was moaning and laughing at the same time. "Crazy woman, that's what you are."

"The heat is good! The more heat, the better. Makes the muscle lubricated!"

"Damn quack."

"You will thank me. When you make the finals at Flushing Meadows, you will say it publicly. 'I owe it all to the great Walda!' "

"I keep telling you . . . I don't have enough time to get . . . ouch! . . . in shape for the Open. Hey—isn't thirty seconds up yet? Damn it, Bets, that hurts!"

"Yes. Now we do the arms. Six sets."

"Oh, Jesus. There's no way we're going to be finished in time to meet Doc."

"We'll be done in plenty of time. We finish here, then we go to the court and do bucket drills, then second serves, then crosscourts and down the line."

"Save the best for last, huh? I hate crosscourts and down the line. Geez."

"Your legs need it. Mine, too. In a few days, I'll be in London tuning up on grass."

"He's taking us fishing at six, after the rain."

"I know. We'll be done. Are you ready?"

Dewey held her arms wide, her back to Bets, feeling her friend's hands cup her triceps, pulling her arms slowly back and up, so that she stood in the room like a diver about to enter the water. Dewey could feel her serratus muscles stretching beneath her skin and the deltoids bunching at her shoulders, her whole upper body beginning to burn as Bets applied pressure.

"Does your elbow hurt?"

"My entire body hurts from this torture. How can I tell?"

"Does it?"

"No."

Dewey could feel Bets's hand squeezing harder, as if trying to squeeze out an answer. "Why do you lie to me?" Said half playfully but half seriously, too. "I don't lie to you."

"I'm not lying. My elbow doesn't hurt."

"There's no difference between lying and not telling."

"As if you tell me everything—hey, not so hard!"

"Name one thing I haven't told you."

"That's a hell of a question to ask. How would I know if you didn't tell me?"

186

"It's because I tell you nearly everything. Only two things I haven't told you."

Dewey could sense the whole mood changing, getting way, way too serious and personal, and she didn't want that; hated it when Bets wanted to talk personal. "Bullshit," she said. "You know what this is like? This is like the old days when they put people on the rack. Stretched them out and interrogated them. Is that what you did in Romania? Put the prisoners through your stretching routine and made them tell you top secrets?"

"That's one of the things I haven't told you. About Romania."

"You did a six-month public relations tour. You told me."

"There was much more."

"Oh, Christ, let's just drop it."

"We didn't stretch prisoners, we shot them. Shot some of them."

"What?"

"We shot them. The lucky ones."

Dewey felt Bets's hands relax. She dropped her arms to her sides and turned slowly, staring through the steam into Bets's sad face. "Are you serious?"

"You asked me what we did. I told you."

"The soldiers shot prisoners. That's what you mean."

Bets said, "I was a soldier."

The two women, one as tall as the other, stood looking eye to eye, their hair dripping as if they'd just come in from the rain. Bets said, "Do you want to hear it? I'll tell you if you want to hear it."

Quickly, Dewey said, "No."

"But you want to know. You've wondered, but never asked."

Dewey said, "I can feel my muscles getting tight. Let's get out there so I can beat your butt and go fishing." Smiling, trying to lighten the mood, but it was too late.

Bets said, "No, I'm going to tell you. You want to know, so I will."

Dewey said, "Damn it, Bets, we came here to practice—"
But Bets was already telling her.

Bets said, "In the city of Timisoara, where the liberation
began, members of the new democracy took me on a tour. The
bodies of two dozen rebels were laid out in the mud. Ceausecu's
secret police, the Securitate, had just left. They had tortured the
rebels as an example. Young boys, old men, women, too. Two
dozen of them, maybe more. Their faces had been burned off
with acid. Their hands had been cut off, their stomachs ripped
open then sewn back so they could live and suffer a little longer.
Ceausecu's people knew how to make people suffer. There was
a girl in the mud, about our age. The Securitate had cut the baby
out of her stomach and let her hold the fetus while she died. That
was on Christmas Eve, the day after I arrived in Romania to lend
moral support to my countrymen."

Dewey said, "My God, Bets," not even aware that now she
was sitting on the wooden bench in the steam room, holding
Bets's hand.

Walda Bzantovski said, "Romanians demanded democracy, so Ceausescu gave them bodies in a field. They asked for
freedom, and Ceausescu cut off their hands. If that was the way
the Communists were going to treat my people, I knew that I
had to do more than make speeches and sign autographs. Romania is the land of my family, but I left because it had become
a prison. When I returned and saw what I saw, I felt ashamed that
I had not stayed and endured the struggle. For what! Money? My
own selfish freedom? For tennis? That's what I learned there,
looking at those people in the mud. Tennis—it is a silly, silly
little thing. It is putting on a mask and dancing around onstage.
It is so . . . easy. And you won't understand that. So damn easy!"

Dewey was holding Bets now, patting her back, saying,
"Bets, Bets, Bets. . . ."

Bets said, "I shot three men and one woman that I know
of for certain. I stood over them and looked into their eyes as
they died. Because I was famous, even Ceausescu's officers and
informants welcomed me into their homes, and that is where I
killed them. I shot them in the chest because I'd only had three

188

days' training with a pistol. I shot them in the chest, then I stood over them and shot them in the head."

Dewey whispered, "Jesus Christ," and began to cry.

Bets squeezed Dewey close. "I'm sorry. You asked me. You are the only one I'd ever trust to tell."

Dewey was whispering into Bets's ear, "It's okay, it's okay. It was something your leaders made you do."

Gently Bets pulled away from Dewey and held her, trying to lock with Dewey's eyes, but Dewey would not look. "Dewey," Bets said, "Dewey! I *was* a leader."

With Dewey and Walda beside him, Ford skimmed his flats skiff through the tidal chop off Sanibel lighthouse, cutting so close to the beach that he could smell suntan lotion, a cloying Coppertone stink that rode with them around Lighthouse Point and along the white sand rind with its feathered border of sea oats and casuarinas.

Beside him, Walda and Dewey seemed subdued; hadn't said much since they'd met him at his stilt house. Maybe they were still hung over from Monday night. Maybe they were squabbling about tennis again. Though she had never come right out and admitted it, Dewey didn't want to play tennis anymore. Ford could see that; Walda refused to see it. So the two women bickered and fenced and tested the edges of what clearly was, to them both, an important friendship. So important that it was out of bounds to a third party, and Ford would not involve himself.

So he rode along with his face in the wind, enjoying the look of the beach, picking out children to watch as they played in the weak surf. Ford admired children and he liked to watch them when he could. The beach people he could see anytime because they were always there.

The beach people came in shifts; moved to and from the houses, hotels, and condos as methodically as a sundial. First came the solitary ones, joggers and fishermen and strollers; early-morning poets out to commune with sunrise. By 10 A.M., suntan freaks had replaced them; the Hawaiian Tropic aficionados basting away, broiling like corn belt hams until the damaged melanin of their skin cells turned black or fiery red from actinic-ray

189

poisoning. By 2 P.M., one shift of sunbathers was replaced with another; a rowdier bunch with radios and Frisbees and coolers.

Now, only an hour before sunset, Ford could see that the late shift was beginning to retreat. Men lugged lounge chairs up the beach while women in bikinis too daring to wear back home in Steubenville or Buffalo folded towels and gathered kids so they could return to their hotel rooms and shower for dinner. The sunbathers were already being replaced by shell hunters. Sanibel and Captiva islands were famous for shelling, and the low tide had drawn them out, men and women in L. L. Bean shorts and floppy hats, shelling bags in hand. A whole wandering line of people looking for whelks and crown conchs and rare junonias. There was no mistaking a sheller. Even in a crowd, they were isolated by their concentration, touching the sand expertly with their bare toes, walking a strange hunched walk as if they were myopics who had strayed from their honeymoon suite and were desperately trying to track their way back.

Over the roar of the engine, Ford said to Dewey, "Good low tide tonight, they ought to find some shells."

Dewey smiled briefly, a forced smile. "It's like they're nuts, shellers. I've gone with some. It could be three A.M., it doesn't matter, as long as the tide's out."

"What's your favorite?"

"What?"

"Your favorite shell—what kind?" Trying to make conversation; snap them out of their funk and share some of his good mood.

Ford did feel good. He had spent two hours with Detective Fuller; had made a convincing show of being unable to find the rental boat from Two Parrot Bight. Finally ran in close enough to the mangroves to allow Fuller to spot it himself, a patch of white fiberglass among the red roots. After wading in, Fuller had lingered over the wreckage, surveying all there was to see before pulling on a single rubber glove. From beneath the broken stern seat, he retrieved sunglasses, then a hat, then fished a soggy business card out of the bilge.

Fuller had held the card up, showing Ford. The card read:

190

Fuller had said, "This is a hell of a thing for a murderer to leave behind."

And Ford had replied, "Sure is," wondering if Fuller suspected that he had planted the card, hat, and sunglasses.

But on their way back to radio for a crime-scene team, Fuller had put his worries to rest, saying, "If this all checks out, your buddy Nicholes should be released by tomorrow afternoon, maybe Friday morning. I never really trusted Sutter from the first time he contacted us."

That's how easy it was to tamper with evidence.

Now, beside Ford, Dewey was saying, "Favorite shell, hum." Because he was sandwiched between the two women, she leaned across him and said to Walda, "Hey, Bets, didn't you find a junonia when you were staying at that hotel?"

Walda, who seemed more relaxed than Dewey, grinned. "One of the hotel guys took me right to it. But I heard the hotels do that, plant junonias. Do they, Doc?"

Ford shrugged.

Dewey said, "That's my favorite, the junonia. A real pretty cone." She leaned her weight against his shoulder, as if she was tired.

Ford thought, *No more Cabbage Key for these two.*

He steered the little boat straight offshore. A brief 4 P.M. thundershower had smothered the afternoon wind, and the open Gulf was slick and smooth, a pale green fairway that ended where the sky ended, far out beneath the sun. In the boat's wake, people on the beach grew smaller and smaller until only casuarina trees and the Sanibel lighthouse floated on the sea behind them.

Finally, Ford dropped the boat off plane, looking over his shoulder to use the old lighthouse as a range. He judged they were about five miles out, probably in about twenty-five feet of water, and it was good tarpon country.

"What we do now," he said, "is look." He was standing at the wheel, steering south. Fort Myers Beach was ahead and off to his left, Bonita Beach a shimmering anomaly in the far distance: its white condominiums, illuminated by harsh late sunlight, looked like the gigantic sails of a sinking ship.

"Look for what?" Walda was using her hand as a visor, her head turned toward Ford, who was backdropped by the sun.

"Splashes in the distance. You look for a flash of silver. Tarpon rolling. A tail sticking out of the water. Anything unusual."

"There!" Dewey was pointing. "A splash. I saw it."

Ford waited until he saw where she was pointing, then he said, "That was a pelican crashing bait. See, he's flying off."

"Ah, crap."

"Keep looking, we'll see them."

Ford idled along and the women, now standing, moved their heads back and forth, back and forth, searching. They idled on for a quarter of an hour. Ford stopped the boat once when he saw a brief flash beneath the water—a school of big permit, large spade-shaped fish traveling in a tight scintillate of golden light. A few minutes later, Dewey grabbed his arm. "Did you see that?"

"What?"

"There it is again!"

Walda said, "I saw it; right, right."

Half a mile away, the flat sea was being pocked by random explosions, as if the sea gulls wheeling above were dropping small bombs.

Ford said, "Hang on," and pushed the throttle forward, running way out around the bubbled craters, then angled back so as not to spook the fish. Then he slowed and shut off the engine, drifting.

Before them, spread out over an acre of water, tarpon were cruising just below the surface. Moving slow, slow, the tips of their great tails punched through the sea membrane, growing ever larger until whole backs of individual fish could be seen

192

before sinking again beneath the water plain. It was like watching plants mature through time-lapse photography, the way their tails breached the surface, growing randomly from this great green field, lifting, tilting.

"There must be a thousand of them. Like they're asleep or something." Dewey spoke in a churchy whisper, focused on the fish.

Ford was watching a ghostly shape, seven feet long, slide beneath the boat. He nudged Walda and pointed. The size of the tarpon and the nearness of it startled her. She jumped. The fish spooked. The panicked fish caused other fish to spook. Inexplicably, suddenly, there was a massive silver form hanging in the air above their heads: huge dark eyes guiding a panel of silver light that arced over the boat and crashed back into the water.

"Christ, they're attacking!" Dewey had collapsed on the deck when the fish jumped; Walda stood frozen, both of them staring wide-eyed at the expanding circle of water where the fish had hit. "I could have . . . touched it!"

Ford was shaken but laughing. "We ought to get some baits out before they attack again." He reached down to take rods out of the holders.

But Walda said, "Ford, you crazy man, I'm not going to try and catch one of those." She was measuring the arc of the fish with her eyes; gauging how close it had come to her head: inches. "These fish, they're *too* big."

Dewey said, "Hell no, not me, either. Hey—do they bite?"

"Huh?"

"Do they bite? People, I mean."

"No. Never. Tarpon don't even have teeth. Not the kind of teeth you mean."

"Could we get in and swim around with them? Can you do that?"

"Sure. That might be more fun."

"I don't know. . . ." Walda was looking at the water, thinking it over.

"I've got a pair of swim goggles and a mask in the storage box somewhere. We'll have to trade off."

"What about sharks? Are there sharks around here?"

"Sure. But you're safer swimming with sharks than driving on any highway in Florida."

"That's not saying much."

Ford had found the goggles and the mask, and was already unbuttoning his shirt. "Still want to try it?"

Dewey took the mask. "Me first." She spit into the mask expertly and slid over the side in her clothes. A few seconds later, she surfaced, pulled the mask up onto her forehead, and whispered, "It's great; you gotta see! They're all around me! *Everywhere.*" Then she made another dive.

Ford held out the goggles to Walda, who was giving him a wry look. "Thank you," she said. Hers was a good face to look into: handsome, with dark eyes that studied him; eyes that had seen a lot.

"Ladies first."

"I don't mean that. I mean her. She needed cheering up."

"Oh. About tennis? Maybe someone should tell her that she doesn't want to play anymore. You, for instance. You could tell her that."

Walda was unbuttoning her blouse. She took it off, folded it neatly, then stood looking at Ford, wearing only a white stretch bra and shorts. She took the goggles and adjusted them on her head. "It wasn't about tennis," she said. "It was about us."

Ford wondered, *Us?*

Walda sat on the gunwale and pushed off into the water.

Walda was in the shower, soaping herself, talking through the shower doors to Dewey. "The most amazing thing I've ever seen. Like Jacques Cousteau. We should have had a camera. You know that? People won't believe us. We really should have."

Dewey had finished her shower, and she stood in front of her bedroom mirror, wrapped in a towel, combing the tangles out of her wet hair. "Yeah, that woulda been neat. Film of it. They were so big! It was like—I don't know what it was like. Like swimming with a bunch of bears."

194

"No—dolphins!"

"Yeah, dolphins!"

"I touched one."

"A dolphin?"

"No, a tarpon, you mullock."

"You told me about a dozen times already. I could have touched one, but I didn't want to scare them again."

Walda shut off the water, slid the shower door open, and stood in the tub drying herself, looking out through the doorway at Dewey. "That Doc, he's a nice man."

"Sure. Everybody likes Doc."

"I don't think you could have picked a better guy."

"I didn't pick him, he just sort of showed up. It's not like he won a contest."

"Well, he did, didn't he?"

"Do you have to keep talking about it?"

"I was just saying that I like him."

"A little dull sometimes, but he's easy to be with."

"Doesn't seem like the marrying kind."

"That's fine with me, because I'm not going to marry anybody."

"You say that now."

"You're damn right I say that now."

"And he's not bad-looking."

"Hoo, he looks like a big old water dog who came back to earth as a man."

"Overall, I mean."

Dewey stopped combing her hair long enough to say, "I guess you'd know more about that than I would."

Walda had stepped out of the tub, into the bedroom. She started to reply but then decided against it. Instead, she said, "At least he's not some overgrown kid. A lot of men are. Almost all of them under thirty, yes? Doc's solid. And he's not pushy. I like being with him."

Dewey said, "That's because you are pushy."

"No I am not."

"Yes you are."

"Am not."

"Are!"

"Am not."

"Bullshit."

"Who shit?" Walda was standing beside Dewey now, and they were both smiling, doing this old routine.

"Says who?"

"Sez me."

"Hah—bitch!"

"Slut!"

"Tramp!"

"Vamp!"

"Whore."

"American . . . cow."

Dewey hooted. "American cow? Now you've gone and done it. Hurt my feelings." She used her comb to flip water at Walda, who caught her by the wrists, both of them laughing. They wrestled around the bedroom, swinging each other hard. Walda lost her towel, so she ripped Dewey's off and flung it toward the bathroom.

"Tart!"

"Romanian pig herder!"

They ended up falling on the bed, face to face, laughing uproariously at their old game, but then they weren't laughing, their eyes wide and noses close, staring at each other.

Walda asked softly, "Are you go to see him tonight?"

A little more laughter escaped from Dewey. "Pushy bitch."

Walda was touching the hair on Dewey's temples. "Nothing wrong with asking, is there?"

"If that was all you did."

Walda said, "We've already talked about that."

Dewey put her hand on top of Walda's and squeezed. "Then I guess I'll stop and see Doc. If it's what you want."

"You owe it to yourself."

Dewey moved her hand, looking hard at Walda. "But not tonight."

196

10

FORD worked in his lab Wednesday night without interruption. He played Gregorian chants on the stereo, then Jimmy Buffett when he was in the mood. Using the microscope, he separated fish eggs from raw sea wrack, and he drank three bottles of beer. He roamed around his lab barefoot and shirtless, burping without apology and talking to the little squid listening from the fish tank outside on the porch. A couple of times, he caught himself thinking of the way Walda looked in her see-through bra, and had to force his attention back to grids and percentages.

"It's not that I don't like women," he told the squid. "It's just that I find biology less complicated."

Ha!

Laughing at his own mild joke. Enjoying this time alone after so much time spent with people.

Tomlinson and Harry didn't return that night, nor was Ford's blue pickup truck in the marina parking lot the next morning when Ford awoke. Standing on his porch and looking at the parking lot, Ford felt a stab of worry. The worry nagged at him all through coffee and the hour he spent getting the nets of his trawl boat ready for the day's work.

Since he had no way of knowing how to get in touch with Tomlinson, he dialed Dewey's number. When Dewey answered, Ford asked, "I don't suppose you've seen my pickup driving around your way?"

"Now you've lost your truck? Ford, if your head wasn't screwed on . . ."

"Tomlinson has it. Thought he might be out cruising Captiva."

"If you need a car, you can use my Vett. We've got Bets's rental."

Dewey had a candy apple red Corvette, sleek as a spaceship and with elaborate anti-theft sensors that ordered *"Back away from this vehicle—you are too close"* when a stranger approached the car.

"Nope. I'm in the boat today. Did you have fun yesterday?"

"Oh man, you know it. Hey, Bets—it's Doc."

Ford could hear Walda talking in the background, but Dewey covered the phone. Dewey said, "Yeah, yeah, I will." Then into the phone, she said, "You going to be around tonight?"

Ford said, "Sure. You two stopping by?"

"I might. Bets has to get ready to leave for London on Sunday."

"It takes her two days to pack?"

"Naw, but she has to do her stretches, and her meditations. Time-alone stuff. She's got Wimbledon tune-ups."

"I thought you might be leaving with her." Ford had assumed it, but was surprised to hear himself come right out and ask.

"To play? Hell, no."

"Not to play. Just to watch Walda."

"Ah, I don't know. She's got an extra ticket, but there's so much terrorist stuff going on."

Ford thought, *Walda just happens to have an extra ticket, right.* He said, "Did you remember about your windows and doors? Keep them locked."

198

"Oh boy, that speech again."

"And when you get in your car—"

"When you get in your car, always check the backseat. Which my car doesn't have. Yes, sir."

"As of yesterday, the pressure on Karl Sutter was turned up about threefold, and there's no telling what the guy might do. I don't trust him."

"Which you've told me about a dozen times."

Except for his own illegalities and his information sources, Ford had kept Dewey apprised of his interest in Jeth Nicholes's arrest, Karl Sutter's behavior, and Marvin Rios's murder—information, he hoped, that had been passed on to Walda.

"Sutter associates you with me. And he hates me. I just want you on your toes, that's all."

"Well, if the creep's a killer, the cops ought to arrest him and be done with it."

"I don't know if he's a killer or not. I truly don't. But he's a liar and he's on the run from something, and that makes him dangerous. Just humor me, okay?"

"Check all doors and windows. Inspect car before entering. Do not leave house alone." Talking as mechanically as a robot, she was making fun of Ford, and it bothered him that she didn't take him seriously.

"You're coming by tonight."

"I might. Probably, yeah."

"Don't forget—"

He began to warn her again, but Dewey said, "I know, I know, I know."

The later it got, the more Ford worried about Tomlinson. He even cut his trawling time short so he could spend more time at his lab, near the phone.

All day long, though, the phone rang only three times, twice from school purchasing agents who placed orders. The third call came from Elizabeth Harper, the public defender who had been assigned Jeth's case.

After pleasantries, Harper said, "I heard through the grapevine that you came up with enough evidence to get Mr. Nicholes released. My client and I appreciate it."

Ford was pleased to hear from her—if for no other reason than to chide her for not trusting him. He said, "And I'm not going to charge the state a cent."

"I guess I deserve that. But I want you to understand. Legally, I just couldn't tell you what you wanted to know. Sorry."

"Call me naive. I thought compromise was the only compelling ethic of legal life."

"So now you've wounded me twice. Feel better?"

"Nope. Feel silly for doing it. You don't deserve it."

She was laughing. "Which is not fair, getting all nice and apologetic just when I was working up a good head of indignation."

"My apologies again."

"See! What I think, Dr. Ford, is that you saved me a lot of work, and that I owe you a lunch. Or a drink."

"A drink. I don't eat lunch. When's Jeth get out?"

"I've just received a copy of the formal release papers. By the time they get to everyone who needs to initial them, probably tomorrow afternoon."

"I'll come in and pick him up."

"No, the police will take Mr. Nicholes anywhere he wishes—and be damn glad to do it. That long drive to Sanibel won't hurt them a bit. Come to think of it, it wouldn't hurt me, either. You were right—I don't know a thing about boats or water, and I should learn at least a little bit if I'm going to work in this area."

Thrown out like self-criticism, Ford knew Ms. Harper was hinting for an invitation to go boating—an invitation he would have certainly offered had he not been so preoccupied with Tomlinson.

"I'll call you about that drink, Ms. Harper."

"Liz. Or call me Elizabeth. Then maybe you can tell me why Mr. Nicholes was so concerned with the time lag between conviction and execution. Do you know?"

Ford said, "When we meet for that drink."

11

ON the barrier islands, in summer, dusk is not just a sterile measure of time. Dusk is a ritual, a cool liturgy of shifting mood and movement. Dusk is a turquoise wedge between the heat of the day and the heat of the night; the breathing void that connects what islanders must do with what islanders want to do. Off go the business suits or panty hose, on go the shorts, the thongs and party dresses, the bird-watching binoculars or pink Hawaiian shirts. On Periwinkle Way, Sanibel's main road, dusk replaces one kind of slow traffic with an even slower, less obsessive line of automobiles—though still bumper to bumper. On Captiva Island, at tourist haunts like The Mucky Duck and the Bubble Room, diners gather over drinks to applaud the sunset, while at local hangouts like Will's Landing and Lazy Flamingo, tables begin to fill with part-time real estate agents—which is to say nearly everyone who works or lives on the islands. The bars call it Happy Hour or Attitude Adjustment, but it is really a little vacation in the day; a time when store clerks and hotel employees and city bureaucrats can tell stories over margaritas or Coronas, get a little drunk, and perhaps even find unexpected romance among their fellows.

Dusk on the islands is a soft time of gathering. Sea wind

collects in the high palms, and the palm fronds rattle. Jasmine flowers sense the temperature change, and bloom. Nightfall pivots on the final, orange axis of sunset, and, all up and down the islands, electric lights go on. To people on boats in Pine Island Sound, the pockets of light mark the night strongholds of human occupation in the mangrove darkness. To a man or a woman out alone on a boat, the little islands of light are a friendly thing to see.

Standing on the porch of his stilt house, Marion Ford watched the marina lights click on and, shortly afterward, noted that a few miles away, people were playing softball at Sanibel Elementary School—he could see the glow of the outfield lights above the mangroves. The mercury glow created a stadium effect in the darkness, reminding Ford of baseball, a sport that he admired. And baseball reminded him of Tomlinson because Tomlinson was such a fan.

Tomlinson's sailboat was dark, unoccupied. Ford's blue pickup truck was still missing from the marina parking lot.

To the squid hidden behind soft corals in the fish tank, Ford said, "You'd at least think that damned old hippie would have the good manners to call." Talking as if he was angry because he was worried.

This would be Tomlinson's second night away from the marina.

Ford stood watching the ball-field lights, mosquitoes buzzing around his ears, until a woman's voice hailed him from the wood-rotted Chris-Craft cruiser tied alongside the newer fiberglass boats at the marina. "Hey, Doc, we're in the mood to talk to a man over here! Could you use a free beer?" Rhonda Lister and JoAnn Smallwood sat on deck chairs, looking at him from the stern of their boat: two meaty, independent young women with big smiles that gauged the breadth of their own enthusiasms. Ford had kept them both at arm's length because he didn't want to get involved with a neighbor, plus he had high hopes for Dewey. But now he thought, *What the hell,* and called back, "I'll put on a shirt and be right over. . . ."

★ ★ ★

. . . Miles away, but at the same moment, Jeth Nicholes stood at the window of his cell, watching darkness absorb the last golden contrail of sunset. He watched closely, hoping to see the green flash once more, but not really expecting it.

The sun slid into a veil of smog, vaporized, and was gone.

No flash. No green flare. Nothing.

Nicholes turned from the window to find one of the guards looking through the bars at him. The guard was smiling. "Last night with us, Captain Nicholes. Sure hope being jailed wasn't too hard on you."

Nicholes stepped over and took the guard's outstretched hand, shaking it. "No, you boys treated me real fine. I hope we can stay in touch. Maybe get out and beat the bushes some time."

"Wasn't a man among us, Captain Nicholes, thought even once you was really a murderer. At least unless the guy damn well deserved it. But the cops is human; they make mistakes sometimes. I'm just glad things got straightened out. After to-night, you should be able to rest easy, huh?"

Nicholes had become so accustomed to touching his head with his hands, feeling, spreading the hair and searching for tender spots, that he didn't even realize what he was doing. "I hope so," he said to the guard. "But you damn sure never know. . . ."

. . . At the plush canal home of the late Marvin Rios, Karl Sutter was lighting Candy Rios's cigarette, the two of them sitting at the patio table by the screened pool. Sutter shoved the lighter into his pocket and said, "Christ, let's get some lights on. It's like a damn tomb out here."

Candy reached through the open doors into the kitchen and the pool was illuminated. The pool lights keyed a memory electrode in Sutter: the brief mental picture of those two tennis women swimming naked; Dewey Nye and the dark-haired one, their bodies so hard and full that it made his breath catch.

Candy Rios touched his arm, concerned. "Are you okay, darling? You look a little pale."

Sutter took a deep breath and squeezed the woman's hand. "Just that I have a lot on my mind. And can't stop thinking of you. How good we are together."

"Boy oh boy oh boy oh boy oh boy, it's so true, Karl. I can hardly believe it myself, but that's just the way I feel."

"We're going to get married."

"You keep saying it."

" 'Cause that's what we're going to do. No more arguing."

"But I really think we should wait for at least a year, just so people won't talk."

Sutter was rubbing Candy's neck, letting his big hands slide down over her breasts, feeling her shiver beneath his fingers. "I don't care what people think. At least we can live as if we're married. You sign your power of attorney over to me. Legally, then, we've done everything but said 'I do,' and I can take care of business at the marina. I can straighten out that mess Marvin got you into with Senator Griffin, too. Sign the papers, and I will help buy you out of a very shady deal. The senator and I are buddies. He'll negotiate."

Candy took the power-of-attorney instrument and read it again. She inhaled deeply from her cigarette, balanced it on the ashtray, then took up the pen. "Tell me the truth, Karl. Was Marv a crook? He was, wasn't he? That's what this is about. Marv was a crook and Senator Griffin caught him; now you're trying to get me out of it and protect me. That's why I have to sign this paper."

Sutter shrugged, trying not to look at the woman's face.

God, she's even uglier than Greta. If I have to see her naked one more time, I may vomit.

He said, "I hate to say anything bad about a man that's dead. Marvin, I mean."

"But he was a crook? I always knew. Christ, this damn pen!"

Sutter was thinking, *If the cops take even the slightest interest, I cash in this bitch's account and I'm gone. New name, new place.* He said, "Let's just put it this way: signing that paper is the smartest thing you can do. . . ."

204

. . . Across the bay, in the middle-class residential area of Iona Cove, Javier Castillo stepped out onto the back *porche* of his three-bedroom rental and sipped the hot demitasse his wife had served him. He had worked hard all day, fishing two different parties, and each party had caught tarpon, so he should have been happy, but he was not. He stood on the stoop, watching the sunset, feeling the dusk take him. The dusk carried his mind far, far away.

Javier thought about Cuba, and the way it smelled at dusk: the jasmine flowers and the frangipani, and the old men sitting beneath streetlights, smoking cigars over a last game of dominoes.

I will never know those things again, he thought. *Nor will my children. I have taken them from their homeland, and they will never know the way it was.*

Javier felt bad. He felt sick in the soul and lonely. In some way, he believed, he had hurt his friend Jeth, and he had harmed his family by spiriting them away from their native island.

Everyone I touch, Javier thought, *I hurt.*

Javier was so intent, staring at the last yellow streak of daylight, that he didn't hear Ellfreda, his wife, step out onto the *porche* behind him. He jumped when she touched his shoulder, causing her to smile. "When you think of younger women," she chided, "your ears go deaf."

"I am not thinking of women," Javier replied, his tone no-nonsense and curt. "I am thinking of important things."

Ellfreda sensed the unhappiness in her husband, and stroked his arm. "You are an important man. It is your place to think about important things."

"Important! That makes me laugh. Have you confused me with an American? Should I remind you? I am an illegal immigrant. A wetback. A wetback who has made wetbacks of his whole family."

Ellfreda said gently, "So that is it."

Javier said, "Yes. That is it."

Ellfreda let her hand rest on her husband's shoulder and sat beside him on the *porche,* saying nothing. She waited as Javier sipped his coffee and watched the pearly afterglow. Finally, he said, "I'm tired of being afraid."

"I know," Ellfreda said.

"I'm tired of being afraid of a knock on the door. Of men in uniform. We came to this country to get away from fear! So why am I still afraid?"

Ellfreda continued patting Javier's shoulder.

"I'll tell you why—because I would not help murder the gringo captain and his crew. Had we murdered them, we could have come right into Key West. The authorities would have welcomed us. We would have been citizens by now! But because I did a foolish thing and saved American lives, I have made criminals of my entire family."

"It was not a foolish thing you did that night on the boat," Ellfreda said gently. "It was a brave thing. A very brave thing."

"But look where it has gotten us. Freda, my little dear one—don't you see this thing? I cannot even go to the jail to help my friend Jeth. Jeth is in jail, but he is not the only prisoner."

Ellfreda heard herself saying very softly, "Then you must do something about this."

Javier did not answer for a long time, but then he said, "Yes. I must."

"What would you do?"

"I would do what the father of good children should do. I will go to the government and tell them the exact truth. I will go after my morning charter and leave nothing out. Tomorrow. At the government building in Fort Myers. They can do what they wish to me, but I will no longer allow my family to live a lie."

Ellfreda stood, saying, "It is the decision only a truly brave man would make." She kissed her husband on the forehead, then went alone into the house to ready the supper.

. . . Harry Rinmon could see sunset residue beyond the bathroom window of the cottage she and Tomlinson had rented for the night. The orange afterglow spread like oily paint upon the water, absorbing light from thickets of bamboo and oak.

They were in Gibsonton, sixteen miles south of Tampa, staying in a place called the Big Top Motor Court and Restaurant, a series of peeling white cabins on the Alafia River abutting a steam table café.

For decades, Gibsonton had been a wintering place for what were known generally, though unfairly, as circus freaks. *Exhibitors* was the more correct term—and locally preferred. The Gibsonton post office had a special drop box built low for midgets, and at local dances, it was not unusual to see the bearded lady dancing with the Alligator Skin Man.

Weddings in Gibsonton were among the best attended and most interesting in Florida.

During the fifties, in Gibsonton's heyday, a circus giant and his wife, known professionally as the Monkey-Faced Lady, purchased land on the Alafia River and built the cottages, which they rented to friends and travelers. The business flourished not only because Americans had fallen in love with automobile travel (though they had) and not just because Florida was beginning its long, suicidal building boom (though it was). The business prospered because the giant and the Monkey-Faced Lady were an intelligent, popular couple and, after so many years on the road working as "freaks," they put their hearts and souls into their new lives in this new place where, for once, they were accepted for the good people they were.

The giant loved to cook, so a restaurant was soon added to the cottage rentals. His specialty was biscuits and milk gravy—which he made every morning of his life right up until the day he died. His wife carried on for a few more years, but then she, too, faltered and the motor court passed into the hands of an investment conglomerate, which planned to replace the motor court with high-rise singles apartments as soon as the demographics warranted.

The demographics would soon warrant.

Neither Tomlinson nor Harry knew any of this; indeed, the knowledge of the motor court's antecedents was all but lost.

Florida's history is a chaotic thing built upon thin layers of human endeavor that are covered or quickly absorbed by more thin layers, then forgotten entirely. Because Florida has always appealed to the provisional and the transitory, what has gone before and what inevitably must come have never been of much interest. Which explains many of Florida's ills, and is also why Florida has always been the nation's tackiest, glitziest state.

Tomlinson and Harry chose the Big Top Motor Court over numerous more modern motels for a couple of reasons. One was that the Art Deco–style motor courts of the fifties were now so rare, the Big Top appealed to Harry's bohemian spirit. Another was that in slowing to look past the bamboo thicket, down the shell drive, Tomlinson received a sensory jolt: the strong impression that this tiny spot had once been a place of great happiness. The final reason was that there was a drugstore nearby, so Harry had said, "You like it?"

"Good vibes," Tomlinson had replied, looking.

"Then it's unanimous." And Harry had pulled in and booked a room.

They were both tired. In two fast days, they had put more than seven hundred miles on the odometer of Ford's old truck. They had been from Sanibel to Mayakkatee County, down dirt roads, along the pretty river, to the county courthouse, then clear north to Tallahassee, poring over newspaper accounts and through public records, assembling data on the proposed development, Mayakkatee River Estates. Tomlinson was certain they had developed precisely the kind of information Ford had requested, and he and Harry both felt good about that. Maybe it would help get Jeth out of jail. And it would certainly help expose a corrupt senator—Robert Griffin.

Now Tomlinson was lying on the bed eating a mango and listening to National Public Radio, and Harry was in the bathroom, having just returned from the drugstore with a paper sack. Wearing soft jeans and a white cossack blouse, she stood at the bathroom window, watching the last orange remnants of day. In that hushed moment of transition, she felt the sweetness and the sadness of her own life, and also an urge to rush, to hurry toward some indefinable destination; what or where, she did not know.

From the other side of the door came Tomlinson's voice: "You fall in, or what?"

She called back, "I'm going to take a shower—go ahead and eat," then stepped away from the window, unbuttoning her shirt collar. She removed her shirt and jeans and panties, then studied herself in the mirror above the sink: wide, heavy breasts, very dark nipples, thin shoulders, oval face in a frame of black hair and dark Japanese eyes.

With each passing week, it seemed to her, that familiar face was increasingly the face of a stranger.

Through the door came Tomlinson's voice once more: "Only one mango left. You'd better get out here, Harry."

The woman smiled. *Harry*.

She had abandoned her old family name of Musashi when, at the age of twenty-eight, she had experienced a spiritual and social awakening that had changed her life and had, over the years, influenced the lives of many of her students—or so Harry hoped.

In that awakening, she received the briefest taste of satori, perfect contentment; an illumined state in which she experienced the letting down of body and mind, and in which she also felt the narrow trail of her own life merge with a greater universal path.

After that awakening, she neither felt nor acknowledged differences in male and female, old and young, healthy and infirm. There was only the infinite breath; the single existing moment, and it was in this moment that she tried to live as bravely and as generously as she could.

After the awakening, she threw away her watch. She wore unisex clothes. She changed her name to Harry, and lived happily and alone for more than five years. Months ago, though, the face that looked back at her from the mirror began to seem increasingly foreign and lacking, and Harry finally acknowledged that there was a change she wanted in her life, a thing she wanted to embrace and experience. That thing was motherhood. Not

209

that she wanted to marry. Nope; never, no way. But she needed a mate, and biology required the mate be male.

So, one night, Harry sat down and listed all the men she knew and admired. It was not a long list, but it was impressive in terms of the power and the credentials represented. Then, in another column, she listed all the qualities she wanted her child to inherit: intelligence, humor, physical beauty, gentleness of spirit.

Tomlinson headed the list in three of the four categories (beauty, Harry hoped, would be passed on through her genes), so Tomlinson was her final choice as father of her child.

Coincidentally, five weeks before, while Harry was still trying to make her decision, Tomlinson had showed up unexpectedly at her apartment outside Boston. Such a karmic sign was nearly too powerful to ignore, and Harry had almost told him then and there of her plan.

But she didn't tell him, even though he stayed several nights.

Now, though, she had told him; asked him, actually, if he would be her temporary mate. To her surprise, Tomlinson had balked at the offer.

"Being a daddy," he had said, "isn't like some dog going out and pissing on a fire hydrant. If I father a child, I want to be with it. It's something I need to think about."

So, in these few nights together, they had slept apart—a fact that made a new realization no easier: After being with Tomlinson five weeks ago, her menstrual period was now a week late.

Harry stared at herself in the mirror, shrugged, stuck out her tongue, made a face, grinned.

Has the hippie knocked you up?

She squatted naked over the old porcelain toilet and, from the paper sack, took the home-use pregnancy test she had purchased at the drugstore, First Response.

From the cardboard box, she took the absorbent stick and held it beneath her. She looked at the ceiling, relaxing, and began to urinate on the little stick. When she was finished, she dried herself and turned on the shower while she held the stick up to the light, watching its tiny clear window for a change in color.

The window seemed to fog, and when it cleared again, it was an unmistakable blue.

Harry put her hand over her own mouth so as not to hoot out loud.

She was pregnant.

She kept looking at the stick, fearful the little window might clear itself. When it didn't, she wrapped the entire kit in the paper sack and shoved it all into the little trash basket beneath the sink.

There is a baby in me!

For some reason, she was crying, and she couldn't stop. Harry soaked for a long time beneath the shower, but, when she got out, she was still crying.

Through the door came Tomlinson's voice: "Are you okay in there, Moontree?"

The sound of her old name caused her to bawl even harder.

Tomlinson opened the door, perplexed, then he was holding her in his arms, kissing her, his chest heaving, saying, "Quit, quit; you know how weepy I get when you do this. . . ." And he was crying with her.

Then she was naked on her back on the little bed, knees bent and legs spread while Tomlinson undressed before her.

"Are you sure?" she kept asking. "Are you sure?"

She spread her legs wider as Tomlinson dropped down onto the bed with her, and she used her hand to help guide him, her abdomen spasming momentarily as he entered her.

"I'm sure," he said.

Harry had one hand tangled in his long hair, the other on his buttocks, trying to press him deeper, deeper. She was still crying, kissing him, and she whispered, "I'm pregnant, dear one."

Tomlinson said, "What? Not yet you're not."

"I'm pregnant!"

"Almost . . . almost! Just give me a little time, damn it!"

★ ★ ★

211

Nightfall pushed dusk westward, the earth's slow rotation measured by cloud mesas and streaks of peach light that were absorbed by a darkening sea. On barrier islands along Florida's Gulf coast, the darkness seemed to seep out of the bays and mangrove breaks, spreading over beaches, condos, and planned communities as quietly as fog.

Darkness came to Cedar Key, Gibsonton, and Clearwater Beach, Longboat Key and Siesta Key, rolling down the tideline like a great cloud shadow.

Darkness came to Boca Grande, Cayo Costa, Captiva Island, Sanibel, and Marco Island, sweeping over the whole chain of west coast barrier islands.

Then the lights of the islands came on in the darkness, one by one by one, like bright pearls on a long string.

To tourists in an airliner, two miles overhead, the islands formed pockets of light on the dark water, as isolated as ships and as distinct as constellations in a night sky.

Standing outside Timmy's Nook bar, Suzie Hemphill, Greta Gideon's best friend, saw the passenger plane passing overhead and thought, *If that weirdo Sutter really did marry Greta, like she said he was gonna, she'da called by now to tell me about some honeymoon they're flying to,* and Suzie resolved to check Greta's apartment first thing before work in the morning.

Opening the gate to the Mayakkatee River Estates construction road, one of the project's backhoe operators, a man named Frank, looked up and saw the plane blinking in the darkness. With him, sitting in the truck, was his supervisor's lonely wife, and he knew just the place for them to have an hour all alone—that little logging trail where he'd glimpsed that white Lincoln parked the day before. Florida was getting so built up, good hiding spots were tough to find, but this was a good one. Frank had the gate keys, he had a six-pack of Pabst, and he had a blanket if they found a soft spot on the ground. . . .

Looking out the window of his cell, Jeth Nicholes saw the airliner, and he thought, *Maybe that's how I ought to spend the next*

212

few months. Traveling. Maybe go clear to New York City. See what that's like.

Turning from the window, Jeth wondered if people did any fishing up that way. *I could always show them a few tricks,* he thought. *While I'm around. . . .*

Standing beside a bamboo thicket on the Alafia River, Tomlinson looked up and saw the plane, and thought, *I wish I was on it, one way to Fumbuck, Egypt. What in the hell have I gotten myself into?* But then he thought of Harry lying inside, the softness of her and the image of her someday swollen with child, and he decided, *Nope, I've done a good thing. Maybe I've finally signed up for the magic bus. . . .*

Sitting on the stern of the wood-rotted Chris-Craft, Marion Ford watched the airliner pass overhead, beginning to bank, descending eastward, its navigation lights flashing.

Luck, he offered, as he always did when he saw a plane about to land or take off. *Safe trip.*

He sat on a folding deck chair between the two owners of the Chris-Craft, Rhonda Lister and JoAnn Smallwood, listening to them talk and laugh, as he drank his third free beer—an Old Milwaukee, which the marina guides called Old Immokalee.

He liked Rhonda and JoAnn just fine; big, plain, healthy women who were full of fun and independent as hell. Smart, too—judging by the sharp looks of appraisal they leveled at him from time to time, and he knew what was going on: the subliminal process of selection, of who would end up with whom.

Sitting in the chair, watching the airliner and pretending to listen, Ford calculated all the possible scenarios. If he took Rhonda to his bed, his friendship with JoAnn would be immediately replaced by a forced cordiality. JoAnn was a modern woman, but she was also human—and no one liked finishing second to a roommate.

Same if he chose JoAnn.

Another option was to make a pass at both of them—an idea not so farfetched, judging from the body language and constant knee contact they kept up with him. But Ford knew, in time, that would alienate them both, and it wasn't worth losing the goodwill of neighbors. Plus, it seemed a little too weird, not to mention demanding.

Nope. Wasn't worth it. As much as he needed to, with one or the other, the uneasiness, the complications and self-recriminations were a price too high. Ford was about to contrive an excuse why he must leave when a car swung into the marina's shell parking lot: a shiny red Corvette.

"Hey," Ford said. "Hey, looks like I have company." Then, to please JoAnn and Rhonda, he added, "Damn it all."

Dewey Nye—tall woman with blond hair—came striding down the dock in dark shorts and fresh dark blouse, squinting through the weak light. "Ford, is that you?"

"How you doin', Dewey? Forgot you were going to stop by." He was standing, already moving across the deck toward the dock.

"We had a date tonight. Get your keister over here."

Ford made his farewells to Rhonda and JoAnn, then he was walking with the tall woman toward his house built on stilts.

Rhonda looked after them, and she said to JoAnn, "That's one pushy bitch."

JoAnn nodded. "Yeah. Blond dye probably leaked into her brain and made her mean."

Both women laughed, then JoAnn said, "Doc could do a lot better than that."

"You're saying she's not pretty? My God, I wish I was as ugly as that."

"I just mean better."

"Like you?"

"At least I'd be nice to him."

"And I wouldn't?"

"You've got Barry."

"Barry's an asshole."

JoAnn watched the tall woman put an arm over Ford's shoulder, the two of them disappearing into shadow. "Doesn't look like either of us can do much about it tonight. Say, why don't we change and go to the Lazy Flamingo, get something to eat?"

Rhonda grinned. "That's what I like about you, Smallwood—you never give up."

12

BECAUSE the door to Ford's house was not locked, Dewey led the way in, turning on lights, the overhead fan, kneeling by the stereo to find music, flipping through albums.

Ford said, "Mind if I get something to drink?" As if it were her house, not his; a mild joke.

"What? Oh." Dewey was still concentrating on the stereo. "Help yourself. You got any wine?" Missing it completely.

"You don't drink wine."

"Hell, I didn't drink margaritas till Cabbage Key. You never know what I might decide to try tonight."

Ford caught the suggestiveness of that, thinking, *What's going on here?*

He made a show of going to the little refrigerator, looking for wine, even though he knew he didn't have any. "Nope," he said finally. "But I can run up to Bailey's Store and get some. I need to get food for Jeth's cat, anyway. Crunch & Des. He's been staying here."

"Naw, I don't need any wine. It was just an idea." She was moving her head around on her shoulders, as if she was tense. "I thought it might help me relax. Bets put me through a hell of a workout today. And it's so damn hot. When are you going to

216

stick an air conditioner in this place? I'm already sweating so bad, I can smell myself."

Ford said, "Or I could ride my bike, get a nice Chablis. That's what they call white wine, right? Or take your car down to Huxters. Wouldn't take two minutes." Thinking, *Every guy on earth keeps wine just for a moment like this, except me. What a maroon.*

"No. Maybe some iced tea. Or a sip of your Coors. Just so long as it's cold."

Dewey was having trouble choosing an album. She kept hesitating and reading, her expression pained. She had on a dark blue pleated blouse that billowed out when she bent over, and she wore her hair in a ponytail. She had recently shaved her legs—Ford noticed the chafed pores on the inside of her thighs, clear up where the black Patagonia shorts were stretched tight against her.

"The Moody Blues," she said, reading an album cover. "This looks pretty weird."

"It's some kind of transcendental experience, the whole album. Tomlinson can explain it. That's the only reason I have it, Tomlinson. There're one or two songs I like, not that I understand any of it."

"Did you ever find Tomlinson? You were looking for him."

"No."

"He'll show up."

"I hope."

She was putting the album on the turntable, placing the needle, her face so concentrated, flushed, that she looked like a fourteen-year-old who'd just gotten out of gym class. But pretty . . . no, not just pretty—beautiful with those eyes and those lips. The crooked nose didn't matter. Ford liked the nose. Eyes set a little too close together, but he liked that, too. And she had those odd kind of hips, where the hinge joints angled out, which he suddenly found endearing.

When Dewey said, "What the hell are you staring at?" he jumped slightly.

"Oh . . . just looking. Your hair looks nice that way."

"Since when did you start noticing my hair?" She pulled the ponytail around so that it was right in front of her eyes. Chiding him, but Ford could tell there was something different about her; something on her mind.

The music was playing now, violins and orchestra with acid guitars, and Dewey took the bottle of beer from his hand and sat beside him on the little couch. She took a drink, made a face, took another, then handed the bottle back. "Tastes like horse piss. I'm not surprised you like it."

Ford said, "I think it's your sophistication—that's what I like most about you."

"Just so long as you like me."

"I do."

"Like a buddy."

"Well—"

"I mean, that's the way we are together . . . buddies. I'm like just one of the guys." She was talking to him like he'd done something wrong; trying to prove a point.

"You don't look like any guy I've ever known."

"You notice that, too?"

"Of course I notice that. A man made out of cobalt would notice it."

She was leaning toward him, nervous or intense—it was hard to tell the difference in Dewey—but not too close, so Ford had to reach a little to get his hand in her hair. He pulled her to him and kissed her tenderly, then harder, and she did not resist.

"See?" he said, expecting her to lean her face against him. Instead, she drew away.

"I was just about to say you'd never tried to kiss me before."

"No longer a legitimate question."

"I was going to ask you why."

Ford took her and kissed her again, holding his mouth on hers, longer, longer, breathing with her, but feeling no passion in return. "Sometimes you talk too much," he said.

Dewey had her big hand on Ford's thigh. "Bets said she

218

went to your room Monday night and you guys made out for a while."

Ford said, "Ah."

"Ah yourself."

"I didn't know who it was, you or her. It was dark. But I'm not surprised."

"But you didn't mention it."

"Nope. Didn't want to get anybody in trouble."

"But if you'd known it was Bets, that would've been okay?"

"I like Walda. I like her a lot. So it would have been just fine."

"You're just flattering as hell, aren't you?"

"I try to keep my lying to a minimum. We're not close enough to be honest?"

Dewey was grinning at him, smiling for the first time. "I think she was trying to get you stirred up; make you decide to come to my room. We've talked about you. Why you never put a move on me."

Ford said, "I did come to your room. Your door was locked." But he was thinking, *A hell of a strange thing for Walda to do.*

"I'm glad you did."

"Are you?"

Dewey moved her hand up Ford's leg, touching the hem of his shorts with her finger, and Ford thought, *She's nervous, but she wants to go through with it.*

Dewey said, "No locked doors around here."

Ford put his hand in her hair and kissed her again.

"Nights in White Satin" was playing, although Ford always thought of it as "Knights in White Satin." A slow, moody, driving song with strange chords that struck a deeper, stranger spirit and fixed the heavy rhythm of Dewey's body atop Ford's.

She had undressed herself quickly, as if ashamed, or as if chilled by the way Ford studied her, for he could not take his eyes off the way she looked in the light of the room's lone

219

reading lamp. Unbuttoning the blouse to reveal the crescent lift of her breasts, wide and round and heavy, nipples pointed up and outward. Reaching to drape the blouse over the table, her ribs showing, blond hair brushing her bare back, muscles flexing beneath the skin, like watching the glossy shoulders of a race-horse.

All Ford could say was, "Good God, you are a picture, woman."

With her back to him, Dewey had slid the shorts down around her ankles, tilting pale buttocks as she stepped out of the shorts, the underside of her showing a hazy tangle of pale pubic hair. Then she turned to him, arms crossed over her breasts, and asked with a nervous laugh, "You going to make me start alone?"

"Not a chance. . . ."

So now they were naked on the foldout bed. Dewey was atop him, a moving weight, lifting and sliding with every stroke of the music, her hands on his shoulders and her face pressed hard against his—her body pounding such a frenzied rhythm that Ford should have been swept up by her passion, but he was not; was not, for he felt no passion in her. Instead, he felt only a grim resolve; a sense of burning determination, as if he were the final station of a difficult exercise course. He could feel it in the way Dewey tensed at his touch; the way she fought him, for an instinctive moment, each time he tried to move her or shift positions.

She had wrestled herself on him, affixed herself as if on a spindle, and now she was going through all the motions, using the proper technique with a sort of tireless precision that had been the hallmark of her sport. Like something she'd read in a book, or seen in a movie: dispassionate passion, and giving it all her concentration, but doing it quickly, as if she was frightened and wanted to get it finished quickly.

Ford lay beneath her, feeling her breasts slap his chest, feeling the sweat of her face on his face, wanting to stop her; wanting to find a way to tell her it was okay to stop, but couldn't, and he'd never felt so alienated from her, so distanced from her friendship than now, when they were making love.

But then his mind would think only of the way she looked, of the way she felt on him, and, for whole minutes, nothing else mattered.

After a time, she said into his ear, "Aren't you getting close?" without missing a repetition in what had become a thumping marathon.

Ford lied, "I'm done. I am."

"What?"

"Already. If you are."

"But you're still—"

"I stay that way sometimes."

"Damn, the girls must love you." Catching herself there, what she'd said. But let it pass without amendment.

Ford helped her roll off, holding her in his right arm, both of them lying on their backs looking at the ceiling fan. He turned and kissed her gently on the cheek, and it was as if they'd never met; like kissing a stranger.

Dewey sighed and said, "I guess I'm not so good at this, huh? Sorry."

"You're beautiful. I think you're great."

"Look at you. You look like a damn sundial, the way you're pointing. Or something for horseshoes."

"Don't talk about it any more. You don't need to."

"I've always been kind of a loser this way. It's not like it'll hurt my feelings."

"Dewey—"

"We're all born different, Doc." She was talking to the ceiling, her eyes open and unblinking, telling him things but speaking to herself.

"Dewey, it doesn't matter to me. Not a bit."

"Hah! You didn't want to become lovers? They all do. They always have."

"It crossed my mind, damn right. But it's not important. I never would have pressed it. The way you showed up tonight, though, it was like the only thing you had on your mind."

221

"I wanted to give it another try, that's all. With someone I care about."

"That's the nicest thing I've heard in a while."

"I do. With someone who didn't try to push me or trick me or try to get me drunk. I've got some decisions to make."

Ford said, "I know you do."

"About tennis. And some things."

Ford found her hand and locked his fingers into hers. "You need to do what you want to do."

"You don't even know what I'm talking about."

"Don't be so sure."

"It'd shock the hell out of you if you knew." Telling him, through the tone of her voice, that she wanted him to know.

Ford said, "If you don't enjoy tennis, quit it. If you enjoy living with Walda, live with her. Either one, you're not doing anything wrong."

Dewey started to say something. Instead, she rolled over and threw her arm across Ford's chest, burying her face into his ribs.

For Ford, in that instant, the sensation of being with a stranger disappeared.

13

BETWEEN 8 and 11 A.M., on Friday, June 24, four telephones calls came into the county police switchboard that were inexorably linked but would be shunted to different offices.

Police departments are often criticized for exactly this lack of coordination, but, in reality, law-enforcement people are usually more competent than their critics—and more efficient than most on the public payroll.

By five that afternoon, three of the calls would be associated, and the fourth would be acknowledged as being peripherally influenced.

The first call that came in was a missing-person report from a woman who identified herself as Suzie Hemphill. According to Ms. Hemphill, her best friend, Greta Gideon, had confided in her that she was going to elope with a guy she'd been dating. Greta had supposedly left with the guy two days before. Now the guy was back on Sanibel Island, but nobody's seen or heard from Greta since—Ms. Hemphill had even gone in and searched her friend's apartment.

As Ms. Hemphill told the officer who took the report, "I know the guy's back, 'cause I just stopped at his marina and they said he was out on an all-day charter. But I had to leave for work, so I taped a note to his dock asking just what the hell's going on—then I thought, hell, he's such a weirdo, I ought to let you guys know, too."

The second call was anonymous and, because it was far more sinister, given priority attention. Within minutes after it was received, a tape of the call had been copied from the main recording bank and was being played back to several of the men and women who worked in homicide—one of whom was Roy Fuller. The recording was of an obviously distraught male. Certain passages were so graphic that Fuller, for one, didn't doubt that the man was sincere:

I wasn't gonna call, but I couldn't sleep all night thinkin' about it, so I got to call, only I'm not gonna give my name. Just believe me, I didn't have nothing to do with it, that's all. See, this girl and me—I wasn't supposed to be with her, which is why I can't tell my name—this girl and me went out parking, and got out and spread a blanket down on the ground where it seemed kinda sandy. We was busy—you know—but I kept smelling this bad smell, and she finally said something 'cause she smelled it, too. So I get up and get a flashlight, and I shine it around, and I can see animals been digging right where we was laying. Maybe hogs rooting. That's why it was so soft. I shine the light down one of the little holes, and, shit, I see a hand. Buried down there— a hand. Hell, I could see fingernail polish! So we got the hell out and wasn't going to tell nobody, but I got to. A couple days before, I saw a car out there, a white Lincoln. And I think somebody ought to know. . . .

And the caller gave directions to the place: a construction road just over the Mayakkatee County line—which meant that the police department of that county had to be notified.

Roy Fuller volunteered to drive up and offer assistance.

The third call was from an officer at the computer center for Federal Crime Information saying they had matched the finger-

224

prints submitted two days ago with a man named Colin Kane, alias Keith Raybourne. Kane was wanted for questioning by federal authorities in a series of rape/murders in the Denver, L.A., and Seattle areas. Kane was to be considered extremely dangerous, and federal agents would arrive that afternoon to help apprehend.

The fourth call that came in was from the secretary at Glades Detention, requesting transportation for a prisoner who was being released.

The ex-prisoner, whose name was Jeth Nicholes, was to be taken to his home on Sanibel Island.

The officer assigned to drive Jeth home was an enthusiastic snook fisherman by the name of Terry. When the ex-prisoner was led through the gate, Terry—who despised this kind of taxicab call—put down his clipboard and began to smile. As the ex-prisoner slid into the front seat, Terry said, "I recognize you! Jesus Christ, you're Jeth Nicholes, the fishing guide!"

By the time Terry and Jeth got across the causeway to Sanibel Island, they had stopped at Fisherman's World for bronze hooks and at a 7-Eleven for diet Coke. At Dinkin's Bay, Jeth gave Terry a tour of the marina, a tour of his boat, and two packs of Kelley Wiggler fishing lures.

Before the police officer drove away, he clapped Jeth on the back and said, "I'm sorry as hell they screwed up and arrested you. That hardly ever happens."

Jeth just laughed it off, not wanting Terry to feel bad. "If I was in charge of police business, I'd get things so screwed up you boys would be wearing moons instead of stars. Everybody makes mistakes."

Jeths stood and waved until the squad car was around the curve of the shell road, then he crossed the parking lot toward the marina building and the door to his apartment.

Through the window, Jeth got a quick glimpse of MacKinley behind the cash register in the office. But he didn't feel like seeing MacKinley right now. He felt like being alone.

Jeth stopped by his Bronco and opened the door. Inside, it

225

was like an oven and smelled of bait gone bad. Battery was probably dead, too—and sure enough, the solinoid didn't even click when he turned the key.

Jeth pulled the hood latch and jumped out to have a look.

Hell, the damn battery was gone, no wonder!

But then Jeth realized that someone from the marina had removed it because they didn't have keys but wanted to keep the battery charged. Probably Mack or Doc.

Jeth felt a little catch in his throat. Being at Dinkin's Bay was like being part of a family, the way people took care of each other.

He went to the front door of his apartment, unlocked it, and went up the stairs quietly, so Mack wouldn't hear him below.

The apartment smelled stale, too. He opened windows, turned on the air conditioner, then checked the first two or three minutes of phone messages on his private number. Nearly all women; all expecting calls; all expecting an explanation of where he'd been and why. Thinking of that was like a weight on his shoulders. Made him tired. Made him want to get on a plane and go someplace.

Over the sink by a stack of dishes someone had washed, there was a note: *I've been taking care of Crunch & Des and getting your mail. Stop by. Doc.*

Jeth Nicholes got a beer out of the refrigerator, then went down the stairs into the heat toward the mangroves at the eastern edge of the parking lot where the path led to Doc's stilt house.

Jeth heard Doc call through the window, "I've got a buddy of yours in here," and followed the voice around the porch to the part of the house called the lab. And there was Doc, with his wire glasses pushed up on his forehead, sitting at a table with his microscope. Behind him, on the steel table, was curled Crunch & Des, the big, sleepy black cat, blinking. Doc said, "He must be happy to see you. He doesn't crack an eye for anyone else."

Jeth shook Doc's hand, patting his shoulder, happier to see

him than he had imagined he would be, then swept up his cat before he found a chair in the corner of the small room.

"Sure appreciate you watching out for my stuff, Doc. Hell, I coulda been gone months. No one knew." Crunch & Des was vibrating beneath his fingers, like a motor running.

It felt good, being here. Jeth liked being in the lab. It smelled good, too, but not like flowers or perfume or food. Not that kind of good. It smelled like old books and wood alcohol and saltwater and something else Doc used in his work, Jeth didn't known what. Plus, there were things to look at: jars of stuff on the shelves, sea horses and starfish, and a lot of other creatures, all labeled if you wanted to know what they were.

Doc said, "You've watched my place for me before. Couple of times. Just returning the favor."

"Even so, I appreciated it."

"They treat you okay in jail?" Doc was looking through the microscope, like it was no big deal for Jeth to have just gotten out of jail, and that was nice.

"Treated me real fine. Lot of the cops want me to take them fishing. They're good guys."

"You talked to MacKinley yet?"

"Nope. Just pulled in and saw your note."

"He's been postponing your charters as best he could, but some he had to farm out to Captain Nels and Felix."

"That's fine with me. In fact, I'm thinking about making it permanent." Jeth, petting the cat with one hand, finished his beer with the other, and decided to toss out the information, just to see how it felt saying it aloud. "I'm thinking about quitting guiding for a while," he said. "Maybe travel around some. You know, I never been out of Florida, unless you count Miami or the Bahamas."

"Many people would count that," Ford said wryly. "Miami, at least."

"Maybe buy myself a airplane ticket and fly clear to New York. Or maybe California. Which one you think?"

"It's a little easier to picture you in California. Women wear bathing suits there."

"Then California it is. You know a good town?"

"Plenty of good towns out there. Depends what you want. Coronado, Monterey, Palo Alto. Maybe visit more than one."

"I'll start with Palo Alto. I like the sound of that."

Doc said, "Good choice. By the way, your mail's on the desk. Beside the dictionary."

Jeth placed Crunch & Des on his chair, then held the stack of mail beneath the desk lamp, shuffling through it.

Ford said, "You got a couple of things there from the University Medical Center in Gainesville."

Jeth stiffened but said nothing.

Ford said, "Is that why you decided to quit guiding? Because you're sick?"

Jeth looked at him, then back at the stack of letters. He said slowly, "You never struck me as the type to read another man's mail, Doc. I don't like that."

Ford pushed the microscope away and adjusted his glasses on his nose. "I didn't read your mail. I didn't have to. You told me."

"I didn't tell you nothing. Not about that."

"Yes, you did. All the last two months, you've been telling me. You went to the eye doctor because you've had headaches, but it wasn't your eyes. I knew that. You've been clumsy as hell, running into stuff, and your hands shake. There's something wrong with your muscles or your coordination; anybody could see. You haven't been yourself, disappearing for weeks at a time. Going off for tests, that's why. You stopped stuttering. And you took the blame for what you thought was a friend's crime because you figured you were going to die anyway, so why not—as long as they didn't electrocute you before you died naturally."

Jeth stood by the window, holding a manila envelope, looking at the address. He stood quietly for a long time, then he said, "You can't tell anybody what you just said to me."

"With the exception of Tomlinson, I promise," Ford answered.

"I guess Tomlinson's okay. I almost told him myself."

"Then I'm right?"

228

"Except that's not why I quit stuttering—because I'm sick. It just happened. Like magic."

"Off Cape Sable," Ford said.

"Right. I saw the green flash. Just like that. I was down there alone, and I was so damn scared. Just so damned scared. That's the only part I didn't tell you."

"You can tell me now, if you want."

Jeth placed the mail on the desk and sat with Crunch & Des on his lap. He said, "I was scared, when I found out. Listening to that doctor made my ears ring, that's how scared." He shrugged. "That feeling, that scaredness, I hope you never know it. It's the sickest, weirdest feeling: like there's warm oil in your spine, but it gives you a cold chill so that your knees are weak, and you have to piss all the time.

"That's the way I felt, for two whole weeks, and I couldn't tell anybody. I didn't have any money for doctors, and I got other payments out the ying-yang. No insurance. Didn't want to go begging. Didn't want to mess up the lives of my sisters or my friends. And I was just so damn scared all the time. But seeing the green flash made me feel . . . *better*. Took the fear right away." He snapped his fingers. "That quick. Like someone was around, making sense of it all. And I knew it. *Really* knew it, for the first time. There's a reason for everything, Doc. Everything means something."

Ford felt that he should speak, but he couldn't bring himself to do it.

Jeth turned, took the sleeping cat in his hands, and sat. He said, "I got something growing on my brain."

Ford said, "I thought it might be that."

"It's like waking up to find some stranger's broken into your house, and you can't get rid of him. I had all sorts of tests done."

"So you know what kind of tumor it is."

Jeth shook his head and pointed to the manila envelope on the desk. "Those are probably the results of the last test, sitting there. I had to lay on a table inside this machine that spun around and around me. The doctors were going to send them. Tell me if the tumor's gonna keep growing, or if it's something else, I forget what—"

"A meningioma?" Ford said. "I hope to hell that's what it is."

"Yeah, that's the word."

"Then, damn it, Jeth, you may not be dying. Hell, it might be something they can fix right off the bat! Open the envelope, and let's take a look."

Jeth shook his head. "Not here."

"Why the hell not? You want to punish yourself a little longer?"

"I been bad enough in my life, I deserve it. But that's not the reason."

"What then?"

"I don't want to read it in front of somebody."

Excited, Ford had stood. Now he sat again. "Exactly right. It's private. Take your cat and your mail and go home. Figure out what you're going to do for the next month or so. Either way, we'll get you fixed up."

Jeth was gathering things, standing. "I told you what I'm doing the next month or so. I'm traveling. Going to California. Palo Alto, like I said."

"But what if the tests say—"

Jeth cut in, "I don't care what the tests say. Either way, they'd have to cut into my brain, and I don't want that. If the results are bad, I'm probably gonna die anyway. If the results are good, I'll probably live anyway. So why the hell should I risk reading 'em and getting scared all over again? You know what the hardest part of all this was, Doc?" Jeth's face had a soft, worn look. "The hardest part was thinking about not being on the water."

Ford's expression was a question: *Why?*

Jeth said, "Because . . . maybe you don't know what it's like to work the same piece of water year after year. Gets to feel like you own that water. Gets to feel like no one has ever known that piece of water better than you. You get to thinking, as long as you keep working it, that piece of water will always be yours.

230

Hell, almost like you're a damn slave or something, because if you quit working it, then that water's not yours anymore.

"But then something happens," Jeth said. "Something happens and you realize that, hell, to the water you're nothing but a gnat. Little blink of the eye, that's all. You don't own it. No one owns the water. Never have, never will. No matter how much you've been out there. Realize that, and it kinda sets you free. Well, I been set free, and I want to feel free for a while."

Ford said, "I see what you're getting at, Jeth. I really do." Smiling even though he didn't feel like smiling. Ford felt shaken and sad that he had been right, and frightened, too; frightened by association of what was implied and what was inevitable. He felt bad for his friend.

Jeth Nicholes said, "When the time's right, I'll have a look at those tests." Then he took his sleepy big cat and his mail, and went out the door.

14

TOMLINSON showed up about 2 P.M.

Ford was out working on the fish tank's subsand filter when he saw him through the mangroves, walking up the shell drive: scraggly hair, long stork legs poking out of khaki shorts, and a baggy khaki shirt stained with sweat and the sleeves rolled up.

Ford yelled to him, "Hey! Where the hell have you been?"

Tomlinson waved casually, unconcerned, and walked up, grinning blandly. He said, "Man oh man, some hot day to hitchhike. Now I know why so many people steal cars in Florida."

"Hitchhike?" Ford demanded. "Where the hell's my truck? You wreck it? Where have you been for the last two days?" Thinking, *Only Tomlinson can make me sound like a nag. Why do I let him?*

Tomlinson walked right past him, up the boardwalk toward the stilt house to get some water. "Out doing research, man. Just like you wanted. Mayakkatee River Estates, remember? Damn, man, don't ever complain about my memory again. And you don't even have synthetic exploration to blame." Meaning substance abuse.

Ford started to reply, then just shook his head, drying his hands on a towel as he followed Tomlinson to the house.

232

Inside, Tomlinson gulped water and explained that he had taken the bus from Mayakkatee County to Fort Myers, then thumbed his way to Sanibel because Harry had stayed to check on a few things, plus he didn't want her riding in a boat.

"Boat?" asked Ford. "Why shouldn't Harry ride in a boat?"

Tomlinson said, "Because she's got your truck." As if that made sense. "But you and I need to see the Mayakkatee development from the water, just to get the big picture. See what's going on and why. I can hardly wait, myself. I want to see what I've been reading about."

"You made a connection between Rios and Senator Griffin?"

Tomlinson said, "Let's load about five gallons of water on your skiff, a six-pack of adult beverage, ice, and a chart, and I'll explain the whole business on the way up. We're supposed to meet Harry at the El Jobean bridge at six, so we'd better get going."

Half an hour later, in the hot, hazy calm of early afternoon, they were in Ford's flats boat, slapping across the banks of turtle grass and bronze sand, running the old Mail Boat Channel to Chino Island. Then up Pine Island Sound on the inside shallows, following the winding scars of propeller tracks, past Demere Key, past the piling houses off Captiva Pass, spooking stingrays and sheepshead, with Ford standing at the wheel, seeing it all through Serengeti Polaroids. Then out toward the main channel, with the white houses of Useppa Island and Cabbage Key shimmering on the rim of sea, as the skiff etched its own trajectory in the green water, an expanding silver wake.

When the water was deep enough for him to relax, Ford sat on the cushion beside Tomlinson, and said, "Okay, so tell me what the connection is between Griffin and Rios."

"You had it. You knew what it was: the land."

Ford said, "Yeah, but how and why—and how did Sutter get involved?"

Tomlinson said, "I'll start at the beginning."

★ ★ ★

233

According to Tomlinson, Griffin controlled twelve hundred acres on the Mayakkatee River where it joined Charlotte Harbor, a great bay northeast of Sanibel. Griffin owned the land with members of his family and through corporations and hidden trusts in which his name was shielded.

"Here's the land and the river right here." Tomlinson had folded a chart into a tiny square so he could hold it in the wind and show Ford. "This acreage comprises the last existing wilderness in the county. Last undeveloped wetlands, anyway. Plus, there are Calusa burial mounds there, set back from the water. More than two thousand years old. Environmentally and historically very valuable ground. Griffin knew if he tried to develop the land, the environmental groups would come down on him with both heels. He couldn't afford that because he's got his eyes on a U.S. congressional seat. Needs all the votes he can get. But he also likes making money. He's a greedy bastard, and he moves in big-digit circles. So he came up with an ingenious plan. At least, that's the way I read what happened."

Tomlinson said he was convinced that Griffin put the word out among his high-roller friends that he was looking for an investor who could not only capitalize a major development project but also organize it—hire the planners and architects, sub-out the jobs.

"He probably wanted a total stranger," Tomlinson said. "A guy who could in no way be associated with Griffin, Inc., past, present, or future. And if the guy had a reputation for playing rough, saying to hell with the rules, so much the better. I think Griffin found exactly the guy he needed: Marvin Rios.

"Less than two years ago, Griffin sold the twelve hundred acres to Rios for nearly twice the going price of raw acreage. Completely screwed up the land appraisals the county had done to set the tax base—for that part of the county anyway. Which would eventually put a tax squeeze on other big landholders, but what the hell did Griffin care? He'd made a respectable profit off Rios, right?"

Tomlinson was looking at Ford, smiling.

234

Over the sound of the engine, Ford said, "You mean Griffin didn't make a lot of money?"

Tomlinson said, "I don't think any money ever changed hands. Not one penny. I think it was all done with paper. Now, if Griffin makes more money than he says he does, that's a crime. But if Griffin makes a hell of a lot less money than he says he does, there's nothing in the world wrong with that."

"But why?" Ford was trying to project; trying to put himself in Griffin's place. "Why would he pay big capital-gains taxes? He'd have had to do that, wouldn't he?"

Tomlinson said, "Because he was looking farther down the road. Instead of just making a respectable profit, he wanted to make an obscene profit. Let me tell you what happens next, see if you can figure it out.

"Rios goes right to work setting up a syndicate, getting blueprints drawn for a giant planned community. I saw copies of the originals up in Tallahassee, Doc. They were like something designed by earth rapers from hell. Canals everywhere. Trees leveled. Five thousand sodded lawns on a concrete table. It was like Rios went way out of his way to make it a bad project—and he *had*. He wanted it to look like a bad project. That was part of the plan.

"A couple of environmental groups got wind of what was going on, and they challenged the proposal when it got to the Southwest Regional Planning Council. And damn if the council didn't reject Rios's application. They cited environmental concerns, plus the lack of roads, water, and sewage facilities. So that should have stopped him, right? No way.

"In steps the Mayakkatee County Planning and Zoning Board," Tomlinson said. "The board is made up of developers and stooges paid by developers, and they allowed Rios to split the proposed development into three distinct tracts. Which is one of the oldest tricks in Florida. County commissions use it all the time. If voters fight them on a big rezoning project, they just break it into three smaller parcels and rezone them one at a time.

"So Rios gets an okay from the Mayakkatee County Commission to go ahead with his project—but chunk by chunk. He brings in the subcontractors and immediately sets them to blasting out canals, cutting mangroves. Rios is not just destroying stuff the commission is allowing him to destroy; he has his people flagrantly violating environmental-protection laws. Four months ago, a circuit county judge fined the development group five grand for cutting mangroves, and you know what Rios's spokesman said? He said it's the price of doing business in Florida. And he's right. All the developers do it. They calculate the fines right into the overhead, which means—for the big-money boys, the ones who can make the nut—there *are* no environmental laws."

They were just crossing inside Boca Grande Pass now, and Ford could see a great fleet of boats drifting the pass for tarpon; could see the phosphate docks and the green storage tank and the white beach beneath the lighthouse. He said, "So how does Griffin profit from all this? I know he must."

Tomlinson said, "Here's how. First—Griffin is the one who warned the important environmental groups about the project. That's right. I've got copies of the letters to prove it. He's the one tipped them about Mayakkatee Development's scorched-earth policy and urged the groups to join forces. Like I said, it's the last wilderness wetland in the county; a damn valuable piece of ground.

"The state of Florida has a special land-acquisition program, acronymn CARL. Through this program, the state can buy environmentally irreplaceable land. With Griffin goading them along, the environmental groups filed an emergency application to CARL to purchase the twelve hundred acres. It's a complicated process: There's a detailed acquisition-proposal form, public presentations, council votes, assessments. The whole bureaucratic jumble. Plus a hell of a long waiting list. But the environmentalists knew that, day by day, Mayakkatee Development was destroying the land and they had to hurry."

Now Ford was nodding. "Enter Robert Griffin to the rescue."

Tomlinson said, "Bingo. I pieced the whole thing together up there in the capitol. Griffin went on record as saying he'd made a mistake selling the land, and now he wanted to help save

236

it. He used his political connections to have CARL immediately consider purchasing the property—or, at least, put the application at the head of the list. Of course, the value of the property doubled when Griffin sold it. And the value of the property more than doubled again when the commission voted a zoning change. Add what the development group is calling 'a projected capital investment recovery,' and you have a piece of property that is going to sell for ten times what it's worth. To the state. Whose checks never bounce. And after only a fourteen-month paper investment in which the only real money that changed hands was to the subcontractors."

Ford said, "So Griffin and Rios probably had a deal on the side where they'd split the profit. The whole thing was planned. Breaking the environmental laws, causing a panic. All of it."

"Harry and I spent hours talking about it, and it's the only thing that makes sense," Tomlinson said. "We don't have irrefutable proof, but we have enough circumstantial evidence to convince any fool. Harry and I have collected copies of thirty-seven memos and letters from Griffin to the various boards and board members that demonstrate that he orchestrated nearly every action relating to that property. He figured he'd come out a winner two ways. The press would see him as an environmental hero. Plus he'd make enough money to buy Learjets and European homes. Not to mention run for Congress."

Ford said, "Rios must have told Sutter. But why would Rios trust a guy like that?" Then Ford amended himself quickly: "Naw, Rios would never trust Sutter. Sutter had to find out somehow after Rios died. Maybe Rios's wife told him."

"If she knew," Tomlinson said. "Or maybe Sutter went through his papers."

Ford was shaking his head, thinking, *The newspapers need to get ahold of this one.*

He knew just the investigative reporter to contact.

To Tomlinson, he said, "We're getting into shallow water. I've got to stand up to run these shoals. That's the mouth of the Mayakkatee River over there."

Tomlinson said, "There's a lot more to the story. Some

237

stuff too nasty to believe. Senator Griffin is not a nice man. But he by God knows how the bureaucracy works."

Ford was watching the flat water as it slid toward him. Ahead, he could see the crescent slicks of oyster bars beneath a running tide. Then more bars; acres of oyster bars. The bars grew in a great maze at the river delta; bulwark striations of hard bottom that could rip the engine off a boat.

The oyster bars deflected water into abrupt tidal cauldrons that slurped and boiled with the speed of the tide. Some of the holes, Ford knew, would be fifteen feet deep or more. To get to the mouth of the river, even in his shallow draft boat, he would have to pick his way through these cuts.

Ford told Tomlinson, "At least we're learning why no one ever built on this river before." Meaning getting to the river was not easy.

Tomlinson was thinking, *Florida has that wildflower look, like a flame in the shade. As pretty as any place in the republic . . .*

Like this pretty place now. They'd hunted their way through the oyster maze, then up the Mayakkatee River. The first few hundred yards of river were a twisting mangrove tunnel that broadened into saw-grass flats. Rising out of the saw grass were dome islands of cypress trees, from which snowy egrets flushed: long-necked birds blooming from the shadows like bright white flowers. There were tarpon rolling at the mouth of the river and, farther up, alligators the color of raw pottery, baking on mud slicks.

"Wild animals," Tomlinson said. He was moving his head all around, looking. " 'Bout a million birds. Lions and tigers and bears, oh my. Like a dang zoo."

Ford had the engine throttled back so that they moved slightly faster than the tide, maintaining steerage. The water of the river was gem black and clear. Beneath the boat, through the water, Tomlinson could see clumps of oysters and scattered mangrove leaves on the bottom. The oysters appeared golden, the leaves an autumn orange. Tomlinson stood on the forward casting deck, holding the bowline. Ford stood at the wheel, the two of them not saying much.

The riverbank changed gradually into oak hummocks draped with Spanish moss, and then the river forked. From the north artery, immediately noticable, flowed a marl gray seepage.

Ford said, "The construction must be up here," and turned into the current.

Just around the bend, they saw the first of a series of newly dug canals. The land had been bulldozed bare; trees piled in smoldering heaps; and the river was a murky, milky white. Only the dinosaur shapes of draglines rose above the flat land. Through the smoke haze, Tomlinson could see that two of the draglines were working, swinging sludge out of the canals and dumping it on the bank. Then abruptly, as they watched, both machines stopped, and their operators—tiny in comparison to the machines—swung down onto the ground.

In the fresh silence, Tomlinson heard what seemed to be voices competing with static.

He looked at Ford, and Ford explained the noise: "Police radios, somewhere over there. A couple of squad cars, maybe more, parked up the river a ways. If you watch, you can see the flashing lights through the smoke."

Tomlinson said, "Maybe they're citing these guys again for cutting mangroves."

Ford shrugged. "I don't see why it would take more than one car to do that. Must be something else. Maybe somebody got hurt."

"You want to go have a look?"

"Nope. I've had enough police business for a while. Is this what you brought me to see? The way it's being developed?"

"After doing all that research, I guess I wanted to have a look for myself. See it from the water."

"I'd have been willing to take your word for it. I've got a lot of work to do."

Tomlinson smiled. Doc always had work to do—his way of isolating himself from those things he did not enjoy or that made him uneasy. Tomlinson said, "You're pissed."

239

"No. If Jeth wasn't already out, your research could have helped. And maybe we can do something with it, anyway. I know a reporter."

"Jeth's out?" On the trip up, Doc hadn't said a word about Jeth; had hardly said a word at all. Just listened and nodded. Which was usually what Doc did.

"Let's get downriver, find some shade, and I'll tell you about it. My eyes are starting to water from the smoke."

An hour later, after they sat and talked, and after they cleared the final oyster bar, Ford checked his watch. It was half-past five.

Over the mainland, storm clouds leaned seaward, feeding on air turbulence generated by cities along the coast, the concrete heat islands. The concrete radiated sunlight; the amassed heat created thermals. The thermals sculpted towering thunderheads that funneled cool air off the bay, spawning nervous crosswinds. The dynamics caused a volatile collision of temperatures, then a buildup of opposed electrical charges: positive charges arcing from the high black clouds to negative charged ions in the earth.

S-z-z-z-BOOM.

Ford could feel the rolling vibrations of thunder through the hull of the boat. To Tomlinson, he said, "We're gonna have to hustle not to get caught in that squall. And we're supposed to meet Harry at six."

Tomlinson could feel the vibrations, too, and he was thinking, *Through the air, through the water, through the fiberglass, through my feet. I am connected to the storm, and to all things. . . .*

Ford said, "Did you hear me?"

Tomlinson was remembering the kinetic jolt he had received from Jeth, the dark electricity of his touch. In that way, he had already known what Ford would tell him. But to have it verbalized aroused in him the old madness, and stirred to the surface grave feelings of fear and pain and wistfulness for the child in Harry's womb, the child whom he had helped give life and, he hoped, would help bring into this world.

As the boat gained speed, Tomlinson took into his mind

240

the refrain that had become his private mantra: *All the way to heaven is heaven all the way to heaven is heaven all the way to heaven is heaven. . . .*

After many minutes, and with the El Jobean bridge within sight, Tomlinson spoke so unexpectedly and loudly that Ford jumped. "It's going to be okay. He'll become a teacher. A great one. Jeth, I mean."

"What?" Ford was irritated. He didn't like being forced into conversation while he was running shallow water—especially when he was trying to outdistance a squall. Plus, he'd been thinking about Dewey, about the way she looked, hoping he would have a chance to hold her again; just hold her. That he felt such a strong surge of affection surprised him, and he didn't want to release the mental picture he had of her, nor the warmth of the emotion. He repeated, "What did you say about Jeth?"

Tomlinson had a soft smile on his face, amused by Ford's pique. "I said everything's going to be okay."

"Huh?"

"He's going to be just fine. Jeth. Whatever happens."

15

DRIFTING two miles off Lighthouse Point, Karl
Sutter heard the rumble of thunder, and said to his four clients,
"Better reel in your baits, folks. Better luck next time, huh?"

He watched them cranking in their lines, two asshole men
and two good-looking ladies wearing bikinis, which is the only
reason he'd agreed to fish them.

They'd come in the day before, right at closing time, begging for a charter. But Dalbert was booked and Javier insisted he
had to go into town in the afternoon on important business,
though what important business a colored spick could have was
anybody's guess. So Sutter told the men that he'd been canceling
all his charters since he'd become an administrator—but they
were such nice folks, he'd take them personally. Thinking: *Just
on the chance your women take their tops off, 'cause they sure have nice
tits.*

Sutter had given them his standard all-day charter. Took
them off Lighthouse Point and drifted frozen bait beneath bal-
loons, so they caught nothing, didn't even get a bite. When the
men suggested they go into the bay and fish for sea trout, Sutter
said, "Why bother? Trout are loaded with worms," which was
his standard reply. He hated fishing for sea trout 'cause it was so

242

much work and he never caught any, so that's the line he always gave them, the bit about worms.

What was wrong with just drifting around out on the ocean?

Which is what they did for eight hours, the two men getting grumpier and grumpier because they weren't catching anything. But the women kept slathering on oil, spread-eagled out there in the sun and drinking frozen daiquiris, pushing their tits out, though still giving him that buggy look, the bitches. But there was a bottle of vodka and an FM radio, so Sutter had a decent time; not like he'd had to work.

But he didn't like being out in storms. Hated them, always had—ever since he was a kid. Hated the smell of them and the way they made his stomach vibrate, and there was no place to hide. Like the night Marvin disappeared, when all those tarpon came squirming to the surface, dead or dying. That lightning scared the hell out of him. Plus, it was time to go in, anyway. Past it really—hell, he'd gotten a little drunk and lost track of the time. Nearly 6 P.M., which is when the marina closed.

Sutter went to the wheel and started the engine. "Grab your seats and hold on tight. We got to try and beat a storm. Damn thing snuck up on me." Figuring to put a little scare into the two asshole men; let the ladies know they had to depend on him for their safety. But, halfway back to the lighthouse, Sutter realized the storm really might catch them: Those clouds were moving fast, like some gigantic train.

Shit.

Damn passengers could keep dry, sitting up there in the little cabin. But he had to stay out in the weather and steer. And he didn't like getting wet when he had a nice buzz going. Ruined the whole effect. The trick was, stay dry.

Trying to watch and hold the wheel, Sutter cracked the storage bin beside his seat and fished around until he felt his rain suit. Heard a clunk and knew it was the Taurus automatic he'd hidden there, but went ahead and pulled the jacket out and put it on. Stored two packs of Marlboros inside one of the Velcro pockets, then settled back to drive.

Now he could see the rain haze hanging over Punta Rassa and Estero Island. The waves beyond the lighthouse bar were a bile green with hard white tops. Sutter steered his boat through them, around the point—and that's where the storm wind hit them: big wall of chilled air that seemed to nearly lift the boat off the water. But no rain; not yet, anyway.

Inside the cabin, the women squealed and Sutter could hear the men swearing. "Jesus Christ, take it easy out there!"

"You people just relax! We're almost to the marina now."

With the storm charging hard off the starboard side, Sutter picked up the markers of the Intracoastal Waterway, pounding through the waves into Pine Island Sound. To his left was the entrance to Sanibel Marina and, just ahead, the causeway: sections of bridge that led to the mainland. Sutter could see heavy traffic backed up on the bridge, like there was maybe a wreck near the tollbooth.

That's the way his mind filed it: *traffic jam caused by a wreck.* That's what he thought when he steered beneath the bridge, holding his breath when it seemed those big waves would swing his boat into the concrete pilings. But he made it, passing beneath all those cars.

Some nasty traffic jam. Musta been one hell of a pileup. . . .

But then some instinct in him, some atavistic sensitivity, brought his mind to focus on the line of cars. Caused him to study the source of the backup. Made him focus on the cluster of police vehicles sitting at the causeway exit ramp, stopping each and every car trying to leave the island.

Uh-oh, uh-oh, uh-oh, not a wreck. A fucking roadblock!

Sutter immediately shoved ahead on the throttle, fighting panic. Turning his face away, as if the cops might look across a mile of green water and spot him.

Wait a minute, it's not for you, you dope. No way they could find out anything about Greta; not this soon. Far as anyone knows, she just packed her bags one day and ran off. Use your head. Relax.

Still, he didn't like it. The causeway was the only way to get on or off the island. With that road blocked, the cops could nail whoever they wanted to nail. Just a matter of time.

Some dumb shmuck probably tried to rob the bank. So they'll just sit on the bridge till they make him.

Sutter took a deep breath and angled off the channel toward Two Parrot Bight, picking up the red and green marker gate that led into the canal. He was going much slower now, taking his time because warning bells were going off in his head. He was sober, too, like all the alcohol in his brain had evaporated with the first rush of fear. That quick, he'd almost forgotten about his four clients.

But there was no forgetting about the storm. The wind was really starting to howl now, and he could see veils of rain sweeping across the water toward him. Normally, he would have gunned his boat and sprinted up the canal to the marina. Been standing beneath the awning before he even got damp.

Now, though, he waited for the rain to catch him. Waited for the rain to envelop his boat, then idled along with the wind, feeling the first fat drops thump his rain jacket. Then it was like standing beneath a fire hose, the rain came down that hard. Sutter tried to shield his eyes with his hands, squinting to see the marina parking lot. Could see the outline of the marina office . . . and the vague shapes of cars . . . and then—

Shit.

Police cars. A couple of them, maybe more. No doubt about it. Parked back in by the pine grove, as if those skinny trees could hide a car, the idiots. But were they waiting for him?

Sutter had pulled the throttle back into neutral, standing there in the rain, thinking.

Maybe the best thing to do was go on in, find out. Hell, he could talk his way out of anything. Cops were so dumb. But what if he couldn't talk his way out of it? And what if it was about Greta? Once they got their hands on him, they damn sure wouldn't let go. Not again. Not after Denver. And sure as hell not after Seattle. Once they found out.

As if it's any of their damn business, the assholes! If only people would mind their own damn business.

Sutter put the boat in gear and made a smooth turn out of the canal, back into Pine Island Sound. Going slow so as not to look suspicious. Though they probably couldn't see him, anyway. Not in this rain.

The little door to the cabin opened, and one of the men poked his face out. "We about to the marina yet? A couple of us are getting queasy down here."

Sutter held up one finger, as if he needed a minute. Then, without warning, he jammed the throttle forward, and the man came tumbling out onto the deck, face-first. Every time the man tried to struggle to his knees, Sutter heaved the wheel over, so the impact of the waves knocked him back onto the deck. The guy had landed on his face pretty hard, and his nose was bleeding.

"That ought to make you feel better, dumb shit!"

Inside the cabin, the women were screaming again, and Sutter held the throttle down hard, his eyes closed, running blind in the rain. He waited for the boat to gain all the speed it could, letting the waves hammer them. Then he slowed suddenly and reached into the storage bin beside the wheel. He took out the Taurus automatic, used the handrailings to make his way forward.

"Hey—get the hell out of the way. Move it!"

The guy on the deck was blocking the door to the cabin, bleeding all over the place. Sutter kicked him in the side. "Can't you hear?"

The man looked up, blinking in the rain. "What did I do? Why are you doing this?"

"You got about two seconds."

"For God's sake, please don't shoot me!"

"Then move it, asshole!"

Sutter kicked the guy once more, and finally got the door open. The little cabin was a littered mess, and three pale faces stared back at him. He waved the gun at them and had to shout to be heard over the sound of the rain on the hull. "Take out all your money. All of it. Traveler's checks, plastic, everything. Put it on the floor, right there by the steps."

The women started crying the moment they saw their buddy with the bloody face. Now the guy in the cabin was bawling, too, saying please don't hurt him, he'd do anything, just please don't shoot. Taking the money from the women and making a real neat pile of cash on the floor, as if neatness might save him.

"Out here! Out on the deck, all of you!"

Sutter waved them out with the pistol, and they had to squat in the rain just to keep their footing on the rolling boat. The women were still in those tiny little bikinis, and Sutter thought, *I would love to, I would love to,* looking at them, knowing he could make them do anything he wanted. Anything. And it might even be better with their men there to watch. That's something he'd tried once or twice, and he liked it.

But he didn't have time for that. He had to use the storm; had to get to a town and find a car. Or a place to hide. Before the weather cleared enough for them to get helicopters out looking for him.

"Jump! Jump or I'll shoot you all dead! Every damn one of you pigs."

Sutter thought maybe he'd have to push them. The moment he said jump, though, all four were up and over the side. Pushing themselves off into a rain so heavy that they couldn't even see shore. He thought about shooting them, plunking them all as they floundered around in the waves. But that would have just made things worse. Not that he would have minded doing it.

The way those bitches gave me the buggy look. If I only had some time alone with them . . .

He returned the pistol to the bin to keep it a little drier, then got the boat up on plane again, but not too fast. He knew he was close to the channel. What he had to do was run from marker to marker—those big steel posts that were placed like road signs, from Key West to Texas, on the Intracoastal Waterway. Even in a storm like this, he could follow those markers. And all he had to do was make it to Boca Grande or Port Charlotte. After that, he could hide the boat, then figure out what he should do next. Use the charge cards to book a flight at one of the small airports. Or rent a car. Something. Right now, though, he had to find one of those damn markers—and there it was, a big red triangle, marker 10.

Hell, he was right by the power lines, not far from Dinkin's Bay, and right on course for Boca Grande!

Sutter began to feel better. It was still raining like hell, and he was soaked and cold, but he felt pretty good. If he could just make it to the mainland and a car, the cops would have a hell of a time catching him. He'd played that game before, and he was good at it. And it would be dark, soon—another thing in his favor.

From marker to marker, Sutter steered, taking his time, being real careful not to get out of the channel. But then, not far beyond marker 24 and the second set of power lines, something went wrong. Sutter kept expecting to see the next marker, but the next marker never appeared. Maybe he'd veered too far to the left. He stopped and tried to retrace his course, but then he couldn't find marker 24, either.

Son of a bitch!

Furious at himself and the damn rain, which made it impossible to see, Sutter pushed the boat faster.

Got to be a marker around here someplace.

Then the boat seemed to lift slightly beneath his feet . . . and he felt the sickening shudder of the hull plowing up and over solid bottom . . . and then the boat jolted, hard aground. Stopped dead as the engine continued to scream, kicking mud and grass up into the haze of rain.

Oh, no no no no . . .

He tried full throttle forward, full throttle reverse. The boat wouldn't move. He shoved the throttle forward once more—and there was the horrible clatter of metal grinding metal. A broken drive shaft.

Sutter switched off the ignition and screamed profanity into the drumming rain. But then he made himself take stock.

Got to find a way out of here quick, or those bastards are going to make me go to prison. Maybe even send me to the chair—they have the death penalty in this state, fucking savages. I've got to do something now!

Ahead and off to the left, he could see the faintest impression of a line of mangroves—not far away, either, maybe a hundred yards. That was good. Land. Maybe Captiva or Sanibel, no way to be sure.

Sutter gathered the money and charge cards he'd taken from the four anglers, put the Taurus automatic in the pouch pocket of his rain jacket, and slipped over the side. The water was only knee-deep, and he began to walk toward the mangroves. As he drew close to the trees, he heard a reassuring sound: the hiss of car tires on wet asphalt.

Hot damn, road up ahead.

Then he saw the ghostly shape of a channel marker, the outline of a dock, and Karl Sutter recognized where he was: Blind Pass, right by that tennis player's house, Dewey Nye. . . .

16

HARRY was at the El Jobean railroad bridge waiting for them at ten after six, which is when they pulled up in the skiff. She was standing in the bed of the blue Chevy truck, smiling in the freshening rain wind.

Ford said, "She is one attractive woman, Tomlinson. A classic." She was, too, with the long black hair and a face that held the light just right.

Tomlinson said, "Yeah, but don't let her catch you with your guard down."

"What?" Ford was holding the skiff at the tide break while Tomlinson climbed out.

"She thinks too much. And she knows where the equipment goes. Life holds no mysteries from that woman."

Confused, Ford said, "I meant that she is physically pretty."

"Exactly!" Tomlinson said. "You spotted it, too. That's the first warning sign. Always is." Half joking, half not, confusing Ford even more. Then Tomlinson said, "Hey—you going to stay and have dinner with us?"

"If I'm going to out run the squall, I need to scoot."

"Domestic life," Tomlinson said miserably. "In the old days, I'd be going with you. Getting soaked, all beat to hell on the run back, maybe killed. Man, I *miss* it! Shit, the days dwindle down, just like the song says."

Ford had already idled away, looking at Harry, who was waving at him from the driver's window of the truck as she turned out onto the road . . . and then he suddenly understood what Tomlinson was telling him.

"Boy oh boy," he said to himself. "Boy oh boy!" To Harry he yelled, "You're pregnant?"

Grinning, she nodded emphatically.

Ford yelled, "You're going to marry that guy?"

Still grinning, she shook her head just as emphatically. "No way! I'd end up a—!" End up a something. Ford couldn't hear, with the sound of the motor and the waves.

Laughing, feeling good for the first time all day, Ford skipped his skiff onto plane, enjoying the way it handled with only him aboard—lighter, faster—and took it hard through the green chop, leaning as he banked southwest, putting the squall over his right shoulder. The sea was following, blowing him in the direction he wanted to go, so he opened the engine a little, cutting through the waves like a cleaver, blasting spray.

A mile past the canal to Miller's Marina at Boca Grande, Ford realized for the first time that he had badly misjudged the storm. Not the squall over his shoulder—that was the standard afternoon shower, and he'd already put it behind him. But boiling out of the east was a long bank of purple thunderheads moving like smoke from a fire, vectoring toward the barrier islands. This front was pushing a lot of wind, carrying a lot of voltage, probably dragging tornadoes behind. Ford could tell by the taut ribbon of light between sea and sky, as if air molecules had been compressed into an explosive vortex of iridescent green.

Ford slowed briefly, watching. He considered turning back to Miller's. Or sitting it out at Cabbage Key. But then he told himself he had already wasted most of a working day allowing Tomlinson to bring him up here. He told himself that the storm probably wasn't as bad as it looked, and his skiff was so fast, he could probably outrun it anyway. Both lies.

251

The fact was, Ford liked storms. In the right mood, and in the right boat, he liked being out in storms. He liked the intimacy of it. He liked having to deal with the elements—people so rarely had to deal with anything elemental. Wind, fire, water—it was all there. He liked being out and alone in the wind and wild light of a blowing rain squall; liked the way it focused his attention and reduced all the threads of his life to one gleaming filament. Not that he went hunting squalls. Nor would he have admitted it, if he did. But there were times when he had the option of sitting one out or riding one out. When he was alone, he nearly always chose to ride.

Ford rode now.

At 6:15 P.M., Dewey helped Walda stack two suitcases of clothes and one trunk of tennis equipment in the trunk of the rental car, and then they stood looking at one another, both of them uncomfortable with good-byes.

"I'll call you when I get to London. In the morning. Morning here, afternoon there."

Dewey said, "I'll be right here, closing up the house."

"You're certain you don't want me to stay and help?"

"Christ, Bets, you keep putting it off. You're a week late as it is. Just get on your damn plane. I'll be there Sunday."

"Monday morning," Walda corrected. "Don't forget the time difference."

"Like I've never traveled. Give me a break."

They both laughed. "I told you I'm staying at the Boar's Head?"

"About a dozen times. God, the names they give hotels over there. You told me."

"And you're sure you don't mind just watching, not playing?"

"Are you kiddin'? I'm looking forward to it."

"Then I'll see you Monday morning."

"Monday morning at Heathrow. Right."

Walda put her arms out, and the women held each other

briefly, then Walda got into the rental car and backed out onto San Cap Road.

Dewey stood in the lawn, watching her, then she looked at the sky.

The wind was blowing, scattering pine needles and leaves. Sand was blowing so hard off the beach that it hurt when it hit her bare legs. It was almost dark, because of the clouds, and Dewey knew a bad storm was coming.

She went into the house to check the windows, and before she'd even gotten to the bedrooms, the storm hit. Lots of rain pouring down. Coming down so hard, she couldn't even see out the glass. Lots of lightning, great big explosions that made the lights flicker.

Dewey put water and a tea bag in a mug, stuck it in the microwave, then went to the bathroom to check the windows there.

When the tea was ready, she found a notepad, pen, and sat at the kitchen table. She wanted to make a list of all the things she had to do before leaving for London.

She had to contact the yardman, the pool man, the plumber, the mailman, the newspaper guy, the island police. So damn much to do, but she'd probably be gone the whole summer, that's the way it looked. Spend the rest of the month in London, stick around for Wimbledon, then back to New York for the Open. Her and Bets.

I shoulda made Bets leave for the airport earlier. It rains every day in the afternoon; I knew that. Her out there driving in this mess . . .

Looking at the tablet, Dewey had the peripheral impression of something passing across the kitchen window.

Abrupt movement; a shadow. Something big.

She turned to look—and saw only a stream of rain blurring the glass.

Probably a tree limb. Or a pelican diving for cover.

She returned her attention to the list she was formulating. But then her mind wandered, and she thought about London, and she thought about Bets, and she thought about last night, the time she'd spent with Ford.

At the top of the tablet, she doodled, *DOC.*

Not that she hadn't tried it before. She had, a couple of times. But never with a guy she'd felt so comfortable with. And, truth was, it wasn't bad. Not with Doc, it wasn't. In fact, it was kind of nice to think about the way he held her; just held her, nothing else. She and Doc, alone, and close, holding. That much of it, she'd like to try again. The rest, it didn't matter. Didn't do a thing for her, and she doubted that it ever would. Doc was right: She was the way she was. But it was too much to ask of him to keep it at just that.

Still, Doc was different. . . .

Why'd I have to tell Bets I'd leave for London Sunday? It's not like I have to get there in time to play.

Dewey tapped the pen on the paper, thinking, considering her options. She could leave for London later in the week, but it wasn't the kind of thing she could explain to Bets. Not on the phone, anyway. Not without upsetting her. Which wasn't fair to do, with Bets getting ready to play the biggest tournament of the year.

Nope. I told her I'd be there, and I will.

Dewey took the tea mug in her hand and, as she did, she heard a faint electronic voice beyond the kitchen door which led into the carport: *"Back away from this vehicle—you are too close!"*

The anti-theft system in her Corvette, probably warning that damn stray dog that he should find someplace else to piss.

But then Dewey had a thought. Maybe the weather was too bad, and Bets had returned. Or maybe she had forgotten something. With ten minutes to talk, face to face, she could explain it all and spend another week on the island. Spend some more time with Doc. Bets wouldn't mind that—she'd said so more than once.

Dewey stood and walked toward the door to the carport.

Then she noticed the doorknob, and she knew the neighbor's dog wasn't waiting for her out there. It had to be Bets, because the doorknob was turning.

★   ★   ★

254

The storm caught Ford just below Captiva Pass as he ran the inside passage from Cabbage Key. The first cold wall of wind slammed past him so hard that, for a microsecond, he thought the skiff might kite upward and flip. He regained control, then slowed long enough to put on his red foul-weather jacket.

Behind him, he could see the rain coming, making patterns on the water as it swept along.

That gust had to be fifty knots, and you're out here in an eighteen-foot boat. Coconut head!

Ford considered fighting his way back to Cabbage Key; pictured himself drinking hot coffee on the porch, talking to Rob and Terry while the rain roared down outside. The prospect was so attractive that he almost did it, almost swung the skiff around. Or thought about ducking into Safety Harbor; maybe the restaurant was open there.

But then the rain hit. Came thumping down on him, a great weighty haze of silver that isolated him from all land everywhere, and narrowed his focus to the water, the steering wheel, and his dripping hands.

Great. Now I've got no choice.

Which, in truth, was the circumstance he desired. To be in a storm without option was to be shed of all affectation and the risk of contrivance. It made an unreasonable action reasonable, so Ford welcomed it. He didn't want the luxury of a choice, because he saw himself as an unremittingly reasonable man.

I'll have to keep going. Wish I hadn't let Tomlinson take the six-pack. A beer would be something good right now.

He got the skiff up, but had to back off, the raindrops were smacking his face so hard. He couldn't go fast anyway, the waves were so ragged. Had to nurse the skiff along, timing the waves, jumping them or chopping through. With the rain and the spray, he was soaked. Even with the foul-weather jacket, cold water dripped down his back, down his arms.

The direction of the storm had changed gradually so that now it was out of the northwest, and Ford decided he could run along the bayside edge of the barrier islands, get a break in the lee. Problem was, he wasn't sure where he was, visibility was so bad, and there were old pilings and bars to worry about.

As Ford well knew, the makeup of all Florida, and all of its bays, was perfectly mirrored by the microcosm of each of its sandbars: a series of washboard swales and ridges on an incline that is pitted and creased by water current. If he could keep moving to the right, keep jumping bars, he would eventually get to the grass swale that edged the mangroves. Then he could follow that mangrove border home.

Which is exactly what he did. He banked west, keeping a close eye on the water beneath his skiff. He trimmed the boat bow down, tilted the engine up, and wallowed along. Kicked sand up on a bar that he guessed was a couple of miles off 'Tween Waters Marina, so he looked hard for the ruins of an old piling house—and found them.

Surprise, surprise—I'm not lost.

Pleased with himself, he turned the skiff shoreward, aware there were more bars, but the tide was up, and the closer he got to Captiva Island, the bigger the break he got from the wind. He was already past South Seas Plantation, so Buck Key and Wulfert Channel were ahead, then Blind Pass, which was near Dewey's home.

Ford considered stopping—he knew Walda was leaving, had probably already left. Which meant the two of them would be alone, just him and Dewey. He also knew Dewey had to make her decision whether to go to London or stay on the island and practice golf—though that decision seemed manifest. She would go. Yet, in some perverse way, that made the prospect of stopping all the more fetching. Like being in a storm without options, Dewey was even more attractive when he knew there was no chance of winning her. Not just because of Walda, but because of the way Dewey was. That he cared deeply about her, there was no doubt. And that he could not lose his freedom to her made him want her even more.

Ford steered toward Wulfert Channel, going slow because there were so many bars. He kept expecting the rain and the wind to slacken, but it did not. He kept looking for markers . . .

looking for markers, thinking: *If I really did care for her, I'd leave her alone tonight. Let her call me if she wants. . . .*

And, gradually, he turned the boat away from Blind Pass, water dripping off his nose; turned away the moment the brain electrons formulated that thought—and instantly yanked back on the throttle because there was a boat only yards in front of him. A big boat; too big for water so shallow.

What the hell is that doing here?

About a twenty-eight-foot Pursuit with a cabin and a big golden Suzuki engine mounted on the transom. Seen through the scrim of rain, it looked like a ghost ship, banging bow high on the sandbar, hard aground.

Ford moved slowly past the boat, looking. He called, "Hello the boat! Anyone aboard?" Called several times, but no reply. He considered boarding the boat, just to make sure no one was hurt, stranded there. But then he thought, *Even if they were injured, they could wade ashore, it's so shallow.*

So he pulled away, picking up speed, finding the rhythm of the waves again . . . but something troubled him. Something about that boat—what the hell was it?

Then he realized: He knew that boat. It was . . . Karl Sutter's—yeah! He'd seen it close only once, that night at Dinkin's Bay, but he recognized it. A boat badly chosen; a boat too big for these waters that no competent back-country fisherman would buy. Which was the main reason he remembered it, and associated it with Sutter.

Ford stopped once more, standing in the pouring rain.

Then he turned his skiff toward Blind Pass, gunned the throttle forward, thinking: *Dewey. . . .*

17

THE door to the carport opened so slowly that Dewey thought Bets must be having trouble with a package or something. Probably had a suitcase in each hand. So she reached to help, calling, "How'd you do at Wimbledon?" and, like an explosion, the door flew open, smacking her on the shoulder and the side of the face. It didn't knock her down; just drove her stumbling back a few steps, where she caught herself on the wall.

Dewey looked up dizzily, still expecting to see Bets.

Maybe the storm wind had caught the door and thrown it open.

But Bets wasn't there. Instead, a huge male shape filled the doorway: a meaty face with jowls, yellow rain jacket the size of a tent, sopping blond hair, and eyes like tiny shards of blue ice looking out from folds of skin. Pointing a great big gun, too; a strange-looking platinum thing with odd tubing, like a pistol from space.

Kicking the door closed behind him, the man said, "Well, well, well . . . looks like I found my port in the storm."

Dewey felt the control mechanism in her snap; an immediate rush of anger, like heat, and she was yelling, "Who the hell are you? And what right do you have to come charging in here?

258

This is my *house,* goddamn you!" Confronting him, standing in his way so he couldn't come into the kitchen—ready to slap the hell out of him, if need be. Then, as if in a dream, she saw his huge fist orbiting toward her. Couldn't even duck, the surprise of it so hypnotized her. . . .

Then she was on her back, skidding across the linoleum of the kitchen floor. Didn't even feel the punch; just a withering pressure on the side of her face, and she couldn't breathe through her nose because there was fluid in it. It was difficult to see, too. In a panic, she touched the left side of her face—maybe he'd knocked her eye out.

No, the left eye was there. She couldn't see out of it, but the eye was there. Blood all over the place: on her hands, on her face, on the floor.

The man was coming toward her, a mild smile beneath the mustache on the tight little mouth. "Don't try to get tough with me again, you rich bitch. See—I'm not like the rest . . . your little yuppie sweethearts. I don't take shit off women. *Comprendo?"*

Dewey lay there unable to take her eyes off the man, unable to move as the man touched his wet shoe to her bare foot, a kind of kick.

"Understand me?"

She watched him, thinking, *This is the guy Doc warned me about, and he's going to kill me. This is him, Sutter. He's going to shoot me with that pistol.*

"Understand?" He was standing over her, yelling down. "Say it!"

"I . . . understand."

"That's better. Are you alone?"

"Yes."

"If you're lying, I'll kill you."

"I'm not; I'm alone."

"Your dark-haired friend with the big tits, she's not here?" Looking around like he was hoping to see Walda.

"She just left."

"When's she coming back?"

"She's flying to London."

259

"Too bad. The three of us coulda had some laughs." The man was looking at her, studying her—legs to face, then he motioned with the gun. "Get on your feet." He was holding his hand out to her, huge fingers spread wide. He wanted her to take his hand.

He was saying, "First thing you and me are going to do is get to know each other better." His face was getting closer and closer as he reached down. "Then you're going to help me get off this island. Use that fancy talking car of yours. Or your buddy Ford's boat, Mister Smart Ass." So close to her now that she felt the nearness of him would smother her.

Dewey tried to edge slowly away . . . heard a *clank* on the floor and realized that she still had the tea mug. The tea had spilled, but she still had the mug, and as he leaned closer, she swung it around with all of her strength—making a heavy crockery thud as she cracked Sutter hard behind the ear. Instantly, then, she lunged away, scampering on her knees; got to her feet and ran.

In a terrible voice, the man cried, "Ouch! You hurt me!" Bellowing like an outraged child; a sound so grotesque that it frightened her as much as the pistol did.

Then he was running after her, making a ponderous, lumbering noise only a few paces behind. So close, she could hear his big lungs sucking air; feel his weight shaking the house; expected him to reach out and touch her at any instant. Once he did touch her—his huge hand sliding down her back, unable to gain a hold.

"When I catch you, you bitch!"

Dewey led him flying through the living room, her bare feet tracking well on the carpet. Then she caught the wall lip of the recreation room and catapulted herself into the dining room, gaining ground.

I've got to put some space between us—and get outside. I can lose him outside. Think of something. . . .

When he was close behind her again, Dewey did a stutter step, as if about to turn . . . then collapsed abruptly in front of

260

him and arched her back to create a higher hurdle. She braced herself for the impact of his knees and rolled into him.

Because he was going too fast to stop, Sutter pitched forward with a wild cry, flying over her, out of control. There was a tremendous thud; the sound of shattering glass—and, in the same instant, a deafening *whap* of thunder as all the lights in the house went out, abandoning them to heavy gray dusk.

Dewey was instantly on her feet, reaching the front door in a few long strides, turning the doorknob frantically, but it wouldn't open; kept slamming back each time she ripped at it—because she had chained the door on the inside, just as Ford had wanted her to do.

Damn!

Fumbling with the chain, Dewey had a woozy, surreal feeling, as if she was living out a slow-motion nightmare. Her hands shook. Couldn't make them work on the lock fast enough. Her brain felt as if it had been drenched with cold ether.

This can't be happening.

Behind her, she could hear the man wheezing, out of breath. Making a strange noise, too—like a bear might sound if it could laugh. Making that noise, but no effort to come after her.

Why?

His voice was terrifyingly calm: "Crazy woman . . . thinking you can get away from me! You don't have the *brains,* baby." Spoken like a growl, followed by that strange chuckling sound again.

Fighting with the chain, Dewey glanced over her shoulder at the huge shape on the floor. It wasn't moving. Just sat there beneath the broken window through which wind and rain gusted. But a strange beam of read light was coming from the shape; a beam so bright and well defined that it was like a tube of glowing plastic; a thread of light that extended clear across the room.

Dewey thought, *The space gun. . . .*

The man turned the beam of light toward her and painted it across her belly, then her breasts, then held it steady on her face, so that she had to block the light with one hand, it was so bright.

"Whatever I touch, whatever I touch, whatever I touch—*I can kill*. Stupid little bitch. . . ."

PLAP . . .

Dewey dropped to her butt, frozen by the noise and the sensation of hot needles on her cheek—the bullet had gone through the door, just over her head, peppering her face with wood fragments.

"You shot me, you bastard!" Screaming at him, holding her face.

The huge figure was moving now . . . standing . . . rising to his full height before the broken window. In the pewter light that filtered through the window, she could see that the man's face was dark on one side, probably bloody from crashing into the glass. But then she couldn't see him at all, because he was shining that red light on the bridge of her nose, blinding her.

"Come here!" he ordered.

"I can't see."

"You better move, damn you! You have about three seconds to live."

Dewey got to her feet and went slowly toward the sound of his voice.

"Closer!"

She took another step.

"Closer, damn you. Get over here in the light so I can see what you look like! And strip those clothes off!" Waving the gun for emphasis.

The man stood before the window and yanked her to him, positioning her only an arm's length away. He reached out and squeezed her left breast hard, then ripped her T-shirt down— and laughed when she slapped his hand away.

"Man, you could play a tune on knockers like yours. That's just what I'm gonna do."

"Keep . . . your . . . filthy hands . . . off me!"

"Big temper, huh? Fiery, yeah—like that night at Cabbage Key. That's right, I saw. Fact, I saw more of you and your friend

262

than you two realized." Laughing, like he'd said something funny, enjoying some private joke.

He was taking something out of his pocket; leaned over momentarily and lit a cigarette, cupping it to get it going in the wind from the window. "Here," he said. "Have a drag."

In the light of a sudden lightning blast, she saw him clearly for a microsecond: deep cut above his eye, face bloody, cigarette braced between the big sausage fingers.

"Smoke it," he said, pushing the cigarette toward her. "I want you to." With his other hand, he was doing something with his pants.

Dewey took a step toward him, hoping he would back up a little, trying to catch her breath, trying to do what was smart, trying to maintain—because she had seen something else in that abrupt flash of white light.

Just outside the window, directly behind Sutter and close enough to touch him, stood Ford.

Dewey took a slow, deep breath and said to the man, "Go piss up a rope, you bastard," and swung her fist at him, as hard as she could.

In all the rain, in all the wind, on the way to Dewey's house a lone bold voice from Blind Pass Bridge yelled at Ford to slow down, no wake zone.

"Ya driving too damn fast, ya bum!"

Screamed at him through the noise of the storm.

Who the hell would be fishing in weather like this?

Some tourist fanatic up there on the bridge, trying to squeeze the last drop of fun out of his vacation, worried about this speeding boat running over his fishing lines.

But Ford didn't slow until he swung up to the first free dock he found; tied his boat and sprinted through the mangroves toward Dewey's house. Halfway there, a lightning blast zapped a casuarina tree, rolling a ball of blue flame across the beach—an eerie sight.

Instantly, the lights in Dewey's house blinked off.

Ford was thinking as he moved, *I don't need this. If Sutter's*

263

in there, I can't let him see me before he sees me. He has worms in his brain.

At the edge of Dewey's lot, Ford stopped in the shadows. Took a good look around. Saw the red Vette in the open carport; saw that Wanda's rental car was gone. Not much else to see. Sandy yard, trees, screened pool, house with aluminum siding, beach.

A world of shadow, mostly. Through the squall haze, the sun was a pale disk in stormy eclipse, the sea a heavy gray presence without form or horizon. It was not yet dark, but there was no light.

Ford sprinted across the lot, and was nearly to the door when he heard *Ka-PLAP* . . .

The muted popping sound of a gunshot inside the house, followed by a whimpering scream and a woman's words he could not decipher.

Dewey, hold on. . . .

Ford was at the side of the house, rain drenching down off the roof as he crawled frantically beneath the side windows. One of the screens had been knocked out—he could see it just ahead. Glass was broken out, too. There were shards piled in the sand.

Above his head, through the window, he could hear the heavy rumble of Sutter's voice shouting orders.

And he heard Dewey: "Keep your filthy hands off me!"

She wasn't dead. And he sure as hell hadn't taken the spirit out of her.

Ford carefully peeked one eye over the sill and saw that Sutter's back was to him.

Just beyond, he could see Dewey.

There was an odd red light moving randomly around the room, and he could see her in that light. Her face looked strange. Not just bloody—but swollen and contorted. Her eyes seemed to be crossed, and her shirt was ripped so that one bare breast showed. She was trying to hold the torn material together with one shaking hand, a pathetic gesture.

Ford knew now—knew for the first time—what he would do to Sutter.

264

Inside, Sutter was pushing something at Dewey, saying, "Smoke it!"

Ford stood. In a sudden flash of lightning, he was looking eye to eye with Dewey. He smiled at her—and had no idea if she had time to define the smile. But she saw him. There was no doubt she saw him. He could tell by the way she straightened herself: *"Go piss up a rope. . . ."*

In that instant, Ford reached for Sutter's belt—and was surprised to hear him grunt, as if something had hit him, driving him backward. Then there was a series of explosions, *PLAP-PLAP-PLAP* as Ford hauled the man back-first through the window, using momentum and adrenaline to force a big body through a small space.

Ford was already yelling as he wrestled Sutter to the ground. "Dewey, you okay?"

Nothing.

"Dewey!"

There was that beam of red light again—a laser sight, Ford finally realized. He dropped knee-first onto Sutter, one knee on his right wrist, the other on his neck. He twisted the pistol out of his hand, grabbed a handful of hair and pulled Sutter's face close.

Sutter's eyes widened in slow understanding, and he croaked, "Shit, it's you."

"If you shot her. . . . *Dewey!*"

Finally, an answer: "Yes!"

"Dewey?"

"I hear you. I'm okay."

"Dewey!"

"Yeah—I'm okay!"

"You sure?"

"That bastard!"

"I've got him; it's over."

"I'm calling the cops—he hurt me!"

"No, don't call. Don't call, not yet. I'm coming in. I'll do it." He was pushing Sutter ahead of him now, toward the door.

★ ★ ★

265

The way this guy was holding him, looking at him with those damn eyes . . .

Sutter's mind scanned frantically for a way to escape, but the only thought that solidified was: *This guy has something missing in him.*

He had seen that void before in Ford's eyes, and it scared him; frightened him as much anything he had experienced since that night in the bathroom with his mother, the night he'd learned how to take control of life. His life, any life, all life.

Sutter wanted to work this situation real easy, skate with the guy and wait for an opening. The way Ford popped the clip out of the Taurus and threw the whole works into the bushes, it was like he knew what he was doing; a guy with a plan. But what? Probably pissed about the bitch, the way she was whining in there, and Sutter didn't want to make any stupid moves. But at least the guy didn't have that damn gun any more. So he must have a knife or something; who the hell knew. Sutter said to Ford, "Man, I thought she wanted me to come on to her. I really did—"

Ford's voice: "That mouth of yours—I'm surprised you've made it this far."

"What the hell does that mean? You know how women are."

"That tongue just keeps digging."

Sutter turned his head a little to see, "You're going to call the police, right?"

Ford was pulling him, making him stand up.

Sutter tried again. "The police . . . right? You're going to call."

Nothing.

Sutter was thinking: *Just run for it, that's maybe what I should do.* He said, "If you don't call the cops, I will. I haven't done anything wrong. I got my side of the story."

Ford had his fingers fixed some way on his wrist so that, with just a tiny push, a burning pain shot up Sutter's arm, straight to his brain.

"Ouch!"

266

"I'm not interested in your side of the story." Talking in a monotone; the way the guy said it was like cold water on the spine.

Shit, this guy's gonna kill me!

Sutter could feel the tears welling in his eyes. "You don't understand—I got problems."

Ford pushed him roughly through the open door into the house, and there stood the blond bitch, holding a lighted candle in one hand, holding her T-shirt up with the other. Face was swollen, bleeding, too. Seeing her, Ford said, "You've got problems all right."

To the woman, Ford said, "Put the candle by the phone, then get in your car and drive somewhere and get some medical attention. To my place, and get Tomlinson. That would be better. If you're okay to drive—"

"I'm okay, but I'm staying with you," she said.

Ford said, "The police call will go over the radio. Journalists keep scanners. They'll be out here, and you don't want them to see you now, do you?"

The blond said, "I don't care."

Sutter was thinking, *If I could get my hands on you one more time,* but she was keeping distance between them, like he was a mean dog or something, giving him that buggy look.

Bitch.

Sutter said, "Tell this guy, lady, you invited me over here. Tell him the truth and, if he lets me go, I won't press the what-you-call-it . . . charges."

"Goddamn you—"

Ford was taking the phone off the wall, holding it between his shoulder and his ear, pressing buttons. "Don't pay any attention to him. Go get in your car." Then, as the girl left, he said into the phone, "My name's Ford, and I have a guy in custody who just tried to murder a friend of mine. That's right, I have him—"

Sutter waited as Ford talked, thinking, *Just you and me alone. That's go-o-o-o-d!*

267

Ford hung up the phone as they heard the Vette start, rumbling down the drive, backing out.

Ford swung Sutter around, looking into his face. "Outside, Karl."

Sutter said, "Sure, we'll wait on the cops and see who they believe," and thinking, *I get outside again, I run for it. . . .*

But outside, he couldn't run, the way Ford had his arm leveraged up behind his back, and pushing him, too.

"Hey, that hurts, damn you! You don't even understand the kind of trouble you're going to be in."

"I do understand, Karl. That's your biggest problem."

Sutter could see where he was being steered: toward the boat dock at the water's edge. "What the hell . . . ? I'm not getting in a boat with you, goddamn it! When the cops get here—"

"The cops aren't coming, Karl."

"Bullshit, I heard you call them. And when they get here—"

Ford was pushing him along now, rougher. "You saw me pick up the phone and dial—"

"Talking to the cops, yeah. Telling them a bunch of shit."

"You heard me talk and made a natural assumption."

A chill moved through Sutter as he realized.

Ford said, "The assumption was that I really had dialed the police."

Feeling real trembly, real scared, Sutter said, "You faked it. That's what you're saying."

Ford said, "So we could spend a little time alone, get to know each other better."

Oh, shit.

"Aw . . . Jeezuz, just don't hurt me. I mean it. I can't take that stuff." Sutter began to snuffle and wobble, but he was thinking, *He left my pistol back there in the yard, dumb shit went off and left it. Moment he lets go of my wrist, I pull out my case knife and hand him his head. . . .*

"You're not being fair!" Sutter was crying aloud by the time they pushed their way through the mangroves to the water's edge—but he had the knife out and open seconds after Ford shoved him away, a Kevlar-handled Gerber. He was palming the knife, a knife as functional as a razor, waiting for Ford to step just a little closer. *Then you wonder why your windpipe is making that funny noise.*

Ford said, "Get in the boat."

"No! You can't make me!"

"I'm going to leave you out on a mangrove island. Let the mosquitoes have a chance to drain you before the cops pick you up. Or maybe you try to swim for it and drown. My little present. Believe me, I'd like to do more."

The guy was nearly close enough, and Sutter turned his body slightly, so he could take a clear swing. "You should have contacted the authorities about me! You didn't even give me a chance!" Taking a short step at him.

Then Ford saw the hand coming; didn't even realize there was a knife in the hand until he hammered the arm up behind Sutter's back—which is when he felt something land atop his foot.

"I wouldn'ta really stabbed you, I just want you to leave me alone!"

Pushing Sutter toward the water, Ford said, "Change of plans, Karl—"

"I'm not responsible! I need a psychiatrist!"

Ford said, "No, Karl . . . you need gills," and ran him down into the fast, black water, where Karl Sutter had, after long moments of screaming panic, a fleeting sensation of peace as he banked down, down beneath a weight that would not relent. As his brain clouded, he thought: *This is the way it must feel to fly.* . . .

Shortly after Ford returned to the house and notified police that Karl Sutter had escaped, a man who had fished through the storm on Blind Pass Bridge got his first bite of the night.

The man's name was Denzler, a retired New Jersey patrolman who loved to fish better than anything on earth. But this night had tried even his patience. It wasn't the weather—hell, up on the Jersey shore, he didn't even bother leaving the house unless it was storming. He loved fishing in storms because that's when the stripers hit best.

But down here in Florida—crap! Two hours of sitting beneath a cheap poncho in lightning and rain, using the best frozen squid he could find for bait, and not the first damn strike.

If so many other New Jersey cops didn't live down here, I wouldn't waste my time on this grease pit. The Ohioans and the New Yorkers could have it.

Denzler was using a Shimano TLD 20 reel with a graphite stand-up rod, all the latest gear, and heavy mono line, because all the magazines said those lunker bridge snook could kick a guy's ass if he didn't. He sat beneath the poncho, watching the reel miserably, but then the reel started to click.

Hey!

Gently, he took the rod in his hands. The line began to fly. He shrugged off the poncho and stood. He was fishing free spool, and he watched with delight as the line on the reel continued to evaporate away.

Run, you bastard. Swallow it.

Denzler waited until he could wait no longer, then he locked the reel and began to ram the hook home with a series of frenzied pelvic thrusts, just like those bass fishermen on television did it.

Cross his eyes!

The fish was taking line. Not fast, but taking it steadily as a steam engine, pulling away at the speed of the falling tide. Denzler followed the trajectory of the fish, moving along the lip of bridge.

This thing's like a damn whale.

A car approached, and Denzler waved it down. He might need help, he told himself. Even if he didn't, he wanted someone to back his story if the fish broke off.

The driver rolled down the window, and Denzler yelled, "I got the mother of all fish here! You mind sticking around?"

The driver yelled back, "Hell no, I'd pay money to watch."

By the time Denzler had battled the fish for half an hour,

a dozen cars were parked side by side on the beach, their lights on, watching. Some of the drivers had formed a pool, betting whether it was a sting ray or a tarpon, and how long it would take to be landed. They called support to Denzler through their cracked windows—complete strangers who had already gotten to know each other by name.

Denzler was thinking to himself, *This is the way I want to die: fighting a hawg, in the rain, before an audience of strangers. Except, it would be nice if some of them wore bikinis,* which is when he got his first look at the fish: a violent spray of water thrown by a gigantic yellow fin.

"Holy Christ," someone yelled, "it's a tuna!"

Denzler was shaking. He'd never caught a giant tuna before. Didn't even know they had giant tuna here. His heart was pounding so hard that he thought it would burst, his knees were weak, and his hands were cramping, but he continued to work the rod: lift . . . lower . . . ree-e-e-el; lift . . . lower . . . ree-e-e-el.

As the fish moved toward him, Denzler moved toward the fish, crossing the shallow bar that had been formed by the currents and the big gray breakers that crashed ashore there. Out of breath, he yelled over his shoulder to the spectators, "Somebody pull their car around so the lights hit the water. Working a fish this big in the dark is dangerous!"

He was up to his knees in surf, and almost had the thing landed, when the car lights finally found the triangulation point of line and water. It was only a few yards away now, that gigantic yellow form.

Denzler gave a massive lift, pulling the creature momentarily into view . . . then stopped reeling, dazed—as he watched a human head and body, hooked just beneath the chin, spin and sink beneath the surface again, catching the current once more.

He felt sickened and weak, but mostly he felt a clammy sense of disappointment.

Denzler thought: *There's no way in hell they're gonna ever let me weigh this big bastard. . . .*

18

BY the beginning of the last week of August, Ford knew things wouldn't work out as he'd planned. . . .

He was in his piling house, on the phone, hearing about one of those disappointments now. Listening to Henry S. Melinski talk about the Mayakkatee River Development project. His investigative reporter friend, Henry Melinski.

Years ago, a corrupt politician had remarked, "In the whole great state of Florida, my family and me only got one thing to fear—now that Ted Bundy's dead and malaria's been cured."

Meaning Melinski.

Melinski had the reputation and he had the journalistic clout, which is why Ford was so surprised the news wasn't more encouraging.

Melinski was asking him, "Do you know why they used so much marble to build the new state capitol at Tallahassee? Because marble doesn't absorb shit, that's why."

Laughing, Ford said, "That's a good one, Henry. I like that."

"The only reason you like it is because you think I'm joking—I'm not. Same with the county courthouses. Why does code require they use metal screens in the urinals? Because if they

272

didn't, this state would lose half its county commissioners the first week. They'd just drain away. Not that that would be bad."

Ford said, "I just thank God journalism hasn't jaded you, Henry."

Standing in the living room with the phone in his hand, Ford could look through the open door to his lab and see the microscope with a fresh slide prepared and lighted, and the postcard he'd just received lying on the dissecting table.

The card was from Jeth, and the first line read: *I started stuttering again. The girl at the desk must of thought I said São Paulo instead of Palo Alto because, goddamn it, instead of California, here I am in Brazil—*

Melinski said, "Go ahead, make your wisecracks. I'm trying to educate you here. Florida attracts the best people in the world, and it attracts the worst people in the world. The best people already have it made, so they go to the beach. And the worst people—"

"The worst people go into politics?" Ford offered.

"Exactly. Government work. About seventy percent of the time, that's actually true. Which brings us to the clever senator, Bob Griffin."

Ford was listening.

Melinski said, "When you brought me the research your friends did, I laid it all out and thought, Beautiful. No shit, a masterpiece of investigative journalism. I mean it. I'd like to meet those people, I really would."

Ford said, "They'll be in Boston a while. But when they get back, I'll arrange it."

Melinski said, "It was so good, I figured I wouldn't have to lift a finger. Just write the damn thing out. I woulda shared the byline with them, which is something I don't often do."

"So what happened?"

"What happened is, I started to look down the road a little. I started thinking, What happens if I try to nail Griffin on this? Even though it's a beautiful bunch of circumstantial evidence, the guy is going to walk. You know why? Because he didn't break a single damn law. You hear what I'm telling you? The whole business stinks like hell, but what he did is absolutely legal."

"The voters ought to know," Ford said.

"Which is the only reason I considered it in the first place. Okay, so I write the story and inform the voters. What's the first thing happens? First thing that happens is, the state immediately stops its efforts to buy the twelve hundred acres on the Mayakkatee River. Bureaucrats despise controversy. Hate it. They'd drop that parcel off the CARL list like a hot potato. You want that to happen?"

Ford said, "Nope. I truly don't."

Melinski said, "Truth is, they're probably going to drop it anyway. It's too closely associated with Marvin Rios, and Rios is too closely associated with Colin Kane."

Colin Kane meaning Karl Sutter.

"You know authorities are now estimating that Kane, coast to coast, raped and murdered more than thirty women? Law-enforcement people are showing up from all over the country, trying to close the books on rape victims. They're tying together all the MO stuff: garbage bags, the cigarette in the mouth, and a couple of other nasty things you probably don't want to hear about."

Ford said, "That's right, I don't want to hear about it."

Melinski said, "You know what gets me? I don't doubt for a second that Colin Kane drowned accidentally in Blind Pass. The bastard was psycho; probably thought he could walk on water. But why in the hell is the DA so quick to agree that Kane also killed Rios? Hell, circumstantial evidence was all they had—and not good evidence at that! Maybe Griffin killed Rios—you ever think about that?"

Ford, who was the only person in Florida who actually knew who killed Marvin Rios, said, "Never did."

"What I'm trying to tell you," Melinski said, "is that an investigative reporter's got to pick his projects carefully. You know what I got before me right now? We got a woman county commissioner who's screwing a local lobbyist. She appoints the lobbyist and his brother to an important county post—and insists

274

there's no conflict of interest. So then one of the department heads commits suicide, and leaves a note saying she's not going to let this county commissioner strong-arm her anymore—see what I mean? This shit just goes on and on and on. I mean shameless, white-trash crap. The morally bankrupt and the terminally stupid have only one occupational hope in this state— government office."

Because Ford didn't agree with Melinski, his attention started to wander. He felt bad about the Mayakkatee River property, but he had done what he could and there was nothing more that he could do. He had borrowed a little portable television from Rhonda and JoAnn, the women on the Chris-Craft, and now he turned it on. The U.S. Open was under way, and Walda was in the quarter finals—though she wouldn't play until that night. Still earlier that morning, one of the networks had played an interview with Dewey—a puff piece on why she was taking a sabbatical from the sport to work full time as Walda's trainer.

Dewey had handled herself well on camera. She was articulate and funny, and she had tugged on her ear to say a private hello, just as she had promised him. She looked happy—and, more than anything else, that's what Ford wanted for her. Sometimes, she had told him, they could hold each other.

Walda had told him the same thing. . . .

But the interview wasn't playing now, so Ford switched the set off. Melinski was saying on the phone, "The point is this, it's like they describe it in war: For an investigative reporter, Florida is a target-rich environment."

Through the screened window, Ford could see a woman coming up the walkway. The public defender, Elizabeth Harper, with hips swinging and a spring in her step.

"Yoo hoo—Dr. Ford?"

Into the phone, Ford said quick good-byes to Melinski, then headed for his microscope in the lab. As he crossed the walkway, he called, "Come on in, Liz. Back part of the house."

Early the previous morning, Ford had accompanied a friend forty-three miles offshore, and there he had done a short drag with a stramin plankton net. There were tarpon in the area; Ford saw them rolling.

In that drag, he had caught a tarpon; the tiny, microscopic tarpon larvae that he had tried but failed to find in the hot shallows of the bay. Not that he was going to give up. He wasn't. Not yet—because he wasn't convinced that tarpon spawned only offshore.

Ford squinted into the microscope, and a draconic creature loomed up at him: a translucent creature with huge eyes, a reptilian tail, and massive curved teeth, like something out of a nightmare.

Marvin Rios had had such a nightmare; had experienced this creature for what it really was: unyielding, instinctive, and elemental. Looking through the lens, Ford had the brief mental image of Rios, the night of the storm, lying terrified beneath a tarpon while that fish pounded him to death, trying to find its way back into the water. . . .

"So here you are?" Liz Harper, not looking nearly so reserved in pink T-shirt and jogging shorts, stood at the door with a smile on her pale, pretty face. "I'm ready for my first lesson in safe boating. Or is it sunbathing? How about you?"

Ford took the slide off the microscope and put it carefully into the stainless-steel sink beside his dissecting table. He grinned at her, thinking, *I like the way this woman looks.*

Turning on the water, he said, "Just as soon as I get rid of this evidence. . . ."